The Girl on the Cliff

ALSO BY LUCINDA RILEY

The Orchid House

ATRIA PAPERBACK
A Division of Simon & Schuster, Inc.
1230 Avenue of the Americas
New York, NY 10020

Originally published in Great Britain 2011 by Penguin Books Ltd.
Published by arrangement with Penguin Books.

Manufactured in the United States of America

ISBN 978-1-62090-667-5

The GIRL on the CLIFF

A Novel

LUCINDA RILEY

ATRIA PAPERBACK

New York London Toronto Sydney New Delhi

For Stephen

So we beat on, boats against the current, borne back ceaselessly into the past.

—F. Scott Fitzgerald, *The Great Gatsby*

Aurora

I am I.

And I will tell you a story.

The words above are the most difficult for any writer, so I'm told.

Put another way: how one begins. I have plagiarized my younger brother's first attempt at storytelling. His opening line has always stuck with me for its simplicity.

So, I have begun.

I must warn you that I'm not a professional at this. In fact, I can't remember when I last put pen to paper. I've always spoken with my body, you see. As I can no longer do that, I've decided to talk with my mind.

I'm not writing this with any intention of presenting it for publication. I'm afraid it's more selfish than that. I am at the stage of my life everyone dreads—that of filling my days with the past, because there is little future left.

It is something to do.

And I think that my story—the story of me and my family, which began almost a hundred years before I was born—is an interesting one.

I know everyone thinks that about their story too. And it's true. Every human being has a fascinating existence, with a big cast of good and evil characters in each.

And almost always, somewhere along the way, magic.

I am named after a princess in a famous fairy tale. Perhaps that's the reason I've always believed in magic. And as I've grown older, I've realized that a fairy tale is an allegory for the great dance of life we all undertake from the moment we are born.

And there is no escape until the day we die.

So, Dear Reader—I can speak to you as such because I must presume that my story has found an audience if you are one—let me tell you mine.

Since many of the characters died long before I was born, I will do my best to use my imagination to bring them back to life.

And as I sit here mulling over the story I will tell you, which was handed down to me by two generations, there is one overriding theme. It is, of course, love, and the choices we all make because of it.

Many of you will immediately think I refer to love between a man and a woman, and yes, there is plenty of that. But there are other precious forms which are equally powerful; that of a parent's love for a child, for example. There is also the obsessive, destructive kind, which wreaks havoc.

The other theme in this story is the vast amount of tea people seem to drink—but I digress. Forgive me, it is what people who feel old do. So I shall get on with it.

I will guide you through and interrupt when I feel it is necessary to explain something in further detail, for the story is complex.

I think I will begin, to complicate things further, somewhere toward the end of my tale, when I was a motherless child of eight years old. On a clifftop overlooking Dunworley Bay, my favorite place in the world.

Once upon a time . . .

I

Dunworley Bay, West Cork, Ireland

The small figure was standing perilously close to the edge of the cliff. Her luxuriant, long red hair had been caught by the strong breeze and was flying out behind her. A thin white cotton dress reached to her ankles and exposed her small, bare feet. Her arms were held taut, palms facing out toward the foaming mass of gray sea beneath her, her pale face looking upward, as if she were offering herself as a sacrifice to the elements.

Grania Ryan stood watching her, hypnotized by the wraithlike vision. Her senses were too jumbled to tell her whether what she was seeing before her was real or imagined. She closed her eyes for a split second, then reopened them, and saw that the figure was still there. With the appropriate messages sent to her brain, she took a couple of tentative steps forward.

As she drew nearer, Grania realized the figure was no more than a child; that the white cotton she was wearing was a nightdress. Grania could see the black storm clouds hovering out over the sea and the first saltwater droplets of impending rain stung her cheeks. The frailty of the small human against the wildness of her surroundings made her steps toward the child more urgent in pace.

The wind was whipping around her ears now and had started to voice its rage. Grania stopped ten yards from the girl, who was still unmoving. She saw the tiny blue toes holding her stoically to the rock, as the rising wind whipped and swayed her thin body like a willow sapling. She moved closer to the girl, stopping just behind her, uncertain of what to do next. Grania's instinct was to run forward and grab her, but if the girl was startled and turned around, one missed footfall could result in unthinkable tragedy, taking the child to certain death on the foam-covered rocks a hundred feet below.

Grania stood, panic gripping her as she desperately tried to think of the best way to remove her from danger. But before she could reach a decision, the girl slowly turned around and stared at her with unseeing eyes.

Instinctively Grania held out her arms. "I won't hurt you, I promise. Walk toward me and you'll be safe."

Still the girl stared at her, not moving from her spot on the edge of the cliff.

"I can take you home if you tell me where you live. You'll catch your death out here. Please, let me help you," Grania begged.

She took another step toward the child, and then, as if the girl had woken up from a dream, a look of fear crossed her face. Instantly, she turned to her right and began to run away from Grania along the cliff's edge, disappearing from view.

"I was just about to be sending out the search party for you. That storm's blowing up well and good, so it is."

"Mam, I'm thirty-one years old, and I've lived in Manhattan for the past ten of those," replied Grania drily as she entered the kitchen and hung her wet jacket over the AGA stove. "You don't have to mind me. I'm a big girl now, remember?" She smiled as she walked toward her mother, who was setting the table for supper, and kissed her on the cheek. "*Really.*"

"That's as may be, but I've known stronger men by far blown off the cliff in a gale like this." Kathleen Ryan indicated the wildness of the wind outside the kitchen window, which was causing the flowerless wisteria bush to tap its twiggy brown deadness monotonously against the pane. "I've just made a brew." Kathleen wiped her hands on her apron and walked toward the AGA. "Would you be wanting a cup?"

"That would be grand, Mam. Why don't you sit down and take the weight off your feet for a few minutes, and I'll pour it for both of us?" Grania steered her mother to a kitchen chair, pulled it back from the table and sat her gently onto it.

"Only five minutes, mind, the boys will be back at six for their tea."

As Grania poured the strong liquid into two cups, she raised a silent eyebrow at her mother's domestic dedication to her husband and her son. Not that anything had changed in the past ten years since she'd been away—Kathleen had always pandered to her men, putting their needs and desires first. But the contrast of her mother's life to her own, where emancipation and equality of the sexes was standard, made Grania feel uncomfortable.

And yet . . . for all her own freedom from what many modern women would consider outdated male tyranny, who was currently the most content out of mother and daughter? Grania sighed sadly as she added milk to her mother's tea. She knew the answer to that.

"There you go, Mam. Would you like a biscuit?" Grania put the tin in front of Kathleen and opened it. As usual, it was full to the brim with custard creams, bourbons and shortbread rounds. Another relic of childhood, and one that would be looked on with the same horror as a small nuclear device by her figure-conscious New York contemporaries.

Kathleen took two and said, "Go on, have one yourself to keep me company. To be sure, you don't eat enough to keep a mouse alive."

Grania nibbled dutifully at a biscuit, thinking how, ever since she'd arrived home ten days ago, she'd felt stuffed to bursting with her mother's copious home cooking. Yet Grania would say that she had the healthiest appetite out of most of the women she knew in New York. *And* she actually used her oven as it was designed for, not as a convenient place to store plates.

"The walk cleared your head a little, did it?" ventured Kathleen, making her way through her third biscuit. "Whenever I have a problem in my mind to be sorted, I'll be off walking and come back knowing the answer."

"Actually . . ." Grania took a sip of tea. "I saw something strange, Mam, when I was out. A little girl, maybe eight or nine, standing in her nightie right up on the cliff's edge. She had beautiful long, curly red hair . . . it was as if she was sleepwalking, because she turned to look at me when I walked toward her and her eyes were"—she searched for the right description—"blank. Like she wasn't seeing me. Then she seemed to wake up and scampered off like a startled rabbit up the cliff path. Do you know who she might have been?"

Grania watched the color drain from Kathleen's face. "Are you OK, Mam?"

Kathleen visibly shook herself. She stared at her daughter. "You say you saw her just a few minutes ago on your walk?"

"Yes."

"Mary, Mother of God." Kathleen crossed herself. "They're back."

"Who's 'back,' Mam?" asked Grania, concerned by how shaken her mother seemed to be.

"Why have they returned?" Kathleen stared off through the window and into the night. "Why would they be wanting to? I thought . . . I thought it was finally over, that they'd be gone for good." Kathleen grabbed Grania's hand. "Are you sure it was a little girl you saw, not a grown woman?"

"Positive, Mam. As I said, she was aged about eight or nine. I was concerned for her; she had nothing on her feet and looked frozen. To be honest, I wondered whether I was seeing a ghost."

"You were of a fashion, Grania," Kathleen muttered. "They can only have arrived back in the past few days. I was coming over the hill last Friday and I passed right by the house. It was gone ten in the evening and there were no lights shining from the windows. The old place was shut up."

"Where would this be?"

"Dunworley House."

"The big deserted one that stands right on the top of the cliff up past us?" asked Grania. "That's been empty for years, hasn't it?"

"It was empty for your childhood, yes, but"—Kathleen sighed—"they came back after you'd moved to New York. And then, when the . . . accident happened, left. Nobody thought we'd be seeing them around these parts again. And we were glad of it," she underlined. "There's a history there, between them and us, stretching back a long way. Now"—Kathleen slapped the table and made to stand up—"What's past is past, and I'd advise you to stay away from them. They bring nothing but trouble to this family, so they do."

Grania watched her mother as she walked over to the AGA, her face set hard as she lifted the heavy iron pot containing the evening meal out of one of the ovens. "Surely if that child I saw has a mother, she would want to know about the danger her daughter was in today?" she probed.

"She has no mother." Kathleen's wooden spoon stirred the stew rhythmically.

"She's dead?"

"Yes."

"I see . . . so who looks after the poor child?"

"Don't be asking me about their domestic arrangements." Kathleen shrugged. "I couldn't care and I don't want to know."

Grania frowned. Her mother's attitude was totally contrary to the way she would normally respond. Kathleen's big, maternal heart beat hard and loud for any poor thing in trouble. She was the first round to a member of the family, or friends, if there was a problem and support was needed. Especially when it came to children.

"How did her mother die?"

The wooden spoon ceased its circling of the pot and there was silence. Finally, Kathleen gave a heavy sigh and turned to face her daughter. "Well now, I suppose if I'm not telling you, you'll hear it soon enough from someone else. She took her own life, did Lily Lisle."

"You're saying she committed suicide?"

"It's one and the same thing, Grania."

"How long ago?"

"She threw herself off the cliff four years ago. Her body was found two days later, washed up on Inchydoney beach."

It was Grania's turn to stay silent. Finally, she ventured, "Where did she jump from?"

"From the sound of things, probably where you set eyes on her daughter today. I'd say Aurora was looking for her mammy."

"You know her name?"

"Of course. 'Tis hardly a secret. The Lisle family used to own the whole of Dunworley, including this very house. They were the lords and masters round here a long time ago. They sold off their land in the sixties, but kept the house up on the cliff."

"I've seen the name somewhere—*Lisle* . . ."

"The local churchyard is filled with their graves. Including hers."

"And you've seen the little girl—Aurora—out on the cliffs before?"

"That's why her daddy took her away. After *she* died, that little mite would walk along the cliffs calling for her. Half mad with grief she was."

Grania could see her mother's face had softened slightly. "Poor little thing," she breathed.

"Yes, it was a pitiful sight and she didn't deserve any of it, but there's a badness that runs through that family. You listen to what I say, Grania, and don't be getting yourself mixed up with them."

"I wonder why they're back?" Grania murmured, almost to herself.

"Those Lisles are a law unto themselves. I don't know and I don't care. Now, will you be making yourself useful and helping me set the table for tea?"

Grania went upstairs to her bedroom at just past ten o'clock, as she'd done every night since she'd arrived home. Downstairs, her mother was busy in the kitchen laying out the table for breakfast, her father was dozing in the chair in front of the TV and her brother, Shane, was at the village pub. Between the two men, they ran the 500-acre farm, the land mostly given over to dairy herd and sheep. At twenty-nine, the "boy," as Shane was still affectionately called, seemed to have no intention of moving into his own home. Women came and went, but rarely across the threshold of his parents' farmhouse. Kathleen raised her eyebrows over her son's still-unmarried status, but Grania knew her mother would be lost without him.

She climbed between the sheets, listening to the rain battering the windowpanes, and hoped poor Aurora Lisle was tucked up inside, safe and warm. She turned the pages of a book, but found herself yawning and unable to concentrate. Perhaps it was the fresh air here that was making her sleepy; in New York she was rarely in bed before midnight.

In contrast, Grania could scarcely remember a night as a child when her mother had not been at home in the evenings. And if she had to go away overnight on a mission of mercy to care for a sick relative, the preparation to make sure the family did not go hungry or the clothes unwashed was a military operation. As for her father, Grania doubted he had *ever* spent a night away from his bed in the past thirty-four years of his marriage. He was up at five thirty every morning of his life and off to the milking shed, coming home from the farm whenever dusk fell. Husband and wife knew exactly where the other was at all times. Their lives were as one; joint and inseparable.

And the glue that bound them together was their children.

When she and Matt had moved in together eight years ago, they'd taken it for granted that one day there would be babies. Like any modern couple, until that suitable moment presented itself, they had taken their lives and careers by the throat and lived fast and hard while they could.

And then, one morning, Grania had woken up and, as she did every morning, had thrown on her track pants and hoodie and jogged along the Hudson to Battery Park, stopping at the Winter Garden Atrium to enjoy a latte and bagel. And it was there that it had happened; she'd been sipping her coffee and had glanced down into the pram parked by the next table. Inside was a tiny newborn baby, fast asleep. Grania was beset by a sudden, overwhelming urge to pick the baby up out of its pram, to cradle its soft, downy head protectively against her breast. When the mother had smiled nervously at her, then stood up and pushed the pram away from her unwanted attention, Grania had jogged back home, feeling breathless at the emotion that had been stirred in her.

Expecting it to pass, she'd spent the day in her studio, immersing herself in molding the malleable brown clay into her latest commission, but the feeling hadn't alleviated.

At six, she'd left her studio, showered and changed into something suitable for the opening of an art gallery she was attending that evening. She'd poured herself a glass of wine and walked to the window that looked across to the twinkling lights of New Jersey on the other side of the Hudson River.

"I want to have a baby."

Grania had taken a hefty gulp of wine. And giggled at the absurdity of the words she'd just spoken. So she'd said them again, just to make sure.

And they'd still felt right. Not only right, but completely natural, as if the thought and the need had been with her all her life and all the reasons "not to" had simply evaporated and now seemed ridiculous.

Grania had gone out to the gallery opening, made small talk with the usual mix of artists, collectors and envelope-openers that made up such events. Yet, in her mind, she was running through the practicalities of the life-changing decision she had made earlier. Would they have to move? No, probably not in the short term—their TriBeCa loft was spacious and Matt's study/spare bedroom could easily be turned into a nursery. He rarely used it anyway, preferring to take his laptop into the sitting room and work there. They were up on the fourth floor, but the freight elevator was quite big enough to take a pram. Battery Park, with its well-equipped playground and fresh river air, was easily walkable. Grania worked from home in her studio, so even if a nanny had to be employed, she'd only be a few seconds away from the baby if she was needed.

Grania had climbed into the big, empty bed later and sighed with irritation that she'd have to keep her plans and her excitement to herself for a while longer. Matt had been away for the past week, and wasn't due home for another couple of days. It was not the kind of thing one could just announce over the phone. She'd finally fallen asleep in the early hours, imagining Matt's proud gaze as she handed him his newborn child.

When he'd arrived home, Matt had been just as excited about the idea as she was. They'd made an immediate and very pleasurable start on putting their plan into action, both of them loving the fact they had their own secret joint project, which would bond and cement them, just as it had her own parents. It was the missing piece that would unite them once and for all into a homogenized, codependent unit. In essence, a *family*.

Grania lay in her narrow childhood bed, listening to the wind howling angrily around the solid stone walls of the farmhouse. She reached for a tissue and blew her nose, hard.

That had been a year ago. And the terrible truth was, their "joint project" had not united them. It had destroyed them.

2

When Grania woke up the next morning, the storm of the night before had blown away like a memory, taking the gray clouds with it. The sun was making a rare winter appearance, lighting the rolling landscape beyond her window, giving definition to the endless green of the fields that surrounded the farm, interspersed with the white, woolly dots of the sheep that grazed on it.

Grania knew from experience that this state of affairs was not likely to last long; the West Cork sun was akin to a temperamental diva, gracing the stage for a cameo appearance, bathing all in her glory and then disappearing as quickly as she had arrived.

Having been unable to complete her normal routine of a morning jog because of the incessant rain of the past ten days, Grania jumped out of bed and rifled through her still unpacked suitcase to find her hoodie, leggings and sneakers.

"Well now, you're up bright and early this morning," commented her mother as Grania arrived downstairs in the kitchen. "Porridge?"

"I'll have some when I come back. I'm going for a run."

"Well, don't you be tiring yourself out. I'd say the color on you isn't healthy—no flush in those cheeks of yours."

"That's what I hope to achieve, Mam." Grania suppressed a smile. "I'll see you later."

"Don't be getting a chill now, will you?" Kathleen called to the disappearing back of her daughter. She watched from the kitchen window as Grania ran down the narrow lane cut into the fields by an ancient drystone wall, which led eventually to the road and the path up to the cliffs.

She'd been shocked at the sight of her child when Grania had arrived home; in the three years since Kathleen had last seen her, her beautiful, bonny daughter—always a head-turner, with her peaches and cream complexion, curly blond hair and lively turquoise eyes—

seemed to have diminished in vitality. As she'd commented to her husband, John, Grania currently resembled a bright pink shirt that had been put by mistake in a dark wash. And emerged a dulled, graying relic of its former self.

Kathleen knew the reason. Grania had told her when she'd called from New York to ask if she could come home for a while. She had agreed, of course, delighted at the unexpected opportunity to spend time with her daughter. However, Kathleen could not understand Grania's motive—surely, this was a time when she and her man needed to be together, to support each other in their grief, not have half the world separating them.

And that lovely Matt telephoned every night to speak to her, but Grania stubbornly refused to take his calls. Kathleen had always harbored a soft spot for him; with his clean-cut good looks, soft Connecticut accent and impeccable manners, Matt reminded Kathleen of the movie stars she'd mooned over as a girl. A young Robert Redford—that's what Matt looked like to her. Why Grania hadn't married him years ago was beyond her. And now her daughter, always stubborn, was surely on the verge of losing him altogether.

Kathleen did not know much about the ways of the world, but she understood men and their egos. They were not built as women—did not have the same capacity for rejection—and if there was one thing she was certain of, it was that his phone calls would soon stop coming nightly and Matt would give up.

Unless there was something that Kathleen didn't know . . .

She sighed as she cleared away the breakfast dishes and dumped them in the sink. Grania was her golden girl—the one Ryan of the clan who'd fled the nest and done everything possible to make her family, especially her mother, proud of her. She was the child the relatives wanted to hear about, poring over the cuttings Grania sent from various newspapers detailing her latest exhibition in New York, fascinated by the well-heeled clients who commissioned Grania to immortalize their children's faces or animals in bronze . . .

Making it in America—it was still the ultimate Irish dream.

Kathleen dried the bowls and cutlery and stowed them away in the wooden dresser. Of course, no one had the perfect life, Kathleen knew that. She'd always presumed that the patter of tiny feet was something Grania had never hankered after, and had accepted it. Did she not have a fine, strong son to give her grandchildren one day? Yet it seemed she'd been wrong. For all Grania's sophisticated lifestyle, living in New York, at what Kathleen saw as the center of the universe, the babies were missing. And until they came along, her daughter would not be happy.

Kathleen could not help thinking Grania had brought it on herself. For all those newfangled drugs, used to help and abet the miracle of nature, there was no substitute for youth. She herself had been nineteen when she'd had Grania. And brimming with the energy to cope with another baby in the space of two years. Grania was thirty-one. And whatever any of these modern career women believed, it was impossible to have everything.

So, although she felt for her daughter's loss, it was her way to accept what she had and not pine after what she didn't. And on that thought, Kathleen climbed up the stairs to make the beds.

Grania sank down on to a damp, moss-covered rock to catch her breath. She was puffing and panting like an OAP; obviously the miscarriage and a recent lack of exercise had taken its toll. Grania put her head between her legs as she caught her breath and kicked at the coarse clods of rough grass beneath them. They stubbornly refused to be dislodged from the strong roots which held them fast beneath the ground. If only the little life inside her had done the same . . .

Four months . . . when she and Matt had finally thought they were fine—everyone knew you'd usually reached a safe place by then. And Grania, paranoid up until that point, had begun to relax and give in to the fantasy of becoming a *mother.*

She and Matt had announced the news to both sets of grandparents; Elaine and Bob, Matt's parents, had taken them out to L'Escale, near their enormous house in the gated community of Belle Haven, Greenwich. Bob had asked bluntly when the two of them would get on with their long-awaited marriage now that Grania was expecting. After all, this was their first grandchild and Bob had made it blatantly clear it must take the family name. Grania had stonewalled—when pushed into a corner her hackles rose, especially with Matt's father—and she'd replied that she and Matt were yet to discuss it.

A week later, at their TriBeCa apartment, the intercom had announced the arrival of a Bloomingdale's van, delivering the contents of an entire nursery. Grania, too superstitious to have the goods placed inside the loft, had directed them down to the basement, where they would be stored until nearer the time. As she'd watched the assortment of boxes being stacked into a corner, Grania knew Elaine had forgotten nothing.

"Bang goes our trip out to Bloomie's to choose a cot, or which brand of diapers I'd like," Grania had murmured ungratefully to Matt later that evening.

"Mom's only trying to help us, Grania," Matt had answered defensively. "She knows I hardly earn anything and your income is healthy, but sporadic. Just maybe I should consider going into Dad's business after all, now that the little one is on the way." Matt had indicated Grania's tiny but visible bump.

"No, Matt!" Grania had expostulated. "We agreed you never would. You'd have no life or freedom at all if you went to work for your dad. You know how overpowering he can be."

Grania gave up trying to dislodge the grass from its roots and stared out to sea instead. She smiled grimly at the understatement she'd used in that conversation with Matt. Bob was a full-time control freak when it came to his son. Although she understood the disappointment he must feel that Matt had no interest in taking over the family investment business, she couldn't understand his lack of interest or pride in his son's career. Matt was doing very well, and had become a renowned authority in the field of child psychology. He held a chair at Columbia University, and was constantly asked as guest lecturer to other universities across the States. Bob also patronized Grania constantly, making small but pointed comments about her upbringing and level of education.

Looking back, Grania was at least relieved they'd refused to accept handouts from Matt's parents. Even in the early days, when she was trying to make her name as a sculptor and Matt was completing his Ph.D. and they'd struggled to pay the rent on their tiny one-bedroom apartment, she'd been paranoid. And with good reason,

Grania thought; the shiny, immaculately dressed Connecticut girls whom she'd met through Matt and his family could not be a greater contrast to an unsophisticated, convent-educated girl from a small Irish backwater. Maybe it had been destined to fail . . .

"Hello."

Grania jumped at the sound of the voice. She looked around her, but could see no one.

"Hello, I said."

The voice was behind her. She turned one hundred and eighty degrees to view the owner. And there was Aurora Lisle, standing at her back. Thankfully, dressed today in a pair of jeans, an anorak that hung from her thin frame and a woolly hat hiding all but the occasional wisp of her magnificent red hair. Her face was tiny and prettily heart-shaped, her huge eyes and full pink lips out of proportion to the miniature canvas in which they were set.

"Hello, Aurora."

Grania's greeting engendered a look of surprise in Aurora's eyes. "How do you know what my name is?"

"I saw you yesterday."

"Did you? Where?"

"Here on the cliffs."

"Really?" Aurora frowned. "I don't remember being here yesterday. And certainly not speaking to you."

"You didn't speak to me, Aurora. I saw you, that's all," Grania explained.

"Then how do you know my name?" Aurora spoke in a high, clipped English accent.

"I asked my mother who the little girl with the beautiful long red hair might be. And she told me."

"And how would she know?" the child asked imperiously.

"She's lived in the village all her life. She said you'd gone away years ago."

"We had. But now we're back." Aurora looked out to sea and swept her arms to embrace the coastline. "And I love it here, don't you?"

Grania had the feeling Aurora's question was a statement with which she was not allowed to disagree. "Of course I love it. It's where I was born and where I grew up."

"So." Aurora settled herself gracefully on the grass next to Grania and her blue eyes bored into her. "What is *your* name?"

"Grania, Grania Ryan."

"Well, I can't say I've ever heard of you."

Grania wanted to smile at Aurora's adult way of expressing herself. "I suppose there's no reason why you should have done. I've been away from here almost ten years."

Aurora's face lit up with pleasure and she clapped her small hands together. "Then that means we have both come back to a place we love at the same time."

"I suppose it does."

"So, we can keep each other company! You can be my new friend."

"That's very kind of you, Aurora."

"Well, you must be lonely."

"Maybe you're right . . ." Grania smiled. "And what about you? Are you lonely here too?"

"Sometimes, yes." Aurora shrugged. "Daddy always has so much work to do and is often away, and there's only the housekeeper to play with. And she isn't very good at games." Aurora wrinkled her delicately freckled retroussé nose in displeasure.

"Oh dear," commented Grania, for want of anything better to say. She was both disarmed and discomfited by the child's quaintness. "You must have friends at school, surely?"

"I don't go to school. My father likes me at home with him. I have a governess instead."

"So where is she today?"

"Daddy and I decided we didn't like her, so we left her behind in London." Aurora giggled suddenly. "We simply packed up and left."

"I see," said Grania, although she most certainly didn't.

"Do you have a job?" Aurora asked.

"Yes, I do. I'm a sculptor."

"Isn't that someone who makes statues out of clay?"

"You're along the right lines, yes," answered Grania.

"Oh, do you know about papier-mâché?" Aurora's face lit up. "I *love* papier-mâché! I had a nanny once who showed me how to make bowls, and we'd paint them and then I'd give them to Daddy as a present. Would you come and make some papier-mâché with me? Please."

Grania was charmed by Aurora's eagerness and genuine excitement. "All right." She found herself nodding. "I don't see why not."

"Will you come now? We could go up to the house and make something for Daddy before he goes away." Aurora reached out her hand and tugged at Grania's hoodie. "Please say yes!"

"No, Aurora, I can't just now. I'd need to go and get the things to make it. And besides, my mammy might think I'd gotten lost," Grania added.

Grania watched Aurora's face fall, saw the light disappear from her eyes and her body sag. "I don't have a mummy. I did once, but she died."

"I'm so sorry, Aurora." Instinctively, Grania reached out and patted the child gently on her shoulder. "You must miss her a lot."

"I do. She was the most beautiful, special person in the world. Daddy always says she was an angel, and that's why the other angels came to take her, so she could go to heaven where she belonged."

Grania quailed at Aurora's obvious pain. "I'm sure your daddy is right," she agreed. "And at least you have him."

"Yes, I do," agreed Aurora, "and he's the best father in the world, and the most handsome. I know if you saw him, you'd fall in love with him. Every lady does."

"Well then, I shall have to meet him, won't I?" Grania smiled.

"Yes." Aurora jumped up suddenly from the grass. "I have to go now. You will be here again at the same time tomorrow."

This was not a request, it was an order.

"I . . ."

"Good." Spontaneously, Aurora launched herself into Grania's arms and hugged her. "Bring all the things for the papier-mâché, then we can go up to my house and spend the morning making bowls for Daddy. Bye-bye, Grania, I'll see you tomorrow."

"Good-bye." Grania waved, and watched as Aurora skipped and danced like a young gazelle along the cliffs. Even in her anorak and sneakers, her movements were graceful.

When Aurora had disappeared from view, Grania drew in a long breath, feeling almost as if she'd been under an enchantment; held in thrall by a small, ethereal being. She rose, shaking her head to clear it, wondering what her mother would say when she announced that tomorrow she was going up to Dunworley House to play with Aurora Lisle.

3

That evening, when her father and brother left the table—and their used plates and cutlery upon it for her mother to clear—Grania helped Kathleen with the washing-up.

"I met Aurora Lisle again today," said Grania casually as she dried the plates.

Kathleen raised an eyebrow. "And was she out in her nightdress again, masquerading as a spirit?"

"No, she was fully clothed. She's an odd little girl, isn't she?"

"Well now, I wouldn't know how she was." Kathleen's mouth was set in a firm, hard line.

"I said I might go up to her house and make some papier-mâché with her. She seems lonely," Grania volunteered.

There was a pause before Kathleen said, "I've told you, Grania, warned you not to get involved with that family. But you're a big girl now and I can't stop you."

"But, Mam, she's simply a lonely, sweet little girl. She seems lost . . . she has no mother. Surely, it can't do any harm to spend a couple of hours with her?"

"I'm not discussing it again with you, Grania. You've heard what I think and you have to make your own decisions. And that's an end to it."

The sound of the telephone ringing broke through the ensuing silence. Grania made no move to answer it, nor did her mother. On the seventh ring Kathleen put her hands on her hips. "You realize who that is, I'm sure."

"No," said Grania disingenuously, "Why should I, Mam? It could be anyone."

"We both know who that is at this time of night, my girl, and I'm too embarrassed to be speaking to him again."

The telephone continued to ring, the abrasive urgency of the sound in direct contrast with mother and daughter's contrived stillness. Finally it stopped and the two women stared into the whites of each other's eyes.

"I'll not be having this, Grania, this rudeness under my roof. I've run out of things to say to him. What has that poor man done to you anyway, to deserve this kind of treatment? You've suffered a loss, but that's hardly his fault, is it?"

"I'm sorry, Mam." Grania shook her head. "But you just don't understand."

"Well, that's the first thing you've said that I agree with. So why don't you tell me?"

"Mam! Please! I can't . . ." Grania wrung her hands in frustration. "I just *can't.*"

"To my mind, Grania, that's not good enough. Whatever's happened is affecting everyone in the house and we all need to be put right on the situation. I—"

"It's Matt, darlin'," said her father as he strolled into the kitchen holding the phone. "We've had a nice chat, but I think it's you he wants to speak to." John grinned apologetically and offered her the handset.

Grania threw her father a killer stare and snatched the handset from him. She moved out of the kitchen and headed up the stairs toward her bedroom.

"Grania? Is that you?" The soft, familiar tones of Matt's voice brought an immediate lump to her throat as she closed the door behind her and perched on the end of the bed.

"Matt, I asked you not to contact me."

"I know you did, baby, but Jesus! I can't figure out what's going on. What have I done? Why have you left me?"

Grania ground her free hand into her jean-covered thigh to keep her calm.

"Grania? Are you still there, honey? Please, if you can explain what it is I'm meant to have done then perhaps I can defend myself."

Still Grania did not answer.

"Grania, *please*, talk to me. This is Matt, the man who loves you. Who you've shared a life with for eight years. And I'm going insane here, not knowing why you've gone."

Grania took a deep breath in. "Please don't call me. I don't want to speak to you. And it's upsetting my parents, you bothering them every night."

"Grania, please, I understand it was real hard on you losing the baby, but we can try again, surely? I love you, honey, and I'll do anything to . . ."

"Good-bye, Matt." Grania pressed the appropriate button to end the call, unable to hear any more. She sat where she was, staring unseeingly at the faded flowers on the wallpaper of her childhood bedroom. It was a pattern she had looked at night after night as she'd indulged in her girlish dreams of the future. In which her own Prince Charming would appear and carry her off to a life of perfect love. Matt had been all those things and more . . . she'd adored him from the first moment she'd set eyes upon him. And it *had* been a fairy tale.

Grania lay down on the bed and hugged her pillow. Now, her belief that love could conquer all—could leap over any boundary, reign victorious over any problem that life might present and emerge triumphant—was gone.

Matt Connelly slumped on to the sofa, his cell phone still resting in the palm of his hand.

In the past two weeks since Grania had upped and left, Matt had racked his brains to think of any reason why she should have gone. None was forthcoming. What could he do to solve this? Grania had made it blatantly clear that she currently wanted nothing to do with him . . . seriously, was their relationship over?

"Goddammit!" Matt hurled the cell phone across the room, watching the battery splay out of the back of it. Yes, he understood how devastated she was about the miscarriage, but surely that was no reason to cut *him* out of her life too? Perhaps he should just get on a plane and go to her in Ireland. But what if she wouldn't see him? What if he made it worse?

Matt stood up, coming to an instant decision. As he marched toward his laptop, he knew anything was better than the uncertainty he was suffering just now. Even if Grania told him point-blank it was all over, it had to be preferable to being in the dark.

Matt logged on and was starting to explore flights between New

York and Dublin when the intercom buzzed. He ignored it. He wasn't expecting any visitors and certainly wouldn't welcome any either. It continued to buzz insistently until, out of sheer irritation, Matt walked across the sitting room and pressed the intercom. "Who is it?"

"Hi, hon, just passing by, thought I'd check in to make sure you're OK."

Matt pressed the entry button immediately. "Sorry, Charley, come up." He left the door ajar, and went back to his perusal of flights. Charley was one of the few people he could stomach seeing. A childhood friend, she'd moved off his radar—along with many of his old buddies—when he and Grania had gotten together. Grania had felt uncomfortable with his old Connecticut group, so he'd given them a wide berth for her sake. A few days ago, Charley had called out of the blue and said she'd heard from his folks that Grania had disappeared back to Ireland. She'd come across town and taken him for a pizza. It had been good to see her.

A few minutes later, a pair of arms snaked around his shoulders and Charley planted a soft kiss on his cheek. A bottle of red wine was deposited on the desk next to his laptop.

"Thought you might need this. Shall I get us a couple of glasses?"

"That would be just great. Thanks, Charley." Matt continued to compare and contrast timings and costs as Charley uncorked the wine and poured it into two glasses.

"What are you looking at?" she asked as she threw off her boots and curled her long legs beneath her on the sofa.

"Flights to Ireland. If Grania's not coming back here, I gotta go to her."

Charley raised a perfectly manicured eyebrow. "You think that's sensible?"

"What the hell else am I meant to do? Hang around here, going half out of my mind while I try to figure out the problem, and hitting a blank wall time and again?"

Charley threw back her mane of glossy dark hair and took a sip of wine. "But what if she just needs some space? To get over . . . well, you know. You might make things worse, Matty. Has Grania said she wanted to see you?"

"Hell, no! I just called her and she asked me to stop contacting her." Matt rose from the laptop, took a large slug of wine and joined Charley on the sofa. "Maybe you're right," he sighed. "Perhaps I should give her some more time and eventually she'll come to her senses. Losing the baby was such a blow to her. You know how eager Mom and Dad were for the next generation to make an appearance. Dad hardly did much to hide his disappointment when he showed up at the hospital after the miscarriage."

"I can imagine." Charley rolled her eyes. "Subtlety was never one of your dad's qualities, now was it? Not that he's ever offended me, but then you guys have been like family, so I'm used to him. But I suppose to an outsider like Grania it might have been hard for her to cope with."

"Yes." Matt rested his elbows on his knees and put his head in his hands. "Maybe I just didn't do enough to protect her. I know how uncomfortable she's always been about the difference in our backgrounds."

"Matty, honey, really—you couldn't have done more. You even put me in the garbage can when Grania came along."

Matt looked at her and frowned. "Hey, you're not serious, are you? That time when we dated could never have worked out long-term, could it? We both agreed on that, if you remember."

"Sure, Matty." Charley gave him a smile of reassurance. "It was always something that had to happen at some point, wasn't it?"

"Sure it was." Matt was pacified by her mirroring of his own thoughts.

"You know," mused Charley, "sometimes, as I watch my girlfriends go through relationship traumas like this, I thank heaven I'm still single. I hardly know anyone that's in a good space with their partners these days, although I really thought you guys had got it right."

"So did we," he replied sadly. "You're not seriously considering spinsterhood for the rest of your life, are you? Out of our Greenwich crowd, you were 'the one most likely to'; Sorority Queen, straight-A student and the most beautiful girl in your class. Now successful magazine editor . . . hell, Charley, you know you could have anyone."

"Yeah, and maybe that's the problem." Charley let out a sigh. "Maybe I'm too darned fussy and no one is good enough. Anyway, now is not the time to be discussing me. You're the one in a real mess. What can I do to help?"

"OK . . . should I get on a plane to Ireland tomorrow to try and rescue my relationship?" he asked.

"Matty, it's so up to you"—Charley wrinkled her nose—"but if you want my opinion, I'd give Grania some space and time. She's obviously got stuff to work out. I'm sure she'll come back to you when she's ready. She's asked you to leave her alone, hasn't she? So why don't you do the lady's bidding, and then maybe think again in a couple of weeks? Besides, I thought you were up to your eyes with work."

"I am," breathed Matt. "And maybe you're right. I gotta give her the space she's asked me for." He reached out a hand and patted Charley's outstretched shin gently. "Thanks, li'l sis. You're always there for me, aren't you?"

"Yes, honey." Charley smiled from under her lashes. "I'll always be here for you."

A few days later, there was another buzz on Matt's intercom.

"Hi, sweetie, it's Mom. Can I come up?"

"Sure." Matt opened the front door for her, surprised at the impromptu visit. His parents rarely graced this part of town, and never unannounced.

"Darling, how are you?" Elaine kissed her son on both cheeks then followed him inside.

"I'm OK," Matt replied, too low and tired to make more of an effort. He watched his mom shrug off her fur coat, rearrange her subtly highlighted blond hair with a quick toss of her head and sit her perfect size six body elegantly on the sofa. He quickly removed his sneakers and a couple of empty beer bottles away from her tiny, stilettoed feet. "What brings you here?"

"I was up in town at a charity lunch and you're on the way home." Elaine smiled. "I wanted to see how my boy is doing."

"I'm OK," Matt repeated. "Can I fix you anything to drink, Mom?"

"A glass of water would do fine."

"Sure."

Elaine watched him as he went to the refrigerator and poured the water. He looked pale and tired and his body language betrayed his unhappiness. "Thanks," she said as he brought her the water. "So, any word from Grania?"

"I called and spoke to her briefly a few days ago, but she sure doesn't care to speak to me."

"Have you found out why she left?"

"No." Matt shrugged. "I don't know what I've done. Christ, Mom, that baby meant everything to her."

"She was real quiet when we saw her that day at the hospital, looked like she'd been crying when she came out of the bathroom."

"Yeah, and the next day I arrived to visit her after work to find she'd checked herself out. I came back here and found a note saying she'd gone home to Ireland to stay with her parents. She hasn't opened up to me since. I know she's hurting, but I don't know how to reach her."

"You must be hurting too, honey. It was your baby as well as hers," Elaine commented, hating the sight of her precious son in pain and suffering alone.

"Yeah, it doesn't feel too good just now. We were gonna be a family. It was, like, my dream . . . shit! Sorry, Mom." Matt did his best to try and stem the tears. "I love her so much, and that little one, who didn't make it, who was part of us . . . I . . ."

"Oh, honey." Elaine stood and reached up to take her son in her arms. "I'm so, so sorry. If there's anything I can do to help . . ."

Matt wished his mother hadn't caught him at such a low moment. He dug deep to find the strength to pull himself back together. "I'm a big boy now, Mom. I'll be OK, really. I only wish I knew what it is that's made Grania run away. I just don't understand it."

"How about you coming to stay with us for a while? I don't like to think of you all alone here."

"Thanks, Mom, but I've got a heap of work. I just gotta believe that Grania will come back in her own time, once she's licked her wounds. She's always been a law unto herself. I guess that's why I love her the way I do."

"She's certainly unusual," agreed Elaine. "And doesn't seem to care for the rules most of us abide by."

"That's maybe because she wasn't brought up with them," countered Matt, not in the mood for any snide parental comments or "I told you so's" about his choice of love.

"Oh no, Matt, you got me wrong," Elaine said hastily. "I really admire Grania, and the two of you, for stepping outside the box and being together simply because you love each other. Maybe more of us should follow our heart, rather than our upbringing." Elaine sighed. "I've got to be getting back. Your father has his golfing buddies coming round for their annual winter dinner."

Matt duly collected then held out Elaine's fur coat for her to put on. "Thanks for coming, Mom. I appreciate it."

"It was good to see you, Matt." She kissed him on the cheek. "You know I'm proud of you, don't you? And anytime you want to talk, I'm there for you, honey, really. I understand . . . how you must feel." A hint of sadness appeared in her eyes, then disappeared as quickly as it had come. "Bye, Matty."

Matt closed the door behind her, sensing that she really did empathize with him. And, loving her for it, he realized for the first time how little he knew of the woman beneath the shiny veneer of perfect Connecticut wife and mother.

4

Once Kathleen had left for Clonakilty to do the weekly shopping the following morning, Grania walked to the barn where the old newspapers were stored and collected a pile of them. She rooted through her father's chaotic workshop and came out triumphantly with a mildewed box of wallpaper paste. Putting them in a carrier bag, Grania set off down the lane and headed up toward the cliffs. If Aurora didn't appear—and as no specific time had been set yesterday for them to meet, it was likely—she would simply come back home.

As she walked, Grania pondered on the numbness inside her. It felt as if her life was happening to somebody else, as if she was walking through treacle and couldn't reach her own feelings. She simply couldn't cry or bring herself to confront Matt, or work out whether her reaction had been rational. That would mean contending with the pain, and the safest and best solution was to shut down. What was done, was done, and couldn't be erased.

Grania sat down on the rock overlooking the sea at the top of the cliffs and sighed. She'd really believed, as the two of them had watched their friends' relationships fall by the wayside, that they were different. Grania blushed in embarrassment for all the smug conversations the two of them had shared. The "it'll never happen to us" and the "aren't we lucky, poor old them" comments burned in her memory. They too had fallen prey to the complex, ever-changing maelstrom; the state of male and female trying to live in harmony together.

Grania stared out at the cold, gray sea and suddenly knew huge respect for her own parents. Somehow they had managed to do the impossible—to compromise, accept and, most important, remain happy for thirty-four years.

Perhaps it was simply because, these days, expectations were so high. The hierarchy of needs had moved on. No longer did a couple have to worry about providing enough food to feed their children, or where the next penny was coming from. Or whether, in fact, their infants would survive through a dangerous childhood disease. Now the concern was not so much to do with keeping one's body warm through a long winter, but what designer label one should wear to do the job. These days, few women in Western society had to kiss their husbands good-bye not knowing when or if they would see them again, as they went off to fight. The bottom line was they were past the business of simple survival.

"Now we *demand* happiness. We believe we deserve it." Grania spoke the words out loud, envying rather than pitying the acceptance and stoicism of her parents. They had little in the way of material possessions, and their horizons were narrow. Inconsequential things made them smile, but that smile was shared in mutual understanding of each other and their lot. Their world was small, but at least it was secure within its boundaries and gave them a bond. Whereas she and Matt lived in a wide-open metropolis, where the sky was the limit for both of them and there were dangerously few limitations.

"Hello, Grania."

Aurora's voice sounded behind her. Grania turned and saw her, thinking how Aurora was like a sprite, appearing soundlessly on the territory she inhabited.

"Hello, Aurora. How are you?"

"I am very well, thank you. Shall we go?"

"Yes. I've brought the things we need."

"I know. I've already seen them in your carrier bag."

Obediently, Grania rose, and the two of them headed up toward the house.

"Perhaps you can meet Daddy," Aurora offered. "He's in his study. He might have a headache though, he gets a lot of headaches."

"Does he?"

"Yes. It is simply because he doesn't wear his glasses and he strains his eyes reading all his business papers."

"That's very silly, isn't it?"

"Well, now Mummy's dead, he doesn't have anyone to take care of him, does he? Except me."

"And I'm sure you do a very good job," Grania reassured Aurora as they walked to the gate that led into the garden of the house.

"I do my best," she said as she pushed it open. "This is my home, Dunworley House. It's been in the Lisle family for two centuries. Have you ever been here before?"

"No," answered Grania as she followed Aurora through the gate, and the wind that had been whistling around them as they'd climbed higher up the cliff suddenly calmed. This was due to a thick hedge of brambles and the wild fuchsia West Cork was famous for, which stood sentinel around the house, protecting it and its occupants as best it could.

Grania stared in surprise at the beautifully tended formal garden that provided an immaculate, soft apron to the austere gray building that stood in the center of it. Low hedges, formed of bay, lined each side of the path that led up to the house. And, as Grania followed Aurora toward it, she noticed the rosebush-filled flower beds—dead and colorless now, but in the height of summer, providing a necessary softness to its bleak surroundings.

"We never use the front door," said Aurora, veering off to the right and following the path along the front of the house and around the corner toward the back. "Daddy says it was locked in the Troubles and somebody lost the key. This is the entrance we use."

Grania was standing in a large courtyard, which provided vehicular access from the road. There was a brand-new Range Rover parked in it.

"Come on," said Aurora as she opened the door.

Grania followed her through a lobby and into a large kitchen. A vast pine Welsh dresser took up the entirety of one wall, creaking under its load of blue-and-white plates and a variety of other crockery. A range took up another wall, and an ancient butler's sink sitting between two old melamine worktops was on the last. In the center of the room stood a long oak table, covered with piles of newspapers.

This was not a room to feel cozy or comfortable in—not a place where a family would gather as the mother stood by the AGA, cooking something delicious for supper. It was spartan, functional and forbidding.

"I needn't have brought any newspaper," Grania commented, pointing at the piles on the table.

"Oh, Daddy uses them to light all the fires in the house. He feels the cold so badly. Now, shall we make some space on the table so we can do our project?" Aurora looked at Grania expectantly.

"Yes . . . but do you think we should tell somebody that I'm here?"

"Oh, no"—Aurora shook her head—"Daddy doesn't want to be disturbed and I told Mrs. Myther earlier that you were coming." She was dumping piles of newspaper on the floor around the table and indicated to Grania the space she had created. "What else do we need?"

"We'll need water to mix with the paste." Grania emptied the contents of her carrier bag, feeling uncomfortable about her unannounced presence.

"I'll get some." Aurora procured a jug from one of the overflowing cupboards in the dresser and filled it.

"And a large container for mixing the paste."

Aurora found this too, and placed it on the table in front of Grania. As she mixed the paste, Aurora watched her, her eyes alive and excited. "Isn't this fun? I love doing things like this. My last nanny didn't let me do anything, because she was too worried about me getting messy."

"I spend my life getting messy." Grania smiled. "I make sculptures from materials very similar to this. Now, come and sit next to me and we'll make a bowl."

Aurora proved to be enthusiastic and, an hour later, a soggy newspaper bowl was placed proudly on the hotplate of the range.

"Once it's dried out, we can paint it. Do you have any paints?" asked Grania as she washed her hands in the sink.

"No. I did in London, but I left them behind."

"Perhaps I can find some at my home."

"Could I come and see your house? I think it would be fun to live on a farm."

"I don't live there all the time, Aurora," explained Grania. "I live in New York. I'm just staying with my parents for now."

"Oh." Aurora's face fell. "You mean you'll be leaving soon?"

"Yes, but I don't really know when." As Grania dried her hands on the towel by the sink she felt Aurora's eyes boring into her.

"Why are you sad?" Aurora asked.

"I'm not sad, Aurora."

"Yes, you are, I can see it in your eyes. Has someone upset you?"

"No, Aurora, I'm fine." Grania could feel herself blushing under the child's continuing gaze.

"I know you're sad." Aurora crossed her small arms over her chest. "I know how it feels to be sad. And when I am, I take myself off to my magical place."

"Where is that?"

"I can't tell you, or it wouldn't be magical. Or mine. You should have one too."

"I think that sounds like a grand idea." Grania glanced at her watch. "I'd better be going. It's lunchtime. You must be hungry. Is someone coming to make it for you?"

"Oh, Mrs. Myther would have left something in there." Aurora pointed airily in the direction of the pantry. "It's probably soup again. Before you go, would you like to see the rest of my house?"

"Aurora . . . I . . ."

"Come on!" Aurora grabbed Grania's arm and pulled her toward the door. "I want you to see it. It's beautiful."

Grania was pulled out of the kitchen and into a large hall, the floor covered in black and white tiles and an elegant oak staircase in one corner leading to the floor above. She was dragged across the hall and into a large drawing room with long French windows that overlooked the garden. The room was unbearably hot, with a big log fire throwing out heat from inside its elegant marble surround.

Grania glanced above the fireplace, and the face in the painting caught her sculptor's eye. It was of a young woman, her heart-shaped face crowned by a mass of Titian curls. Her facial features were delicate and, Grania noticed, symmetrical, which was the mark of a true beauty. Her striking blue eyes, set in her white skin, were innocent yet knowing. From a professional point of view, Grania knew that this had been painted by a talented artist. She turned to look at Aurora and immediately saw the resemblance.

"It's my mother. Everyone says I'm the image of her."

"You are," Grania answered softly. "What was her name?"

Aurora took a deep breath. "Lily. Her name was Lily."

"I'm very sorry she died, Aurora," said Grania gently as the child stared intently at the painting.

Aurora did not answer, just continued to stare at her mother.

"And who might this be, Aurora?"

A male voice from behind them made Grania jump. She turned

around, wondering how much of the conversation the interloper had overheard, and caught her breath.

Standing by the door was—Grania berated herself for falling into cliché, but this was *fact*—the most beautiful man she had ever seen. Tall—at least six foot—with thick, ebony hair, tidily combed but just a centimeter too long, so that tendrils of it curled at the nape of his neck. Lips that were full, but not too plump as to be feminine, and a pair of deep, navy blue eyes, fringed with thick, dark eyelashes.

As she was trained to do, Grania took in and admired his immaculate bone structure; the razor-sharp cheekbones, strong jaw and perfect nose. It was a face Grania wanted to remember in detail, so she could sculpt it for herself at a later date.

And all of this sat atop a lean, perfectly proportioned physique. Her eyes were drawn to the slim, sensitive fingers that were clenching and then relaxing, indicating some form of inner tension. The overall picture was one of singular elegance, a quality she wouldn't normally associate with the male sex. But one which guaranteed that this man would turn every head in the room—be it male or female—the moment he entered it.

Grania sighed involuntarily, her professional response to a man that verged, in her opinion, on physical perfection, conspiring with a natural feminine reaction to it that rendered her temporarily silent.

"Who are you?" he asked again.

"This is my friend Grania, Daddy." Aurora broke the silence, to Grania's relief. "Remember? I told you I'd met her on the cliffs yesterday. We've had such fun in the kitchen this morning, making a bowl out of glue and newspaper. When it's painted I'm going to give it to you as a present." Aurora walked to her father and put her arms around him.

"I'm glad you've had fun, darling." He stroked her hair affectionately and gave Grania a half-smile, which contained an air of suspicion. "So, Grania, are you a visitor to Dunworley?"

His dark-blue eyes appraised her. Grania did her best to compose herself, found her mouth was dry and swallowed before she said, "I'm from the village originally, I was born there, but I've been living abroad the past ten years. I've come home to visit my family."

"I see." His eyes traveled toward the long French windows and the magnificent view of the sea beyond the garden. "This is a rare and magical place. And you love it, don't you, Aurora?"

"You know I do, Daddy. It's our real home."

"Yes, it is." He brought his attention back to Grania. "Forgive me, I haven't introduced myself." With Aurora still clinging to his hips, he walked toward her and extended a hand. "Alexander Devonshire." His long, slim fingers clasped hers.

Grania did her best to drag herself back from the sense of the surreal she was experiencing. " 'Devonshire?' I thought this was the Lisle family?"

A pair of dark eyebrows rose almost imperceptibly. "You are right in the sense that this is the Lisle family house, but I married into it. My wife"—Alexander's eyes darted to the painting—"Was the heiress to Dunworley House and one day it will pass to our daughter."

"I'm sorry . . . I didn't realize."

"Really, Grania, I'm used to being called 'Mr. Lisle' around here." Alexander pulled his daughter closer to him, lost in his own thoughts.

"I'd better be getting home," said Grania uncomfortably.

"Oh, Daddy, does she have to go? Can't she stay for lunch?" Aurora looked up at her father, imploring him with her eyes.

"Thank you for the offer, but really, I must go."

"Of course," said Alexander. "It's very kind of you to spend time with my daughter."

"She's far more fun than the old nanny, Daddy. Why can't she look after me?"

"Darling, I'm sure Grania has lots of other things she needs to do." Alexander smiled apologetically at her over Aurora's head. "And we mustn't take up any more of her time."

"Really, it was no bother. I enjoyed it."

"Will you come back tomorrow with the paints when the bowl is dry?" pleaded Aurora.

Grania looked to Alexander for approval and got it. "Of course, I'll see what I can find." Grania started to move toward the door, and Alexander moved aside and held out his hand again.

"Thank you, Grania. It's very kind of you to take the time to amuse my daughter. Please, feel welcome to drop in any time. If I'm not here, Mrs. Myther lives in with Aurora to take care of her." He guided Grania out of the drawing room across the hall and back toward the kitchen, Aurora holding his hand. "Aurora, will you go and find Mrs. Myther and tell her that we're both ready for lunch now?"

"Yes, Daddy," she said obediently. "Good-bye, Grania, see you tomorrow." Aurora turned and disappeared up the stairs.

Alexander led the way across the kitchen to the back door. As he opened it, he turned to her. "Please, Aurora can be very persuasive. Don't let her talk you into spending more time with her than you wish to."

"As I said, I enjoyed it." The proximity of Alexander's presence only a few inches from her as he held the door open was turning Grania's brain to putty.

"Well, just be careful. I know how she can be."

"I will."

"Good. I'm sure we'll be seeing you here again soon. Good-bye, Grania."

"Good-bye."

As Grania walked across the courtyard, and then along the path that led back down to the gate that opened on to the cliff, she was desperate to look behind her to see whether he still stood by the door. After the gate, she set off at a brisk pace along the cliff path until she reached her favorite rock. She slumped on to it, feeling breathless and disoriented.

She put her head in her hands to try to gather her senses. An image of Alexander's face appeared in her mind's eye. She felt overwhelmed and almost fearful that a man with whom she'd had no more than five minutes contact could have such an effect on her.

She lifted her head, and looked out to sea. It was calm today, tranquil—a sleeping monster that could rise up and create havoc within the space of a few minutes.

As she stood up and set off for home, Grania pondered whether the analogy could also be true of the man she had just met.

"Hi there, it's me. Can you let me in?"

"Sure." Matt pressed the entry button and walked back disconsolately to his perusal of a baseball game.

Charley appeared at the door, and closed it behind her. "I've bought us take-out from the Chinese. It's your favorite, hon, crispy duck," she added as she headed for the kitchen. "You hungry?"

"Nope," stated Matt as Charley sourced a couple of plates from the kitchen and opened the bottle of wine she had brought with her.

"You need to eat, sweetie, you'll waste away." She eyed him as she set the food and the plates on the coffee table in front of him. "Here." Charley rolled strips of duck and hoisin sauce into a pancake and offered it to him.

With a sigh, Matt sat forward, bit into and chewed the food without pleasure.

Charley rolled him another pancake and took a sip of her wine. "Wanna talk about it?"

"What is there to say?" Matt shrugged. "My girl has left me for reasons I don't know or understand and refuses to speak to me to explain them." He shook his head in despair. "At least if I knew what it was I'm meant to have done then I could do something about it." He put another pancake in his mouth. "And by the way, your tactic of silence hasn't worked. Grania hasn't called me once. So much for playing it cool, hey?" he added morosely.

"I'm sorry, Matty. I really thought that if you gave Grania some time and space she might respond. I thought she loved you."

"So did I." Matt grimaced bitterly. "Maybe I was wrong. And, just maybe, this is more to do with her feelings for me. Maybe"—Matt ran a hand through his hair distractedly—"it's as simple as her not wanting me anymore. Because I have racked my brains, and I can't think of a single damned thing I have done to hurt her."

Charley put a comforting hand on Matt's knee. "Perhaps it was losing the baby, maybe her feelings have changed . . ." Charley shrugged. "Sorry, I'm all out of platitudes."

"No, there is nothing to say, is there? She's gone, and as each day passes I lose belief that she'll be coming back." He looked at Charley. "Do you think I should do as I originally planned and get on a plane to Ireland?"

"I don't know, Matty. I don't mean to be negative, but it seems to me she's making it pretty clear she doesn't want anything to do with you just now."

"Yup, you're right." Matt drained his wineglass and poured himself another. "I'm just deluding myself, trying to believe it isn't over, when she's real certain it is."

"How about giving it till the end of the week and seeing if she calls? Then maybe if she does, you could suggest that you jump on a flight to Ireland?"

"Maybe, but I'm sure getting tired of feeling that I'm the bad guy. Besides, I've got a heap of work and I'm away on and off lecturing for the next two weeks."

"Poor old Matty," Charley crooned, "You really are going through it just now. Promise it'll get better, one way or the other. You know, we all have bad times like this . . . when it seems like the world has come to an end."

"Yup, I admit it—I'm in Self-Indulgent City," agreed Matt. "Sorry. I suggest you leave me be just now. I'm not great company, I know."

"That's what friends are for, Matty, to be there when you need them. Changing the subject for a second, I came by to ask you a favor," said Charley.

"What's that?" Matt, lost in his own misery, was hardly listening.

"I have the decorators coming into my apartment in a couple of days' time. They're gonna be there for a month or so, and I was wondering if I could use your spare room while they're working? I'd pay rent, of course," Charley added. "And you know me, I'm out most evenings and weekends."

"Hey, no need to pay me. As I said, I'm slammed with work and have a big lecture tour cominng up soon, so feel free to move in whenever you want." Matt stood up, rummaged through his desk and produced a key, which he handed to her.

"Thanks, hon."

"No problem. And to be honest, despite what I just said, I could probably use the company. You'd be doing me a favor."

"Well, if you're sure, that would be great. I really appreciate this."

Matt slapped her leg. "And I appreciate you being here for me."

"No problem, Matty." Charley smiled at him. "No problem at all."

5

And where are you off to today?" Kathleen eyed Grania as she buttoned up her coat. "Your hair is washed and you have makeup on."

"In answer to your question, I'm going to see Aurora. Is it unusual for a woman to wash her hair and wear mascara around these parts?" Grania answered defiantly.

"You're off up to Dunworley House, then?"

"Yes."

Kathleen folded her arms. "I have warned you, Grania, it's not a good idea to get involved in their goings-on."

"Mam, I'm helping amuse a lonely little girl, not moving in with them! What is the problem?"

"I've said to you before and I'll say it again: that family are trouble to this one. And I'd say you have enough problems of your own, without adding theirs to it."

"For pity's sake, Mam! Aurora's a motherless child who has just moved back here, and knows no one. She's lonely!" Grania said in exasperation. "I'll see you later."

The door slammed behind Grania and Kathleen sighed. "Yes," she whispered to herself, "and you're a childless mother."

Kathleen went about her morning chores with a heavy heart. She pondered whether to speak to John about Grania and her visits to Dunworley House. For the past week, Grania had been going up there every day, and yesterday had not come home until after dark. The look in her daughter's eyes was enough to tell her mother that something was drawing her there, just like it had drawn others before her . . .

"Well, my girl," Kathleen said to herself as she made Shane's bed, "the sooner you get yourself back to New York and your man, the better. For all of us."

• • •

Grania knew now that somewhere along her walk up the cliffs toward the house, Aurora would appear and run down the hill to escort her back up to the gate. Grania loved watching her as she did so; she had never encountered such a graceful child. When Aurora walked, she floated, and when she ran, she danced. And here she was now, circling her like a will-o'-the-wisp, an ethereal creature straight out of the story books her mother had once read to her of the legends of old Ireland.

"Hello, Grania." Aurora hugged her, then took her hand and led her up the hill. "I was watching for you to come from my bedroom window. I think Daddy has something to ask you."

"Does he?" Grania had not seen Alexander at all in the past week. Aurora had said he'd been plagued by a bad migraine and was lying down in his room. When Grania had expressed concern as to his health, Aurora had shrugged nonchalantly.

"He gets better quickly, as long as he's left alone in peace and quiet."

Even though she'd berated herself, thoughts of Aurora's father had filled her head in the quiet moments before she fell asleep. And the fact that Alexander was somewhere upstairs and might appear at any second, created a guilty sense of pleasure inside her. She didn't understand the effect he'd had on her—all she knew was that she was spending less time thinking of Matt than she had previously. And that had to be positive.

"Why does he want to see me?" Grania couldn't help herself asking.

Aurora giggled. "It's a secret." She pirouetted toward the gate and had it open by the time Grania reached it.

"Did you ever take dancing lessons in London, Aurora? I think you might be good at it."

"No, Mummy wouldn't let me. She always hated ballet." Aurora rubbed her nose as she closed the gate behind them. "I'd like to learn though, and I found some old books in the attic, full of pictures of beautiful ladies standing on their toes. If Mummy didn't hate it so much, I think that's what I'd like to be."

Grania watched as Aurora skipped up the path in front of her, wanting to tell her that Lily was dead, and surely wouldn't mind if she learned, but it was not her place to do so. So she followed Aurora silently into the kitchen.

"Now"—Aurora smiled up at her and put her hands on her hips—"what are we going to do today? What do you have hidden in your magic bag?" she asked eagerly.

Grania duly produced a tin of watercolors and a small canvas. "I thought, as the weather's fine, we might go outside and paint the view. What do you think?"

Aurora nodded. "Don't we need an easel?"

"I'm sure we can make do, but if you find you like it, I might take you into Cork city to the art shop there and we could buy one."

Aurora's face lit up. "Would we go on a bus?" she questioned. "I've always wanted to go on a bus."

Grania raised an eyebrow. "Have you never been on a bus before?"

"No, there aren't many here, and when we lived in London, Daddy's chauffeur took us everywhere. Perhaps you could ask Daddy if I might, when you see him?"

Grania nodded in agreement, and just as they were making their way into the drawing room to go out on to the terrace, Mrs. Myther, the housekeeper, came down the stairs with a basket of laundry. Grania had met her before on a couple of occasions and she seemed a pleasant enough woman.

"May I have a word, Grania?" Mrs. Myther asked her. "In private," she whispered.

"Aurora, you go outside and try to find the best spot from which to paint the view. I'll be there in two seconds."

Aurora nodded and opened the French windows to move out on to the terrace.

"Mr. Devonshire wanted me to ask you if it was possible for you to join him for dinner either tonight or tomorrow? He would like to talk to you about Aurora."

"I see."

Grania must have looked concerned, for Mrs. Myther patted her arm and smiled. "It's nothing to worry about. Mr. Devonshire, and I for that matter, are very grateful for all the time you've been spending with Aurora. May I tell him whether tonight or tomorrow will be best for you? He obviously doesn't want Aurora to be involved in the conversation, you see."

"Tonight will be fine."

"Shall I tell him you'll be here at about eight?"

"Yes."

"Good. And may I say that you're just what that child needs," added Mrs. Myther. "She's come alive since she met you."

Grania wandered through the drawing room and out on to the terrace to join Aurora, doing her best not to second-guess what it was Alexander wanted to speak to her about. The two of them passed a pleasant morning in the weak sunshine, Grania teaching Aurora the basics of perspective. When it became chilly, they went back into the kitchen to paint the sketch. Aurora climbed onto Grania's knee as she showed her how to mix a little red with blue to achieve the soft purple of the faraway cliffs at the end of the bay. When they'd finished and were surveying their handiwork, Aurora threw her arms around Grania's neck and gave her a hug.

"Thank you, Grania. It's beautiful and I shall hang it in my bedroom wherever I live, so it will always remind me of home."

Mrs. Myther had appeared in the kitchen and was stirring soup over the range. Grania took her arrival as a cue to leave and stood up.

"What shall we do tomorrow?" asked Aurora eagerly. "Will you ask Daddy tonight if I can go on the bus to Cork city?"

Grania glanced down at Aurora in surprise. "How did you know I was coming tonight?"

"I just did." Aurora tapped her nose. "You will ask him, won't you?"

Grania nodded. "I promise."

Grania had told her mother she would not be in for supper that evening. This had elicited a raised eyebrow but no comment.

"I'm off," Grania said as she came down the stairs. "I'll see you later."

Kathleen eyed her. "I'd say you were dressed up for a gentleman. Are you, Grania?"

"Oh, Mam, Aurora's father simply wants to talk to me about her. I've only met him once; this isn't a date or anything." Grania headed for the lobby as swiftly as she could, and grabbed a torch from the shelf.

"And what am I to tell your man about where his woman is, if he calls?"

Grania did not grace this comment with a reply, simply slammed the door behind her and marched off in the direction of the house. There was absolutely no reason for her to feel guilty, and no reason for her mother to question her motives either. And Matt no longer had a right to tell her who she should see or what she should do. It was *he* who had destroyed their relationship. The fact her mother had always had a soft spot for Matt couldn't be helped. And after nearly three weeks at home every evening, it would do her no harm to get out.

Armed with defiant thoughts, Grania switched on the torch and marched off up the lane.

When she arrived at the back door of Dunworley House, she knocked to no answer. Not knowing what else to do, she let herself in and stood uncertainly in the empty kitchen. Eventually, she opened the kitchen door tentatively and walked into the hall. "Hello?" she called, again receiving no answer. "Hello?" She walked across it and knocked on the drawing-room door. Pushing it open, she saw Alexander sitting in a chair by the fire, reading a document. He started as he saw Grania and stood up, embarrassed.

"My apologies, I'm afraid I didn't hear you arrive."

"No problem," said Grania uncomfortably, again feeling tongue-tied in his presence.

"Please, let me take your coat and come and sit down by the fire. I find it so cold in this house," he commented as he helped her remove her coat. "Can I get you a glass of wine? Or a gin and tonic perhaps?"

"Wine would be lovely."

"Make yourself comfortable, and I'll be back shortly."

Grania did not head for the chair on the opposite side of the fireplace—the heat in the room was oppressive. Instead, she sat down on an elegant but uncomfortable damask-covered sofa and thought how cozy this room was at night.

Alexander arrived back with a bottle of wine and two glasses.

"Thank you for coming, Grania," he said as he handed her the wine and returned to his chair by the fire. "Amongst other things, I wanted the chance to tell you how grateful I am to you for keeping Aurora amused for the past week."

"Really, it's been my pleasure. I've enjoyed it as much as she has."

"Nevertheless, it really has been most kind of you. Aurora tells me you're a sculptor. Do you practice your trade professionally?"

"Yes. I have a studio in New York."

"How wonderful to use one's talent to earn oneself a living." Alexander sighed.

"I think so," Grania ventured. "On the other hand, I've never had the ability to do anything else."

"Well, far better to excel in one thing alone, than to be average at many. That's me to a tee," he stated.

"If you don't mind me asking, what exactly is it that you do?"

"I shovel money around the world; other people's money, that is. And from making them rich, I make myself rich too. You could say I'm a vulture. What I do gives me no pleasure whatsoever. It's totally meaningless," Alexander added morosely.

"I think that's being hard on yourself," commented Grania. "After all, it's a skill. I wouldn't know where to start."

"Thank you for your kindness, but I create nothing, whereas you create something material which brings pleasure to the beholder." Alexander took a sip of his wine. "I've always admired people with artistic talent, having absolutely none whatsoever myself. I'd love to see your work. Do you hold exhibitions?"

"Yes, occasionally, although these days most of the sculptures I do are private commissions."

He looked at her. "So, I could commission you?"

"Yes." Grania shrugged. "I suppose you could."

"Well then, I just might." He smiled tightly. "Are you ready for supper?"

"Yes, whenever you are," Grania replied faintly.

Alexander stood up. "I'll go and tell Mrs. Myther we're ready."

Grania watched him leave the room, puzzled as to how a man such as he could seem so ill at ease. In her experience, rich, successful men who looked like Alexander had an arrogance and a natural confidence that came with being universally admired.

"Everything's ready," Alexander said as he put his head around the door. "We're in the dining room, I find it far warmer than the kitchen."

Grania followed Alexander across the hall and into a room on the other side of it. The highly polished, long mahogany table was set at one end for two. Another large fire was burning in the grate and Grania headed for the chair furthest away.

Alexander sat down at the head of the table next to her, and Mrs. Myther entered the room carrying two plates which she set down in front of them. "Thank you," he said as the housekeeper left the room. He glanced at Grania and gave a wry smile. "I apologize for the basic qualities of the dish in front of you, but fancy cooking is not her strong point."

"As a matter of fact, ham, colcannon and gravy is one of my favorites," Grania reassured him.

"Well, when in Rome . . . and this is one dish I can always rely on for Mrs. Myther to cook adequately. Please," he indicated, "start."

They ate in silence for a while, Grania casting surreptitious glances at her companion. Eventually, she broke the silence. "So, what was it you needed to see me about?"

"I wanted to ask about your plans for next month," Alexander explained. "Presumably, if you're merely visiting your family, you'll be returning soon to New York?"

Grania put her knife and fork together. "To be honest with you, I haven't decided what I'm going to do."

"Do I gather then, from that, that you are running away from something?"

It was a perceptive observation, coming from somebody she hardly knew. "I suppose you could put it like that," she admitted. "How did you know?"

"Well . . ." Alexander finished his supper and wiped his lips with his napkin. "For a start, you have an air of sophistication about you that's unlikely to have been nurtured in the village of Dunworley. For seconds, I saw you, probably before Aurora did, taking walks along the cliffs. You were obviously deep in thought about something; I deduced it was most likely you were wrestling with a problem. And lastly, it is unlikely that a woman such as yourself would normally have the time or inclination to spend every day in the company of an eight-year-old child."

Grania could feel her cheeks reddening. "I'd say that's a fairly accurate assessment of my current situation, yes."

"My daughter seems awfully fond of you, and you are not averse to her either, from the look of things—"

"I think she's a delightful little girl, and we've had a fine time together," Grania butted in. "But she's lonely."

"Yes, she is lonely," Alexander conceded with a sigh.

"Would you not think of sending her to school? There's a very good primary only a mile away; it might mean she meets some friends of her own age."

"That would be pointless." He shook his head. "I have no idea how long we will be here, and forming ties she will then have to break is the last thing Aurora needs."

"What about boarding school? Surely then, wherever you are, she could at least have a sense of stability?" Grania suggested.

"Of course, that thought has crossed my mind," Alexander said. "The problem is, after her mother died, Aurora developed problems—emotional problems—that prohibit it. So, even though it's less than ideal, she has to be educated at home. Which brings me to the reason I invited you here tonight."

"Which is?"

"Mrs. Myther worked for us in our London house and kindly consented to come over here with us when we left, just for the first few weeks. But her family is back in London and she obviously wishes to rejoin them as soon as possible. I've been in contact with a number of agencies to try to source a nanny for Aurora and a housekeeper for Dunworley, but so far I've had no luck. And I must leave in a few days' time. What I want to ask you, Grania, is whether you would be prepared to come and live in with Aurora here, and look after her until I have found a suitable set of staff to take over?"

It was the last thing Grania had expected to hear. "I—"

Alexander put up a hand to stop her speaking.

"I understand that you are not a nanny, and nor would I see you like that. However, on this occasion, Aurora cannot accompany me and I must find someone, as a matter of urgency, whom I can trust and whom she feels comfortable with, to take care of her. I hope you're not insulted by my asking you."

"Not at all," she replied. "I'm honored that you feel you could trust me, considering you hardly know me."

"Oh, I know you, Grania," he smiled. "You're all Aurora ever talks about. I've never seen her so attached to anyone since her mother died. So forgive me for asking. I completely understand you may have other plans. I promise you it would be no more than a month, just to give me the time to do what I need to . . ." his voice trailed off, "and find someone to care for her long term."

"A month . . . Alexander"—Grania bit her lip—"I honestly don't know."

"Please take time to think about it. Don't decide now. And the other thing I wish to ask you is whether, while you're here, I could commission you to do a sculpture of Aurora? Which would mean you'd be working at the same time. And I'd pay you for both the sculpture and the care of my daughter. Handsomely, I might add."

Grania could feel herself sinking into the deep blue of his eyes and checked herself. "I need to go home and think about it, because I'm not really sure what I'm doing."

"Of course," Alexander nodded. "Perhaps you could let me know as soon as possible? I leave on Sunday."

Sunday was four days away.

"What will you do if I say no?" she asked.

"I have absolutely no idea." Alexander shrugged. "Perhaps persuade Mrs. Myther to stay on and double her salary. Anyway, that isn't your problem, and I apologize if you feel I've put you in a difficult position. You must do whatever is right for you. Forgive me for asking, but Aurora begged me to."

"May I give you my answer tomorrow?"

"Yes. And now, if you'll excuse me, I'm afraid I have a dreadful migraine."

"Of course. Can I do anything to help?"

Alexander stared at her, a look of deep sadness in his eyes. "No, I only wish you could." He reached out a hand and put it on hers. "Thank you for asking."

As Grania made her way home along the cliffs by torchlight, she felt ashamed that the touch of Alexander's hand on hers had rendered her compliant. At that moment, she would have done anything to help him. Who he was and what he was, she just didn't know. But the pain she had seen in his eyes stayed with her as she crept into the farmhouse, climbed the stairs to bed and sank, for some reason exhausted, between the sheets.

The whole idea was ridiculous . . . she was a successful sculptor in New York, with a life . . . what was she doing even *contemplating* moving into a godforsaken house on a cliff, to care for a little girl she had never laid eyes on up until a week ago? To please a man she knew nothing about? On top of which, the Lisle family heritage and Grania's recent association with it was obviously causing her mother inexplicable pain.

And yet . . . and yet . . .

Grania felt, as the clock ticked away the night hours, that she was entering dangerous waters. She suddenly and urgently longed for the safety, security and normality of the existence she'd known for the past eight years.

Was her relationship with Matt over?

She'd run away so quickly, so hurt . . . like a frightened animal . . .

And never given him the chance to explain. What if she had got it *wrong*? What if it had been a series of unfortunate events she had linked together to create a scenario that could be easily, and innocently, explainable? After all, she'd just lost her baby . . . her longed-for baby. Had she really been in any kind of emotional position to equivocate? And had she, due to shock and the hormones coursing through her body, overreacted? Grania sighed and turned over yet again in the narrow bed. She missed the huge king-size one that she and Matt had shared. And what they had shared in it. She missed the life . . . she missed *him*.

Grania came to a decision. Maybe it was time to find out, give Matt a chance to tell his own version of events.

She looked at the clock and saw it was 3:00 a.m., which meant it was 9:00 p.m. in New York. At worst, Matt's cell phone would be switched off, and the answering machine in the loft on. At best, he might answer either.

Grania sat up, switched the light on and reached for her cell phone. Without thinking any further, she pressed Matt's name, and the number began to dial. Matt's voice mail clicked in immediately and Grania pressed the "off" switch. She then dialed the loft number and, after two rings, a voice answered.

"Hello?"

The voice was female, and she knew the owner of it.

Grania stared wordlessly into space as the voice said again, "Hello?"

Oh God, oh God, oh God . . .

"Who is this?"

Grania punched her thumb on the button to end the call.

6

Alexander appeared in the kitchen expectantly the following morning as Grania and Aurora arrived up at the house.

"I'll do it. Take care of Aurora, that is, for a month anyway."

"That's wonderful! Grania, thank you. You can't know what it means to me to know that Aurora will be safe here with someone she likes." Alexander glanced at his daughter. "Are you happy, Aurora?"

Neither of the adults needed a vocal answer. It was written all over Aurora's face. "Oh, yes!" She went to hug her father, then moved to Grania and hugged her too. "Thank you, Grania. I promise I won't be any trouble."

"I'm sure you won't." Grania smiled.

"And perhaps there might be time to open some of those schoolbooks that are lying upstairs, eh?" Alexander raised an eyebrow at Grania. "She came here with enough work to see her through for a month from her old governess in London. I doubt she's opened them once."

"But, Daddy, I've been learning to do art."

"Don't worry, I'll see to it that Aurora does some work," said Grania hurriedly.

"Did you ask Daddy about going to Cork city on the bus?" Aurora asked eagerly, turning to her father. "Grania needs to buy some art supplies, and she said I could go with her. Can I, Daddy? I've never been on a bus before."

"I can't see the harm in that, as long as Grania doesn't mind you tagging along."

"Of course I don't," said Grania.

"And perhaps, at the same time, you could acquire what you need for the sculpture we talked about last night?" Alexander questioned.

"Yes, if you're sure you'd like me to do it. I could show you some of my work on the Internet."

"As a matter of fact, I looked you up this morning," he said. "I'm happy for you to go ahead and, of course, we must discuss payment, both for your care of Aurora and the sculpture. I was also wondering whether you knew of anyone in the village who might be happy to come up for a few hours a day to take care of the house? I don't regard that as something that's included in your remit as well."

Grania thought of her mother's antipathy to the Lisle family and wondered how many others in the village felt similarly too.

"I can ask," she said uncertainly. "But . . ."

Alexander put his hand up to stop her. "I understand our family does not have a good reputation locally. I've never really got to the bottom of the exact reason, being a relative newcomer, but I can assure you that it's all based on ancient history."

"People in Ireland have long memories," Grania agreed. "But I'll see what I can do."

Aurora tugged at Grania's sleeve. "If we don't go soon, surely we'll miss the bus?"

"There's one at midday. We have ten minutes."

"Then I'll leave you girls to it," Alexander said. "Thank you once again, Grania, and I'll see you before I leave to sort out the details."

Having taken an exuberant Aurora on the bus to the city and returned laden with supplies from the art shop, Grania arrived home just as her mother was serving supper.

"And where have you been all day, miss, I'd like to ask?"

"In Cork city." Grania dumped her shopping bags in the lobby and took off her coat. "I needed to go and buy some materials."

"I hear you had a friend with you," said Kathleen as she doled the beef stew into bowls.

"Yes. I took Aurora with me. She'd never been on a bus and she was very excited. Can I help you, Mam?"

Kathleen ignored her offer and placed the bowls on the table.

As Grania sat down, and her father and brother joined them, she felt as though it was *she* who was eight years old, caught on the bus playing truant from school.

After supper, once Shane had disappeared to the pub and her

father was installed in his chair next door, Grania helped her mother clear the plates. "Why don't I put the kettle on and we'll have a cup of tea?" she ventured. "I have news for you."

"You're going back to New York to your lovely man?" Kathleen's face brightened for an instant, but Grania shook her head.

"No, Mam, I'm sorry, but I'm doubtful that will ever happen now," she said sadly as she placed the kettle on the AGA to boil.

"Well, Grania, what I can't understand is the reason for this. I know it was a terrible shame you lost the baby, but—"

"It's more than that, Mam, please, and I really don't want to speak about it."

"But from the sound of him, whatever it is Matt has done, he wants to make amends. Won't you give him a chance, pet?" Kathleen urged.

Grania made two cups of tea and brought them to the table. "I swear, Mam, if there was any way this could be sorted, I'd want it to be. But I think it's too late. And as you've always said, there's no use crying over spilled milk. I have to move on."

"So, what are your plans?"

"Well, I know you're not going to like this," Grania sipped the burning hot tea, "but Aurora's father has to go away for a month and I have agreed to take care of her up at Dunworley House while he does so."

"Holy Mary, Mother of God!" Kathleen raised her hands to her cheeks. "It gets worse, so it does."

"Please, Mam, as Alexander said to me today, whatever has happened is ancient history. And nothing to do with that poor little girl. And nothing to do with me either," Grania emphasized, trying to remain as calm as she could. "Alexander wants me to make a sculpture of Aurora while I'm there. He's going to pay me, and until things are sorted out with Matt, I could use the money, Mam, I really could. Especially as I have no idea whether I'll be returning to New York."

Kathleen's head was now buried in her hands. "Jesus, it's like history is repeating itself. But you're right." She looked up at her daughter. "Why should the past have anything to do with you?"

"Well, Mam, maybe if I knew what the past *was,* I would understand. As it is, I'm going to take Alexander's offer. Why shouldn't I?"

"Why shouldn't you . . . ?" Kathleen whispered. She made a mental effort to pull herself together. "Well now, the trouble is that both of us seem to be working in the dark. I'd have no idea what has gone wrong with you and Matt, and you can't understand why it upsets me, you becoming involved with the Lisle family. You say Himself will not be there while you're staying up at Dunworley House?"

"No, he has to go away."

"And what do you think of Aurora's father?"

"He seems like a nice man." Grania shrugged. "I don't know him terribly well."

"I think he was . . . *is* . . . a good man. But anyone who has the misfortune to get themselves mixed up with that family seems to be tainted by it, and that goes for you too, Grania." Kathleen wagged a finger at her daughter fiercely.

"Mam, the last thing I want to do is upset you, but until I know—"

"Yes, you're right," Kathleen interjected. She smiled weakly and patted her daughter's hand sadly. "There was me thinking you were the one that got away."

"It's only for a month, Mam," Grania underlined. "And at least I'll be out from under your feet."

"And is that really what you think I want, Grania? After ten years of never seeing you? 'Tis a pleasure to have you here and it always will be."

"Thanks, Mam. I was also wondering whether it might be possible to bring Aurora here to meet you?" ventured Grania. "I'm sure, once you did, you'd understand. She's such a lovely little girl . . ."

"Don't you be pushing it, Grania. I'm sure she is as you say, but feelings run high in this house. Best leave it for now."

"I understand." She yawned. "Excuse me, I didn't get much sleep last night. I'm for my bed." Grania stood up and rinsed her mug in the sink. She walked over and kissed her mother on the top of her head. "Night, Mam. Sleep tight."

"And you, pet."

When Kathleen had heard Grania's door close at the top of the stairs, she stood up and wandered into the sitting room to speak to her husband.

"I'm worried about our girl," she said with a sigh as she sat down in the armchair opposite John. "She's gone and agreed to go up to Dunworley House for a month to take care of the Lisle child."

"Has she now?" John turned his attention from the television to study his wife's anxious expression.

"So, what can we do?" Kathleen asked him.

"I'd say, nothing. She's a big girl now."

"John, can you not see what's happening? You know how Grania has always shut down whenever there's been emotional bother in her life. She's doing it now. You can see the pain she's feeling inside, but she won't open up."

"'Tis the way she is, Kathleen. Just like her father," John said with a smile. "We all cope with our problems differently and none are right or wrong."

"Do you not think it odd she hasn't shed a tear over losing that baby?"

"As I said, we each have our own ways, darlin'. Let her be."

"John." Kathleen could feel herself losing patience with her husband's usual calm approach to what she could see was impending disaster. "Our daughter is pouring all her maternal feelings into that child. She's using Aurora as a substitute for what she's lost. And on top of that, perhaps seeing the girl's father as a replacement for Matt. And while she's concentrating all her energies on them, she doesn't have to think about her own life, or try to sort it out."

"Ahh, Kathleen," John replied, finally responding to his wife's distress, "I can understand how this situation is upsetting you, and you're wanting to protect our girl, but I don't see there's anything we can do. Do you?"

"No," Kathleen said after a long pause, knowing she was searching for solutions John could not give her, but irritated with him for failing to do so nevertheless. She stood up. "I'm off to bed."

"I'll be up shortly," John replied to his wife's back. He sighed. When Kathleen was in a state about one of her beloved children, he knew there was little he could do or say to comfort her.

Three days later, Grania was given a lift up the hill to Dunworley House by her brother.

"Thanks, Shane," Grania said as she climbed out of the car.

"No bother, Grania." He smiled. "You just let me know if there's any lifts you need with that young'un. Take care."

Grania took her holdall from the boot and entered the kitchen through the back door. A small thunderbolt catapulted itself into her arms.

"You're here! I've been waiting for you all morning."

"Of course I'm here," Grania said with a smile. "You didn't think I wouldn't come, did you?"

Aurora pursed her pink lips. "Sometimes adults say they will do something, and then they don't."

"Well, I'm not one of those adults," Grania comforted her.

"Good. Now, Daddy said if you arrived, I'm to show you to your room. I've put you next to me, so you don't get lonely. Come on." Aurora took Grania's hand and pulled her out of the kitchen, through the hall and up the stairs. She led her along the landing to a pretty bedroom containing a big wrought-iron bed with a white lace counterpane. The walls were pink, with flower-sprigged curtains at the window, framing the stunning view out over the headland.

"Pink's my favorite color," said Aurora as she bounced on the big bed. "Is it yours?"

"I love pink and blue and purple and"—Grania joined Aurora on the bed and tickled her—"Yellow and red and orange and green . . ."

Aurora giggled with pleasure, and that was how Alexander found them when he knocked on the door and walked in.

"My goodness! What a racket."

"Sorry, Daddy." Aurora sat up immediately. "I hope we didn't disturb you."

"No, darling, you didn't." He smiled, which, Grania noticed, seemed to be almost more of a grimace. He looked deathly pale.

"If Aurora will allow you out of her clutches for half an hour, Grania, we can go through a few things before I leave," Alexander suggested.

"Yes." Grania clambered off the bed and turned to Aurora. "Why don't you go and find those schoolbooks your father was telling me about, and I'll see you down in the kitchen shortly."

Aurora nodded obediently and went off into her bedroom next

door as Grania and Alexander walked downstairs. He led her into a small library, which was equipped with a desk and computer.

"Sit down, Grania, please."

Grania did so as Alexander handed her a sheet of typed paper. "Listed here are all my contact numbers. I've added the name of my solicitor, Hans, too, and if you can't get hold of me, he's the best person to speak to. He knows you may be calling."

"May I ask where you're going?"

"To the States, and then possibly Switzerland . . ." Alexander shrugged. "I apologize for being unable to be more specific. I've also added the names of a plumber and electrician, in case there are any problems with the house. The heating and the water are set on a timer by the boiler in the utility room, which is just off the kitchen. A gardener comes in once a week and also provides logs for the fireplaces."

"Right," said Grania, "and I think I may have found a temporary cleaner. She's the daughter of the lady who runs the village shop and seems like a nice girl."

"Good. Thank you, Grania. You'll note that there is a check attached, made out to you, which includes what I think is a fair sum for your time this month, plus payment for the sculpture. I've also added enough to cover general expenses such as food, with a sum for emergencies, out of which you can pay the cleaner. You'll find it all detailed on the sheet. If, by any chance you need more, as I said, please contact my solicitor."

Grania glanced at the check. It was written out for twelve thousand euros.

"But this is far too much—I . . ."

"I know your sculptures sell for a minimum of ten thousand dollars each, Grania."

"Yes, but normally the client wants to see the finished product before he pays in full."

"I don't need to do that," said Alexander. "Now, enough of finances. If it weren't for you, I'd be unable to leave."

"Really, it's a pleasure," Grania reiterated. "I'm terribly fond of Aurora."

"And you must know that it's mutual. I haven't seen my daughter respond to anyone the way she has to you since her mother died. I find it"—Alexander sighed—"very moving."

The look of innate sadness appeared again in his eyes, and it was all Grania could do to restrain herself from reaching out her hand to comfort him. "I promise I'll take care of her for you," she said softly.

"I know you will. And I should warn you . . . it's difficult to know how to put this . . . but Aurora sometimes talks about her mother still being here, in this house." Alexander shook his head. "We both know this is simply a fantasy of a bereaved child. I assure you there are no ghosts here, but if Aurora chooses to be comforted by the thought, then I really can't see the harm."

"No," Grania agreed slowly.

"Well then, I think that's everything. I'll be leaving in approximately an hour. A taxi is taking me to Cork airport. You may, of course, have full use of my car, the keys to which hang on the key rack in the pantry."

"Thank you." Grania stood up. "I'll go and see where Aurora has got to, and try to persuade her to put her nose in some books."

Alexander nodded. "I'll call as often as I can, but please don't worry if you don't hear for a while. And Aurora mustn't either. Oh, by the way"—he indicated the top left-hand drawer of his desk—"if by any chance something should happen to me, all the papers you might need are locked in here. My solicitor will direct you to the whereabouts of the key."

Grania shivered suddenly at the look on Alexander's face. "Let's hope I don't need to make that call. I'll see you in a month. Have a safe trip."

"Thank you."

She turned to walk toward the door.

"Grania?"

"Yes?"

Alexander gave her a sudden, wide smile. "I'll owe you dinner when I get back. You've saved my life, literally."

Grania nodded and silently scurried out of the room.

Grania and Aurora sat on the window seat in the child's bedroom and watched as Alexander's taxi snaked its way down the hill. Grania put an instinctive arm around Aurora's shoulders, but the little girl seemed calm. She looked up at Grania. "It's all right, I'm not sad. I'm used to him leaving me when he has to go away to work. And this time it's better, because I have you here." Aurora knelt up and threw her arms around Grania's neck. "Grania?"

"Yes?"

"Do you think we could go into the sitting room, light a fire and toast marshmallows on it, like they do in the Enid Blyton book I've just read?"

"I think that sounds like a wonderful idea. As long as you spend an hour doing sums at the kitchen table while I make supper. Deal?" Grania held out her hand.

Aurora grasped it and smiled. "Deal."

Later that evening, once Grania had settled Aurora into bed for the night, and had been cajoled into reading to her for far longer than they'd originally agreed, Grania walked back downstairs and went into the sitting room. As she knelt in front of the fire to stoke it she listened to the silence in the house, and wondered what on earth she had done by agreeing to this. Grania realized it was simply a knee-jerk reaction to the shock of hearing Charley's voice in *her* loft the other night. Was imprisoning herself in a house for a month, alone with a little girl she hardly knew, a sensible thing to do?

She wanted Matt to call her parents' house, wanted her mother to tell him she was no longer there, needed him to *know* that what he had done to her would not destroy her, that she was already moving on . . .

With effort, she replaced Matt's face in her mind's eye with that of Alexander's. Had she imagined the look on his face when he'd offered her dinner on his return? And was she so vulnerable that she'd cling on for dear life to a few words that could have been spoken out of politeness without any other resonance? Grania sighed, realizing that whatever Alexander's motive, she had at least a month to ponder it without resolution.

Turning off the downstairs lights, she made her way up the stairs to her bedroom. She took a long soak in the deep, clawfoot tub adjacent to her room, before donning her pajamas and climbing into the big, comfortable bed. She lay back on the pillows, luxuriating in its space after weeks in her narrow one.

Tomorrow, she thought, as she switched off the light, she would start to sketch Aurora, get a feel for the shape of her face, decide which expression appeared most often in her eyes . . .

Grania settled herself down for sleep and closed her own eyes.

Kathleen sat at the kitchen table, nursing a mug of tea. She could hear from next door that the ten o'clock news had just finished. Once he had listened to the weather forecast, John would switch off the television along with the lights, and make his way through to the kitchen to fill a glass of water to take up to bed.

Kathleen stood up and went toward the back door. She opened it, and peered out to her left. There were no lights on at the house on top of the cliffs. Grania must have already gone to bed. Kathleen closed the door behind her and shivered slightly as she locked and bolted it, wondering at the sense of unease she had about her daughter's whereabouts tonight. As she walked back into the kitchen, John was standing by the sink, running the tap for his glass of water.

"I'm for my bed, pet. You too?" He glanced down at his wife and gave her a gentle smile.

Kathleen gave a big sigh, and rubbed her face with the palms of her hands. "Oh, John, I hardly know where to put myself."

John placed his water glass down on the draining board, came toward his wife and took her into his arms. "What is it? It's not like you to be in a state. You'd better tell me what the problem is."

"It's Grania . . . up there in *that* house, all alone. I realize you'll say to me I'm being silly now, but"—she raised her eyes to her husband—"You know my feelings about that family and the bad it has brought us."

"Yes, I know." John gently tucked a graying tendril of his wife's hair behind her ear. "But it was all long in the past. Grania and the child are a new generation."

"Should I tell her?" Kathleen entreated him with her eyes to provide her with the answer.

John sighed. "I'd not be knowing whether that's a good idea or bad. But not saying anything to her is clearly unsettling you. If it would make you feel better, then you should speak to her. Not that it will make any difference to the outcome. You know as well as I do that the next generation can't be blamed for the sins of their fathers."

Kathleen laid her head against her husband's broad chest. "I know, John, I know. But what *they* did to our family . . ." She shook her head. "They almost destroyed us, John, so they did." She looked up with fear in her eyes. "And I've seen Grania's face when she talks of Aurora's father. Two generations ruined because of the Lisles, and now I'm seeing it happen again in front of my very own eyes."

"Come now, pet, our Grania is made of stronger stuff," John comforted. "You know as well as I there's no persuading our daughter of something she doesn't want."

"But what if she wants *him*?"

"Then there'll be little you can do about it. Grania is a grown woman, not a child, Kathleen. But, surely, you're fearing the worst? He's not even in the house with them, she's only minding his daughter while he's away, there's nothing to suggest that—"

Kathleen pulled away from John, and wrung her hands in despair. "No! You're wrong! I've seen that look, John, and it's there in her eyes for *him*. What about Matt? Perhaps I should call him, tell him to come . . . she doesn't know, doesn't understand."

"Kathleen, calm yourself." John sighed. "You can't be going around interfering in our daughter's affairs. There's something she isn't saying about Matt, and it's not our business to know until she does. But perhaps it would make you feel better to tell her of the past. It can do no harm and Grania might understand why you've taken it so hard she's up there."

Kathleen raised her eyes to him. "You think so?"

"Yes. Then she can make her own decisions. Now, my decision is that it's high time we were away to our bed. And as long as I'm her father, I swear to you I'll let no harm come to our daughter."

Calmer now, Kathleen smiled weakly at her husband.

"Thank you, pet. I know you won't."

• • •

Grania was awoken by a loud bang. Sitting up and reaching for the light switch, she wondered whether the noise had been part of a dream. She checked the time on the clock by her bed, and saw that it was a few minutes past three. There was total silence now, so she turned off the light and settled back down to try and sleep.

The faint sound of floorboards creaking on the landing beyond her bedroom made her sit up again. She listened, and heard the sound of footsteps, then a door being opened somewhere along the corridor. Climbing out of bed, Grania tentatively opened the door to her bedroom and peered out. A door at the end of the landing was ajar, letting a faint chink of light through. Grania walked toward it, hearing the floorboards creak under her own footsteps. Reaching the door, she pushed it open and saw that the bedroom was bathed in moonlight, coming from a set of French windows that led on to the small balustraded balcony beyond. The room was freezing cold and Grania noticed the French windows were ajar. Walking nervously toward them, her heart now beating fast against her chest, she stepped through the doors and onto the balcony.

And there was Aurora, a ghostlike figure in the moonlight, arms outstretched toward the sea, just as Grania had first seen her. "Aurora," Grania whispered, her senses alert to the fact that the balustrade separating the child from a drop to the ground of at least twenty feet only rose to her thighs. "Aurora," she called gently, again to no reaction. Instinctively, she reached out and grabbed her by the arm, but still she did not respond. "Come in now, darling, please. You'll catch your death out here." She could feel the iciness of Aurora's body beneath her thin nightdress.

Suddenly, Aurora pointed her hand toward the sea. "She's there, just there . . . can you see her?"

Grania followed Aurora's fingers to the edge of the cliffs and caught her breath. A shadowy figure, silhouetted against the moonlight, standing just where she had first seen Aurora . . . Grania swallowed hard, closed her eyes and reopened them. She looked again and saw nothing. Panic seizing her, she tugged at Aurora's arm.

"Aurora! Come in, now!"

In response, Aurora turned, her face as white as the moonlight. She smiled up at Grania wordlessly and let her lead her inside, through the bedroom and along the landing to her own room. As Grania tucked her in, adding an extra blanket from the end of the bed to try and warm her, the child said nothing, merely rolled over and closed her eyes. Grania sat with her until she heard her breathing was steady and she knew Aurora was asleep. Then, shaking with cold and fear herself, she tiptoed out and went back to her own bedroom.

As she lay there, the silhouetted figure on the cliffs was clear in her memory.

Surely . . . surely, she'd imagined it? She'd never been one prone to fear of the unknown; she'd always laughed at her mother when she talked of the spirit world she believed in, putting it down to an overactive imagination.

But tonight . . . tonight . . . out there on the cliffs . . .

Grania sighed. She was being ridiculous.

She closed her eyes and tried to sleep.

7

Grania woke to find a weak sun lighting her windows. She stretched, rolled over and saw that it was past eight o'clock. Normally, at home, she'd be woken by the sound of her father and her brother leaving at dawn for the milking sheds. She lay back on her pillows and remembered the strangeness of last night with a shudder. Surely it had simply been her imagination? And, in the brightness of the morning as she climbed out of bed and got dressed, it was easy to believe it must have been.

Aurora was already in the kitchen, eating a bowl of cereal. Her face dropped as she saw Grania. "I was going to bring you breakfast in bed," she said, pouting.

"That's very sweet of you, but I'm happy to make it myself." Grania filled the kettle and put it on the range. "How did you sleep last night?" she asked carefully.

"Very well indeed, thank you," Aurora answered. "And you?"

"Yes, fine," she lied. "Would you like some tea?"

"No, thank you. I only drink milk." Aurora paused, with a cereal-laden spoon between her mouth and the bowl. "Sometimes, Grania, I have very strange dreams."

"Do you?"

"Yes"—the spoon was still hovering—"sometimes I dream I see my mother, standing out there on the cliffs."

Grania said nothing, but continued to make her tea and watch the cereal spoon enter Aurora's mouth. As Grania sat down, Aurora chewed thoughtfully. She looked up at Grania.

"But it's only a dream, isn't it? Mummy's dead, she can't come back because she's in heaven. That's what Daddy says, anyway."

"Yes." Grania put a comforting hand on Aurora's thin shoulder. "Daddy's right. People who go to heaven can't come back, however much you want them to . . ."

It was Grania's turn to feel the sudden pain of loss. Her precious, tiny baby had never had a chance to experience any form of life, had died inside her before taking its first natural breath. But that didn't mean to say she hadn't imagined who her baby would become . . . the life he or she would live. Tears came to her eyes and she did her best to blink them away.

"But sometimes I feel she's here," Aurora continued, "and I'm sure I see her. But when I tell Daddy, he gets cross and sends me to a doctor, so I don't tell him any more," she added sadly.

"Come here." Grania reached out her arms and pulled Aurora on to her knee. "I think, Aurora, that your mummy obviously loved you very much, and you loved her too. Even if Daddy's right and people can't come back from heaven, you can still feel as if they are with you, looking after you and loving you."

"And you don't think that's wrong?" Aurora looked at her earnestly for reassurance. "You don't think I'm mad?"

"No, I don't think you're mad." Grania stroked the red-gold ringlets and twisted a coil around her finger. "Now"—she kissed Aurora on the forehead—"I was thinking that this morning we'd do some schoolwork to please Daddy, and I can take sketches of you for the sculpture I'm going to make for him. And then this afternoon is ours to do what we want. Any ideas?"

"No." Aurora shrugged. "You?"

"Well, I thought we might pop into Clonakilty for a sandwich, and then go to the beach."

Aurora clapped her hands together in delight. "Oh! Yes, please. I love the beach!"

"That's settled then."

Aurora sat at the table, diligently doing sums, then working through a geography question sheet. Grania sketched her swiftly from different angles until she had a feel for Aurora's bone structure. Halfway through the morning, as Grania was making herself some coffee, she realized what was missing. "Aurora, do you have a radio or a CD player in this house anywhere?" she asked. "When I'm in my studio, I love to listen to music."

"Mummy didn't like music," she stated without looking up.

Grania raised an eyebrow, but did not pursue it. "What about television?"

"We had one in our house in London. I used to like watching it."

"Well, Daddy's left me some money, so how about we go and buy one? Would you like that?"

Aurora's face lit up. "I'd love it, Grania."

"You don't think Daddy will mind?"

"Oh no, he used to watch it in London too."

"Well then, we'll get one in town before we head to the beach. And I'll ask my brother, Shane, to come and set it up for us later. He's good at things like that."

"And can we have ice cream at the beach?"

Grania smiled. "Yes. We can have ice cream."

Having bought a television, the two had lunch in Clonakilty, then Grania drove them to the nearby magnificent Inchydoney beach, for which the town was famous. She watched as Aurora twirled and danced along the deserted expanse of clean white sand, beset by an urge to capture the sheer grace of the child's movement. For a young girl who professed never to have had a dancing lesson in her life, her natural ability was breathtaking. Her arms moved about her, forming beautiful shapes and exquisite lines as her legs lifted her effortlessly from the ground in a perfectly formed jeté. Aurora arrived next to Grania and flung herself down on to a sand dune, a healthy pink flush coloring her cheeks.

"You love dancing, don't you?" Grania commented.

"Yes." Aurora put her hands behind her head and looked up at the clouds skulling across the sky. "I don't really know how to do it, but I . . ." she paused.

"Yes?" Grania prompted.

"It's as if my body knows what to do. When I'm dancing, I can forget everything and I'm happy." A sudden shadow passed over Aurora's face and she sighed. "I wish every moment could be like this."

"Do you think you would like to learn to dance? Properly, I mean, at a ballet class?"

"Oh, I would love it. But Daddy once suggested it to Mummy, and she said no. I don't know why." Aurora wrinkled her tiny, upturned nose.

"Well," said Grania carefully, "perhaps it was because she thought you were too young. I'm sure she wouldn't mind if you tried it now, don't you?"

Grania knew it was vital that this be Aurora's decision, not hers.

"Maybe . . . but where could I go to learn?" Aurora asked doubtfully.

"There's a ballet class in Clonakilty, every Wednesday afternoon. I know because I used to go to it."

"Then the teacher must be very old."

"Not *that* old, young lady." Grania giggled at her cheek. "And nor am I. Well? Should we give it a try tomorrow?"

"Won't I need some ballet shoes, and one of those things that dancers wear?" Aurora enquired.

"You mean a leotard?" Grania thought about this. "Well, I think that we try it tomorrow, and if you think you're going to like it and want to carry on, we could go to Cork city again and find you the things you need."

"Won't the other girls laugh at me if I'm in my normal clothes?"

It was the textbook response of a shy eight-year-old. "I think that once they see you dance, they won't even notice what you're wearing."

"OK then," Aurora replied uncertainly. "But if I don't like it, I never have to go again, do I?"

"Of course you don't, sweetheart."

Later that evening, Shane came to set up the television in the drawing room. Aurora bounced around him excitedly, and listened as he patiently explained to her how to access the various channels through the remote control. With Aurora settled in front of it, brother and sister went into the kitchen.

"Drink?" asked Grania. "I treated myself to a bottle of wine when I was in town," she added, opening it.

"I'll have a small glass, but I'm not really one for the wine," said Shane as he sat down. He looked around him. "This house could do with a lick of paint, couldn't it?"

"It could, but then it's been empty for the past four years. Maybe if they stay here, Alexander will decide to renovate it."

"Godforsaken place, though." Shane drank his wine in two gulps, the way he would his pint of Murphy's. "I'd say you were brave staying up here by yourself with just the small one for company. It'd not be for me, that's for sure. And Mam's not happy about it either."

"She's made that very plain." Grania poured some more wine into his glass. "Mam was never one for hiding her true feelings, was she? Have you any idea why she's so set against this house and the family?"

"Not a clue." Shane repeated the gulping exercise with his wine. "But it'll be something to do with the deep and distant past. Don't you worry, Grania, we all suffer from it. Last year, I took up for a while with a girl whose mother had once been in her class at school. Mam had never liked her, and she made my life hell, so she did." Shane smiled. "Good job she wasn't the *one,* but Mam's heart's in the right place, Grania, you know that."

"Yes," Grania sighed, "I do. Sometimes, though, it's difficult to know if there's any real reason behind what she feels."

"Well, I know she was talking to Dad last night about you, so you might get a visit tomorrow. Now then, I'd better be off; tea'll be on the table and she doesn't like us to be late." Shane stood up. "And that pet in there"—Shane indicated Aurora—"is a sweet little thing that needs a mammy and some love, I'd reckon. If you need anything while you're up here, Grania, give me a buzz on my mobile, there's no need for Mam even to know I've been. One thing's for sure," he added as he pecked Grania on the cheek, "she's never going to change. I'll be seeing you."

Before she climbed into bed that evening, Grania walked down the corridor and opened the door to the bedroom that led to the balcony where she'd found Aurora last night. Switching the light on, she recognized a faint hint of perfume hanging in the air. Grania's eyes strayed to the elegant three-mirrored dressing table, on which were placed the accoutrements of femininity. She approached it and picked up a beautiful ivory hairbrush, the initials *L L* engraved on to the back of it. She turned it over, and saw a long, red-gold hair still wound around the bristles. Grania shuddered—she'd always found what the dead left behind them strange and unsettling.

She turned away from the dressing table and looked at the bed, covered in a lace counterpane and dressed prettily with pillows, as if still waiting for its former occupant to climb into it. She looked at the heavy, mahogany wardrobe and, unable to stop herself, walked to it and turned the key. As she'd suspected, Lily's clothes still hung there, and the smell of the perfume that pervaded the room was strong on all of the garments.

"You are dead . . . gone . . ."

Grania spoke the words out loud to convince herself of the fact. Leaving the room, she removed the key from the lock, then relocked it from the outside. She walked back down the corridor and stowed the key in her bedside drawer. Climbing into bed, she pondered whether, for Aurora's sake, it was a good thing that her mother's bedroom had obviously been left untouched since she died. It was the equivalent to a shrine, invoking and perpetrating the idea that Lily still lived.

"Poor little thing," Grania whispered to herself sleepily. And thought that, even if her own mother's view of the Lisle family was over-dramatized, there was no doubt that the house and its occupants were decidedly strange.

Grania jumped awake and saw her bedside light was still on. She heard footsteps outside her door and tiptoed to open it. The small figure was standing at the end of the corridor, trying to turn the handle to her mother's bedroom.

Grania switched the landing light on and walked toward her. "Aurora," she said softly as she put a hand on the little girl's shoulder, "it's me, Grania."

Aurora turned toward her, her face full of anxiety and confusion.

"Darling, you've been dreaming again, come back to bed." Grania tried to steer her away from the door, but Aurora shrugged her off and turned back to the locked handle, twisting it with growing frustration. "Aurora, wake up! You're dreaming," she repeated.

"Why won't it open? Mummy's calling me, I have to go to her. Why can't I get in?"

"Aurora." Grania shook her gently. "You must wake up, darling." She tried to pry the little girl's fingers from the knob, finally succeeding. "Come on now, sweetheart, I'll take you back to bed and tuck you in."

All the fight suddenly left Aurora's body and she collapsed against Grania, sobbing. "She was calling me, I heard her . . . Grania, I heard her."

Grania felt Aurora shivering, swept her up in her arms and carried her down the corridor and into bed. She gently wiped Aurora's tears from her face and stroked her hair.

"Darling Aurora, don't you see that this is all a dream? It isn't real, I promise you."

"But I hear her, Grania, I hear her voice. She asks me to go to her."

"I know, darling, and I do believe you. Lots of people have vivid dreams, especially about people they've lost and miss very much. But Aurora, darling, your mummy has gone, gone to heaven."

Aurora wiped her nose with her hand. "Sometimes, I think she wants me to go to heaven with her. She says she's lonely and needs me to keep her company. They think I'm mad . . . but I'm not, Grania, I'm really not."

"I know you're not," Grania murmured soothingly. "Now, why don't you close your eyes and I'll stay here until you've gone to sleep."

"Yes, I do feel a little tired . . ." Aurora did as she was bid and Grania stroked her forehead. "I love you, Grania, I feel safe when you're here," she murmured.

Finally, Aurora drifted off to sleep, and Grania tiptoed back to her own room, feeling exhausted herself.

8

Grania drove a nervous Aurora into Clonakilty the following afternoon. "Really, if you don't like the ballet class, you never have to go again," she offered as comfort.

"I know I will like the dancing bit, it's the girls staring at me that I'm frightened of," Aurora admitted. "Other girls my age don't seem to like me."

"I'm sure that's not true, Aurora. And as my mother says, you should always try something once."

"Your mother sounds nice," said Aurora as she climbed out of the car. "Do you think we could go down to your farm one day, so I can meet her?"

"I'm sure that can be arranged. As a matter of fact, I'm seeing my mam for a cup of tea while you're having your lesson." Grania shepherded her through the door of the village hall.

Miss Elva, Grania's old ballet mistress, whom she had spoken to earlier, kissed Grania and gave Aurora a warm smile. "Grania, 'tis grand to see you. And this must be Aurora." Miss Elva knelt down in front of the child and took her hands. "You do know, don't you, that you are named after the beautiful princess in the ballet of *The Sleeping Beauty*?"

Aurora, wide-eyed, shook her head. "No, I didn't."

"Now then"—Miss Elva offered her hand—"You come along with me, and I'll introduce you to some of the other girls in your class. We'll say good-bye to Grania and be seeing her back in about an hour."

"All right." Aurora shyly put her hand in Miss Elva's and followed her through the doors into the studio.

Grania left the building and walked along the narrow, bustling street, the houses painted in gay colors, as was the way in Ireland. She saw her mother through the window, already sipping a cup of tea in O'Donovan's Café.

"Hello, Mam, how are you?" Grania kissed her and sat down opposite her.

"Grand altogether. You?"

"I'm good, Mam." Grania surveyed the short menu and ordered another pot of tea and a scone.

"So now, you say the child has gone off for her first dancing class?"

"Yes and I really think, although I'm no expert, that she has the potential to be very good. She's so graceful, Mam, I sometimes find myself staring at her just because of the beautiful way she moves."

"Well, of course." Kathleen nodded sagely. "I'd think she'd have a gift in that direction. It's in the blood," she sighed.

"Really?" Grania raised an eyebrow as her tea arrived. "Was her mother a dancer?"

"No, but her grandmother was. And, in her day, very famous."

"I'm surprised Aurora hasn't mentioned it." Grania bit into her scone.

"Maybe she doesn't know. So, how has it been up at Dunworley House?"

"It's . . . fine." Grania needed to talk to her mother about Aurora's nighttime wanderings and the strange atmosphere in the house, but didn't wish to provide further fuel to feed Kathleen's displeasure. "Aurora seems to be relaxing and coming out of her shell with me. As you know, I bought a TV for her, and she's been enjoying that. I feel she needs . . ." Grania searched for the appropriate phrase. "Some normality. She seems to have been isolated from the outside world for so much of her life and I don't think it's healthy. The loneliness gives her far too much time to be in her own head, and her imagination to run riot."

"Imagination, is it?" Kathleen gave a wry smile. "I'd say she's been talking about seeing her mother."

"Yes . . . but we both know she's dreaming."

"So then, you haven't spied her mammy standing on the cliffs yet?" There was a twinkle in Kathleen's eyes.

"Mam, be serious! You are joking, aren't you?"

"Not wholly, Grania, no. For myself, I've never seen her, but I could tell you some from the village who swear they have."

"Well, of course, it's ridiculous." Grania nervously took a sip of her tea. "But the problem is, I think Aurora really believes her mother *does* appear to her. She . . . sleepwalks, and when I try to wake her, she tells me her mother is calling to her."

Kathleen crossed herself out of habit and shook her head. "Well now, what came over her father to bring her back here, I really can't think. Anyway, it's not our business to wonder. Although you're the one left dealing with the poor little mite."

"I don't mind. I love her and I want to try to help her if I can," Grania replied defensively. "So, what was it you wanted to talk to me about?"

"Well now, Grania," Kathleen leaned forward and lowered her voice, "I had a word with your daddy, and he thinks it's best if I tell you part of the reason why I'm finding your involvement with that family so unsettling." Kathleen reached inside her shopping bag and pulled out a thick wad of letters.

Grania could see from the browning edges that the letters were old. "What are they, Mam? Who are they from?"

"They are from Mary, my grandmother."

Grania frowned, racking her brains for a memory. "Did I ever meet her?"

"No, sadly. She was a wonderful woman and I was very fond of her. Some would say she was ahead of her time. She was feisty and independent, and I'd go as far as to admit that you take after her, Grania." Kathleen grinned.

"I'll take that as a compliment, Mam."

"So you should, and you certainly look like her." Kathleen opened the top envelope and passed Grania a small sepia photograph. "There she is, that is your great-granny."

Grania studied the picture and couldn't disagree. In a bonnet and old-fashioned clothes, it was her own features and coloring that stared back at her. "When was this taken, Mam?"

"Mary was in her twenties then, so it was probably taken in London."

"London? What was Mary doing there?"

"Well now, that's what you'll discover from the letters."

"You want me to read them?"

"I'm not forcing you, but if you want to start to understand where all this began with the Lisles, I'd suggest you do. Besides, it might while away some lonely nights sitting up at the big house by yourself. And it'd be a grand place to read them too, seeing as Mary herself spent time there."

"So, you say it'll explain everything?"

"No." Kathleen shook her head. "I'm not saying that. It'd be up to me to tell you the rest." She checked her watch. "I'd better be off."

"And me." Grania signaled for the waitress. "You go, Mam, I'll pay for this."

"Thank you, Grania." Kathleen stood up and kissed her daughter. "Take care and I'll be seeing you."

"That reminds me, would you really mind if I brought Aurora down to the farm? She's desperate to meet you and see the animals."

"What harm, I suppose?" Kathleen sighed in surrender. "Just give me a buzz before you come."

"Thanks, Mam." Grania smiled. She paid the bill, tucked the thick wad of envelopes into her handbag and set off back down the street to collect Aurora. When she arrived, she saw the other girls had left the studio to get changed, but Aurora was still inside with Miss Elva. The teacher saw Grania peering through the glass panes and said something to Aurora, who nodded. Miss Elva then came out of the studio to speak to Grania.

"How did she get on?" asked Grania eagerly.

"Well now, that child," Miss Elva lowered her voice as her other students started to file out of the changing room to leave the building, "is amazing. You say she has never had a ballet class in her life?"

"No." Grania shook her head. "That's what she tells me, and I don't see why she would lie."

"Aurora has *everything* one would look for in a future ballerina. A natural turnout, a high instep, perfect physical proportions . . . to be honest now, Grania, I can hardly believe what I've just seen."

"You think she should continue?"

"Absolutely. And fast too. She's already four years behind, and once her body starts to mature it will be that much harder for her to learn. But this isn't the right class for Aurora to be in. She'll have outgrown them all in a couple more lessons. I don't know what the situation is at home, but I'd certainly be prepared to give her a couple of private lessons every week."

"The question is, is that what Aurora wants to do?" asked Grania.

"Well, I was asking her just now what she thought and she seemed very eager. Grania, once that child has grasped some technique, I can see her getting a place at the Royal Ballet School in London in a couple of years' time. Perhaps I could speak to her parents?"

"Aurora's mother is dead and her father is abroad. I'm in charge of her. Why don't I have a chat with Aurora and see if she's happy to continue?"

Miss Elva nodded as Aurora, bored of waiting by herself in the studio, joined them outside.

"Hello, sweetheart, Miss Elva says you enjoyed yourself. Did you?" asked Grania.

"Oh, yes!" Aurora's eyes were alight with pleasure. "I loved it," she said.

"Good, so you want to come back again?"

"Of course. Miss Elva and I have already discussed it, haven't we? I can come back, can't I, Grania?"

"I'm sure you can, yes. But perhaps I should speak to Daddy to make sure that's all right."

"OK," Aurora accepted reluctantly. "Good-bye, Miss Elva, and thank you."

"Hope to see you next week, Aurora," Miss Elva called as Grania and Aurora left and walked back to the car.

That evening, Aurora was full of excitement about the class, showing Grania the positions she had learned, pirouetting and jumping and pointing her feet around the kitchen as Grania cooked them supper.

"When can we go to Cork city to get my ballet things? Can we go tomorrow?"

"Perhaps," said Grania after supper, "but I really feel I should ask your daddy about this first."

"If it's what I want," Aurora pouted, "he won't say no, will he?"

"I'm sure he won't, but I just need to make sure. Story?"

"Yes, please," Aurora said eagerly as Grania took her hand and they climbed the stairs. "Do you know *The Sleeping Beauty,* about the princess I'm named after? I'd love to dance that part one day," she said dreamily.

"And I'm sure you will, sweetheart."

After Aurora had subsided, Grania went downstairs and opened the door to Alexander's study. She checked the contact list for his phone number and dialed it. His voice mail clicked in immediately.

"Hello, Alexander, it's Grania Ryan here. Aurora is very well indeed, and I'm sorry to bother you, but I just wanted to check that it was all right for Aurora to take some dancing lessons. The one she did today she really enjoyed, and she wants to continue. Perhaps you could give me a quick call back or even send me a text, and"—Grania thought about it swiftly before she continued—"if I don't hear from you in the next two or three days, I'll take it that it's fine. Hope all is well with you, bye."

Despite herself, Grania felt apprehensive as she climbed into bed at eleven that night. Her senses were alert to hear footsteps along the corridor, and however hard she tried, sleep would not come. At three o'clock—the time she had woken on the previous nights—Grania tiptoed into Aurora's room to find the child peacefully asleep. Tiptoeing back out again, she reached for the heavy pile of envelopes her mother had given to her. Undoing the string that bound them together, she opened the first one, and began to read . . .

Aurora

So, the story has begun. And some of our characters are in place. Including me, of course. As usual, I take center stage. I look back and see what a precocious child I was. But also "troubled," for which adults forgive a lot.

I will not spoil the story by giving too much away about my midnight wanderings. But I have put in little for "effect," especially about me. Besides, in act two of The Sleeping Beauty, *the gossamer curtain between reality and dreams is opened by Princess Aurora herself, with the help of the Lilac Fairy.*

Who is to say what is real or imagined?

I told you from the start I believed in magic.

I've also discovered today that not only am I named after a princess in a fairy tale, but a mystical set of lights that brighten the night sky. I like the idea of being a star, shining down forever from the heavens, although I'm quite glad my second name isn't "Borealis."

Now, we move back in time, and I must start to exercise my writing powers more proficiently. Up until this point, I've known the living, breathing protagonists:

Grania, who grieved so much for the baby she had lost, and was in such a muddle about the man she loved. I can see now how vulnerable she was. Easy prey for a child needing a mother, and for a handsome father struggling to cope.

Kathleen, whose past knowledge makes her desperate, yet impotent, to protect her child.

And Matt, dear Matt, so confused and helpless, and at the mercy of the strange breed, which men, it seems to me, can't do with or without—

Women.

We will meet many females in the next hundred pages. We will meet good men and bad too—a cast of characters to do justice to any fairy tale. It was a darker time then, a time when little value was placed on human life, when survival for the most part was all we strove for.

I wish I could say that we have learned our lesson.

But humans rarely look back to the past, until they have made the same mistakes. By which time their opinions are considered irrelevant, as they are apparently too old to understand the young. Which is why the human race will always remain as flawed yet as magical as we are.

We are returning now to that same clifftop in Dunworley Bay, where my story began . . .

9

West Cork, Ireland, August 1914

"My mobilization papers have come. I'm to leave for Wellington Barracks in London tomorrow."

Mary, who had been enjoying the unusual blue of the sea below her—the hot August day turning the murky, forbidding colors of Dunworley Bay into a picture postcard of the French Riviera—stopped dead in her tracks and released Sean's hand.

"What?!" she exclaimed.

"Mary, pet, you knew as well as I did that this was coming. I'm a reserve in the Irish Guards and now that war has broken out against Germany, I'm needed to help the Allies win it."

Mary stared hard at her fiancé, wondering if the sun had gone to his head. "But we're to be married in a month's time! We're halfway through building our house! You can't just up and leave!"

Sean smiled down at her, his gentle eyes understanding her shock. It had been a shock to him too, even though he was a reserve. But a thought in your mind and the reality of it happening were two different things altogether. He reached down to pull Mary to him—at six foot three to her five foot one, it was a big reach—but Mary resisted.

"Come now, Mary, I must go and fight for my country."

"Sean Ryan!" Mary put her hands on her hips. "'Tis not your country you'll be fighting for! It's Britain, the country that's oppressed *this* country for the last three hundred years."

"Ah, Mary, even Mr. Redmond is urging us to fight for the British; you know yourself about the bill that is going to be passed by Parliament giving us independence here in Ireland. They've done us a favor and now we must repay it."

"Favor! Letting those to whom this land belongs have a say in its rule? Ah well—" Mary sat down abruptly on a convenient rock. "I'd say 'tis a pretty big favor they've granted us." She crossed her arms and stared staunchly ahead of her into the bay.

"You'll be signing up for the Nationalist Party soon too, will you?" Sean understood her need to blame anyone else for the catastrophe he'd brought to her life.

"If it will keep my man by my side where he belongs, I'll do anything."

Sean crouched on the ground beside her, his long legs almost to his ears as he bent them. He reached for her hand but she nudged him away. "Mary, please. All it means is that our plans will be delayed, not canceled."

Mary continued to stare out to sea, ignoring him. Eventually she sighed. "And there was me thinking the soldiering business was a boy's game, a chance for you to play with guns and feel big with yourself. Never did I think it could be real. And I would lose you to it," she added softly.

"Sweetheart"—Sean offered his hand again and this time she accepted it—"it wouldn't matter whether I was a reservist or not. John Redmond is wanting all us Irish boys to volunteer. The way I see it, at least I've had some training, whereas some of the other fellows will have none. And the Irish Guards—'tis a true and proud institution. I'll be with my own out there, Mary; we'll give Jerry a lesson he'll never forget. And I'll be returning to you and Ireland soon, don't you worry."

Another long silence ensued before Mary was able to voice her thoughts, choked with emotion now. "Ah, Sean, *will* you be back? There's no guarantee of that, you know it as well as I do."

Sean stood up, pulling himself to his full height. "Look at me, Mary, I've the kind of build that was made for fighting. Your husband-to-be is no wimp of a man who can be brought down by a few Germans. I could take on three of them at one go and they'd not be a match for me."

She looked up at him, tears in her eyes. "But a single bullet in the heart doesn't worry about the size of you."

"Don't you be thinking thoughts like that, pet. I can take care of myself. I'll be back to you sooner than you know it."

Mary studied his eyes and saw the glint of excitement there. While all she could see was the possibility of his death, Sean was imagining glory on the battlefield. She realized this was what he'd been waiting for. "So, you leave for London tomorrow?"

"Yes. There's transport from Cork city, taking us Munster reservists up to Dun Laoghaire to catch the boat to England."

Mary dropped her eyes from the skyline and stared instead at the thick, coarse grass beneath her feet. "When will I see you again?"

"Mary, I can't be knowing that," Sean replied softly. "But they'll give us leave and I'll be straight home to you." He took her hand in his. "It's not grand timing, but there's not much to be done about it."

"How will your daddy manage without you on the farm?" Mary asked plaintively.

"The women will do what they always have at a time like this; they'll take on the man's work. Sure, when my daddy was fighting in the Boer War, my mammy did a grand job altogether."

"Have you told her yet?"

"No, I wanted to break the news to you first. Telling her is my next task. And I must do that now. Ah, Mary. What can I say?" Sean put his arms around her shoulders and hugged her to him. "We'll get wed as soon as I return. Now, pet, will you walk back down to the farm with me?"

"No." Mary shook her head slowly. "I think I need to be by myself for a while. You go off and tell your mammy."

Sean nodded silently, kissed her on top of her head and straightened up. "I'll be calling round later to see you, to . . . say good-bye."

"Yes," she whispered to herself as Sean began to walk slowly back down the hill. She waited until he was out of sight, then she put her head in her hands and wept. Inwardly, she raged at the God she'd spent so many hours confessing her sins to. Yet Mary could not think of one thing she had done wrong to deserve this catastrophe.

In her old life—the life that had existed up to twenty minutes ago before he'd broken the news—she was to be Mrs. Sean Ryan in under four weeks' time. She was to have, for the first time in her life, a home of her own, a family and respectability. And, above all, a man who wasn't bothered about her unknown provenance, but simply loved her for being her. On the day she wed, her past was to have disappeared.

She would have left her position as a maid at Dunworley House, scrubbing floors and fetching and carrying for the Lisle family. And would have her very own floors to scrub.

Not that young Sebastian Lisle, her employer, had been anything but kind to her during her time at the house; he had come to the nuns who ran the orphanage nearly four years ago, when she had been fourteen, looking for a girl to fill a place on his household staff. Mary had begged to be considered for the position. The Reverend Mother had been less than keen—Mary was a bright girl and a hard worker who'd been able to help the other orphaned children with their reading and writing. She was an asset to the convent, and Mary knew that the Reverend Mother's greatest desire was for her to take the veil and remain at the convent for the rest of her life.

This was not Mary's wish; she had too many doubts—kept to herself—about a God who allowed his flock so much suffering. Motherless babies left on the doorstep of the convent, merely to die unloved and in pain a few months later during a diphtheria outbreak, or perhaps measles. She'd been taught that suffering was part of the path on the way to Heaven and God Himself, and so she tried hard to believe in His goodness. But a life spent devoted to Him, never moving on or seeing the world, cloistered inside the walls of a convent, was not what she believed was right for her.

The Reverend Mother had given in gracefully; she could see that Mary, blessed with her intelligent, inquiring mind and quick wits, would not settle for what she herself had chosen. However, she was unhappy at Mary beginning her life as a servant.

"I was thinking that you could be taking a position as a governess," she'd urged. "You have a natural gift for teaching children. I could make inquiries . . . to see if there is such a position available when you turn eighteen."

To fourteen-year-old Mary, the idea of waiting another four years for her life to begin had been unthinkable. "Reverend Mother, I'll not be caring what I do. Please, I'd like at least to be given the opportunity to meet Mr. Lisle when he comes here," Mary had begged.

Finally, the Reverend Mother had agreed. "You may meet him, and then it will be God's will to decide if you go."

Happily for Mary, this seemed to be the case. Out of the six girls the Reverend Mother had put forward for the position as "tweeny"—the in-between maid—Sebastian Lisle had chosen her.

Mary had packed her few possessions and left the convent without a backward glance.

As the Reverend Mother had suggested, her position was far below Mary's capabilities but, after her years at the convent, she was not afraid of hard work. The room in the attic, which she shared with one other maid, was enough to thrill her after spending her entire life in a dormitory with eleven other girls. Mary gave of her best and worked diligently.

And it wasn't long before the young master noticed.

In the space of a few months, Mary was promoted to parlormaid. As she served the master and his guests, Mary watched, she listened and she learned. The Lisle family were English. They had come to Dunworley House two hundred years ago, to take control of the heathen Irish who inhabited the land the British believed was theirs. Mary learned to decipher their clipped accent, became used to their strange, formal traditions and their instilled and unshakable sense of superiority.

It was not a demanding household to be part of. The master, Sebastian Lisle, a young man of eighteen, lived there with his mother, Evelyn, who had lost her husband to the Boer War and now relied on her son to run the house for her. Mary learned that Evelyn Lisle also had an older son, Lawrence, who had followed his father into the diplomatic service and was currently abroad. The Lisles had another residence in London; a grand, white house that reminded Mary of a wedding cake, from the painting she had seen.

One day, Mary dreamed, she would leave Ireland and go off and see the world. But until then, she saved up the few shillings she was paid every week and stored them under her mattress.

And it had been two years later that she'd met Sean Ryan.

The housekeeper had been laid up with her chest, and had not wanted to walk down the hill to the farm in the pouring rain to collect the eggs and the milk. So she had sent Mary.

Mary had walked down the cliff and arrived, soaking wet, in the yard in front of Dunworley Farmhouse. Knocking on the door, she had stood dripping outside it.

"Can I be helping you there, miss?" came a deep voice from behind her. Mary turned around and looked up, and up again, into the gentle green eyes of a young man. He was unusually tall and broad-shouldered—built for the land, she felt. This was a man who you just knew for sure would protect you through any bother. With those strong, muscled arms around your shoulders, you'd be as safe as houses, whatever the trouble.

After that initial meeting, no longer did Mary spend her afternoon off wandering aimlessly along the cliffs near the house. Sean would meet her in his trap and they would ride off down to the village of Rosscarberry, or take tea in Clonakilty. Or simply, on a fine day, walk along the nearby beach together. They talked endlessly about anything and everything, taking knowledge from each other. While Mary had her convent education, Sean had knowledge of the land. They'd aired their opinions on Ireland, the Troubles, and discussed hopes and dreams for the future, which included leaving Ireland to try their luck in America. And, sometimes, they simply didn't talk at all.

The day Sean had taken Mary home to meet his family, her knees had shaken as he'd ushered her through the door into the kitchen. But Bridget, his mammy, and Michael, his daddy, had been welcoming and kind to Mary, and agog to know stories of what went on at the Big House. And the fact she could recite entire passages from the Bible, and the catechism in Latin too, brought smiles of wonder to their weatherbeaten faces.

"You've got yourself a good 'un there," Bridget had proclaimed. "I'm hoping you'll be making an honest woman of her soon. It's time you got yourself married, son."

So, after a year and a half of courting, Sean had proposed, and a wedding date was set for a year's time.

"Now then," Michael, Sean's father, had said a few days later over one too many glasses of poteen. "Your mammy and I have been talking about the future. Our farmhouse, 'tis old and damp and small. We need to be thinking of building us a new house altogether. And I'd be thinking that the other side of the barns is a grand spot for such a place. Your mammy and me, we're too old to move, but for you and Mary and the small ones that will arrive, and for their children's children, we should be planning for it." Michael had put a rough drawing in front of Sean. "How does this look to you?"

Sean had studied the drawing—a good, big kitchen, sitting room, dining room and a place at the back for an inside lavvy. Four bedrooms upstairs, with an attic that could be made habitable as the family grew further. "But, Pa, where will we find the money to build this?" Sean had asked.

"Don't you worry about that, son, I have some put by. And there will be no costs in labor." Michael had thumped the table. "We'll be building it with our own bare hands!"

"Still," Sean said with a sigh, "all that money and work, and 'twill not be ours to own. We only rent this land and what's upon it from the Lisles, after all."

Michael took another healthy gulp of poteen and nodded in agreement. "I know, son, and for now that's the case. But I'm thinking there's a lot going to change in Ireland in the next few years. The Nationalists' voice is growing stronger every day now, and the British government is starting to listen. I reckon that one day the Ryans will be standing right here on land that they own. And we must think of the future, not the past. So now, what do you think of my idea?"

When Sean had told Mary of his father's plan, she clapped her hands together in delight.

"Oh, Sean, an inside lavvy! And a new home for us and our children. Can it be built soon?"

"Yes, pet," Sean had affirmed. "The lads from around these parts will lend me a helping hand."

"But what about our plans?" Mary's smile had faded. "What about the thoughts we had to see the world, to get on that boat to America?"

"I know, I know," he'd agreed, putting his hand over hers. "And that must still be in the back of our minds. But even if we left, the Ryans still need a good new roof over their heads. And wouldn't it make us both feel better to know we were leaving them with one, if we did decide to go?"

"I thought we had decided," Mary had answered.

"We have, pet, we have, but everything in time."

So, in the past year, having gained permission from Sebastian Lisle to build a new farmhouse—as Michael had said, it was no skin off his nose, it simply made the land more valuable—the foundations for the house were laid and the walls began to go up. Mary would often pass it, and stop and stare in wonder.

"My house," she'd whisper to herself in disbelief.

Every spare hour Sean had, he'd worked on it, and as it had grown, and the rooms that would one day be hers began to take shape, the talk was less of leaving for America than it was of the furniture Sean would make in his workshop. And those they would invite in to see their grand new home once they were wed.

Having no family of her own, Mary had adopted Sean's. She helped his younger sister, Coleen, with her letters, his mother with baking soda bread, and learned from his father how to milk the cows in the dairy. And they in turn responded to her generous, capable self.

Although the family were not wealthy, their one hundred acres brought them a steady income. The farm itself provided for many of their needs, with milk, eggs, meat from the sheep and wool for their backs. Michael and Sean worked from dawn till dusk making sure the farm yielded its potential.

Mary was aware from the looks on the faces of the other local families when they came around to be introduced to her, that she'd won herself a good catch.

And now, thought Mary as she wiped her eyes roughly on her shawl, it was to be taken away from her. It was all very well Sean believing that he'd return to her safe and sound, but what if he didn't?

Mary sighed. She should have known it was all too good to be true. She had already handed in her notice at the Big House, and was to leave next month in preparation for her marriage. Mary wondered whether, under the new circumstances, this was still the right thing to be doing. If she slipped under the Ryans' roof and waited until Sean returned from war, she'd have no independence *or* money of her own. If Sean didn't return, the chances were she'd die an old maid under her dead fiancé's roof.

Mary stood up and turned toward Dunworley House. Even though Mrs. O'Flannery, the housekeeper, didn't like her, she appreciated her hard work and there'd been a look of dismay in her eyes on the day she'd given her notice. Sebastian Lisle too, and his mother, had expressed their sadness that Mary was leaving.

As she walked back up the cliff toward the house, Mary was sure she'd be able to keep her position for longer. At least, until Sean returned. Mary set her jaw as she walked into the kitchen. Even though she would be swallowing her pride to ask, and then see the gleam of pleasure at her misfortune enter the housekeeper's eyes, Mary decided it was the lesser of the two evils.

She'd been "owned" for most of her life and had finally escaped. She did not wish to go back to prison now.

10

After Mary had waved Sean off to war, gritting her teeth to keep her emotions in check, she gave herself a good talking to on the way up to Dunworley House and went back to work.

The months passed, with news from the front filtered through to her via Sebastian Lisle, who had *The Times* delivered to him from England once a week. There was the occasional letter from Sean, who said he was already in France and had fought in a battle in a place called Mons. From his letters, he seemed in high spirits, enjoying the camaraderie of the other "Micks," as the Irish Guards were known. But already there were fatalities in his battalion; he wrote of friends lost or wounded.

Occasionally, Mary popped down to see the Ryans, but the sight of the half-finished house—untouched since Sean and the other young men of the village had left—upset her.

She was in a holding bay, waiting for fate to decide her destiny.

Nine months on, and Sean's letters had become less frequent. She wrote to him every week, asking him when he thought he might be having the leave he'd been promised. In his last letter, he'd mentioned he'd been shipped back to the Irish Guards' London barracks for four days—not nearly enough time to make the trip all the way down to West Cork. Mary read in *The Times* that thousands of Allied soldiers had lost their lives in a place called Ypres.

Sebastian Lisle had left Ireland five months ago; not to fight, on account of him suffering from asthma, but to help out in what he called the Foreign Office.

A pall fell over Dunworley House; with only Evelyn Lisle to care for and no guests, there was little for the staff of three to do. The tweeny was dismissed, which meant Mary took on her tasks too.

And, along with every soul across Europe, Mary held her breath and waited.

Eighteen months on, Sebastian Lisle came home. It was a pleasure to at least have someone to serve at table; Evelyn roused herself from her torpor and came downstairs to eat in the dining room with her son. Two days later, Mary was summoned to Sebastian's study.

"You'd be wanting to see me, sir?" Mary said as she entered.

"Yes." Sebastian's watery blue eyes seemed to have sunk further into their sockets; he looked haggard and drawn, double his real age. His red hair was receding, and Mary thought that breeding did not necessarily bless you with looks. "There's a position of housemaid available at our London home. I have suggested you for it, Mary. How would you feel about that?"

Mary looked at him, astonished. "Me? Go to London?"

"Yes. Now I'm back here, we can manage with Mrs. O'Flannery and a daily from the village. Whereas in London, what with the war effort and more girls going into the munitions factories and taking over the men's jobs driving the buses, et cetera, it's becoming increasingly difficult to find household staff. My brother asked me if I could find someone here in Ireland, and you are the obvious choice."

"London . . ." Mary breathed. That was where Sean's barracks were. Perhaps next time he got some leave from France, she'd be able to meet him. Besides, it was an adventure and an opportunity she knew she must grasp.

"I'm thinking that might be grand, sir. Would my duties be similar to here?"

"More or less, yes. It's a far larger house than this, and used to have a staff of twenty. We are now down to ten and everyone is mucking in. You'll be given a smart uniform, a room shared with one other maid and a salary of thirty shillings a month. Would that suit you?"

"Well now, I think it might, sir, yes."

"Jolly good, Mary. Please let me know as soon as you've decided and I'll arrange your passage to England."

"Yes, sir. I'll do that, so."

• • •

A few days later, Mary went down the hill to see Sean's parents and tell them of her decision. Not surprisingly, they weren't keen on their son's fiancée leaving Ireland's shores while he was away.

"But, Bridget," Mary comforted as she sipped tea with her in the kitchen, "I'd want to be going so that maybe I can see Sean when he next gets leave."

"To be sure, that's all well and good, but my cousin's daughter went off to London only last year. They don't like Irish maids there, so she said. They'll be looking down on you, like all the English do with the Irish," Bridget sniffed.

"As if I'd care about that! I'll put them right, never you mind." Unperturbed, Mary smiled, unable to keep the glint of excitement out of her eyes.

"Just promise me, Mary, when the war is ended, you'll be coming back home here to your man, won't you?" Bridget entreated.

"You know there is nowhere else I'd rather be than by Sean's side. But while I can be doing something useful as I wait for him, and earn a few more shillings to put away for our future, I'd be thinking it was a good plan."

"Well now, you take care of yourself in that heathen city." Bridget shuddered at the thought of it.

"Don't you worry, I will, I swear."

Mary felt not a glimmer of fear as she embarked on her long journey. First, up to Dublin, and across on the boat to Liverpool, then down south on an overcrowded train. It came to a halt in a vast station. She hauled her valise up the platform and looked around her. She'd been told she was to be met by someone who would be holding up her name. She gazed through the sea of khaki, engaged in sorrowful good-byes or happy hellos, and finally spotted a man in a smart uniform, holding a piece of card with her name on it.

"Hello there," she smiled as she walked up to him. "I'm Mary Benedict."

The man nodded solemnly. "Follow me, please."

Outside, the man motioned for her to get into the back of the gleaming black car. She did so, marveling at the soft leather on the seat. As they set off, Mary felt like a princess. She had never been in a car before.

She gazed out of the windows at the gas lamps above her—like oversized sherbet-lemons suspended on big sticks—at the crowds of people flowing along the pavements and the tall buildings that lined them. Trams moved ceaselessly up and down the center of the streets. And the women, she noticed, were wearing skirts that showed their *ankles.* They drove along a wide river, but it was too dark to see much. Then the chauffeur turned right, away from the river, and finally into a large square, lined on each side with enormous white houses. They drove along a narrow mews, where he parked the car and indicated for her to step out.

"This way please," he said as Mary followed him along the mews. "This is the servants' entrance to Cadogan House, and the one you will always use." He led her down the flight of steps and opened the door into a small lobby.

Another door led to a low-ceilinged but warm kitchen, in the center of which was a table occupied by a number of people, all dressed in smart uniforms.

"Your new parlormaid is here, Mrs. C," said the chauffeur, nodding to a large woman sitting at the head of the table.

"Come here where I can see you." The woman beckoned her over, surveying Mary as she did so.

"Hello, ma'am." Mary curtsied. "I'm Mary Benedict."

"And I'm Mrs. Carruthers, the housekeeper." The woman finished her inspection and nodded. "Well, at least you look healthy enough, which is more than I can say for the last Irish maid we had here. She was dead of bronchitis within a week. Wasn't she, Mr. Smith?" She turned to the balding man sitting next to her and broke into a hearty chuckle, her ample bosom heaving as she did so.

"I believe I'm healthy, ma'am," answered Mary. "In fact, I've never had a day's illness in my life."

"Well, that's a start, I suppose," Mrs. Carruthers agreed.

Mrs. Carruthers spoke English in a strange accent. Mary strained to understand what she was saying.

"I suppose you'll be hungry. You Irish always are." She pointed to a seat at the end of the table. "Take off your bonnet and your coat and sit down. Teresa, get Mary a plate of stew."

"Yes, Mrs. Carruthers." A young woman wearing a mobcap and brown dress rose immediately from the table. Mary removed her hat, gloves, coat and shawl and was directed to hang them in the lobby. She sat down next to a girl dressed in a maid's uniform.

"So, Mary, I suppose you can't read and write? Your kind usually can't. It makes life so much more difficult for me," sighed Mrs. Carruthers.

"Oh yes, ma'am, I can." Mary nodded as a plate of stew was put in front of her. "I used to teach the small ones at my convent school."

"School, is it?" Mrs. Carruthers smirked. "Well, I'm sure you'll be teaching me to lay the table next!"

The others around her laughed dutifully. Mary determinedly ignored the jibe and gulped back her stew silently, hungry from her long journey.

"You've been working for Mr. Lisle's brother at his house in Ireland, so I hear," continued Mrs. Carruthers.

"Yes."

"Well, I don't know how they go on there, but I think you might find things a bit different here in London. Mr. Sebastian Lisle tells me you know how to serve at table, is that true?"

"I'd be thinking I do, so," agreed Mary. "But I'm sure you're right. Things will be different here."

"You're to share with Nancy, our upstairs maid." Mrs. Carruthers indicated the girl sitting next to Mary. "Breakfast at five thirty prompt; if you're five minutes late, it won't be saved for you, understand?"

Mary nodded.

"Your uniform's laid out on your bed. And make sure your pinny is clean. Mr. Lisle is very particular about spotless uniforms."

"Pinny?" Inquired Mary.

"Your apron, girl." Mrs. Carruthers raised her eyebrows. "After breakfast tomorrow morning, I'll inform you of your duties. When Mr. Lisle is in residence, this is a busy household. He's a very important man and he likes things just so. Luckily for you, he's away at the moment, but we don't let our standards slip, do we?"

Those at the table nodded in agreement and began to rise from it.

"Nancy, take Mary up to her room."

"Yes, Mrs. C," the girl next to her said dutifully. "Follow me," she said to Mary.

A few minutes later, Mary was hauling her valise up the steps and into a vast hallway. A huge chandelier hung in the stairwell, full of electric lightbulbs. They climbed another three flights of stairs until they arrived on the attic floor. "Jesus, Mary and Joseph! This house! 'Tis the size of a palace!" she exclaimed.

"That one's yours," said Nancy, leading her into a room that housed two beds and not much else. She pointed to a bed by the window. "You're last in, so you get the draught."

"Thank you." Mary smiled wryly and dumped her valise onto her bed.

"We take it in turns to get hot water for the washbasin, and there's a pot under the bed for the other," indicated Nancy, sitting down on her own bed and surveying Mary. "You're pretty, you are. How come you don't have that red hair that all you Irish have?"

"I don't know, I'm sure," Mary replied, unpacking her meager items of clothing and stowing them in the drawer by the bed. "But not all of us have it, you know."

"All the ones I've met have. No, you've got lovely blue eyes and fair hair. Do you put a bottle on it?"

"You mean, do I dye it?" Mary chuckled and shook her head. "You wouldn't be getting that kind of thing where I'm from. We're still waiting for the electricity to come to our part of the world."

"Blimey," Nancy giggled, "couldn't imagine what it's like to live without it no more, though when I was a little'un, we didn't have none. That's why I got so many brothers and sisters!" she cackled. "You got a young man?"

"Yes, but he's away off fighting Jerry, and I haven't seen him for eighteen months."

"There's always more where he came from, you know"—Nancy grinned—"'specially here in London."

"Well, I'd not be interested in any other fellow. There won't be anyone else for me," Mary replied staunchly.

"You wait till you've been living here a few months, then we'll see. There's a lotta lonely soldier boys here in the city on leave, looking for a pretty girl to spend their wages on, you mark my words." Nancy began to undress, her stays barely covering a magnificent set of breasts and Rubenesque hips. As she let down her long blond hair, she resembled a ripe cherub. "If we get our days off together, I'll take you out and show you the sights. There's plenty to keep you occupied here in the Smoke, that's for sure."

"So, what are the master and mistress like?" Mary asked as she climbed into bed.

"Oh, we have no mistress yet. Mr. Lisle lives alone, at least when he's here. No lady seems to have taken his fancy. Or maybe he hasn't taken theirs!" Nancy chuckled.

"Well now, to be sure, neither has his brother Sebastian married," said Mary, pulling the thin blanket tighter around her, understanding why the bed she was in was not favored.

"Mrs. Carruthers says the master might be a spy," said Nancy. "Whatever it is he does is important. He entertains lots of famous people for dinner here. Once we even had Lloyd George himself! Can you imagine, the British Prime Minister sitting in our dining room?"

"Holy Mary, Mother of God! You mean I might have to serve him at table?" Mary's eyes were round with horror.

"The way I always think of it when we have someone famous to the house, and I see 'em with my very own eyes, is that they all have to use the lavvy. So, I just imagine them sitting on that and then I'm not frightened any more."

Mary giggled and warmed to Nancy. "How long have you been in service?" she inquired.

"Since I were eleven, when my ma sent me to be a pot washer. Now that were hard, emptying all them slops." Nancy shuddered. "Whether you're a lady or a skivvy, yer piss and shit smells the same."

Mary's eyes were beginning to close, the apprehension and excitement of coming to London getting the better of her. As she drifted into sleep, Nancy continued to talk, but Mary listened no more.

11

In the first few weeks, life at Cadogan House was full of wonder for Mary. The house was run on a grand scale, even when there was no master in residence. She could not help but gape at the vast, beautiful rooms, their huge windows draped in thick damask curtains, the finely hewn furniture and the enormous fireplaces with elegant mirrors atop them.

Apart from the ongoing jokes about her Irishness, Mary found the other servants a friendly bunch. Nancy proved to be a fine guide to London, having lived in the city for all of her life. She took Mary on trams to Piccadilly Circus to eat hot chestnuts under the statue of Eros, and up the Mall to look at Buckingham Palace. They had tea and buns in Lyons Corner House, where a couple of young soldiers "gave them the eye," as Nancy put it. Nancy was all for giving it back, but Mary would have none of it.

Mary loved her new and exciting world. The bright lights and hubbub of London made it hard to remember this was a country at war. So far, the British mainland had remained untouched and, apart from the surprising sight of women driving the trams and buses and serving behind counters in shops, the city had remained unchanged.

That was until the zeppelins came.

Mary heard the huge explosion in the middle of the night, and woke up with the rest of the city to the news that the Germans had bombed a site in the East End, killing two hundred people. Suddenly, London became a hive of activity, with barrage balloons hanging above the skyline, the shadowy profiles of machine guns sitting on the tops of tall buildings and preparations for further attacks taking place in the cellars of every house.

During the summer of 1917, when Mary had been in London more than a year, the air-raid sirens rang out with regularity. The staff would scuttle down to the cellar to eat dry biscuits and play cards, while the sounds of the guns rattled above them. Mrs. Carruthers sat on her wooden chair, brought down from the kitchen, and take surreptitious swigs from her hip flask to steady her nerves. Yet even during the worst moments, where it seemed a zeppelin must be directly overhead and Mary watched the fear on the candlelit faces around her, she knew little of her own. She felt . . . *invincible*—as though the horror of what was happening could not touch her.

One morning, in the spring of 1918, Mary finally received a letter from Sean. Even though she'd told him of her new address, Mary had received no letters in return. She had no idea where he was, or whether he was alive or dead. Guiltily, she berated herself every time she and Nancy got dressed up on their day off to go up to town, for the giggles they shared and above all the sense of freedom she felt in this wide open city, where anything seemed possible.

And because, if she was being honest with herself, she could hardly remember what Sean looked like. Opening the letter, she began to read.

France

17th March

My lovely Mary,

I am writing to tell you that I am well, although we seem to have been fighting this war forever. I've a week's leave soon, and I received your letters telling me that you are working in London. When I arrive there, I will be calling round to see you.

Mary, pet, we must both believe that this war will be over soon and we can return to our life in Dunworley together.

You are all that gets me through the days and nights here.

With all my love,
Sean x

Mary reread the letter five times. Then she sat and stared silently at the whitewashed wall opposite her bed.

"What's up?" Nancy was regarding her thoughtfully.

"My young man, Sean. He'll be getting some leave soon and coming to see me."

"Mercy be!" said Nancy. "He ain't a figment of your imagination, after all."

Mary shook her head. "No. 'Tis true, he's real."

"And bulletproof and Jerry-proof too, if he's been in them trenches for the past three years. Most of them soldiers don't make it through the first few weeks. Ain't you the lucky one, that you have a fella still alive? What's the rest of us girls gonna do, eh? Gawd knows how many thousands of young men us girls have lost to this war. We're all going to end up dying old maids. You hang on to yours, you lucky bugger!" Nancy cautioned.

Mary was stoking the fire in the drawing room a few weeks later when Sam, the footman, poked his head around the door.

"There's a gentleman by the name of Ryan asking for you at the front door, Mary. I've sent him around the back to the servants' entrance."

"Thank you, Sam," said Mary. Her legs trembled as she walked down the stairs toward her past, praying the kitchen was empty so she could at least be allowed a moment with Sean alone. However, with the constant monotony of their daily routine, the staff were eager for excitement. Consequently, the kitchen had a full complement of servants.

Mary walked across to the back door as fast as she could, hoping to get there first, but Nancy had beaten her to it. Nancy's hands were on her hips and she was smiling broadly at the gaunt, barely recognizable soldier on the threshold.

Nancy turned toward Mary. "Seems this young man is called Sean, and he wants to speak to you."

"Thank you," said Mary.

"He might be a Paddy, but he's a looker, he is," Nancy whispered to Mary as she went back into the kitchen.

Mary gazed up into Sean's eyes for the first time in three and a half years.

"Mary, my Mary, I can hardly believe I'm staring right at you. Come, give your fiancé a hug." Sean's voice was choked with emotion as he opened his arms and she went to them.

He smelled different, yet the same. As she hugged him, she could feel his thinness against her.

"Mary," he crooned, "'tis really you, right here in London town. And I'm holding you in my arms . . . you don't know how many times I've dreamed of this, so I have. Let me look at you." Sean took hold of her shoulders and surveyed her. "I swear, you have grown even more beautiful."

He was smiling down at her, his gentle eyes full of tenderness.

"Don't be daft," Mary said, blushing, "sure, I'm the same as I always was!"

"Can you get away today? I'll only be having two nights in London before I must leave again."

Mary looked at him doubtfully. "'Tis not normally my day off, Sean. But I can ask Mrs. Carruthers if I may."

She turned from him to walk back into the kitchen, but he stopped her. "You go and get yourself ready to walk out with me. I'll be asking your woman myself. There's not many in London town that can resist a soldier."

And sure enough, by the time Mary was back in the kitchen in her best skirt and new hat, Sean was sitting at the table with Mrs. Carruthers, a glass of gin in his hand, while she and the rest of the servants listened avidly to his tales of life at the front.

"They don't tell us nothing," Mrs. Carruthers complained. "We don't know what's going on, we don't, they just tell us what they want us to hear."

"Well now, Mrs. Carruthers, I'd say another six months and we'll have them beaten. To be sure, Jerry is suffering more casualties than we are. We've learned, you see, how to fight them. It's taken time, but I'd reckon we're on the winning side now."

"Let's hope so," said Mrs. Carruthers fervently. "The shortages here are getting worse and it's more difficult to put food on the table every day."

"Don't you be worrying, Mrs. Carruthers. We've a brave bunch of soldiers defending this nation, and I'll see to it personally that there's a goose on your table next Christmas," added Sean, with a wink.

Mrs. Carruthers chuckled and looked up at Mary. "You've got a fine man there, miss, even though I say so meself. You two had better be getting off. I'm sure you don't want to be wasting a second of your leave talking to an old duck like me!"

"Ah now, Mrs. Carruthers, you're exactly the kind of fine woman us boys are fighting to keep safe." Sean looked at Mary and smiled. "Are you ready?"

"Yes." Mary turned to Mrs. Carruthers. "What time will you be needing me back?"

"Take as much time as you want, dear. I'm sure Nancy won't mind covering your duties just for once, eh, Nancy?"

"No, Mrs. C," Nancy agreed reluctantly, her nose pushed firmly out of joint by the turn of events.

"'Tis awfully kind of you to spare Mary, Mrs. Carruthers. And I promise I'll have her back here by ten o'clock sharp," added Sean.

"As I said, any time will do," Mrs. Carruthers agreed happily.

Mary and Sean left the house and stopped in the mews beyond it.

"I'd forgotten how you could charm the birds out of the trees, Sean Ryan." Mary gazed up at him in admiration. "Even that old battle-axe I work for. Where should we go?"

Sean looked down at her and shrugged. "You'll be the one with the knowledge of London, Mary. I must leave it to you."

"Well now, I'd say that for a start we should go somewhere quiet. So why don't we go and sit in the gardens just across from here for a while, where no one will bother us?"

Sean took her hands in his. "I don't care, as long as I can stare into those beautiful eyes of yours."

They walked across the road to the square gardens, opened the wrought-iron gate and sat down on a bench.

"Ah, Mary." Sean kissed Mary's hands. "You can't know what it means to me to see you, I—" He choked suddenly on his words and sat, silent, next to her.

"What is it, Sean?"

"I—"

And then he began to sob. Great racking sobs which shook his body. Mary looked on in dismay, not knowing what to say or how to help.

"I'm sorry, Mary, I'm sorry . . ." Sean wiped the tears away roughly with one of his big hands. "I'm being daft, so I am, but the hell . . . the *hell* I've been to and seen . . . and there you are, beautiful as you always were. I"— his shoulders heaved—"can't explain."

"Perhaps 'tis best if you try and tell me, Sean. I'm not promising I can help, but maybe I can listen," said Mary softly.

Sean shook his head. "I swore to myself I wouldn't do this, wouldn't break down when I saw you but . . . Mary, how can I tell you what it has been like? How I've wished for death so many times because life is"—his voice cracked—"beyond endurance."

Mary stroked his hand gently. "Sean, I'm here, and whatever it is you need to tell me, I can cope with it, I promise you."

"The stink, Mary, the smell of dead, rotting corpses . . . it fills my nostrils even now. Just a-lying there in the mud, trampled over—bits of bodies everywhere you look. And the smell of gunsmoke and gas, and the bangs that would frighten the life out of you going on and on, all day, all night, without end." Sean put his head in his hands. "There's no respite, Mary, no respite at all. And you'd be knowing every time you went over the top that, at best, you'd lose your friends and, at worst, you'd lose yourself. And wouldn't that have been fine! To escape from that living hell I've been in for almost three and a half years!"

Mary gazed at him in horror. "Sean, we hear only that our boys are doing well now. That we are winning."

"Ah, Mary." Sean was no longer crying. His head hung heavy still in his hands. "They don't want to tell you of the suffering, of course they don't. To be sure, they wouldn't get another human being into the trenches if they knew the truth." He looked up at her suddenly. "And I shouldn't be telling you now."

"Sean," Mary reached out her hand and stroked his head, felt his wiry hair beneath her fingers, " 'tis right you're telling me. I'm to be your wife as soon as you're out of this. And it can't be long, I'm thinking, can it?"

"I've been thinking the same thing every day for three and a half years, Mary, and I'm still there," he replied desolately.

They sat in silence for a while.

"You know," Sean said eventually, "I've forgotten what we're fighting for. And I'm not sure I can go back and face it again."

Mary continued stroking his hair. "'T'will be soon you're out of it, and home with me in Dunworley and our fine new house, where we both belong."

"You must never tell my mammy any of this." Sean looked up at her, anxiety on his face. "Do you promise me, Mary? I couldn't bear to have her thinking and worrying, now. And you're right." He reached for her hand and squeezed it so tight that the blood left Mary's fingers. "It will be over soon. It must be."

When Mary arrived back at the house and crept upstairs to her bedroom a few hours later, she was greeted by Nancy, sitting upright in bed, waiting for her to come in.

"Well? How was it? I never seen Mrs. C so taken before. He's a real charmer, your Sean."

"Yes, he is that." Mary wearily began to remove her clothes.

"Where did you go? Did he take you dancing?"

"No, there was no dancing tonight."

"Did he take you to a club for supper?"

Mary pulled on her nightdress. "No."

"Well then, what did you do?" said Nancy, with a hint of annoyance in her voice.

Mary climbed into bed. "We sat in the gardens in the square."

"You mean, you didn't go nowhere?"

"No, Nancy." Mary put out the light. "We didn't go nowhere."

12

The following evening, Sean came back to Cadogan House to collect Mary again. This time, she took him by tram up to Piccadilly Circus and they bought fish and chips, sitting under Eros to eat them.

"I wish 'twas longer, Mary, and that I could take you somewhere special."

"This is special for me, Sean." Mary kissed him on the cheek. "Better than going to a crowded place and having to mind how we behave, don't you think?"

"'Tis fine by me, if 'tis fine by you," Sean agreed, stuffing the chips hungrily into his mouth. "Mary, I want to say how sorry I am about last night. You didn't deserve to hear all that. And I'm better today."

"It's no problem, Sean." Mary shrugged. "You needed to let it out, and it's only right you did it with me."

"Well now, I don't want to be talking anymore about all that. I'll be back soon enough in the midst of it. Tell me about you, Mary, and your life here in London."

Mary did so as they walked hand in hand down to St. James's Park. Finally, Sean took her face in his hands. "Mary, it won't be long now, and we'll both be going back home." He looked suddenly anxious. "You will want to come back to Dunworley, won't you? I mean"—Sean threw his arms wide and indicated what was around him—"'tis hardly London town."

"No, it isn't, Sean," Mary agreed. "And I'd say both of us have grown up since we met all those years ago. And the world has changed too. But we'll build a life together, wherever that is."

"Mary, oh Mary." Sean wrapped his arms around her and kissed her hard. He pulled away from her suddenly. "I'll be getting too carried away with myself if I'm not careful." He took a few deep breaths then hugged her again. "We'd better be walking back now. I don't want you in trouble with Mrs. Carruthers."

The two of them strolled through the streets, still humming with activity at eleven o'clock at night. "Just like Clon village on a rainy Sunday evening," Sean teased. "So, how do you find Lawrence Lisle? Is he like his brother, Sebastian, a bit of a limp rag? For all his land and his big house."

"I couldn't tell you, Sean," said Mary. "I haven't seen sight nor sound of him since I arrived."

"Where is he?"

"No one knows for sure, but he works for the British government overseas. The rumor is he's in Russia."

"Well, you might have heard what's going on there now. I'd say that if your Mr. Lisle is in Russia, you'd be seeing him back here pretty soon. The Bolsheviks are becoming more powerful as each day passes. Ah," Sean sighed, "I'd say the world is in a right old state just now. And I'm wondering where it will all end."

They'd arrived in the mews and stood silently at the top of the stairs, neither of them knowing how to say good-bye.

"Come here, my Mary, hold me and give me the strength to turn away from your softness and walk back into hell," Sean murmured as she put her arms around him.

"I love you, Sean," she whispered. "Come back to me safe, won't you?"

"I've got this far, haven't I?" he reassured her. "I'll write to you as often as I can, but don't be worrying yourself now if you don't hear for a bit. I've a feeling things are to be mighty difficult. There's another big push coming which'd sort it out once and for all."

"I won't. Bless you, my sweetheart, and may God bring you back safe home to me soon. Good-bye, Sean." Mary wiped her tears on Sean's greatcoat and stood up on tiptoe to kiss him.

"Good-bye, pet. 'Tis only the thought of you that is going to get me through."

Sean turned away from her reluctantly, tears in his own eyes. And, shoulders hunched, walked slowly away down the mews.

• • •

"Don't know what's eating you at the moment," Nancy commented in bed a few days later. "I suppose it's seeing your fella and him going off again back to it all, is it?"

"Yes." Mary sighed into the darkness. "The things that he told me about what it's like out there. I can't be getting the pictures out of my mind."

"Perhaps he was exaggerating to get your sympathy, and maybe an extra kiss!"

"No, I don't think so, Nancy. I wish it was so, but Sean isn't a liar."

"Well, from what the papers are saying, sounds as though it'll be over soon, and then your fella can whisk you off back into the bog you both came from," Nancy chuckled. "Want to go up to town on Thursday, do some window-shopping and have our tea at Lyons? Might cheer you up."

"I think I'll just see how I feel."

"Suit yourself," Nancy huffed.

Mary rolled over, closed her eyes and tried to sleep. Ever since she'd said good-bye to Sean three days ago, she had found it impossible to rid her head of the dreadful images he'd conjured up. And, since then, she had begun to notice the countless men milling around London with eye patches, a lost arm or a leg. And this afternoon, a soldier standing in the center of Sloane Square, shouting to passersby as though his wits had left him. Sean had said the noise of the continual shelling affected the soldiers' brains. Mary had turned away from the poor, demented soul with tears in her eyes.

The newspapers were full of the Bolshevik revolution in Russia, and the fact that the Russian Imperial family had been arrested en masse. The talk in the kitchen was that they'd be seeing the master home any day soon. Mrs. Carruthers had apparently received a telegram to tell her to prepare the house for his imminent arrival. She immediately went into overdrive, having Mary and Nancy polish the silver three times, until Smith, the butler, gave his approval.

"As if the master's going to notice whether his teaspoons have a couple of marks on them!" Nancy exclaimed irritably. "After being in all that Russian hoo-hah, I should think he'll just be glad to be comfy in his own bed."

Although the house was on red alert, there was still no sign of

Lawrence Lisle. Then, four days later, a bleary-eyed Mrs. Carruthers notified the staff that the master had just arrived home at three o'clock in the morning.

"And for reasons you'll find out later, I ain't had no sleep since," she complained. "Honestly"—she raised her eyebrows at Smith—"Who'd have thought it of him?" They shared a moment of disbelief, before Mrs. Carruthers said, "Mary, the master and I want to see you in the drawing room at eleven o'clock sharp."

"Am I in trouble?" she asked nervously.

"No, Mary, it isn't you who's in trouble . . . anyway, I'm saying no more about it until the master's seen you. Make sure you're in a clean uniform and there's not a wisp of hair hanging out of your cap."

"Yes, Mrs. C."

"I wonder what all this is about?" said Nancy as Mrs. Carruthers left the kitchen. "She looks like she's in a right two and one. Why do they want to see you?"

"Well now, I'll be finding out, won't I, in a couple of hours." Mary answered tightly.

Mary presented herself in front of the drawing-room doors at eleven o'clock prompt and knocked. Mrs. Carruthers opened the door.

"Come in and meet Mr. Lisle, Mary."

Mary did so. Standing by the fireplace was a tall man, who bore a strong resemblance to his younger brother, Sebastian. To Mary's mind, Lawrence Lisle seemed to have gleaned the best out of their joint gene pool.

"Good morning. I am Lawrence Lisle. Er . . . Mary, isn't it?"

"Yes, sir." She curtsied.

"Mary, there has arisen in this household a . . . delicate situation. And, having consulted with Mrs. Carruthers, she thinks you are the one person who may be able to help us with it."

"I'm sure I'll do my best, sir. When I know what it is," Mary replied nervously.

"Mrs. Carruthers says you were brought up in a convent orphanage."

"That's correct, sir."

"And while you were in the convent, you helped take care of the other children there, especially the younger ones?"

"Yes, sir, when the babes were left on the doorstep by the poor mothers, I'd help the nuns care for them."

"So, you like babies?"

"Oh yes, sir, I love them."

"Jolly good, jolly good." Lawrence Lisle nodded. "Well, Mary, the situation is this: I have brought home with me from my travels a baby, whose mother, just like those poor women who left their children on the convent doorstep, found herself . . . unable to take care of it. She has asked me to do so, until further notice."

"I see, sir."

"Now, I have talked with Mrs. Carruthers about employing a nursemaid, but she suggested that you might be the person to fulfil the role temporarily. At present, your duties as parlormaid are rarely utilized, and almost certainly won't be for the next few months to come. So Mrs. Carruthers and I would like you to take over the care of the baby immediately."

"I see, sir. Well now, how old is this baby, sir?"

"She must be well . . ." Lawrence thought for a moment. "I should say she is no more than four or five months."

"Right, sir, and where is she?"

"She's there."

He pointed to a small bassinet sitting on a chaise longue at the other end of the drawing room. "Go and take a look if you would like to."

"Thank you, sir."

As Mary walked over to the basket and tentatively peered inside, Lawrence added, "I think she's quite attractive for a baby, although I wouldn't have much experience in these matters. And rather good too. On the boat-train from France, the child barely whimpered."

Mary stared at the shock of dark, downy hair, and the pale but perfect complexion. The baby's thumb was in its mouth and she was fast and contentedly asleep.

"I fed her just an hour ago," commented Mrs. Carruthers. "She can certainly holler when she wants her grub. I presume you know how to bottle feed a baby and change a napkin?"

"Of course, Mrs. C." Mary smiled down at the baby. "What is her name?"

Lawrence hesitated, before he said, "Anna, her name is Anna."

"To be sure," Mary whispered, "she's a beautiful little thing. And yes, sir, I'd love to take care of her for you."

"Good, then that's settled." Lawrence looked relieved. "The baby will be sleeping on the second floor and the nursery has already been prepared. You are to move into it with her today, so you can attend to her feeds in the night. You will be released from all your household duties for the present. You and Mrs. Carruthers must buy whatever is appropriate for the child; perambulators, clothes, et cetera."

"Did she not come with any clothes, sir?"

"The mother packed a small bag for traveling. That is all she has. So"—he indicated the door—"I suggest you take her upstairs now and settle into your room."

"May I ask you what country this baby is from?" said Mary.

Lawrence Lisle frowned and paused for a moment. "From this moment on, the child is English. If anybody inquires, *including* any members of the household staff, she is the child of a close friend of mine, whose wife fell sick giving birth to her. Her father was killed in action a month later. I have taken her in as my ward, until her mother is strong enough to care for her herself. Do you understand, Mary?"

"I understand, sir. And I promise I'll be taking the best possible care of Anna for you."

Mary bobbed a little curtsy, left the room and carried the bassinet carefully up the stairs to the second floor. She waited on the landing until Mrs. Carruthers joined her.

"You're in here." Mrs. Carruthers led her down the corridor to a bedroom that overlooked the square gardens. "I've put you in this room because it's furthest away from the master. Whatever he may say, that baby don't half caterwaul if she's hungry, and I don't want him disturbed."

Mary gazed in awe at the pretty room. It contained a dressing table and a comfortable wrought-iron bed, with a counterpane spread atop it.

"Don't you be getting any ideas above your station, young lady,"

Mrs. Carruthers added. "You're only in here because you need to attend to the baby at night."

"I won't," agreed Mary quickly, knowing that her sudden elevation in rank might be threatening to Mrs. Carruthers's own position.

"It's only temporary, mind. I'm sure that, as soon as he can, the master will want to employ a professional nursemaid. But, as I pointed out, with the war on, it'd be like finding a needle in a haystack. I hope you're grateful that I suggested you for this, my girl. Don't you go letting me down, will you?"

"I'll do my best, Mrs. C, I promise you, so," Mary reassured her. "And there's no need for us to go spending money on clothes for the baby. I'm handy with my needle and thread, and I enjoy sewing."

"Right then. Remove your belongings from your old bedroom when you can. There's a water closet and a bathroom next door. No more pissing in pots for you, my girl. Ain't you the lucky one?"

"Yes. Thank you for the chance, Mrs. C."

"Even though you're Irish, you're a good girl, Mary." Mrs. Carruthers walked to the door then paused. "I dunno," she said, "there's sommat funny about all this. After you'd left with the baby, the master asked me to call Smith to collect a small suitcase and store it in the attic. He said it was to be held here for the baby's mum until she arrived to collect it. That little'un doesn't look English to me," she added, peering into the bassinet. "Does she to you?"

"She's an unusual color," agreed Mary carefully. "All that dark hair and white skin."

"My betting is she's one of them Russian babies," surmised Mrs. Carruthers. "But we'll probably never know, will we?"

"Well now, all that's important is the little pet's safe and sound with us here," said Mary.

"Yes, you're right," agreed Mrs. Carruthers. "I'll see you downstairs later."

Finally, Mary was left alone with her new charge. She sat on the bed with the baby in the bassinet next to her and stared down into Anna's tiny face. Eventually, as though the baby knew she was being observed, she twitched, stirred and opened her eyes sleepily.

"Hello, little pet," Mary cooed, looking straight down into the deep, brown eyes. She watched the expression in them change, and realized that the observing was being done by the baby.

Mary grasped the baby's hand with her fingers. "Hello, Anna, I'm here to take care of you."

It was love at first sight.

13

The war continued to drag on for the next few months and Mary received only one further letter from Sean. He said he believed the Allies were finally winning the battle. Mary wrote faithfully to him every week, and prayed for him every night.

Yet now, her every waking thought was no longer just for Sean, but for the small, exquisite human being she was caring for. She was with the baby twenty-four hours a day. During the morning, after her feed, Anna would sleep outside in the garden, while Mary soaked her napkins and washed the tiny clothes she had sewn for her. After lunch, she would put Anna in the big perambulator and take her for a walk up to Kensington Gardens. They would sit near the statue of Peter Pan and listen to the gossip of the other nursemaids who gathered there with their charges.

They didn't speak to her—Mary knew they looked down on her, attired as they were in their plain gray dresses, whereas she still wore her parlormaid's uniform.

After their walk, and if the master was not at home, Mary would take the baby into the kitchen to feed her, where she was cooed over by the household staff. Anna loved being the center of attention; she would sit upright in her wooden baby chair and bang her spoon on the table, singing along to the sound of it. Every milestone she passed as she grew was admired and commented on by her audience. There was no animosity from the other servants at Mary's new position. She was in charge of the little ray of sunshine that lit up the kitchen. Anna was adored by all of them.

At night, as she sat by the bassinet, Mary would sew dresses, the collars decorated with delicate embroidery, and crochet cardigans and bootees. Anna was growing more bonny by the day, as her pale cheeks filled out and the fresh air provided a rosy glow to them.

Lawrence Lisle popped into the nursery occasionally to glance at the baby, inquire after her health and then depart swiftly. Sadly, Mary's eagerness to show off her charge to him was mostly ignored.

One night in late October, as news of an imminent victory ran rife through London, Mary sat by Anna's cot and watched her sleep. The atmosphere in the house, due to the good news, was one of excitement, with everyone holding their breath to see if the promised armistice would finally come.

Like thousands of other women with their men at the front, Mary had often imagined how she would feel when it was announced that the war was over. Now, she thought with a sigh, she wasn't sure.

Anna stirred and murmured in her sleep. She went to her immediately and gazed down at her, stroking the soft cheek.

"What will become of you, if I'm not here to take care of you?"

Tears came unbidden to Mary's eyes.

The Armistice was eventually announced three weeks later. Mrs. Carruthers agreed to care for Anna for a few hours while Mary, Nancy and Sam, the footman, joined thousands of other Londoners in celebration. Mary was propelled down the Mall toward Buckingham Palace in an ecstatic crowd, waving flags, singing and cheering. Everyone roared as two small figures appeared on the balcony—she was too far away to see them properly, but she knew it was King George and his wife, her namesake, Mary.

She turned and saw Nancy kissing Sam passionately and then found herself swept up in a pair of strong arms.

"Isn't it wonderful news, miss?" said the soldier as he swung her around then set her down. "It's the start of a whole new world."

Nancy and Sam had met up with a crowd who were all going back down the Mall to Trafalgar Square to continue the celebrations. Mary walked back through the packed streets alone, enjoying the infectious happiness around her, yet not able to participate fully.

The end of the war meant the end of her time with Anna.

A month later, Mary received a letter from Bridget, Sean's mother. Bridget had never been good with her letters, and this one was short and to the point. All the boys who had gone away to fight and lived to tell the tale were apparently back home in Dunworley village. Sean was not among them. Someone remembered seeing him alive in their last battle at the Somme, but a week ago Bridget had received a letter from the War Office telling her that her son was officially Missing in Action.

Due to the restraints of Bridget's literacy, it took Mary a few minutes for the meaning of the letter to sink in. Sean was Missing in Action. Presumed dead? Mary didn't know. She'd heard it was chaos out in France as the soldiers began to make their way home. Huge numbers of them were still unaccounted for. Surely then, she thought desperately, there was still hope?

As the rest of the world slowly began to look to the future for the first time in five years, Mary felt her own was still as much in limbo as it had ever been. And she could not see the point in returning to Ireland until there was news of Sean. At least, here in London, she was busy, and the amount of shillings under her mattress grew by the month.

"Surely, it's best if I stay here with you, for now?" she cooed to Anna as she bathed her. "There's nothing for me back in Ireland until Sean returns, pet, nothing."

As Christmas approached, guests began to appear back at the dinner table in Cadogan House. One morning in mid-December, Lawrence Lisle called Mary into the drawing room.

With her heart in her mouth, Mary bobbed a curtsy and waited for the axe to fall.

"Mary, please, sit down."

She raised an eyebrow in surprise. It was not the custom for servants to do this in front of their masters. She did so tentatively.

"I wanted to ask you how Anna is progressing?"

"Ah now, she's wonderful, so she is. She's crawling, and I have a deal of a job to keep up with her, she goes so fast! She'll be walking soon, and then we're in trouble." Mary smiled, affection in her eyes.

"Good, good. Well now, Mary, you've probably noticed how the house is coming back to life. To that end, we must look to reinstating the position of parlormaid to wait at table."

Mary's face fell and her heart thundered in her chest. "Yes, sir."

"This was your old position and by rights you should now return to it."

"Yes, sir." Mary's eyes were downcast and she had to grit her teeth to stop herself crying.

"However, Mrs. Carruthers seems to think that you have a natural affinity with Anna. She has indicated that the bond the two of you have formed is strong, and excellent for the development of the child. I agree with her. So, Mary, I wish to ask you what your plans are. I am sorry to hear your fiancé is still missing in action, but the point is this: I am prepared to offer you the permanent post of nursemaid to the child. *If* you are not imminently preparing to scamper back to Ireland the moment your young man is found."

Master and servant shared a look that said the possibility of that happening was fading by the day.

"Well now, sir, I can't be knowing whether he will, but while he . . . isn't, I'd be happy . . . more than happy to continue to care for Anna. But if he did . . . come home, that is," Mary stuttered, "I'd be thinking I would have to go back with him to Ireland. And it's only fair to tell you so, sir."

Lawrence Lisle thought for a moment, mentally weighing up the odds. "Well, perhaps we should cross that bridge when we come to it, eh?"

"Yes, sir."

"We're all having to take each day as it comes, and Mrs. Carruthers assures me that your care of Anna has been impeccable. So, if you accept the position, you will receive a raise of ten shillings a month and I'll have Mrs. Carruthers do something about finding you a more suitable uniform. I do not wish my friends to think that I am not doing right by the child."

"Thank you, sir. And I promise you that I will continue to take the greatest care of Anna. She is such a beautiful child. Perhaps you'd like to visit the nursery to see her. Or I could bring her down here?" she offered eagerly.

"When I have time, you may bring her down to see me. Thank you, Mary, and keep up the good work. Could you please ask Mrs. Carruthers to join me in here, so we can discuss the engagement of a new parlormaid?"

"Of course, sir." Mary stood up and walked toward the door. She turned back. "Sir, the baby's mammy, do you think she'll ever be coming for her?"

Lawrence Lisle sighed then shook his head. "No, Mary, I doubt that very much. I'd doubt it very much indeed."

Mary walked down the stairs to the kitchen with a guilty spring in her step. She may have currently lost her beloved Sean, but she was mighty relieved she hadn't lost Anna too.

The months passed and there was still no word. Mary had taken herself down to the War Office, and queued with the other poor souls who had loved ones as yet unreturned to them. The man behind the desk, harassed by the line of desperate women, looked Sean up on his lists of missing persons.

"I'm sorry, madam, but there is little more I can tell you than you already know. Sergeant Ryan has not yet been identified, either living or dead."

"Does that mean that perhaps he is alive somewhere and has maybe"—Mary shrugged in desperation—"lost his memory?"

"Certainly, madam, amnesia is a common phenomenon with many soldiers. But it's also likely that, if he was alive, he would have been spotted. The Irish Guards' uniform, in particular, is very noticeable."

"Yes, but should . . . should I and his family be holding out hope for his return?"

From the look on the man's face, it was a question he was obviously asked many times a day.

"While, no erm . . . body has been found, there must always be hope. But it's not for me to advise yourself or your family how long to keep that hope alive. If Sergeant Ryan is not found in the next few weeks, the War Office will be in contact and his status will be changed to 'Missing, Presumed Dead.'"

"I see. Thank you."

Without another word, Mary stood up and left the office.

• • •

Six months later, Mary received a letter from the War Office:

Dear Miss Benedict,

Further to your inquiry about the whereabouts of Sergeant Sean Michael Ryan, it is my sad duty to inform you that his jacket, bearing his army number and containing identification papers, has been recovered from an enemy trench in Somme, France. Although no remains have so far been found in the vicinity, we would sadly presume that, under these circumstances, Sergeant Ryan met his death in the theater of war while serving his country.

Our heartfelt condolences are sent to both you, and to his family, whom we will be informing separately. On a personal note, the fact that his jacket was identified in an enemy trench provides a fitting footnote to his record. Which, I can inform you, has already been mentioned in dispatches.

At present, Sergeant Ryan is under consideration for a posthumous award for bravery.

We understand that this is little compensation for the loss of a beloved relative, but it is due to men like Sergeant Ryan that the war has been concluded in a satisfactory manner and peace has been attained.

Yours sincerely,
Edward Rankin

Mary took Anna down to the kitchen and asked Mrs. Carruthers to mind her for an hour while she took a walk.

Mrs. Carruthers's rheumy eyes were filled with sympathy as she looked at Mary's white face.

"Bad news?"

Mary nodded. "I'm after needing some fresh air," she whispered.

"You take yerself off for as long as you want. Me and Anna will be fine, won't we?" she cooed. "I'm sorry, dear." She reached out a tentative hand and placed it on Mary's shoulder. "He was a lovely chap, and I know how you have waited all these long years for him to come back."

Mary nodded numbly and walked into the lobby to don her coat and boots. Mrs. Carruthers's uncharacteristic sympathy had brought tears to her eyes and she didn't want Anna to see her cry.

Mary sat in Cadogan Place Gardens, watching the children play and a couple strolling arm in arm. This new world, a world which was now at peace, and allowed the pursuit of happiness and the enjoyment of simple pleasures, was a world that Sean had helped to preserve and protect. Yet had not lived to see.

Mary sat on the bench, even as dusk fell and the other visitors in the garden left. She ran through the gamut of emotions: sorrow, fear, anger . . . and more tears than she had ever shed in her life.

She reread the letter twenty times over, the words fueling her thoughts.

Sean . . . that huge, vital *bear* of a man. So strong . . . so young . . . *Dead.*

No longer breathing. No longer part of the earth. Gone. No more gentle smile, or chiding, or laughter . . .

Or love.

It became dark, but Mary still sat where she was.

Once she was calmer, over the initial shock, Mary began to consider the implications for herself. They had not been married, so there was no widow's pension for her. The life she had once imagined many years ago—a man to love her and take care of her, to protect her and provide a roof over her head and her very own family—was at an end.

She was once again alone. Orphaned for the second time in her life.

Mary was sure, if she went back to Ireland, that Sean's parents would welcome her with open arms. But what would her life be? Even though she had no intention of finding a man to replace their son, Mary knew that any happy activity she cared to take part in would be a bittersweet pill for parents in mourning. And her presence would remind them of what they had lost.

Mary rubbed her face slowly with her palms. The March air was becoming cooler now and she found she was shivering; from shock or a chill, she didn't know. She stood up and looked around her desolately, remembering the time she and Sean had sat here together.

"Good-bye, pet. God bless and sweet dreams," she whispered, and left the gardens to return to the only life she now had.

14

Anna was almost three now, her hair grown into a black, shiny mane, contrasting with her ivory skin. She toddled around the nursery, rarely falling over, and her natural grace entranced the entire household. Even Lawrence Lisle took to having Mary bring her into the drawing room and perform the perfectly executed curtsy Mary had taught her.

Somehow, instinctively, Anna knew the stranger who sometimes called for her was important in her life. It would seem to Mary that Anna did her best to charm him, giving him her most beautiful smile and throwing her arms open to him for a hug.

Despite her physical development, Anna was still not talking properly, although she made repetitive sounds and uttered some words, so Mary tried not to worry about it.

"How is her speaking coming along?" Lawrence Lisle asked one day as Anna sat with him in the drawing room.

"Slow, sir, but from my experience, little ones develop at their own pace, so they do."

When it was time to go, Anna threw her arms around Mr. Lisle's shoulders.

"Say 'good-bye' to me now, Anna," Mr. Lisle encouraged.

"G-Good . . . bye," Anna managed.

Lawrence Lisle raised an eyebrow. "Say it again, Anna, there's a good girl."

"G-Good . . . b-bye," the little girl said accommodatingly.

"Mmm . . . Mary, it sounds to me as though Anna has a stutter."

"No, to be sure," Mary glossed over it nervously. The master was voicing her own fear. "She's simply learning to put the words round her tongue."

"Well, you're the expert in small children, but I would watch that carefully."

"Yes, sir, I will."

Sure enough, in the next few months, as Anna learned more words, her stutter became too obvious to be put down to a developmental stage. Mary fretted over it, and asked advice from the kitchen.

"Nothing to be done, I'd say." Mrs. Carruthers shrugged. "Just try not to let the little'un say too much in front of the master. You know how the gentry don't like imperfections in their kids. And as Anna's the nearest he's got to his own, I'd hide it from him as much as I could."

Undaunted, Mary visited the local library and found a book on the problem. She learned that any situation in which Anna felt nervous would make the stutter more pronounced. And, as Anna's primary carer, to make sure she herself spoke clearly, so that Anna could hear the words and copy them as best she could.

The kitchen laughed at Mary as she spoke to Anna slowly, over-enunciating her words, and encouraging the rest of the staff to do the same.

"You'll have the little'un stuttering in all manner of Irish and Cockney accents if you're not careful," chuckled Mrs. Carruthers. "I'd leave her be, if I were you, let nature take its course."

But Mary was not prepared to do so and persevered with the child. Heeding Mrs. Carruthers's words, she also taught Anna to remain silent when she was in front of the master, hoping her pretty curtsy and charm would mask the problem, as she worked with Anna on the few basic words she needed to communicate with him.

Mr. Lisle mentioned Anna's relative silence on a number of occasions, but Mary continued to brush it off.

"W-why can't I speak to h-him, M-Mary?" the little girl whispered as Mary took her from the drawing room and back up to the nursery.

"You will in time, pet, you will in time," Mary comforted her.

It seemed that Anna, however, had developed her own method of communication with her guardian.

A few months later, after their allotted half an hour together, Mary knocked on the door to collect Anna.

"Come."

Mary pushed the door open and found Lawrence Lisle standing by the fireplace, his focus on Anna, who was moving around the room to the music he'd put on the gramophone.

"Look how she dances . . . she is exquisite." His voice was no more than a whisper as he watched, enchanted. "It's as if Anna knows what to do instinctively."

"Yes, she loves to dance." Mary watched proudly as the little girl, lost in her own world, flitted around the room to the music.

"She may not be able to communicate with words as well as others, but look how she expresses herself with her body," commented Lawrence.

"What is the music, sir? It's lovely, so," inquired Mary as she watched the child stretch and bend and turn.

"It's the music to *The Dying Swan,* a ballet by Fokine. I saw it once, at the Mariinsky Theatre in St. Petersburg . . ." He sighed. "I've never seen anything quite so beautiful."

The music finished and the needle spun around and around, the sounds of the cracks on the vinyl beneath it the only noise in the room.

Lawrence Lisle pulled himself out of his reverie. "Well now, there we are," he said. "Anna, you dance beautifully. Would you like to take lessons?"

The little girl hardly understood what she was being asked, but she nodded.

Mary glanced at Anna nervously and then at Lawrence. "Do you not think she's a little young to be taking lessons in dancing, sir?"

"Absolutely not. In Russia, they start at just this age. And there are many Russian émigrés whom I know living in London at present. I shall find out who they think is a suitable teacher for Anna and inform you."

"Very good, sir."

"I l-lo-love you, M-Mr. Lisle," Anna said out of the blue, and gave him a beaming smile.

Lawrence Lisle was taken aback by his ward's sudden spoken words of affection, as Mary took Anna's hand and walked her smartly toward the door before she could speak anymore.

"Mary, I am wondering whether it is appropriate for my ward to be calling me 'Mr. Lisle'? It sounds . . . so formal."

"Well now, sir, do you have any suggestions?" asked Mary.

"Perhaps 'Uncle' would be more appropriate under the circumstances? After all, I am her guardian."

"I think 'tis perfect, sir."

Anna turned back toward him. "G-Good n-night, Uncle," she said, and the two of them left the room.

Lawrence Lisle was true to his word, and a couple of weeks later Mary found herself in a bright, mirrored studio in a house called the Peasantry along the King's Road in Chelsea. The teacher, one Princess Astafieva, gaunt and turbaned, smoking a Sobranie through a holder and clad in a multicolored silk skirt that trailed behind her as she walked, looked suitably exotic and unwelcoming.

Anna grasped Mary's hand even tighter, her pale face pinched and fearful at the sight of the strange woman.

"My good friend Lawrence tells me zis leetle one can dance."

"Yes, Madam," Mary replied nervously.

"Zen we shall put on some music and see how the leetle one respond. Take off your coat, child," she ordered as she signaled the pianist to play.

"Just be dancing like you do in front of Uncle," Mary whispered and pushed Anna to the center of the floor. For a few seconds, Anna looked as though she might burst into tears. But as the beautiful music caught her ear, she began to sway, and her body to move as it always did.

Two minutes later, Princess Astafieva banged the wooden floor of the studio with her stick and the pianist stopped playing.

"I have seen enough. Lawrence, 'e is right. The child moves naturally to the music. So, I will take her. You will bring Anna here every Wednesday at three o'clock."

"Yes, Madam. Can you be telling me what she will need?"

"For now, nothink, only her body and her bare feet. So, I will see you zen." With a nod, Princess Astafieva swept out of the room.

Mary had to cajole Anna to persuade her to return and bribe her with a pink dress with a tulle skirt which she made for her to wear to the lesson, then tea and buns in Sloane Square afterward.

The rest of the household too, had raised their eyebrows at Lawrence Lisle's notion.

"He's having her dancing before she can walk and talk proper!" Mrs. Carruthers raised her eyebrows. "Must be all that time he spent in Russia that's turned his head funny. He plays that miserable music on the gramophone over and over again. All about swans dying or sommat."

Nevertheless, when Mary arrived to pick up Anna after her first lesson, the child was smiling. Over the promised tea and buns, Anna explained that she had learned to put her feet in a funny position like a duck. And hold her hands in different positions in the air.

"She isn't a w-witch really, Mary."

"But you're sure you want to go again?" Mary confirmed.

"Oh, y-yes, I want to go again."

In the spring of 1926, Anna celebrated her eighth birthday. As Lawrence Lisle had little idea of her actual birth date, they had invented one in mid-April.

Mary looked on proudly as Anna cut the cake the master had bought for her. Anna tingled with excitement as she opened his present to her, and found a pair of pink satin ballet slippers inside.

"Th-Thank you, Uncle, they're beautiful. Can I p-put them on now?" asked Anna.

"After you've eaten, you can. We don't want chocolate crumbs spoiling them now, do we?" Mary admonished, a twinkle in her eyes.

"Absolutely right, Mary. Perhaps a little later on you will come into the drawing room and dance for me in them, Anna?" suggested Lawrence.

"Of c-course I will, Uncle." She smiled. "And maybe you could d-dance with me?" she teased.

"I'd doubt that," he replied with a chuckle. He nodded at his staff, gathered in the dining room, then left while everyone ate the cake.

An hour later, Anna, in her new pink ballet slippers, disappeared off to the drawing room.

Mary smiled as she closed the door behind her. There was no doubt that the bond between Lawrence and Anna had grown. When he had to go away on business for the Foreign Office, Anna would wait eagerly at her bedroom window if she knew his return was imminent.

He too lit up when he saw her, the dour expression leaving his face as she ran into his arms.

These days, she couldn't have a more caring daddy if he were her real one, Mary often commented in the kitchen. He'd even decided to engage a governess for her. "Probably best we educate her here at home. We don't want her being teased about her stutter," he'd commented.

Yet the passion that took up Anna's every waking moment was ballet. She lived and breathed it, waiting eagerly for her lesson and spending every day practicing the new positions Princess Astafieva taught her.

When Mary chided her for her lack of concentration in her lessons, Anna would give her a bright smile. "I w-won't be needing to kn-know about history when I g-grow up, because I am going to be the best b-ballerina in the world! And you will c-come to my first night, Mary, when I dance Odette/Odile in *Swan L-Lake*!"

Mary did not disbelieve her. If it was simply down to determination alone, she reckoned Anna would fulfill her dream. And as Princess Astafieva had indicated, Anna displayed the talent as well.

When Mary went upstairs to fetch Anna for her bath, she found her pirouetting around the bedroom, excitement written on her face.

"G-Guess what?! I am going to see the D-Diaghilev's *Ballets R-Russes* with the Princess and Uncle! They are performing at C-Covent Garden. Alicia M-Markova is dancing Aurora in *The Sleeping Beauty*!" Anna ended her dance by leaping into Mary's arms. "Now how about th-that?"

"I'm thrilled for you, pet," Mary smiled.

"And Uncle says we are to go out tomorrow to b-buy me a new dress! I'd like velvet, with a b-big, wide ribbon round my middle," she clarified.

"Then we'll have to see if we can find it for you," agreed Mary. "Now, away with you into the bath."

Although Mary wasn't to know it, the night that Lawrence Lisle took Anna to see her first ballet was to change all of their lives.

Anna returned home after the performance, clutching her program in her small hands, her eyes wide with wonder. "Miss M-Markova was so beautiful," she said dreamily as Mary tucked her into bed. "And her partner, Anton Dolin, lifted her above his head as though she w-was as light as a feather. Princess Astafieva says she knows Miss M-Markova. Perhaps one day I can meet her. Imagine that," she added as she put the program beneath her pillow. "G-Good night, Mary."

"Good night, pet," Mary whispered. "Sleep tight."

A few days later, Mrs. Carruthers came into the kitchen in a state of high excitement.

"The master's up there, in the drawing room. He's asked me to take in afternoon tea. And he's with . . ." Mrs. Carruthers paused for full effect, *"a woman."*

At this, all the servants' ears pricked up.

"Who is she? Do you know?" inquired Nancy.

"No, I don't. I could be wrong, but there was a look in the master's eyes as he watched her that made me think . . . well now." Mrs. Carruthers shrugged. "Perhaps I'm getting ahead of meself, but I have a feeling our confirmed bachelor might be about to change his spots."

In the next few weeks, Mrs. Carruthers's intuition looked as if it was going to be proved right. Elizabeth Delancey became a regular visitor to the house. Between them, the servants managed to piece together the information they had all gathered. It seemed Mrs. Delancey was the widow of an old friend of Lawrence Lisle from his school days at Eton. Her husband, an officer in the British Army, had lost his life at the Somme, like Sean.

"That Mrs. Delancey's a one!" huffed the parlormaid as she brought the tea tray down from the drawing room one afternoon. "She told me the scones tasted stale, and to tell Cook."

"And who does she think she is to be making such comments!" exclaimed Mrs. Carruthers. "She told me yesterday there was smudges on the mirror in the drawing room and could I see to it the maid was more careful next time."

"She looks like a horse," added Nancy, "With that long face and them droopy eyes!"

"She's no beauty, that's for sure," agreed Mrs. Carruthers, "and nearly as tall as the master. But it's not her looks that worry me, it's her character. She's getting her feet under his table, well and good, and it will be trouble for all of us if she's here permanently, you mark my words."

"And he's never after asking Anna to go to the drawing room since she arrived here," Mary said quietly. "In fact, he's hardly seen her at all in the past month. The little pet keeps asking me why he doesn't call for her any more."

"She's a cold one, she is, and she won't want to be having no competition for her man's affections. And we all know how the master is about Anna. She's been his two eyes, and Lady Muck won't like that at all." Mrs. Carruthers wagged her finger at no one in particular.

"What if he marries her?" Mary asked, her fear raising the question they all wanted to ask.

"Then there's trouble for all of us," Mrs. Carruthers repeated grimly, "and there ain't no two ways about it."

Three months later, Mr. Lisle called his servants into the dining room to speak to them. Elizabeth Delancey stood next to him as he announced proudly to his household staff that the two of them were to be married as soon as the wedding could be arranged.

The mood that night in the kitchen was subdued. Each one of the servants knew their comfortable world was about to change. As the new mistress of the house, Elizabeth Delancey would, on her marriage, take charge of the running of the house. And the staff would be answerable to her.

"D-do you like Mrs. D-Delancey?" Anna asked Mary quietly as she read her a story before bedtime.

"Well now, I'd say I hardly know her, but I'm sure if Uncle thinks she's grand, she must be."

"She told me my speech was f-funny and I looked . . ." Anna searched her mind for the word. "Scraggy. W-what is scraggy, Mary?"

"Ah, it means you are a pretty little thing, pet," Mary comforted her as she tucked her into bed.

"She said that I must call her 'Aunt' when she b-becomes Uncle's wife." Anna lay down on her pillows, her huge dark eyes nervous. "She won't b-become my mother, will she, Mary? I mean, I know you're not really my m-mother, but I feel like you are."

"No, pet. Don't you be worrying your head over that, you know I'll always be here to take care of you. Night, night, sleep tight." Mary kissed Anna gently on the forehead.

As she turned off the light and began to leave the room, a voice came through the darkness.

"Mary?"

"What is it, pet?"

"I don't think she l-likes me."

"Don't be daft! How can anyone not like *you*? Now, you stop your worrying and close your eyes."

The wedding took place in a church near Elizabeth Delancey's parents' home in Sussex. Mary was asked to bring Anna to sit in the congregation. The bride's nieces performed the role of bridesmaids.

Cadogan House held its breath for a month while the newlyweds took a honeymoon in the south of France. The day they were due back, Mrs. Carruthers ordered the house to be cleaned and polished from top to bottom. "I will not have that woman suggesting I don't know how to take care of her new home," she muttered to her staff.

Mary put Anna in her best dress to greet her uncle and her new aunt, her heart heavy with a sense of unease.

Mr. and Mrs. Lisle arrived home at teatime. The servants lined up in the hall to greet them and clapped reticently. Their new mistress had a few words with each of them. Anna stood with Mary expectantly at the end of the queue, waiting to perform her perfect curtsy. Mrs. Lisle simply nodded at Anna then moved on and into the drawing room. Mr. Lisle followed suit.

"She wants to see each of us individually tomorrow," Mrs. Carruthers huffed later. "And you too, Mary. Gawd help us all!"

• • •

One by one the next morning, the servants filed into the drawing room to meet their new mistress. Mary stood nervously outside, awaiting her turn.

"Come," said the voice, and Mary stepped inside. "Good morning, Mary," said Elizabeth Lisle.

"Good morning, Mrs. Lisle. May I be offering you my personal congratulations on your marriage?"

"Thank you." Her thin lips did not curl into a smile. "I wish to inform you that, from now on, any decisions regarding Mr. Lisle's ward will be taken by myself. Mr. Lisle is very busy at the Foreign Office, and it is not acceptable for him to be bothered with the details of a child."

"Yes, Mrs. Lisle."

"I'd prefer it if you call me 'ma'am,' Mary. That is what I am used to in my own home."

"Yes . . . ma'am."

Elizabeth Lisle swept over to the desk, on which were laid out the ledgers containing the monthly accounts. "I shall also be taking over these,"—she indicated the ledgers—"from Mrs. Carruthers. It seems to me, having studied them, that there has been sloppiness in the use of finances. I will be putting a halt to this immediately. Do you understand?"

"Yes, ma'am."

"For example . . ." Mrs. Lisle pulled her horn-rimmed glasses, hung by a chain around her neck, up on to her nose to read the ledger. "It says here that Anna's costs are running at over a hundred shillings per month. Can you explain where this money goes?"

"Well, ma'am, Anna has two ballet lessons a week, costing forty shillings a month. She also has a governess to come in and help her with her lessons every morning at a cost of fifty shillings a month. Then there are her clothes, and—"

"Enough!" snapped Mrs. Lisle. "It is patently clear to me that the child has been indulged and the expenses you talk of are unnecessary. I will be speaking to Mr. Lisle about them later tonight. The child is eight, is she not?"

"Yes, ma'am."

"Then I would hardly think it necessary for her to be taking two ballet lessons a week." Mrs. Lisle raised her eyebrows and sighed as an indication of her dissatisfaction. "You may go, Mary."

"Yes, ma'am."

"B-but, Mary, why can't I go twice a week to my ballet lessons? One isn't enough!" Anna's eyes were full of anguish.

"Perhaps you will again, pet, but for now, Uncle can't afford the money it costs."

"B-but he's just g-got a new p-posting! And everyone in the kitchen was talking of the big diamond necklace he's just b-bought Aunt. How c-can he not have ten shillings a week if he c-can b-buy that?' Emotion making her stutter worse, Anna burst into tears.

"Now, now, pet." Mary put her arms around the child. "The nuns always told me to be grateful for what I was getting. At least you have one lesson still."

"B-but it's not enough! It's not enough!"

"Well now, you will just have to practice more in the meantime. Please try not to go upsetting yourself."

But Anna was inconsolable, just as Mary had known she would be.

After his marriage, Lawrence Lisle was rarely at home. When he was, Anna would wait in an agony of anticipation for him to call her into the drawing room. Mary's heart broke as she watched the disappointment on the child's face when he didn't.

"He doesn't l-love me any more. Uncle doesn't l-love me. He loves Aunt. And does everything she t-tells him."

The kitchen was in full agreement with Anna.

"She's got him where she wants him, good and proper," sighed Mrs. Carruthers. "I didn't think the master had it in him to be so cruel," she added. "Poor little mite. He hardly speaks to Anna these days, doesn't even spare a glance for her, from what I've seen."

"Probably get a clip round the ear from the mistress if he did!" put in Nancy. "I reckon he's as scared of her as we are. She's never satisfied, that one, always finding fault with whatever I do. If it continues, I've half a mind to leave. There's other employment for women these days, and well paid too."

"I'm of the same mind," agreed Mrs. Carruthers. "My friend Elsie tells me they're looking for a housekeeper just around the Square. I might go and apply."

Mary listened to them wistfully. She knew that leaving would never be an option for her.

The household staff lived in a constant state of tension, knowing whatever they did and however hard they worked would never be enough to satisfy the new Mrs. Lisle. The parlormaid left, and then the cook. Smith, the butler, decided it was time to retire. Mary did her best to keep herself and Anna out of the way, going about their business as quietly and invisibly as possible. But, often, the call would come from the drawing room. Mary was not allowed to accompany Anna and would hover nervously outside waiting for her to emerge, usually tearstained. Whatever Elizabeth Lisle could find to criticize in Anna, she did. From her halting speech to the bow in Anna's hair being untied and dirty footprints up the stairs, Anna got the blame.

"She h-hates me, she hates me," Anna cried on Mary's shoulder one night.

"She doesn't hate you, pet, that's just the way she is. With everybody."

"It's not a very n-nice 'way,' is it, Mary?"

Mary couldn't disagree.

15

In the autumn of 1927, when Anna was nine, Lawrence Lisle left for his new, permanent posting as British Consul in Bangkok. Elizabeth Lisle was to follow him in three months' time.

"Well, we got to look on the bright side—at least we only have to suffer a few more weeks of her," said Mrs. Carruthers. "With any luck, they won't be back for years."

"Maybe she'll die of some tropical disease and never come back," sniffed Nancy.

Lawrence Lisle offered a curt, unaffectionate good-bye to Anna as his wife stood next to him, watching his every move. Then it was Elizabeth Lisle's turn to say good-bye to her husband.

Lawrence put his arms around her. "So, darling, I will see you in Bangkok."

"Yes." She nodded. "And don't worry about anything here. Rest assured, I will make sure the house runs smoothly in your absence."

Two days later, Mary was called into the drawing room.

"Mary." Elisabeth Lisle attempted a tight smile. "I've asked you here to tell you that your services in this house are no longer required. Due to my imminent departure to join my husband in Bangkok, it has been decided by me that it's best if Anna enters a boarding school. Mr. Lisle and I will be in Bangkok for at least the next five years and this house is to be closed up. It is a waste of money keeping the staff on while we are away. I understand that you have been with Anna for nine years and it will be a wrench for both of you. Therefore you will be paid a month in lieu. I will be taking Anna down to her new school at the end of the week, and you will leave this house on the same day.

I will tell her tomorrow she is to go away to school. But I think it is perhaps best if you say nothing to her for now about you leaving. We don't want the child becoming hysterical."

Mary heard a ringing in her ears. "But—but, ma'am, surely I must be allowed to say good-bye? I—can't—have her thinking I'm abandoning her. Please, Mrs. Lisle . . . I mean, ma'am," Mary pleaded.

"Anna will be fine. You are not, after all, her real mother. She will be with girls of her own age and class," Elizabeth Lisle added pointedly. "I am sure she will cope."

"What will happen to her during the holidays?"

"Like many orphaned children, or in fact children whose parents are residing abroad, she will simply stay at school."

"You mean the school will be her new home?" Mary was aghast.

"If you wish to phrase it like that, yes."

"May I at least be writing to her?"

"Under the circumstances, I forbid it. I feel it will be too unsettling and upsetting for her to receive letters from you."

"Then"—Mary knew she mustn't cry—"may I know where you're taking her?"

"I think it is best that you don't. Then you will not be tempted to contact her. I have organized everything she will need for her new school. There is nothing more you need to do other than name her clothes, and pack her trunk and your own belongings." Elizabeth Lisle rose. "You must understand, Mary, that a child in the care of Mr. Lisle and myself cannot spend her life being brought up by servants. She must learn manners and decorum to enable her to become a lady."

"Yes, ma'am." Mary choked the words out.

"You may go, Mary."

Mary walked toward the door then stopped. "What about her ballet lessons? Do they do ballet at her new school? She is so talented . . . everybody says . . . and Mr. Lisle was so very keen—"

"As his wife, and acting ward of the child while my husband is abroad," Elizabeth cut in, "I think it is up to me to know my husband's thoughts. And what is best for Anna."

Mary knew it was pointless saying any more. She turned and fled the room.

• • •

The following few days passed in a miasma of misery. Unable to say or do anything to warn Anna of her own imminent departure, Mary did her best to comfort the child as she sewed name labels on her uniform and organized the trunk she would be taking with her to her new school.

"I don't w-want to g-go away to school, Mary. I don't w-want to leave you and all the other servants and my b-ballet lessons."

"I know you don't, pet, but it's what Uncle and Aunt think is best for you. And you might be enjoying the company of other girls of your age."

"Why do I need them w-when I have you and all my other friends in the kitchen here? Mary, I'm frightened. Please tell Aunt not to make me g-go. I promise I won't be any trouble," Anna begged. "P-please ask her to let me stay!" Mary put her arms around the child as she sobbed pitifully into her shoulder. "You will tell the Princess I'll be b-back in the holidays, w-won't you? Tell her I'll still keep practicing hard at school and I w-won't let her down."

"'Course I will, pet."

"And the time w-will pass quite quickly, won't it? It's not long until the holidays and I'm b-back here w-with you, is it?"

Mary held her own tears in check as she saw the child trying to reassure herself in the face of the inevitable. "No, pet, it's not."

"And you'll be here w-waiting for me, won't you, Mary? What w-will you do when I'm gone?" Anna raised an eyebrow. "You might get awfully b-bored."

"Well now, I might just take myself on a little holiday."

"Well, make sure you're b-back for when I arrive home from school, won't you?"

"I will, pet, I promise."

At nine o'clock on the morning on which Anna was to leave, there was a knock on Mary's door.

"Come in."

Anna appeared wearing her new school uniform, bought with

room to grow into. Her slight body looked drowned in material and her heart-shaped face was pinched and white.

"Aunt says I must c-come to say g-good-bye to you. She said she didn't want a show d-downstairs."

Mary nodded and walked toward her, held her in her arms and said, "Do me proud now, won't you, pet?"

"I'll t-try, Mary, but I'm so fr-frightened." Anna's stutter had become progressively worse over the past week.

"There now, a couple of days and you'll be loving it, I'm sure."

"No, I w-won't, I know I'm g-going to h-hate it," came the muffled response into her shoulder. "You w-will write to me every day? W-won't you?"

"Of course I will." Mary pulled Anna gently away from her, looked at her and smiled. "Now, you'd better be on your way."

Anna nodded. "I know. G-Good-bye, Mary."

"Good-bye, pet."

Mary watched as Anna turned away from her and walked slowly toward the door. When she reached it, she paused then turned back. "W-when the other g-girls ask me about my mother, I'm g-going to tell them about you. Do you th-think that's all right?"

"Oh, Anna . . ." Mary could not keep the emotion from her voice any longer. "If that's what you'd like to do, I'm sure 'tis grand."

Anna nodded silently, her huge eyes full of pain.

"And just remember," Mary added, "one day you'll be a great ballerina. Don't give up on your dream now, will you?"

"No." Anna smiled weakly. "I promise, I w-won't."

Mary watched from her window as Anna followed Elizabeth Lisle into the car, then stood silently as it drove off down the road. Two hours later, Mary was also packed and ready to go. Elizabeth Lisle had already paid her her final salary and, through Mrs. Carruthers, she had secured a room in a boardinghouse in Baron's Court a few miles away, to tide her over until she'd cleared her head and decided what to do.

Unable to face any further emotional good-byes, Mary left letters on the kitchen table for Mrs. Carruthers and Nancy. She picked up her suitcase, opened the back door and walked out into an empty future.

Aurora

So . . . poor, kindhearted Mary has been thrown out onto the streets by the wicked stepmother. Perhaps she is the Cinderella of my tale—a mixed metaphor in a fairy-tale sense, so forgive me. And Anna—the Little Orphan—not lacking in privilege, but in love, left to fend for herself at boarding school.

Mary's letters to her prospective mother-in-law, Bridget, which Grania read so assiduously far into the night, ended here. In retrospect, I understand that Mary's pride would not have allowed her to continue writing home to Sean's parents.

I know that Grania, on coming to the end of the letters, went to her mother and begged her to tell her what happened to Mary after that. For the purpose of fluidity in the narrative—Reader, I'm becoming rather good at this writing business—I will not bore you with the details of that journey down to the farmhouse, or the cups of tea over which Grania was bound to have heard the rest of the story.

Tea was a big part of our lives at Dunworley Farmhouse.

I rarely drink it these days. It makes me feel sick, but then, most things do.

I digress, again. Now, in any good fairy tale the sad Princess finds happiness with her Prince.

What has always fascinated me is what happens after the "Happily Ever After."

For example, Princess Aurora from The Sleeping Beauty *wakes up a century later. Gracious! Can you imagine? Technically, she is one hundred and sixteen years old. Her prince is eighteen. Which is what one might call an age gap. And that's before she's dealt with what would be, even in those days, a very different world one hundred years on.*

Personally, I wouldn't put much money on their relationship surviving.

Of course, you might answer, that's how fairy tales are. And yet, are the trials Princess Aurora would face when she wakes up in Happy-Ever-After Land any different from those Mary may find? If, by chance, she does meet her prince? After all, war—especially one as vicious as that which Mary lived through—inflicts dreadful changes, leaving indelible marks on one's soul.

Well, we shall see . . .

16

The hardest thing about Mary's new life was the amount of time she had to think. So far during her twenty-nine years, every day that she could remember had been packed with things to "do" for other people. There had always been a task, a *duty* to fulfill for someone else. Now there was no one to please but herself. Her time was her own and it was endless.

She'd also realized that she'd lived her entire life surrounded by other people. Used to the common parts of every home she had lived in, Mary found the hours alone in her one cramped room unbearably lonely. Thoughts of those she had lost—her parents, her fiancé and the young girl whom she'd loved like her own daughter—assailed her as she sat in front of the mean flame of the gas fire. Others might think it grand to no longer be woken by a bell or a sharp knocking at the door, but for Mary, the lack of being "needed" was an unpleasant revelation.

She had no problem with money—her fifteen years in the Lisle households had provided her with a solid nest egg that could easily keep her going for the next five years. In fact, she could afford to live in far more comfortable surroundings than she was at present.

Mary found herself most afternoons sitting in Kensington Gardens, watching the familiar faces of the nursemaids caring for their charges. They hadn't talked to her then and they didn't talk to her now. She belonged to no one and no one belonged to her. She watched people walking past her, on their way to Somewhere Else.

In her darkest moments, Mary believed there wasn't a soul who cared whether she lived or died. She was irrelevant, replaceable and unnecessary. Even to Anna, whom she'd poured so much love into—she knew the child would adapt and move on. That was the spirit of youth.

To pass the time, Mary whiled the lonely evening hours away by making herself a whole new wardrobe. She purchased a Singer sewing machine and, by the light of the dim gas lamp, sat at the small table by the window which overlooked Colet Gardens. When she was sewing, her mind was numb, and the creation of something from nothing comforted her. As she sewed, her right arm weary from turning the wheel of the machine, she'd pause and look down at the life outside. Often, she'd see a man leaning against a lamppost directly beneath her. The man looked young—no older than she was—and he'd stand there for hours, staring into the distance.

Mary began to wait for him to appear, usually around six o'clock in the evening, and watched him as he stood by the lamppost, unaware he was being observed. Occasionally, dawn would be breaking before he'd disappear.

His presence comforted Mary. He seemed as lonely as she did.

"Poor pet," she'd whisper to herself as she toasted a crumpet on the gas fire. "He's touched in the head, the lamb."

The nights drew in and winter approached, yet still the young man appeared by the lamppost. As Mary put on the warm layers of clothes she had made for herself, the man below seemed to pay no heed to the lowering temperature.

One night in November, as Mary arrived home late from having tea with Nancy, she passed him. Stopping, she turned around and studied him. He was a tall man, with fine features—an aquiline nose, a proud chin, his skin pale under the lamplight. He was gaunt to the point of emaciation, but Mary could see that, filled out, he'd be a handsome chap. She carried on up the steps and turned the key in the lock of her front door. Entering her room, she walked immediately to the window and pondered how he could stay still for so long in the bitter cold. Shivering, then lighting the gas fire and wrapping a shawl tightly around her shoulders, Mary had an idea.

A week later, she walked down the steps of her boardinghouse and went up to the young man, standing in his usual spot.

"Here, take it. 'Twill keep you warm as you hold that lamppost up." Mary proffered the bundle in her arms and waited for a response. For a long time, the young man didn't acknowledge her, or what she was offering to him. Just as she had decided to turn away, realizing he was obviously beyond help, he moved his head toward her, looked down at what she held and gave a weak smile.

"'Tis a coat, made of wool. To keep you warm while you stand here," she prompted.

"F-F-For me?" It was as if he was not used to speaking. His voice was hoarse and forced.

"Yes," she reiterated. "I live up there," Mary pointed to the lighted room above them, "and I've been watching you. I don't want you to die of pneumonia on my doorstep," she added, "so I made it for you."

He looked down at the bundle, then back at her in astonishment. "Y-You made this, f-for *me*?"

"Yes. Now, will you be taking it from me? 'Tis heavy and I'd be glad if you did."

"B-But . . . I have n-no money with me. I can't pay you."

"It's a present. While I'm tucked up cozy in there, it upsets my eyes to see you shivering down here. Look at it like I'm doing myself a favor. Take it," she urged.

"I . . . it's awfully k-kind of you, miss—?"

"Mary. My name is Mary."

He took the coat from her and, with a pair of shaking hands, tried it on.

"It f-fits p-perfectly! How d-did you . . . ?"

"Well now, I did have you standing there every night to look at while I made it."

"It's . . . the b-best present I've ever b-been g-given."

Mary noticed that, although the man stuttered, he spoke in a clipped English accent, like Lawrence Lisle.

"So now, at least I can sleep easier in my bed knowing you'll be warm. Good night, sir."

"G-Good night, M-Mary. And—" the look in his eyes as he gazed at her was one of such gratitude, Mary felt the tears spring into her own—"th-thank you."

"Think nothing of it," she replied and hurried up the steps to her front door.

• • •

A couple of weeks later, just as Mary was on the point of deciding that her only escape from loneliness was to return to Ireland and live her life as an old maid with Sean's family, she met Nancy for tea in Piccadilly.

"Blimey! You look smart!" Nancy commented as they ordered tea and buttered toast. "Where did you get your new coat? I've seen it in the magazines, but it costs a bloomin' fortune. Have you come into the money or what?"

"I saw it in the magazines too, so I just copied it from the picture."

"You made it *yourself*?"

"Yes."

"I know you've always been handy with the needle, but that looks like the real thing!" Nancy said admiringly. "Can you make one for me?"

"I'm sure I could, if you tell me what color you'd be wanting it in."

"How about scarlet? Would it suit my complexion?" She patted her blond curls.

"I think that'd suit you well," Mary agreed. "I'd have to charge you for the material, mind."

"Of course. And your time. So how much?"

Mary thought. "Well now, I'd say it would be ten shillings for the material, and then a few bob for the making of it . . ."

"Done!" Nancy clapped her hands together. "Sam's taking me out next Thursday. And I think he's going to propose. Can it be made by then?"

"A week . . ." Mary thought about it. "I don't see why not."

"Oh, Mary, thank you! You are a star, girl, you really are."

The Red Coat, as Mary would always remember it, marked a turning point in her life. Nancy showed it off to her friends and soon they were all clamoring at Mary's door to ask if she could make one for them too. Even Sheila, the girl who lived in the next house along and worked in one of the smart department stores near Piccadilly, had commented on Mary's coat in the street, and asked her to make one. Sheila came up one evening for a fitting and the two girls chatted over a cup of tea afterward.

"You should set up as a proper dressmaker, Mary. You have real talent."

"Thank you, but I'd say is it right to make a business of something that you enjoy?"

"Of course it is! I have lots of friends who'd be willing to pay for you to make them the latest styles. We all know what they charge in the shops."

"Yes." Mary was leaning out of the window, looking down at the young man standing under the lamppost, snug in his black wool coat. "Do you know who *he* is?"

Sheila came to the window and looked down.

"My landlord told me his girl used to live here before the war, when she was training to be a nurse at St. Thomas's hospital. She was trampled on by a terrified horse at the Somme and died. And he came back with shell shock, poor love." Sheila sighed. "Out of the two of them, I think I'd be her. At least she doesn't have to suffer anymore. Not like him; reliving the horror day after day."

"Does he have a home?"

"Apparently his family is very well-to-do. He lives with his godmother, just up the road in Kensington. She took him in when his parents refused to. Poor chap, what kind of future can he look forward to?"

"I really don't know." Mary sighed, feeling guilty and churlish for ever feeling sorry for herself in the past few weeks. "It must somehow comfort him, being here. And in this life, we must take our comfort wherever we find it."

Mary had been at Colet Gardens for almost three and a half months. Her days were now taken up with customers, sewing the coats, blouses, skirts and dresses they were ordering. She was considering taking on an assistant, and moving to a larger set of rooms so one could be dedicated to her work. Even though she was busy, with less time to think, her pen often itched to start a letter to her darling Anna. To tell her how she'd been forced to leave her, that she loved her more than anything and thought of her every day. But she knew, for Anna's sake, it was best she kept silent.

Time no longer hung in Mary's hands like an empty void; but her heart, lacking someone to pour her love into, was numb and closed. Yet whenever she was in danger of becoming self-pitying, all she had to do was look below her at the poor young man standing by the lamp-post.

As Christmas approached and her customers demanded their clothes be ready beforehand, Mary had no time to wonder how she'd feel spending it without Anna. Nancy had invited Mary over to spend Christmas day at Cadogan House.

"It'll be the last one there for all of us," Nancy had said. "We're all on a month's notice—got to leave in January after the house has been closed up. I'm sure that snotty cow would have had us out on the streets before Christmas if she could, but luckily there was things to do."

"Has she left for Bangkok?" inquired Mary.

"Yes, last month. And did we throw a party in the kitchen! Anyway, me and Sam have got ourselves fine jobs working as housekeeper and butler in Belgravia. The day I step out of that kitchen, I won't be looking back. It's that poor little girl I feel sorry for. She's been expecting to come home for Christmas. It does make you wonder how people can be so cruel, doesn't it, Mary? And men so blind as to fall for it," Nancy added.

Mary stayed up the whole night before Christmas Eve to make sure her customers received their clothes on time. At four the following afternoon, all her orders collected, she sank exhausted into the armchair by the fire. She was awoken by a soft knocking on her door.

"Hello?"

"It's me, Sheila, from next door. You've got a visitor."

Mary roused herself from her chair and walked over to let her in. And could hardly believe her eyes when she saw who was standing next to Sheila, looking pale and anxious.

"Mary!" Anna threw herself into Mary's arms, hugging her so tightly the breath almost left her.

"Jesus, Mary and Joseph! Anna, what are you doing here? How did you find me?"

"You know her then?" Sheila smiled. "Found her like a waif and stray, sitting on your doorstep."

"Oh yes, I know her. She's my Anna, aren't you, pet?" Mary's eyes were full of tears as she looked down at Anna's beloved face.

"Well, I'll leave you to it. Seems like your Christmas present has just arrived, Mary."

"To be sure, it has."

Mary smiled, then shut the door, walked Anna over to the chair and sat her down. "Now, tell me exactly what you're doing here. I thought you were meant to be at school?"

"I w-was . . . I am. But"—Anna's face set a determined line—"I've run away and I'm n-never, ever g-going back."

"Now, now, Anna, pet, don't be saying such silliness. Surely you don't mean it?"

"I do, I mean every w-word. And if you try and make me I shall simply r-run away again. Th-the headmistress is hateful, the g-girls are hateful! They make me r-run around playing something called lacrosse, which is b-bad for my knees and more hateful th-than anything! Oh, Mary!" Anna buried her head in her hands. "I've b-been so miserable. I was l-living for the Christmas hols, and seeing you and everyone else at C-Cadogan House, and then the headmistress called me into her office and t-told me I wouldn't be going home. That Aunt had gone to B-Bangkok with Uncle and the house had b-been closed up. Mary, *please* don't make me go b-back to that terrible place, p-please."

At that, Anna's last reserves left her and she burst into tears.

Mary settled the child on her knees, and Anna leaned herself against her chest, pouring out her dreadful stories of loneliness, abandonment and misery.

When she was calmer, Mary spoke to her softly. "Anna, we must let the headmistress know as soon as possible that you're safe. She'll be having half the country's police force out by now, I shouldn't wonder."

"I only r-ran away this morning," Anna pouted, "and Mrs. G-Grix, the headmistress, has gone away to stay with her sister in J-Jersey for Christmas. She left me with Matron, who drinks so much g-gin she sees two of me, rather than none of me."

Mary couldn't help but smile at Anna's turn of phrase. "Well now, we must at least contact Matron, then. We don't want to be causing anyone a worry, do we now? However we might feel, Anna, it just isn't right."

"As long as you p-promise not to say where I am. They might c-come to get me and I am not g-going back. I'd rather die."

Mary knew the child was completely exhausted and there was no arguing with her tonight. "I will only say you have turned up at Cadogan House safe and sound, and that we will be in contact with her after Christmas. How about that?"

This seemed to pacify Anna, who nodded, albeit reluctantly.

"Now then, you look to me as though you could do with a bath. It'd be not quite what you're used to in Cadogan House, but at least you'll be clean, pet."

Mary led Anna to the communal bathroom down the corridor and filled the tub. As she scrubbed the child, Mary asked how she'd managed to find her way to London and then on to her in Colet Gardens.

"It was easy," Anna replied. "I knew where the station was because we'd been on a day trip to London once b-before to see St. Paul's C-Cathedral. So I sneaked out of the school and walked. Then I g-got on a train, which took me to a big station called Waterloo. I caught a bus to Sloane Square and walked the rest of the way to Cadogan House, then Mrs. Carruthers put me in a taxi to bring me to you."

"But, Anna, you'd been told that the house had been closed up. What were you going to do if no one was there?" Mary helped Anna out of the bath and wrapped her in a towel.

"I hadn't really thought that f-far," Anna admitted. "I knew the latch on the kitchen window was b-broken, so I could easily have opened it and climbed through. But Mrs. Carruthers was there and t-told me where you lived."

Mary looked at Anna in admiration, despite her anxiety about what she had done. The little girl who had left her four months ago had grown up. And shown the kind of initiative and backbone Mary hadn't known she possessed.

"Now then," Mary said as she led Anna back down the corridor to her room. "I'm going to tuck you up in bed then I'm going to go downstairs to ask if I may borrow my landlord's telephone. I'll speak to Mrs. Carruthers at Cadogan House and tell her she must call Matron at the school immediately to say that you're safe and sound." Mary saw

Anna's anxious face. "And no, we won't tell her you are here with me. Besides," Mary comforted herself as much as Anna, "We'll be going there tomorrow for Christmas lunch."

Anna's face brightened considerably. "Really? How l-lovely. I've missed everyone very much."

Mary watched as Anna's head sank against the pillows and her eyelids began to droop.

"You sleep, pet, and we'll wake up to Christmas in the morning."

17

Back at Cadogan House, small gifts for Anna had been hastily collected by the servants. When the two of them arrived the following morning, Anna was greeted with affection and excitement by the six remaining members of staff. Mrs. Carruthers, as was her custom on Christmas Day, cooked lunch for them all. After Anna had opened the gifts, they sat down in the kitchen to enjoy a goose with all the trimmings. At the end of the lunch, Nancy stood up and proudly showed off a sparkling gemstone on the fourth finger of her left hand. "I'd like to announce that Sam and me, well, we've decided to tie the knot."

The news was cause for a toast. Sam was dispatched downstairs to the cellar to procure a bottle of port with which to make it.

After everyone had chipped in to clear up, Nancy, with a gleam in her eyes, suggested they go up to the drawing room and play charades.

"Oh, y-yes!" Anna clapped her hands together. "I love charades. Let's go!"

As they climbed the stairs up to the ground floor, Mary said, "Do you really think us lot should be playing games in *their* drawing room?"

"Who's here to stop us?!" Mrs. Carruthers, tipsy on gin and port, gave a snort. "And besides, we have the young lady of the house with us, and she has invited us in, haven't you, Anna?"

At eight o'clock, after a raucous game of charades, everyone walked back down the staircase to the kitchen, feeling exhausted and content.

Mrs. Carruthers turned to Mary. "Will you and Anna be staying here tonight?"

"I hadn't thought about it," said Mary honestly.

"Well now, why don't you put her in her old room, then come downstairs and have a chat with me. I'll make us a nice brew."

Mary agreed, and took a weary Anna upstairs to her old bedroom.

"Oh! I've had such a lovely day, it's been one of the b-best Christmases ever!" Anna sighed with pleasure as Mary tucked her in.

"I'm glad you have, pet. 'Twas certainly better than I was expecting myself. Good night, sleep tight."

"Good night, Mary. Mary?"

"Yes, pet?"

"You and Nancy and Sam and Mrs. Carruthers . . . you're my f-family, aren't you?"

"I'd like to think so, pet, I'd like to think so," said Mary softly as she left the room.

"So now, what are we to do about the young miss upstairs, then?" asked Mrs. Carruthers as Mary settled herself at the kitchen table and sipped her tea.

"I'm sure I don't know," Mary sighed.

"Of course, what we should do is send a telegram to Mr. and Mrs. Lisle, saying that Anna has turned up here."

"Yes, we should," agreed Mary. "But, well now, the thing is, I've made a promise to Anna that she never has to go back to that school. I'd have a worry that if we *did* take her back there, she'd only run away again."

"True," agreed Mrs. Carruthers, "true. Maybe we could speak to the master, tell him how unhappy Anna is at the school, and see what ideas he has."

"And how will we get past the mistress?" Mary rolled her eyes.

"You just have to hope to be lucky and speak to the master. Could you send him a telegram directly?"

"Even if Mrs. Lisle didn't intercept it, he'd talk to her about it. And she would say Anna must be returned to the school as soon as possible."

"Well, I'm sure I don't know what the solution is," Mrs. Carruthers sighed. "That poor child has been abandoned by the very person who promised to protect her. And I can hardly bear to witness it."

"I know. And I mustn't abandon her too." Mary took another sip of tea and breathed slowly. "She's told me stories of the bullying and the way the teachers all turned a blind eye. She says besides everyone knowing she's an orphan, they're after teasing her about her stammer. What can I do to help her?" Mary implored.

"I don't know tonight, dear, I really don't. But I'm fond of Anna too, and the last thing I want to see is that poor little'un suffering. Tell you what, let's have a night's sleep, then put our heads together tomorrow morning and see what we can come up with."

"You know I'll do anything to protect her, don't you?" said Mary.

"Yes, Mary," said Mrs. Carruthers, "I do."

Mary did not sleep that night. She paced around her bedroom, trying to decide the best course of action to safeguard Anna. She only wished she could spirit her away, but the child, whatever her own instincts and emotions told her, was not hers to take.

Or was she . . . ?

Mary was in the kitchen by six the following morning. A yawning Mrs. Carruthers joined her. They made a brew and sat back down at the table.

"I've been thinking . . ."

"Thought you would have been, Mary. So have I, and I can't say I've come up with much."

"Well now, maybe I have, but I need to ask you some details . . ."

Forty minutes later, they were on their third cup of tea.

Mrs. Carruthers, her palms clammy with tension, sighed. "I understand what you're suggesting, Mary, but you know it's a long shot, don't you, girl? And a criminal offense, I'd warrant. You might get yerself locked up if it goes wrong."

"I know, Mrs. C, but it's the only way I can think of to protect Anna. And I'd be having to trust you to never say a word that you knew."

"You know you can count on me, dear. I'm as fond of the little love as you are."

"One more question: when the master first brought Anna home, did he ever say anything about her birth certificate?"

"No. It was never mentioned," said Mrs. Carruthers.

"Was there *anything* he brought with the baby to indicate who she was and where she'd come from?"

"Well, remember I said at the time there was a small suitcase which Mr. Lisle brought with him? He said it was from the baby's mother and he was to mind it until she came to collect her child."

"Where is it now?"

"Still up in the attic, I'd suppose. The mother never came to pick it up, now did she?" Mrs. Carruthers shrugged.

"Do you think it would be wrong if I went to have a look to see if it was still there?" asked Mary.

"Well, if it gives you any clues as to where Anna came from, I can't see the wrong in it. Shall I ask Sam to go up to the attic and see if he can find it?"

"If you would, Mrs. C. Now, in the meantime, as we discussed, I'll be needing anything you can find that can show me Elizabeth Lisle's handwriting and signature. And a piece of headed notepaper for me to write the letter on."

"You're serious about this, aren't you, Mary? Rather you than me," breathed Mrs. Carruthers. "I'll go and get Mrs. Lisle's precious accounts ledger. The one she took from me to fill in herself, because my bookkeeping was sloppy."

Later on that day, Mary left with Anna to return to her lodgings. When Anna had fallen asleep, Mary sat at her desk and practiced the letter she would write on pieces of scrap paper. She thanked God that she'd spent many a childhood hour copying out the scriptures to perfect her writing and spelling. Mary had also noted that the ledger confirmed next term's fees had been paid to Anna's school just before Mrs. Lisle had departed for Bangkok.

Then, when she felt confident, Mary took the ink pen Mrs. Carruthers had handed her from Elizabeth Lisle's desk and began to write.

Three days later, and now returned from holidays with her sister in Jersey, Doreen Grix, the headmistress of Anna's school, sat down and began to sift through the post.

Cadogan House,
Cadogan Place,
London, SW1

26th December, 1928

Dear Mrs. Grix,

My departure to Bangkok was unfortunately delayed until after Christmas, following the death of a relative. And who should appear on my doorstep but my ward, Anna. Due to her obvious distress at being away from my husband and myself, the decision has been taken that Anna will accompany me to Bangkok and receive her education there. I understand that we will forfeit a term's fees, but as the amount has already been paid, I will presume the matter is closed. Please address any correspondence to my London address, c/o Mrs. J. Carruthers, my housekeeper, who will forward it on to me in Bangkok.

Yours sincerely,
Elizabeth Lisle

Doreen Grix did not feel pained by the loss of the girl. Anna Lisle had been a strange little thing who had not added to the school. And had to be catered for during the holidays.

The headmistress filed the letter in her drawer and considered the matter closed.

A few days later, when all the servants had left to move on to their new employment, and only Mrs. Carruthers remained at the house, Mary left Anna with Sheila and returned to Cadogan House. She'd explained to the child that she was off down to Kent to see Anna's headmistress and tell her she was not returning to school.

Mary found Mrs. Carruthers upstairs, packing bedding into trunks. "I've come to say good-bye," she said.

Mrs. Carruthers wiped the sweat from her brow and pulled herself to her feet. "You're going through with it, then?"

Mary nodded. "Yes. I can't see that I have any choice."

"No . . . as long as you're aware of the risks you're going to be taking. Does Anna know she'll never be able to come back to Cadogan House?"

"No, she doesn't." Mary sighed in agitation. "Do you think I'm doing wrong?"

"Mary, sometimes in life we have to follow our heart. And . . . all I can say is that, when I was younger, I wish I'd have followed mine." Mrs. Carruthers stared out of the window, her face contorted with the sudden pain of memory. "I once had a gentleman, you know, and a babe of my own. The gentleman vanished, I had to work, so I gave it up for adoption. I still regret that decision every day of my life."

"Oh, Mrs. C, I'm very sorry. I had no idea . . ."

"No. Well, you wouldn't, being as I never told you," she answered briskly. "But I can see that your love for Anna is like that of a proper mum. And in my opinion, what you're doing is in her best interests. But not necessarily in yours. If you get found out . . ."

Mary nodded stoically. "I know."

"You know I'll never give you away, don't you, dear?"

"Yes, I do."

"But you must understand that once you've done what you're suggesting, we can't see each other again. I'd be seen as an accomplice in the stealing of a child, and I'm not keen to spend my last years in Holloway Prison."

"Yes," said Mary, "I understand. Thank you." Mary instinctively threw her arms around Mrs. Carruthers.

"Don't go thanking me. I'll well up, I will. You'd better be getting off now."

"Yes."

"Good luck," called Mrs. Carruthers as Mary reached the door.

Mary nodded and left the house, wondering why her life had been punctuated by a series of painful and final good-byes.

Mrs. Carruthers walked back inside to make herself a fresh brew, and it was only then she noticed the small leather suitcase sitting in the lobby by the back door. She went outside, but saw the mews was empty and Mary had gone. "Ah well, too late now," she said to herself, and picked up the suitcase to take it back upstairs to the attic.

• • •

Mary arrived at Tunbridge Wells station two hours later. Stepping off the train, she asked for directions to the nearest post office. Walking the short distance toward it, she entered and stood patiently in the queue, trying to stem the beating of her heart. When it was her turn, she approached the counter and spoke to the young girl behind it in her best English accent.

"I wish to send a telegram to Bangkok. Here is the address, and here are the words."

"Very well, miss," replied the girl, surveying her chart. "To Bangkok, that will be six shillings and sixpence."

"Thank you." Mary counted out the money required and passed it across the counter. "May I ask when it will be received?"

"By the latest, tonight. We send all the telegrams at the close of business."

"And when can I expect a reply?"

The girl looked at her oddly. "Whenever the recipient wishes to send one. Come in tomorrow afternoon. We may have something for you by then."

Mary nodded. "Thank you."

She spent the night in a small bed-and-breakfast in the center of the town. She did not venture out of her room to eat, partly because she had no appetite, but also it was important that as few people as possible saw her. She passed the long hours pondering her actions, wondering if she was clear in the head for what she had done.

On paper, she was killing the child she loved. Or, at least, her chances of a future under the umbrella of a wealthy family.

But instinct told her that Anna's hopes of being embraced by either the guardian who had promised to protect her, or the woman he'd married who resented her, were small. Besides, it was five years before they would return. Five years in which, if she didn't act, Anna would spend the rest of her childhood lonely and abandoned in a place she hated. And whatever it took, and whatever she must sacrifice if she was caught, it had to be worth the risk. In fact, as Mary approached the post office the following morning, her heart drumming in her chest, she knew that her entire plan depended completely on her belief that Anna's sudden removal from the Lisles' lives would be a relief, rather than a curse.

Elizabeth Lisle walked into her husband's office holding the telegram. Before she'd entered, she'd set her face into an appropriate expression of shock and grief.

"Darling, I"—she moved toward him—"I'm afraid there's been some very sad news."

Lawrence Lisle, exhausted from another night of relentless Bangkok heat, took the telegram Elizabeth offered him. He read it in silence then placed his head in his hands.

"I know, my dear, I know." Elizabeth put a comforting hand on his shoulder. "How terribly tragic."

"My Anna . . . my poor little girl . . ." Tears came to his eyes as grief and guilt assailed him. "I must, of course, return immediately. The funeral arrangements . . ."

Elizabeth held him silently as he wept.

"I failed her, Elizabeth. I promised her mother I would take care of her. I was wrong to have left her behind in England—she should have come here with us."

"My dear, it's always been obvious to me that Anna was fragile. She was so pale and thin, with that terrible stammer. It is indeed unfortunate that there was a bout of influenza at the school, and she was not strong enough to fight it. But it is very likely, given her frail health, that she may well have contracted one of the many tropical diseases here if she had accompanied us."

"But at least she would have been with those who loved her. Not alone in some godforsaken school," Lawrence moaned.

"Lawrence, I can assure you I would not have trusted your ward to any establishment I did not feel could offer Anna the very best of care," Elizabeth reprimanded him. "As it says in the telegram, the headmistress was terribly fond of Anna."

"Darling, my apologies," Lawrence said hastily. "I was not trying to suggest you were at fault. No." He shook his head. "It is I that am at fault. And now Anna is dead . . . I can hardly bear it. I must sail for

England as soon as possible. The very least I can do is organize and attend the funeral. Be there for her in death, when I failed her in life."

"Really, my dear, you must not punish yourself. You did what so many others would not have done. You took her away from harm, gave her a home and love and kindness, and treated her like your own for ten years." Elizabeth knelt beside his chair and took his hands in hers. "Lawrence, you must know that it is impossible for you to attend Anna's funeral. Such things cannot wait for the six weeks it would take you to return to England. Anna deserves her soul to be laid to rest as soon as possible in a Christian burial. The headmistress is offering to make the arrangements for us. And for Anna's sake, we must accept her help."

Eventually, Lawrence nodded. "You are, of course, right," he agreed sadly.

"I will reply to the telegram for you," Elizabeth said gently. "Perhaps, if you could consider where you feel would be appropriate for Anna to be buried, I can inform the headmistress. She mentions a local church she feels would be suitable. Unless you have any other suggestions."

Lawrence looked out of the window of the Consulate and sighed. "I don't even know what faith Anna was. I never thought to ask at the time. There were so many things I failed to ask . . . so, yes, whatever the headmistress suggests," he replied numbly.

"Then I will reply immediately, thank her for her kindness and ask her to make the necessary arrangements."

"Thank you, my dear."

"And, Lawrence, there is something I must tell you." Elizabeth paused, inwardly making a decision. "I was going to wait a little longer, but perhaps, under the circumstances, it might help." She stood up. "My dear, we are to have a child of our own in seven months' time."

Lawrence stared at his wife, trying to switch his emotions from grief to joy. He had dearly wished for this. "Why, that is the most wonderful news! Are you sure?"

"I am sure."

He rose and put his arms around her. "Forgive me, I am overwhelmed. It is almost too much to take in."

"I understand. But I thought, my dear, that it might lessen the blow of this dreadful news."

"Yes, yes . . ." Lawrence murmured as he stroked his wife's hair. "And perhaps, if it is a girl, we might call her 'Anna,' after the child we have just lost."

"Of course, my dear." Elizabeth gave a tight smile. "If that is what you would like."

Mary took the telegram from the girl behind the counter. Her hands were trembling as she walked outside and sat down on the nearest bench to read it. *Everything* depended on this reply.

DEAR MRS. GRIX (STOP) IT IS WITH TERRIBLE SADNESS WE LEARNED OF ANNA'S PREMATURE DEATH (STOP) AS IT IS IMPOSSIBLE FOR EITHER OF US TO RETURN HOME WE ARE MOST GRATEFUL FOR YOUR HELP IN ARRANGING THE FUNERAL (STOP) WE WILL BOW TO YOUR SUGGESTIONS AND PLEASE INFORM US OF THE COSTS (STOP) WE THANK YOU FOR YOUR KINDNESS AND CONSIDERATION TOWARD ANNA (STOP) ELIZABETH LISLE (STOP)

Mary let out a small yelp of relief. Even though it had been doubtful that Lawrence and Elizabeth Lisle *would* decide to board a ship bound for England forthwith, it had always remained a possibility. Mary took out her pencil and drafted a reply on the back of the telegram. There were a few loose ends that were vital to tie up. As she knew from the Sherlock Holmes books she had always loved, it was the attention to detail in circumstances like these that was important. Ten minutes later, she walked back to the post office and gave the girl behind the counter her response.

"I'll be back in a few days to check for a reply," said Mary as she counted out her shillings and handed them to the girl.

"You know you can have them delivered to your home if that's more convenient," commented the girl.

"I'm . . . moving and I'm not sure of my new address," Mary replied quickly. "Anyway, it's no bother to use my own feet and come and collect it."

"Whatever suits you." The girl shrugged and moved on to the next customer.

Mary left the post office, readying herself to move on to a new life with her beloved Anna.

Elizabeth Lisle took the reply to her telegram into her husband's office.

"Mrs. Grix is organizing everything for Anna. She says that there are no costs to pay for the funeral as we had already paid this term's fees. Any monies remaining after that, she will forward to us. It is to be held in a week's time and she will inform us of the exact spot where Anna is buried, so that we may go and visit her when we return to England. She will post Anna's death certificate to Cadogan House."

"Death certificate . . . the poor child, I—"

Lawrence watched his wife sway a little and immediately rushed to her side. "My dear, I understand how stressful this must have been for you, especially under the circumstances." He sat her down in a chair and held her hands in his. "What is done is done, and as you rightly said, I did my best for Anna. I must move on and not upset you further by talking of it. And"—he indicated his wife's stomach—"think of life, not death."

18

Anna, pet," Mary said as they sat toasting crumpets over the gas fire, "I've spoken to your headmistress and she knows you'll not be returning."

Anna's face lit up with joy.

"Oh, Mary! That's w-wonderful." Then she frowned. "And have you t-told Uncle and Aunt about this?"

"Yes, and they agree." Mary took a deep breath. She hated herself for lying, but knew Anna must never know what she had done.

"You see? I told you that Uncle wouldn't have me stay there if I was unhappy. So when can we go b-back to Cadogan House?" Anna bit into the buttered crumpet Mary handed her.

"Well now, that's the thing, pet. As you know, the house is being closed up while your Aunt and Uncle are living in Bangkok. And even though they love you, they don't feel they can afford to run a house the size of Cadogan House just for one little girl to live in. Do you understand?"

"Yes, of course I understand. So where am I to l-live?"

"Well now, they've suggested that you might want to stay here with me."

Anna looked around the small room, her privileged upbringing suddenly betraying itself in her eyes. "You mean, l-living here always?"

"Well, my friend Sheila next door is getting wed next month and moving out of her flat. Her landlord said that we could be having that if we want. It's got two bedrooms, a sitting room, a kitchen and its own bathroom. I was thinking we might take a look."

"All right," Anna agreed, "and it means we don't have to leave the p-poor man who stands outside by the lamppost."

Mary glanced at Anna. "You've noticed him, then?"

"Oh, yes." Anna nodded. "I've spoken to him. He looked so sad and l-lonely, all by himself out there."

"You *spoke* to him?"

"Yes." Anna was busy devoring her crumpet.

"And did he answer?"

"He said the weather was getting even c-colder." Anna wiped the butter from her mouth. "Does he have a home?"

"He does, pet."

"So he's not an orphan like me?"

"No, he's not an orphan."

"So, where am I to go to school?" Anna returned to the conversation.

"Well now, I was thinking that we might go back to the old days of teaching you from home. Especially if you want to continue your ballet lessons." Mary dangled the appropriate carrot. "A school might not be too happy to let you have afternoons off to do that. But, of course, it's up to you."

"Can I go b-back to Princess Astafieva?" asked Anna. "I do think she's a very good teacher."

"Unfortunately, the Princess isn't well just now, but I've been making inquiries and we have a wonderful teacher just five minutes from here. His name is Nicholas Legat and he used to be Anna Pavlova's partner!" said Mary encouragingly.

"Anna Pavlova . . ." Anna's eyes were wide at the thought. "The greatest ballerina that has ever l-lived!"

"Yes. So, I'm thinking in the next couple of days we'll go down to his studio to see if he'll take you. How about that?"

"Oh, Mary!" Anna clapped her hands together. "I can hardly believe two weeks ago I was in that dreadful place thinking I'd n-never be able to dance again." She threw her arms around Mary. "And here you are, like my guardian angel, c-come to save me."

"Ah now, pet, you knew I'd never let you come to any harm."

"When you didn't write to me at school, I thought"—Anna bit her lip—"I th-thought you'd abandoned me."

"Well, everyone felt it was better if I let you be while you settled in."

Anna eyed her. "You mean you were t-told not to write by Aunt?"

"Yes, but only out of your best interests."

"Mary, you're so kind about everyone, but we both know that Aunt h-hated me." Anna kissed her on the cheek. "And whatever you are to me, I don't think there's a girl in the world that c-could have a better mother."

Mary eyes welled up with tears, wondering whether Anna would agree with that if she told her the truth about what she had done. "Well now, pet, that's enough of that. But as you'll be living with me for at least the next few years, it might be easier if you took my surname."

"W-well, as I don't seem to have one anyway, I think it would be wonderful to be called the same as you," agreed Anna.

"You know too, that the nuns named me 'Benedict,' so I have no real surname either. I'd say we both start again," Mary smiled, "and make one up!"

"Can we really do that?"

"I wouldn't see why not."

"How exciting! Am I allowed to ch-choose?"

"Of course you are, as long as it's not after some unpronounceable Russian ballerina that no one can get their tongue around!"

As always, when Anna was thinking, her index finger went into her mouth and she chewed it. "I know!"

"Do you, pet?"

"Yes! I was thinking of my favorite piece of b-ballet music, *The Dying Swan,* and that my name is Anna, the same as Anna P-Pavlova. So, I would like our surname to be 'Swan.'"

"Swan . . ." Mary tested the name on her tongue, then turned to Anna. "I like it."

A day later, it was Anna Swan who walked into the studio of Nicholas Legat. And Mary Swan, her mother, who took her. Anna was immediately accepted into his class and began to take three ballet lessons a week.

Within a month, the two of them moved to Sheila's old flat in the building next door and Mary set to work to paint and brighten their new home. She produced pretty floral curtains from her sewing machine for Anna's bedroom, and treated herself to some duck-egg blue chintz for the small sitting room that would double as her sewing room. As she hung them and stepped back to admire her handiwork, Mary thought of the new house in Dunworley that was to have been hers all those years ago. But that dream was gone, so she poured her homemaking energies into the cramped space that would be the nearest thing to it she would ever have.

"You have m-made a miracle," Anna declared when Mary proudly showed her the finished bedroom. "And I love you. Can we ask Nancy and Mrs. Carruthers around here for t-tea? I'd love them to see our new home."

"I'm so sorry, Anna, but they've both moved out of Cadogan House and I've no idea of their addresses," Mary replied calmly.

"Oh, but I think it's terribly rude of them not to let us know, don't you? They were our f-friends, after all."

"I'm sure they'll be in contact when they're ready, pet," Mary answered guiltily.

The two of them settled into a routine. Mary did her best to make sure Anna sat down at the small desk in the corner of the sitting room to work at her lessons. She used the local library to source books on history and geography and encouraged Anna to read as much as she could. She was aware it was hardly the kind of education a girl such as Anna should be receiving, but it was the best she could do. Besides, she knew the child's mind was elsewhere.

Three afternoons a week, Mary walked with Anna across Colet Gardens to drop her at her ballet class. Mary glanced behind her nervously as she entered and exited the building. It was something she would do for the rest of her life. She knew it was the price she must pay for her actions.

When the idea had first come to Mary, she had thought that perhaps the best thing to do was to spirit Anna abroad. But as she'd worked out the details, Mary had known it was not an option. Anna had no birth certificate, passport or, in fact, any official papers detailing who she was, so they were trapped in England. She had also considered moving away from London, but she had to think of her income. Besides, she thought, in a small town or village, the two of them would be far more noticeable. In a big city such as London, they had more hope of remaining anonymous. And the fact that so much of Anna's childhood at Cadogan House had been lived inside its walls and she'd met few people during her time there, made the chances of Anna's being recognized small.

However, Mary kept far away from their old Chelsea stomping grounds, comforting herself that, as Anna grew into a young woman, few would ever associate her with the little girl who had suffered such a tragic and early death.

As for the future . . . Mary could not think about that. She had done what she believed was right to protect the child she loved. And if there was one thing she had learned from the loss of Sean and her hopes and dreams along with him, all you could do was to seize the day.

One balmy spring evening, when Mary and Anna had been living their new life together for three and a half months, Anna came into the flat accompanied by a visitor.

Mary looked up from her sewing machine in surprise. For there, standing shyly by Anna, was the young man who stood outside under the lamppost.

"Mary, this is Jeremy. He's my friend, aren't you, Jeremy?"

The man looked down at Anna nervously and nodded.

"I said to Jeremy that he should c-come in and meet you. I said you wouldn't mind. You don't, do you, Mary?"

"Why, I . . . no, of course I don't." Mary felt flustered as Jeremy's dark, haunted eyes fell upon her. "Jeremy, come and sit yourself down and I'll be making a brew."

"Th-Th-Thank you."

Mary went into the kitchen and busied herself with setting a tea tray, hearing Anna chatting away comfortably next door. Her high-pitched voice was interspersed with the odd deep grunt from Jeremy.

"Here we are then," Mary said as she set down the tea tray on the table. "Jeremy, will you be taking milk and sugar?"

"B-Both." After a long pause, there was a "Th-Thank you kindly."

Mary poured the tea and handed it to him. As Jeremy took it, his hands shook, making the cup clatter against the saucer. She removed it from him gently and set it down on the table next to him.

"Isn't this nice?" commented Anna. "Much b-better in here than it is out there." She indicated the lamppost. "And besides, I said to

Jeremy that my mother didn't have any friends either. So I thought you could b-be each other's friends."

Jeremy nodded, glancing at Anna. Mary caught a glimmer of emotion in his eyes and read that this strange, sad man was obviously fond of his young friend.

"Well now, it's very thoughtful of you to be thinking of me, Anna. Isn't it now, Jeremy?"

"Y-Yes."

Mary busied herself pouring her own tea, and sat in silence, wondering what on earth she could say to him. Asking what he did with himself seemed daft, when she knew he spent most of his time communing with the lamppost outside their window.

"Th-Thank you f-for the *coat*," Jeremy said, the effort of saying the words visible. "K-Kept me w-warm."

"See?" said Anna. "He speaks like I do sometimes." She patted his hand affectionately.

"Well, 'tis nice that you two have been talking."

"A-Anna t-tells me she l-loves dancing," ventured Jeremy. "L-Loves Tch-Tchaikovsky's *Swan Lake*."

"Yes," Anna said eagerly. "And Mary has said that as soon as we get enough money, we can buy a gramophone like we used to have at Cadogan House. Then we can b-buy the record and you can come and l-listen to it, Jeremy."

"Thank you, Anna." Jeremy picked up his tea cup gingerly and put it with shaking hands to his lips. He gulped the contents down, relieved the liquid had made it to his mouth. Then he placed the cup back on the saucer with a clatter. "And th-thank you for the t-tea, Mary. M-Mustn't b-bother you for l-longer."

"You don't bother us, does he, Mary?" Anna said as he stood up.

"No, not at all." Mary walked with Jeremy to the door of the flat. "Now you feel free to come in for a brew whenever you'd be wanting to."

"Th-Thank you, M-Mary." Jeremy smiled at her with such gratefulness that Mary instinctively reached out her hand to pat his thin one.

"We'll be seeing you again, I'm sure."

• • •

A couple of afternoons later, Anna appeared in the flat with Jeremy, who was carrying something under a blanket.

"Jeremy says he has brought us a present! I can't wait to see what it is." Anna flitted around excitedly as Jeremy asked Mary where he should place the bundle.

"Put it on there." Mary indicated the sideboard, and Jeremy did so. With a flourish, he removed the blanket to reveal a gramophone and, placed on the spindle, a pile of records.

"F-For you and Anna."

"Oh, Jeremy!" Anna clasped her hands together in excitement. "What a wonderful p-present. Isn't it, Mary?"

"Well now, it is, but this is only to be borrowing, isn't it, Jeremy?" Mary underlined.

"N-No, it's for you. T-To k-keep."

"But these machines cost a fortune. We can't—"

"You c-can! I h-have m-money. W-which record, Anna?"

As Anna and Jeremy discussed whether it should be *Sleeping Beauty* or *Swan Lake,* Mary recognized the glint of determination in Jeremy's eyes. Even in his broken state, she saw a glimmer of what he might have been before the war destroyed him.

He turned to Mary suddenly as Anna was placing a record on the spindle, and smiled at her. "In r-return for the c-coat."

And that was that.

It was also the start of Jeremy Langdon becoming a permanent fixture in Mary's sitting room. Every afternoon, Anna would sweep Jeremy away from his lamppost and bring him in for a cup of tea. As Mary sewed, Anna and Jeremy would listen to the ballet music. Anna would pirouette around the room, Jeremy applauding loudly at the end of the piece. As Anna dropped him a graceful curtsy, Mary realized the child was re-creating the moments she had spent with Lawrence Lisle in the drawing room of Cadogan House.

"S-She's very g-good, Mary," Jeremy commented one day as he made his way out of the flat.

"Do you think so? She's certainly determined, and that's for sure."

"T-Talented," Jeremy nodded. "I s-saw the b-best before the war. Sh-She could be too. G-Good-bye, Mary."

"Where will you be getting your supper from tonight?" Mary ventured. "You look as though you haven't had a square meal in a long time. I've some chops in the oven and there's plenty to spare."

"Oh, Jeremy, do stay!" persuaded Anna.

"Y-you're very kind, but I don't want to be a b-bother."

"He's not, is he, Mary?"

"No, Jeremy, you're no bother." She smiled.

19

Soon the lamppost was bereft of its old friend, as Jeremy spent more and more time with Mary and Anna. He'd arrive with an offering; some chocolate for Anna, or a piece of fresh fish that Mary would cook for their supper. As his confidence grew, Jeremy's speech became less halting. With the gentle encouragement of woman and child, he began to communicate more easily. Over the weeks, Mary watched as some of the gauntness left his thin features, due in part to Mary's heaped plates at suppertime, and his hands became more capable of holding a knife and fork to his mouth. Mary saw flashes of humor start to emerge, began to glimpse a man who was obviously not only educated, but had a quiet wisdom to complement it. Jeremy's gentleness, thoughtfulness and kindness, especially toward Anna, endeared him more to Mary as each day passed. And as his haunted expression left his deep green eyes and his body filled out, Mary saw what a handsome man he was.

One night, Mary tucked Anna into bed, thinking too how the child had blossomed since Jeremy had arrived in their lives.

"I'm so happy, Mary," Anna sighed as she rested her head on the pillow.

"I'm glad you are, pet."

"Yes . . ." Anna murmured, "You and me and Jeremy, it's almost like we are a real f-family, isn't it?"

"Yes, I suppose it is. Now you shut your eyes and get yourself to sleep."

Mary left the room and went back to her desk to continue sewing, but found she couldn't concentrate. She gazed out the window and saw that the lamppost was abandoned, as it often was these days after Jeremy had departed from their flat. She still had little idea of who he was. There was no guarantee that one day Jeremy wouldn't simply disappear, never to return. Mary's stomach churned as she thought of Anna losing yet another person she loved.

And her too . . .

Mary felt a sudden jolt in her stomach as she realized that Anna was not the only one to have become more than fond of their regular visitor. There was something about Jeremy that reminded her of the last time she'd seen Sean. She had that same feeling of protectiveness toward him. *And* attraction . . .

Mary pulled herself up short. She had to end this nonsense at once. She was an orphaned Irish spinster and former domestic servant, whereas Jeremy Langdon was obviously a gentleman. He was simply a friend and a companion, someone who had known the kind of terrible pain in his life which she could empathize with. And that was the way it must stay.

A few days later, there was a knock on Mary's door. Startled, as Anna was out at her ballet lesson and she wasn't expecting a client, Mary went to the door and opened it.

"Jeremy," she said in astonishment. Never had Jeremy come to the flat without Anna bringing him in. "I . . . are you all right?"

"N-No."

Mary could see by the ghostly color of his skin and the expression in his eyes that something had happened. "Come in. Anna's not back yet, but we'll be having a cup of tea while we wait, shall we?"

"I w-wanted to speak to you. W-Without Anna."

"Well now, you sit down and make yourself comfortable. I'll be off to make the tea."

"N-N-No! N-Need to speak, not d-drink!"

Mary noticed his speech was far more stilted than it had been in recent weeks. She led him into the sitting room and sat him down in his usual chair.

"Are you sure I can't be getting you anything, Jeremy?" she asked as she took the chair opposite him.

"My go-godmother d-died l-last night."

"I—oh, Jeremy . . . I'm so sorry, pet."

"I . . ." Jeremy put a shaking hand to his forehead. "S-Sorry," he offered as tears began to fall down his face. "Only p-person who"—he choked—"c-cared for me! L-Loved me! How I am *n-now*!"

Mary watched as his shoulders heaved in despair. Unable to bear his suffering, she did the only thing she could. She went to Jeremy and put her arms around him. "There now," she whispered, cradling him as if he were a child, stroking his soft hair, "You have a good cry. Nothing wrong with crying, is there?"

As Jeremy continued to sob, she wrapped her arms tighter around his chest. "I'm here, Jeremy, and so is Anna. And we both care for you."

Jeremy turned his anguished eyes up to Mary. "D-Do you c-care? For a b-broken wreck like me? How c-can you?"

"Because you're a good, kind man. And whatever happened to you out there in the trenches was not your fault. It doesn't change who you are inside, now does it?"

Jeremy's head dropped forward and Mary bent down on her knees and reached up to hold him. He buried his face in her shoulder. "Th-That's n-not what my parents think, they *h-hate* what I've b-become. So ashamed! W-Wanted to h-hide me."

"Holy Mary, Mother of God!" Mary shuddered, horrified. "I'm so sorry for what you have suffered. But I promise, it does not change the person that you were and still are. There now, you must remember that, Jeremy. The war did terrible things to men like you. Us at home had no idea what you went through to win us our freedom."

"You th-think so?"

"I *know* so." Mary felt the wetness of his tears dampening her shoulder. "I had a . . . somebody, who was out there for years. And, right at the end, didn't survive to see us win."

At that, Jeremy lifted his head from her shoulder and looked directly at Mary. "Y-You l-lost your s-sweetheart?"

"My fiancé. And any idea of the life we had planned along with him."

"M-Mary, I th-think you must b-be an angel. The way you c-care for Anna, and *m-me*. Listening to everything we t-talk of and yet you have l-lost so much yourself."

"Yes. But I haven't faced the fear and pain and the memories of those things which you must live over and over."

"Yes, but you too have suffered b-because of the d-damned war! Mary." Jeremy took her hands from his shoulders and curled them in his. "I have been thinking of this f-for a while. And what I th-think is th-that I l-love you. I love you." With huge effort, Jeremy repeated the phrase without stuttering.

There was a pause as Mary looked into Jeremy's eyes. Her natural common sense and pragmatism won over what he was saying. This was a moment of high emotion and need for him. And she mustn't believe it. "Jeremy, you are in so much pain, you're not after knowing where you are. It's the shock, you see. And—"

"*N-No!* It's not the shock. You are so b-beautiful and so kind. I've l-loved you from the moment you handed me the c-coat. Since then, I haven't been coming to stand by the l-lamppost to think of my dead sweetheart. But to catch a g-glimpse of *you*."

"Jeremy—stop it, please!" Mary said desperately.

"It's true! I watched Anna, knew she was your d-daughter, spoke to her. To give me a chance to meet you p-properly. And t-today, when I've l-lost the only person who c-cared for me, I had to tell you my feelings! L-life is very short!"

Mary looked up into his tear-filled eyes in wonderment. Not only because Jeremy professed to love—to *love* her—but because he had just managed to utter at least two paragraphs in the same breath.

"Well now, Jeremy, I'd be saying that is very kind of you, but I think, if I'm honest, you've had a bit of a nasty shock, so."

"Mary." Jeremy's tears had dried now. His eyes softened as he looked at her. "I understand that you and I, we b-both know what pain is. Trust me, I would never play with your f-feelings. And I'm not getting mine c-confused either. Perhaps you feel nothing f-for me anyway."

Mary sat at Jeremy's feet, her eyes downcast, her hands still held in his.

"I understand." Jeremy nodded. "How c-could anyone l-love somebody like me?"

Mary dragged her eyes up to his again. "No, 'tis not that. It's simply that I've loved before and lost. I"—Mary drew in her breath—"*do* care for you. In fact, I'd be saying I care for you a deal too much. And if you were to go out of my life, I'd be worrying that I'd miss you."

"Well, I understand that we've both l-lost someone. We share that. Could we share the fact we've f-found someone too?"

"Oh, Jeremy, you know nothing about me." Mary shook her head sadly. "There's many things I've done, many things about me—"

"M-Mary, I've killed other human b-beings! Nothing you could ever tell me would shock me, after what I have s-seen. And whatever it is, my love, I would want to share it! So tell me and I will t-tell you of the things I've d-done. That's what l-love is all about, isn't it? Trust?"

"But, Jeremy, pet," Mary whispered, "I'm an orphan from nowhere. You are a gentleman, and you need a lady. I can never be that, not even for you."

"Do you think I care?! My mother is a real l-lady and when I came b-back from the t-trenches, she put me into an"—Jeremy struggled to say the word—"asylum! Her own ch-child!" He gulped back his tears. "War has changed everything, there is nothing I n-need to know about you. Other than that you are the k-kindest person I have ever met. And you have a b-beautiful heart."

"Ah, Jeremy . . ." Mary took her hands away from his and wiped her eyes roughly.

It was Jeremy's turn to reach down, pull her from the floor and fold her into his arms. And what she felt there, after years of loneliness, she could hardly describe. The smell of him, a man's smell—so familiar, yet unknown.

He tipped her chin up and placed a soft kiss on her lips. "Mary, I'd never h-hurt you. You must believe me. I c-can read the fear in your eyes. I've seen it so m-many times b-before."

He planted gentle kisses on her forehead, her eyes, her cheeks. Finally, she gave up trying to analyze whatever this might mean, and gave in. Feelings were aroused in her as he kissed her and caressed her which Mary thought she'd never experience again. For all Jeremy's outward disabilities, Mary felt his maleness and his strength.

Twenty minutes later, Mary glanced at the clock on the mantelpiece and put her hand to her mouth. "Oh, Jesus, Mary and Joseph! Anna will be waiting for me." She climbed off Jeremy's knee and straightened her hair in the mirror.

"May I accompany you to c-collect her?"

Mary turned and smiled at him. "If you'd be wanting to, yes."

A disgruntled Anna was sitting on the steps outside the studio when Mary and Jeremy appeared around the corner. Her expression changed immediately as she saw them.

"Hello, you two! You're late." She smiled.

"Yes, sorry about that, pet, but Jeremy came round to see me. He's had some bad news today, haven't you?"

"Yes."

Anna looked at him quizzically. "You look very happy for someone who's had b-bad news," she responded.

Jeremy gave Mary a secret smile as they set off toward home. Anna danced happily along in front of the two of them. "It's all right, I know why. I've been waiting for this to h-happen for weeks!" She stopped suddenly on the pavement to turn around to face them. "You two love each other, don't you?"

"Well now, I . . ." Mary blushed furiously.

Jeremy took her hand firmly in his. "Yes. Do you m-mind?"

"Of course I don't! I think I'm about the happiest girl in the world. It means that if you two get married, I have a mother and a father. And we can be a p-proper family." Anna threw her arms spontaneously around both of them. "Because I love both of you l-lots and lots and lots!"

20

The death of Jeremy's godmother had left him the owner of a large house in West Kensington, enough money to provide him with a small income for life and a smart black Ford car. A week after his godmother's funeral, Jeremy took Mary and Anna to see his house.

Anna ran from room to room happily. "It's almost as big as Cadogan House, b-but not quite."

Mary shifted uncomfortably when Anna made the comparison. Although she trusted Jeremy implicitly, any talk of the past, especially to someone who came from the same social class as her former employees, had to be dangerous.

As Anna ran down the stairs into the entrance hall, she stopped and turned to look at Mary and Jeremy, who were walking down with more decorum behind her. "Are you going to ask us to come and l-live here with you, Jeremy? It's a big house for just you. And it seems silly, Mary and I l-living in our little flat, when you have all this space."

"Now then, Anna." Mary blushed at Anna's lack of guile. "Jeremy's only showing us his house. Don't be asking him such impertinent questions."

"Sorry, Mary. It w-was just that I thought . . ."

"You th-thought right, Anna." Jeremy smiled. "The l-logic of a child. Well, Mary, would you l-like to come and l-live here?"

"*Please . . . !*" It was all too much. Mary fled down the rest of the stairs, across the hall and out of the front door. She didn't stop running until she arrived in the safety of her own sitting room.

Jeremy arrived at the front door of her flat ten minutes later. She let him in, tears streaming down her face. "Where's Anna?" she asked.

"I've told Mrs. Hawkins, the housekeeper, to give her t-tea. I th-thought that you and I should have a ch-chat. Can I come in?"

Mary nodded tearfully, then turned and walked back into the sitting room. "Jeremy, I don't know what you want from me, but whatever it is, it's not something I can ever give you. You don't know who I am! I'm not a lady, as I said before. And your housekeeper knew it. I could see it in her eyes. I should be serving you, not being your *girlfriend*!"

Jeremy took out a handkerchief and offered it to her as she sank into a chair. "Mary, I've b-been in your company almost every day for months now. You are everything a l-lady should be. And as for your so-social position, I learned in the trenches that class has nothing to do with one's c-character. As for the secrets you keep, I can only say I will l-listen. I've said to you before, there is nothing that can ever sh-shock me." He knelt down in front of her, wiping a stray piece of hair from her cheek. "And I believe that love can f-forgive and understand anything. Tell me, Mary, tr-trust me," he urged.

Mary sighed deeply, knowing that to tell him would perhaps be the end of their possible future. But to give that future a chance, she *had* to do as he asked.

Mary asked for help from up above. And, finally, she nodded.

"I'll tell you."

Twenty minutes later, Mary wrung her hands. "The fact is, I have committed a sin against God. I've pretended Anna is dead and I've stolen her away. I've stolen a child. Oh, God save me . . ."

Jeremy went to her and held her tight in his arms. "Mary, Mary, please d-don't punish yourself anymore. Yes, you've done a wrong thing, but for the r-right reasons. You did it because you love Anna, and wanted her h-happy and safe."

"But did I do it for Anna?" Mary looked up at him in anguish. "Or for me, because I needed her?"

"From what you've t-told me, and the danger you'll face if the secret is ever discovered, I would b-believe your motives were unselfish."

"You really think that?"

"Yes." Jeremy took her hands and squeezed them hard. "I d-do. Mary, is it any different from telling a relative that their son d-died in the trenches painlessly, when in fact he was screaming in agony? And"—Jeremy looked away—"perhaps taking days to die. Or a platoon captain sending his men over the t-top every day, knowing they were going to their d-deaths?" Jeremy's gaze fell on her once more. "You have done your best to pr-protect someone you love, and you should n-never be ashamed of that! Never! And I l-love you even more for what you've done."

"You do?"

"Yes. You are brave and g-good and strong."

"Ah, Jeremy, I'm not. I'm so frightened of being discovered and Anna taken away from me. I look behind me every time I'm out of the flat."

"Protecting an orphan, just like yourself, is something to be proud of. B-besides"—Jeremy smiled at her—"I just m-might be able to help you and Anna. If you m-marry me, that is."

"Even after all I've told you, you still want to?" Mary was astonished.

"More than ever, Mary. I p-promise you."

21

Three months later, Mary Swan, orphaned child of parents unknown, became Mrs. Jeremy Langdon, chatelaine of a large house in Kensington. The only other person present at the wedding was Anna Swan, a girl of ten.

In the following year, three things happened to make Mary believe there truly was a God protecting her. She found herself pregnant, which brought untold joy to all of them. Then Jeremy, through channels which Mary did not wish to know about, discovered that Lawrence Lisle had died nine months earlier of malaria in Bangkok. Elizabeth Lisle, so he'd heard, had miscarried her baby soon afterward, but, equally, had lost no time in finding herself another suitable husband. Jeremy's contacts had discovered the chap had been posted to Shanghai and Elizabeth Lisle had accompanied him.

"You d-do understand what this means, Mary? It means you're free. Lawrence Lisle can n-never come after you now. And from what I heard, I'd d-doubt Elizabeth Lisle would be interested."

Mary crossed herself, feeling guilty at the relief she felt that Lawrence Lisle was dead. "'Tis sad news, but I'd be lying if I said there wasn't part of me that's happy. Mind you, Jeremy, I doubt I'll ever be able to relax again."

"I know, darling, but he c-can't get you where he's gone, I promise. Which means I think I should investigate our going through the process of officially adopting Anna."

"But she has no birth certificate. And not even a second name."

"Leave it to me, darling." Jeremy waved this away as a mere detail. "I may be a wreck of a man now, but C-Captain Jeremy Langdon can still call in a few favors at the H-Home Office. One chap in particular owes me his life." He patted Mary's hand and gently moved it to the small, but visible, outline of the baby nestling inside her.

• • •

Six weeks before their own baby was due to be born, Mary and Jeremy signed the adoption papers that would legally make Anna their own child.

"No one can touch her now, darling. Or take you or her away from m-me," he'd whispered softly into her ear.

Mary watched with tears in her eyes as Anna danced around the kitchen table with her certificate of adoption.

"Anna Langdon," she mouthed in contentment, and then threw her arms around both of her new parents. "I'm so happy, I can hardly b-breathe!"

The baby arrived, much to Mary's frustration, ten days late, but otherwise without incident. Mary lay in her beautiful bedroom, a baby to her breast, her beloved husband and newly adopted child cooing over both of them. She only wished that time could stand still, wished she could die at this very moment, because she could not feel any greater contentment. The baby, a plump, rosy-cheeked girl they named Sophia, after Mary's favorite saint, was placid and happy. Mary watched with pleasure as Jeremy gently cradled his daughter in his arms.

She noticed how, these days, his stammer was barely discernible when he spoke to her. And the terrible nightmares he'd suffered—waking up screaming and drenched in sweat—were lessening as time passed. Mary had read all she could about shell shock, knew it rarely disappeared, but could at least be controlled by a peaceful and tranquil existence. Jeremy rarely left the house, other than to stroll through Kensington Gardens on his way home from buying *The Times,* but if he did so and they were in a noisy London street, he'd jump every time a horn sounded. Both his stammer and his shaking hands would become more acute for a while afterward. Yet the restrictions placed on their life were not a problem to Mary. As long as her family was calm and content, so was she.

Jeremy took to painting and proved himself a more than adequate artist. When Mary looked at the black darkness of the trenches he reproduced, she shuddered, but she knew it was cathartic for him, an outward expression of all the pain, fear, loss and death he relived every single day of his life.

While Jeremy painted, Mary cared for her growing baby, taking both Anna and Sophia to the park on sunny afternoons, or sometimes up to Piccadilly so that Anna could browse through racks of the clothes she loved. It still amazed Mary that whatever Anna picked out she could purchase for her daughter, with no thought for the amount of money it would cost. She was a woman of substance, married to a wealthy gentleman.

Meanwhile, as the years passed in the tranquil cocoon of their comfortable home, Sophia learned to crawl, toddle, walk and then run through the house. And Anna's passion to achieve her ambition of becoming a ballerina grew apace. One evening, when Sophia had just turned four, Anna, starting to show signs of womanhood at fifteen, came into the kitchen where Mary was preparing supper.

"Mother, have you heard that Ninette de Valois has opened her new ballet school?" she asked.

"No, I hadn't, Anna."

"Can I go, Mother? Audition for her and see if she will teach me? Then perhaps one day I might be accepted into her company and dance at Sadler's Wells. Can you imagine th-that?" Anna sank gracefully into a chair, sighing in sheer pleasure at the thought.

"But I thought you wanted to dance for Diaghilev's *Ballets Russes*?"

"I did, b-but how much better to be part of the first *British* ballet company." Anna stretched out a leg, flipped off her shoe and pointed a highly arched foot. "Can I go, Mother, p-please?"

"Perhaps you should talk to your father and see what he thinks," suggested Mary.

"It would mean I'd be d-dancing all day, with no time for English and arithmetic, but how much more can I learn? I can read and write and add up, which is as about as much as any d-dancer needs to do, surely? And I c-can tell you the dates of the Battle of Hastings, Trafalgar and—"

"Anna," repeated Mary, "go and speak to your daddy."

As Mary had suspected, Jeremy was putty in Anna's convincing hands. It was agreed that she should go to audition for Ninette de Valois, to see if she could win a place at the Sadler's Wells Ballet School.

"It is doubtful that our darling Anna will settle to anything else, until she has at least t-tried this," said Jeremy, secretly proud.

Three days later, Mary accompanied Anna on the bus over to Islington where the Sadler's Wells Royal Ballet School ran its classes. Mary had never been backstage at a theater, and as she was led through the warren of passageways to a small room containing a barre and a piano, she felt both unnerved and excited to be entering a different world. Anna was asked a few questions about her previous training, and then Miss Moreton, the teacher, put her through her paces, first at the barre and then in the center of the room. Mary could not help but marvel at the way Anna had improved over the last few years. She'd always had a natural grace and turnout, but her burgeoning maturity had added a new poise to her movements.

After the last *enchaînement,* Miss Moreton paused as she studied Anna. "You dance like a Russian, and you have the look too. Are you Russian?"

Anna stole an anxious glance over to Mary, who gave a small shrug and shake of her head.

"No. I'm English."

"But she was taught by the Princess Astafieva and Nicholas Legat for a while now," put in Mary nervously, wondering whether this was a plus or a minus.

"Well, it shows in your movements. As I'm sure you know, Anna, we here at Sadler's Wells are of course Russian-influenced, but as the first British ballet company, Miss de Valois is trying to develop our own style. You're raw, but talented. Can you start on Monday?"

Anna's dark eyes, filled with anxiety, lit up with joy. "You mean I'm in?"

"Yes. Now, I'll hand your mother a list of practice clothes you'll need, and you must buy your ballet shoes from Frederick Freed. We'll see you bright and early on Monday morning."

At home that night, there was much cause for celebration. Anna was beside herself with excitement, and the entire family was swept up in it.

"Now you really w-will see me dancing Odette/Odile onstage, Sophia." Anna cooed in delight as she danced her little sister around the kitchen.

"There'll be no stopping her now, darling," Jeremy commented as he lay in bed next to Mary that night. "Let's just hope she can achieve her d-dream."

Over the next five years, it seemed Anna's determination, dedication and natural ability were starting to pay off. She made her debut as the young Master of Treginnis on the stage of the newly opened Sadler's Wells Theatre in Rosebury Avenue. Dressed in a little Lord Fauntleroy suit and wearing a close-cropped wig, Anna's character both opened the ballet and was left alone onstage at the end. Mary, Jeremy and nine-year-old Sophia clapped and cheered as the company took their curtain call. The part was far removed from Anna's dreams of a frothy white tutu, but it meant that Ninette de Valois, the queen of the company, was noticing Anna. Other small parts began to follow, such as one of the four Cygnets in Act II of *Swan Lake* and the Creole girl in *Rio Grande*.

In January 1939, just short of her twenty-first birthday, Anna made her debut as Odette/Odile in *Swan Lake*. The Sadler's Wells Theatre was packed—this was the first time that homegrown talent from England, rather than imported or exiled Russian dancers, would lead the cast of the British company. Word about Anna and her talent had started to spread through the balletomane world. Mary, in a new evening dress, with her hair professionally styled for the occasion, sat with Jeremy and Sophia in a box. The strains of Tchaikovsky's poignant overture hushed the audience to silence. Mary held her breath, sending up a prayer that this moment, so long dreamed of by Anna, would be perfect for her.

Mary had no cause to doubt. As the bouquets rained onto the stage to crown the rising young star, she held Jeremy's hand tightly and tears rolled down her face. The dressing room afterward was packed with well-wishers, and Mary could hardly get through to congratulate her daughter. Anna, still in her tutu, her eyes huge with heavy stage makeup, made her way through to her family and threw her arms around her mother.

"Ah, pet, I'm so proud of you. You said you'd do it and look at you! You have!"

"It's all due to you, Mother." Tears glittered in Anna's eyes. "Thank you," she whispered, "thank you for everything."

Mary looked back on the moment when Anna had achieved her goal with mixed emotions. In retrospect, she realized it was when she had begun to lose her daughter. The world Anna inhabited, full of colorful, artistic characters, with their exotic clothes, strange habits and sexual proclivities, was far removed from Mary's experience. As Anna was proclaimed the young queen of British ballet, and others gathered around her to bask in her reflected glory, she began to move away from the cocoon of her Kensington home.

Mary had always waited up for Anna to arrive home after a performance, wanting to hear how it had gone and provide cocoa and biscuits for her exhausted daughter. Now, often, she wouldn't hear Anna's footsteps on the stairs until three in the morning. Anna would talk the next day of a posttheater dinner with her friends at the Savoy Grill, or dancing at a fashionable nightclub with no less than junior members of the royal family.

Mary no longer had control over her daughter's life. And, as Anna was now earning a good wage of her own, she could not complain about some of the daring dresses she wore—often without a corset—or the amount of red paint she applied to her lips. She was aware from the number of bouquets that were delivered to their home that Anna had a stream of male admirers. Whether there was one in particular, Mary didn't know. Any inquiries made in this direction were always stonewalled.

When Mary complained to Jeremy that Anna's social life was a worryingly unknown quantity, especially the male element of it, Jeremy would comfort her gently. "My dear, Anna is a young and very b-beautiful woman. She is also a star. She will behave as she wishes."

"That's as may be," Mary commented irritably one evening, "but I'm not happy about the smell of cigarette smoke that drifts into our bedroom in the small hours. And I know she's drinking."

"Smoking and the occasional gin are hardly crimes, Mary. Especially for a young woman who is under so much pressure to give of her best every night."

Mary turned and eyed him, frustrated that Jeremy always seemed to be on Anna's side. "I worry for her, that's all. The crowd she runs with . . ."

"I know, darling, but she's a b-big girl now. And you have to let her go."

The tension between Mary and Anna came to a head a few weeks later, when Anna decided to invite, unannounced, a posse of her friends back home after the performance. The sound of Cole Porter on the gramophone and the shrieks of laughter from Anna's guests in the drawing room kept both Mary and Jeremy awake until the early hours. The following day, determined to speak to Anna and lay down some ground rules, Mary knocked on Anna's door and entered the bedroom. Anna was fast asleep. So was the young man lying in bed beside her. Breathless and choking with horror, Mary slammed the door behind her and left the room.

Ten minutes later, Anna appeared downstairs in the kitchen in her robe. She smiled sheepishly at her mother, who was crashing breakfast plates into the sink. "I'm sorry if I kept you awake last night. I should have asked. It was late and I th-thought—"

"Never mind about that! What was . . . *who* was . . ." Mary could not bring herself to voice the words.

"You mean Michael?" Anna pulled her cigarettes from the pocket of her robe, lit one and perched gracefully on the edge of the table. "He's my d-dancing partner, Mother. And we are . . . lovers." She took a drag of her cigarette. "You don't mind, d-do you? After all, I am over twenty-one now."

"*Mind?* Of course I mind! *You* might live in a world where that kind of behavior is acceptable, but you have a sister of ten years old. And while you're under my roof, you will behave with some common courtesy. What were you thinking of, Anna? Sophia could have walked into your bedroom at any time and seen—*him*!"

"I'm sorry, Mother." Anna shrugged. "I mean, the world has changed, and these d-days, no one minds about se—"

"*Don't* even say the word!" Mary shuddered. "How could you even think of being so *brazen*? You should be ashamed of yourself! And I'm ashamed that I failed you, that I brought you up to believe that kind of behavior wasn't a sin!"

"Mother, you're sounding awfully p-parochial, and rather Catholic and—"

"Don't you *dare* talk to me like that, my girl! I don't care how big a star you are on the stage, when you're under my roof you abide by our rules! And I will not have"—Mary pointed upward to the ceiling—"*that* kind of shenanigans beneath it!"

Anna sat calmly, smoking her cigarette. Mary watched as the ash fell to the floor and Anna made no move to prevent it. Eventually, Anna nodded. "All right, Mother, I understand. And if you d-don't approve of my life, well, I'm a big girl now, with my own income. Maybe it's time I found my own roof."

Without another word, Anna removed herself from the kitchen, slamming the door behind her.

A day later, she packed her suitcases and moved out.

Jeremy tried to comfort his wife, assuring her that Anna's behavior was normal for a young girl in the modern age. A girl who was not only finding her feet as an adult, but was increasingly fêted by an adoring public. Despite the sense in what Jeremy said, Mary struggled to come to terms with Anna's abrupt departure.

In the following weeks, Anna made no attempt to contact her mother. Anything Mary heard of her was gleaned through the many newspaper articles and gossip columns, of which Anna seemed to be a regular feature. She was pictured with stars of stage and screen at glittering gatherings, and on the arm of various aristocratic men. The shy little girl who Mary had sacrificed so much to rescue had turned into a creature she did not know or understand. And yet . . . Mary acknowledged there had always been a rod of steel running through her daughter. Whatever Anna had wanted, she'd usually achieved. The fact she was now at the top of her chosen profession was testament to that. And the ease with which Anna had cut her mother, her father and her sister so completely from her life, illustrated a hitherto unseen callousness.

However, as the storm clouds of war gathered over Europe again, Mary had problems enough under her own roof. Jeremy, who had come so far from when she had first met him, began to have nightmares again. The tremor in his hands and the stutter became more pronounced. Every morning he would read *The Times* and his face would grow gray. His appetite diminished and Mary watched as he withdrew into himself. No matter how many times she told him that if there was war, no army would want him, Jeremy's fear of returning to his nemesis grew apace.

"Y-You d-don't understand, Mary. They may not want me initially, but as they grow desperate for ca-cannon fodder they'll take anyone to throw at the Krauts. Believe me, I've seen it, men older than me thrown over the top to keep the n-numbers up."

"Jeremy, pet, it's in your medical records that you suffered from shell shock. Of course they won't want you back."

"I was sent b-back to the t-trenches four times, Mary. In a far worse state than I am t-today." He shook his head despairingly. "You can't understand war, Mary. Please don't t-try."

"But everyone says it'll be different this time. There won't be trenches, pet," she entreated time and again. "This war, if it comes, will be fought with the new modern equipment that's been developed. No one in their right minds will be after losing a whole generation of men like last time. Please, Jeremy, things have changed."

Jeremy would stand up, anger, frustration and fear plain on his face, and leave the room.

As the news became worse and the inevitability of another war became more certain by the day, Mary keened inside for her husband. Jeremy no longer joined his wife and daughter in the kitchen for supper, preferring to eat alone in his study.

"What's wrong with Papa?" Sophia would ask as Mary tucked her up for the night.

"Nothing, pet, he's just not feeling himself at the moment," Mary would comfort.

"Will there be war? Is that why Papa is so worried?" she'd question, her huge green eyes, so like her daddy's, staring up at Mary from the pillow.

"Perhaps. But if there is, there is. Don't you be worrying, pet. Your daddy and I lived through the last one to tell the tale, and we'll do it again."

"But everything's different now, Mother. Anna's gone, and Papa feels . . ." Sophia sighed. "As if he's gone too. Nothing is the same as it was. I'm scared, Mother, I don't like it."

Mary would hold her daughter in her arms, stroking her hair, just as she had held Anna long ago, and murmur soothing words she no longer believed.

The summer dragged on, and signs of preparation for impending war began to appear in the city. Mary felt as if the entire country was in a state of suspended animation, holding their breath for the inevitable. Jeremy was catatonic. He had even moved out of their bedroom and now slept in his dressing room, citing the fact that his nightmares were disturbing Mary's sleep. Brow furrowed with anxiety, Mary begged him to contact his old regiment and allay his fears.

"You were invalided out, pet. There's no chance they're going to want you. Please, Jeremy, write a letter and put your mind at rest. At least once you've heard for definite, it will make you feel better."

But Jeremy would sit there in his chair in the study, staring out into the distance and not hearing her.

When war was announced at the beginning of September, Mary felt a sense of relief. Perhaps now, they'd all know where they were. Ten days later, Mary was lying in bed reading a book when there was a knock on the door.

"M-May I c-come in?" Jeremy asked.

"Of course you can. For pity's sake, this is your bedroom." Mary watched Jeremy as he shambled over toward her. He'd lost considerable weight and his face was as gaunt and drawn as when she'd first met him. He sat down on the bed next to her and took her hands in his.

"Mary, I w-wanted to tell you that I l-love you. You and Anna and Sophia have made my l-life worth l-living."

"And you mine," said Mary gently.

"I'm s-sorry for being d-difficult in the past f-few weeks. I won't be anymore, I p-promise."

"I understand, pet. I hope that now it has begun, you'll start to feel better."

"Yes." The word was no more than a whisper. Jeremy reached forward and took Mary into his arms. "I l-lo-love you, my darling. N-never f-forget that, will you?"

"I won't."

"Be as strong and b-brave and kind as you've always been." He released her, kissed her on the lips and smiled at her. "W-would you mind if I s-slept in here w-with you tonight? I don't w-want to be alone."

"My love," replied Mary tenderly, "this is your bed and I am your wife."

So Jeremy climbed in next to her and Mary held her husband in her arms, stroking his hair, until she heard the telltale signs of his regular breathing. Unable to sleep herself, she watched over Jeremy. And, only in the early hours, when she was content he was sleeping deeply and peacefully, did she let herself sleep too.

22

The following morning, Mary left Jeremy in bed and went downstairs to make breakfast for Sophia. The two of them left the house at eight fifteen to make the ten-minute walk to Sophia's school, just off the Brompton Road.

"Have a good day, pet, and I'll be here as usual to collect you afterward."

Mary watched as Sophia turned away from her and headed into school. The day was sunny and bright, and as Mary walked toward the row of shops where she routinely bought her meat and vegetables, she felt more cheerful than she had for a while. At least Jeremy had communicated with her last night and had seemed calmer. Even though this new war promised to be hell all over again, Mary knew that as long as she and Jeremy clung to each other, everything would be all right. She lingered for longer than normal, listening to the other women chattering to the butcher about the likelihood of rationing, and when the Germans would begin to bomb London in earnest. Whatever came, Mary thought as she made her way home, she and Jeremy could face it together.

There was no sign of her husband when she arrived at the house. But this was not unusual; Jeremy took a stroll out in the mornings to buy a newspaper, and would then meander through Kensington Gardens on his way home.

Mary went about her usual chores, thinking how many would feel it strange that she preferred to do the menial work herself when it was entirely possible to employ someone to do it for her. She had dismissed the housekeeper when she'd first wed Jeremy, feeling uncomfortable under what she had perceived as a patronizing eye, and had only a daily maid to help her run the big house. But there was still a pleasure and a joy in providing a neat, clean, well-run home for her husband and child.

At midday, when she had prepared a light lunch for Jeremy and herself, but had not heard the key turn in the front-door lock, Mary wondered if exhaustion had caught up with him, and he was still sleeping where she'd left him.

"Jeremy? Jeremy?" she called as she went from room to room downstairs. Jeremy's study was empty, as was the drawing room, the library and the dining room. An edge of panic filled Mary. One of the ways in which Jeremy had survived since his ordeal was with routine. It was unheard of for him not to be in for lunch at the appointed hour. She climbed the stairs with a sense of foreboding, pushed open the door to their bedroom and saw the bed was empty.

"Where are you, pet? Are you here?" she called as she walked along the landing toward his dressing room. She knocked on the door and received no answer, so she opened it.

It took a while for her eyes to adjust to what she saw. A pair of highly polished shoes dangled in front of her nose. She looked up, and saw the rest of his body attached by a rope to the light fitting above him.

After the doctor had arrived, pronounced Jeremy dead and called for the police to come and cut his body down, Jeremy was laid on the bed. Mary sat with him, unable to stop herself from stroking his pale, gray skin. Catatonic with shock, she couldn't process what had happened.

"Do you have any reason to suggest why Mr. Langdon might have taken his own life, madam?" the policeman asked.

Mary, holding her dead husband's hand, nodded. "Perhaps."

"I'm sorry to ask these questions at what is a very difficult time for you, madam, but I'd be grateful if you could elucidate. And then we won't have to bother you again."

"He"—Mary cleared her constricted throat—"he thought he was to be called up again. He suffered from shell shock, you see."

"And was he? To be called up?"

"He'd been invalided out of the army after the last war. I told him, over and over, they wouldn't want him, but"—Mary shook her head in despair—"he wouldn't believe me."

"I see. If it's any comfort, madam, my uncle was the same way.

Nothing you could do or say would take away the fear. You mustn't blame yourself."

"No. But I do . . . *I do* . . ."

The doorbell rang downstairs. "That's probably the ambulance, madam, come to take your husband away. I'll pop downstairs and let them in. While I do that, would you be kind enough to check your husband for anything you might wish to keep?"

Mary nodded. She watched as the policeman left the room then slowly laid her head on Jeremy's chest. "Oh, my darling, why did you have to leave me and Sophia? Could you not have trusted us to help you make it better? I loved you, pet, with all my heart. Didn't you know that? Couldn't you feel it?"

Mary shook her head despairingly into the silence, understanding he would never answer her again. As the policeman had requested, she removed his watch, then moved her hands inside Jeremy's pockets, searching out anything that might be there. Her hands felt paper in the left-hand pocket, and she pulled out an envelope. Sitting up, she saw the words *On His Majesty's Service* in the left corner. It was similar to the brown envelope Sean had received when he'd been called up for duty in the Irish Guards.

Mary turned it over and saw that it was unopened. Slowly, she tore the paper and pulled out the letter, knowing now what had caused her husband to take his own life.

Army Pensions Department

5th October 1939

Dear Mr. Langdon,

This is to inform you that your army pension will be rising from £5.15s a month to £6.2s. This will be effective from January 1940.

Yours sincerely,

The stamped signature at the bottom was illegible.

The letter fell from Mary's hands as she laid her head back down on her husband's chest and wept as if her heart would break.

• • •

Mary and Sophia alone attended Jeremy's funeral. Mary had no idea of the whereabouts of Jeremy's parents. More painful still was the absence of Anna, whom Mary had written to and informed.

All that got Mary through the dark month of October was Sophia and her need for comfort. Mary thought it was a blessing she didn't have time to focus on herself. For she too might have chosen the same way out as Jeremy, so deep was her pain. She also knew there were things she must investigate soon. For example, Jeremy had provided her each week with an amount of housekeeping money. She was currently using her own savings from the days she had been in service. And although there was no likelihood of their running out in the near future and she could always resort to dressmaking again, she had no idea where she stood in terms of the house, or whether she had been provided for in his will.

The situation was made clear for her a week later, when the doorbell rang and a balding gentleman, dressed in black, doffed his bowler hat to her.

"Mrs. Langdon, I presume?"

"And who may be asking?" said Mary suspiciously.

"Sidney Chellis, of Chellis and Latimer, Solicitors. I've been sent here by Lord and Lady Langdon, your late husband's parents, to discuss a business matter. May I come in?"

Wearily, Mary nodded. As she led him to the drawing room, she realized Jeremy had never said he was the son of a lord. Or, in fact, much about his family at all.

"Please, sit down. May I get you some tea?" she asked him.

"That will not be necessary. What I have come to say should not take very long." The solicitor was pulling some papers out of his briefcase, which he placed on his knee.

Mary sat down nervously opposite him. "Have I . . . done anything wrong?"

"No, Mrs. Langdon, you are certainly not in any trouble. That I am aware of anyway." He looked over his glasses at her and raised his eyebrows. "You know, I'm sure, that your husband made a will, leaving this house, his war pension and his private income to you?"

"No, Mr. Chellis, I have not so far thought to investigate the matter. I've been too occupied with grief," Mary replied truthfully.

"Well, he lodged his will with our firm, who have been the Langdon family's solicitors for over sixty years. However, there is one small problem."

"And what might that be?"

"This house was originally given to Mr. Langdon's godmother by his grandfather. It has been in the Langdon family since it was built, two hundred years ago. The codicil in his godmother's will indicates that your husband was to have use of the house for his lifetime. But on his death, it would return to the Langdon family."

"I see," said Mary quietly.

"Now, you and Mr. Langdon have produced one child. A girl named"—Mr. Chellis consulted his papers—"Sophia May. Is this correct?"

"Yes."

"And she is currently ten years old?"

"That is correct."

"The problem we have here," and Mr. Chellis removed his glasses and wiped them on his waistcoat, "is that, put simply, Sophia is a girl. When she marries, she will take her husband's name. And if, say, Sophia and her husband were to divorce, or in fact Sophia herself was to die, there would be a problem keeping the house in the Langdon family. Are you following what I am saying?"

"Yes, Mr. Chellis. Unfortunately I am."

"I must tell you that, in the eyes of the law, if you wished to challenge the codicil in the will, it might be possible that a court would uphold it. After all, you are Mr. Langdon's widow, and you have his progeny. However, this would be a costly business and"—Mr. Chellis visibly shuddered—"quite undignified. Therefore, Lord and Lady Langdon have made a suggestion. In return for your vacant possession of this house, they are prepared to offer you a substantial sum in compensation. And, on top of that, as a gesture for relinquishing the rights to your late husband's private income, a substantial settlement would be made on the head of your daughter, Sophia."

"I see." Mary digested what the solicitor was saying. "So, Mr.

Chellis, the truth is that Lord and Lady Langdon wish for myself and my daughter to be out of their lives, like their son?"

"I wouldn't put it quite like that, Mrs. Langdon. It is obviously unfortunate there has been an estrangement between Lord and Lady Langdon and their son, but that is not for me, as their solicitor, to comment on. The settlement they have suggested in return for the house is a sum of one thousand, five hundred pounds. On top of which, the sum of five thousand pounds will be made in favor of Sophia."

Mary listened silently. As she had little idea of what the house was worth or, in fact, what Jeremy's private income would amount to, she could not comment on whether what she was being offered was fair. Besides, the whole business brought bile to her throat.

"I have set the offer down here for you to consider. My address and telephone number are at the top of it. When you have thought about it and made a decision, I'd be grateful if you would contact me directly."

"And what about Lord and Lady Langdon? Do they not wish to see their granddaughter?" she mused, almost to herself. "After all, Sophia is their flesh and blood."

"As I indicated earlier, Mrs. Langdon, I am simply the messenger. Certainly, it was not indicated to me that they wished to meet Sophia."

"No . . . of course not." Mary raised her eyes and stared at Mr. Chellis. "After all, the child of an Irish nursemaid wouldn't be acceptable to the gentry, now would she?"

Mr. Chellis lowered his eyes in embarrassment. He busied himself with replacing his papers inside his briefcase. "As I indicated, if you would be so kind as to contact me when you've made your decision, I will see to it that the arrangements are made." He rose and nodded to her. "Thank you for seeing me, and I fervently hope that all can be worked out to the satisfaction of both parties."

Mary followed him silently to the door. "Good-bye, Mr. Chellis, I'll be in touch when I've had the time to think on your offer."

Over the next few days, Mary began to make some inquiries about her late husband's mysterious family. She discovered that Jeremy was the second son of Lord and Lady Langdon, whose family estate stood in five hundred acres of Surrey countryside and was known for its plentiful pheasant and duck shoot. And a collection of valuable Holbein paintings. Mary also investigated how much the house she currently called her home would be worth if she placed it up for sale.

Even though the process was painful, Mary's thoughts were simply for Sophia. And what was rightfully hers as Jeremy's daughter. A few years ago, she'd have turned her back on any offer, but Mary was older and wiser now, and understood clearly how the world worked. And on behalf of her child, however much what amounted to blackmail galled her, she knew she must see it through.

Mary also knew that what she had done in the past precluded any thought of fighting Jeremy's family in court. Who knew where it might lead if the case reached the newspapers? What if someone from the past recognized her and her connection with Anna? And put two and two together . . .

Mr. Chellis's office was in Chancery Lane. Mary presented herself in front of his secretary and sat, waiting to be shown in, steeling herself to keep her nerves and emotions under control.

"Mrs. Langdon." Mr. Chellis appeared at the door of his office. "Please step inside and come and sit down."

"Thank you." Mary followed him in and sat on the edge of an uncomfortable leather chair. "I have thought about your offer, Mr. Chellis." Mary gathered her strength to say the words. "And if you are prepared to double the amount I will receive in lieu of my home, I will accept it."

Mr. Chellis hardly raised an eyebrow. As Mary had suspected, this had been expected.

"I shall have to consult with Lord and Lady Langdon, but I think somewhere in that region may well be acceptable to them. You would obviously be asked to sign a legal document, negating all rights to your husband's will. *And* any claim Sophia might make in the future on the Langdon estate."

"I understand that." Mary stood up, not wishing to prolong this pact with the devil any longer than she had to. "I'll wait to hear from you. Good day, Mr. Chellis."

• • •

Two months later, Mary stood in the entrance hall of her home and took one last glance around the house in which she had enjoyed such happiness. The car would arrive at any moment, and the two trunks which held clothes for herself and her daughter, plus a third trunk full of mementoes, would follow on behind them. Mary sat down on the bottom stair, feeling drained of energy. She comforted herself that even had she been able to stay here in the house, it was unlikely she would have done so. Every sight, every smell inside these walls, reminded her of what she had lost.

She saw Sophia walking down the stairs toward her and held out her arms for her daughter. Sophia went into them and Mary stroked her hair. "All set?"

"Yes." Sophia nodded. "I'm scared, Mother."

"I know you are, pet. But it's for the best. I've spent one war already in London town, and they say this time the bombs will be far worse."

"I know, Mother. But—"

There was a knock on the front door. "The car's here, sweetheart." Mary released her from her arms, then smiled at her and took her hand. Together, they walked slowly to the front door, both saying a silent good-bye to the life they were leaving behind. Mary led her outside and into the car.

It was time to go home.

Aurora

Oh dear. It's probably not done for authors to cry at their own stories, but I find Mary and Jeremy's tale so dreadfully sad. They loved each other so much yet, at the end, not even love could win through and make it better. Sometimes, as I am learning on my voyage through my history, love cannot overcome the terrible wounds inflicted on a person by the past. If only Jeremy had opened that envelope, had seen it contained a raise in his army pension, not his call-up papers . . .

If only.

Well. I suppose one could say that about everything in life . . . especially mine.

But then, if Jeremy had opened that envelope, the rest of my story would be very different, and perhaps not worth writing. I'm starting to understand how pain gives you strength and wisdom—I have certainly changed—and is as much a part of life as happiness. Everything has its natural balance, and how would you know you were happy if you weren't sad sometimes? Or feel healthy if you were never ill?

I've been thinking about the concept of "time" recently. Mary and Jeremy had a moment in time together when they were exquisitely happy. And perhaps those moments are as much as we humans can hope for. As is always the way in fairy tales, bad has to happen as well as good. We human beings survive on hope that those good moments will come again. And when all hope of that has disappeared, like Jeremy's did, what is there left?

To be truthful, I am currently struggling to hold on to mine. I have little left.

But where there's life . . .

Anyway, enough of me. I'm going to move back to more modern times now, after Grania has been told her great-grandmother's story by Kathleen. And I was taken down to Dunworley Farmhouse for the first time . . .

23

Dunworley, West Cork, Ireland

So, I presume 'home' was Ireland?" Grania was sitting at the kitchen table in her parents' house, nursing a mug of tea. She'd decided to bring Aurora down to the farmhouse and, at the same time, ask Kathleen what more she knew of Mary's story.

"Yes. Mary came back with Sophia and bought a pretty cottage in Clonakilty."

"And never married again?"

"No." Kathleen shook her head. "From what my mother told me, Mary had enough heartbreak in London town to last a lifetime."

"But the connection with the Ryan family continued?"

"Yes, and there's irony there, to be sure," agreed Kathleen. "Of course, it wasn't Mary who ended up marrying Sean, but her *daughter,* Sophia, who married Seamus Doonan, the son of Sean's younger sister, Coleen, and had me!"

"Oh my goodness, Mam!" Grania listened in amazement. "So, Bridget and Michael Ryan were your great-grandparents? And if he had lived, Sean would have been your great-uncle?"

"Yes. Coleen moved into the new farmhouse that had been originally built for Sean and Mary, when she married Owen, my grandfather. Then they handed it over to their son, Seamus, who married my mammy, Sophia. And when my daddy died, me and your father took up the reins on the farm," explained Kathleen.

"So your mother, Sophia, had English blood in her, and titled blood at that?" added Grania. "Your other grandfather was Jeremy Langdon?"

"Yes. Which means you and Shane do too." Katheen's eyes twinkled. "There now, not such an Irish peasant as you thought yourself, Grania! Not that you'd ever have noticed it in Sophia. My mammy was just like her mother, Mary: kind, home-loving, not an air or grace upon her. Not like that adopted sister of hers, that Anna."

Grania read the timbre in Kathleen's voice and watched her face darken.

"Did you know her?" Grania asked in surprise. "I thought she and Mary were estranged?"

Kathleen sat down heavily at the table. "Well, Grania, pet, there's more to this tale yet. Haven't you put two and two together?"

"No." Grania shook her head. "Should I have done?"

"Being up at Dunworley House, I thought you might. There's enough clues around the old place. Well now, the—"

At that moment, Aurora entered through the back door, one of the newborn collie pups cradled in her arms. "Oh, Grania! Mrs. Ryan!" Aurora's eyes were shining with happiness as she looked down at the pup. "She is adorable! And Shane says I can be the one to name her! I thought Lily, after my mother. What do you think?"

Grania saw the expression on her mother's face, but ignored it. "I think that would be perfect."

"Good." Aurora planted a kiss on the top of the newly christened pup's head. "There wouldn't be a chance, I mean a possibility that . . ."

"We'd have to ask your father first, Aurora." Grania read her mind. "Besides, Lily's not ready to be taken from her mother just yet."

"But can I come down and see her every day?" Aurora begged. "Can I, Mrs. Ryan?"

"I . . ."

Grania could see her mother grudgingly softening in the face of such an engaging and excited little girl.

"Well now, I don't see why not."

"Thank you!" Aurora walked up to her and planted a kiss on Kathleen's cheek. She sighed with pleasure. "I love it here at your house. It feels like a proper . . ." Aurora searched for the word. "Home."

"Thank you, Aurora." Kathleen's last shred of reserve crumbled. "And what will you two be doing for your tea tonight, then?"

"We hadn't really got that far, had we, Aurora?" said Grania.

"Then why don't you both stay here and have it with us?"

"Yippee! That means I can stay longer with Lily. I'm going back to see Shane now. He said he'd take me into the milking shed."

Grania and Kathleen watched Aurora as she returned outside.

"Despite how you feel about the Lisles, you have to admit that Aurora is a lovely little girl," Grania ventured carefully.

"You're right." Kathleen banged the table and stood up, heading for the pile of potatoes waiting to be peeled. "It's nothing to do with her, poor little pet. How are her nightmares?" she asked Grania as she took a knife from the drawer and began peeling.

"She seems better. No more night wanderings at least. Mam . . ." Grania wanted to lead the conversation back. "When you asked me if I had put two and two together before Aurora came in, I—"

It was her father's turn to interrupt. "Make me a brew, Kathleen, I've a raging thirst on me," John said as he strode into the kitchen.

"You be going upstairs for a shower while I do it." Kathleen wrinkled her nose. "You smell of cow and you know I can't stand it."

"I will, pet," John said as he planted a kiss on Kathleen's head to annoy her. "And I'll be back down smelling of roses for that tea."

That evening, Grania did not get another chance to talk to her mother further about the past, but instead enjoyed the sight of Aurora sitting at the table with the Ryans and questioning them eagerly on all aspects of living on a farm.

"I think I'd like to be a farmer if I can't be a ballerina," she commented to Grania as they walked up the cliff path on their way to the house. "I love animals."

"Have you ever had a pet of your own?"

"No. Mummy didn't like animals. She said they smell."

"Well, I suppose they do a bit," agreed Grania.

"But humans do too," Aurora said equably as they arrived in the darkened kitchen and Grania put the lights on.

"Right, madam. Straight upstairs for you. It's late."

Once Aurora was settled for the night, Grania—still thinking about Mary, her great-grandmother, and what a remarkable woman she had sounded—prowled around the house, unable to settle. Still unaware of what the connection to the Lisles was, and what, in her mother's words, she had not yet put together, there was something that was pricking at the back of her consciousness. Some fact she could not place, which would tie the strands together. It was not in the drawing room, or the library, or Alexander's study . . . Grania opened the door to the dining room, remembering the one night she'd spent having dinner with Alexander in it.

And there, hanging over the fireplace, was the answer. When she'd sat here before, she'd barely glanced at it, but it had obviously stuck in her memory. An oil painting of a ballerina in a white tutu, swansdown gracing her dark head. Her arms crossed over her legs, her face invisible as it rested on her knees. At the bottom of the painting, the words read: ANNA LANGDON AS "*THE DYING SWAN*."

"Anna Langdon . . ." Grania said the name out loud. This was the connection she had missed. The reason her mother had mentioned that Aurora had inherited her talent from her grandmother.

Grania climbed the stairs an hour later, unable to confirm her theory as the face of the dancer in the painting was hidden. But if it was the same as the dark-eyed woman in the black-and-white photographs strewn around the house, Grania knew she'd made the connection.

At breakfast the next morning, Grania asked casually, "Aurora, did you ever meet your grandmother?"

Aurora shook her head. "Mummy said she died before I was born. Granny was quite old when she had Mummy, you see."

"Can you remember her name?"

"Of course I can!" Aurora was insulted at the question. "Her name was Anna, and once upon a time she was a ballerina. Just like I'm going to be."

Back at the farmhouse that afternoon, with Aurora happily up on the hills counting sheep with Shane, Grania tackled her mother again.

"So, Mam, how did it happen that Anna Langdon and Lawrence Lisle's younger brother, Sebastian, met and got married? I'm right, aren't I? Anna Langdon, famous ballerina, became Anna Lisle? Lily's mother and Aurora's grandmother?"

"Yes." Kathleen nodded. "She did. You can't really ask me the ins and outs, Grania, because I was no more than a baby when they married. Even though I met her, I can only guess at what happened before that. And there was no love lost between my mother and her sister, so my mammy hardly spoke of it."

"But why did Anna follow her mother and sister to Ireland? When she'd obviously become so famous?"

"Well now, you have to remember that Anna was in her late thirties when she came home to Ireland to roost. And all ballerinas and beauties have a shelf life, don't they?" Kathleen added pragmatically.

"Do you remember her at all, Mam?"

"Oh, I remember her." Kathleen's busy hands paused on the pastry she was rolling. "For a child like me, brought up in this small place, Aunt Anna seemed like a movie star. The first time I met her, she was dressed in a coat of real fur. I remember the softness against my face, when she hugged me . . . and then she took it off, to sit down and have a brew in our front room. She had the tiniest figure on her I'd ever seen. And heels that seemed the height of mountains to me. And then she lit a black cigarette." Kathleen sighed. "How could I ever forget her?"

"So, she was beautiful?"

"She was . . . a presence . . . a force of nature. And it's hardly surprising that the first time old Sebastian Lisle set eyes on her, he fell passionately in love with her."

"How old was he?"

"He would have been sixty or so. A widower, who had married late to begin with. Adele, his first wife, was thirty years younger than him. She died giving birth to . . . *that boy*."

"Sebastian had a son already?"

"Yes," Kathleen shuddered. "His name was Gerald."

"So Anna and Sebastian Lisle married?"

"They did so."

"What was Anna wanting with an old man after the life she'd led, Mam?" pondered Grania.

"Who knows? Money, maybe. My mam always said Anna was a terrible spendthrift, enjoying the life of luxury. As for Himself, he must have thought all his Christmases had arrived at once in the shape of Anna. They married within three months of their first glance of each other."

"The brother of Anna's guardian, Lawrence . . ." mused Grania. "Did Sebastian know who Anna was?"

"Oh, yes," Kathleen continued, "they both thought it a huge joke that Anna had been presumed dead for all these years."

"But what about Mary? Didn't the fact that Anna came to Ireland cause a problem for her?"

"Well now, when Anna turned up in Ireland at Mary's cottage, then met Sebastian a while later, Mary knew she had to be telling her what she'd done to protect her when she was younger," said Kathleen. "'Twas for all the right reasons she did it—who knows what would have become of Anna if Mary hadn't intervened? Anna knew that without Mary's telling Lawrence Lisle she was dead and taking her in, she'd not have had the chance to pursue her ballet career."

"And Mary forgave her daughter for not contacting her for all those years?"

"Well, after what they'd been through together in London, there was a bond. And you've already heard how Mary loved Anna as her own. She'd have forgiven her anything. My mammy, Sophia, was the one who took it hardest. She referred to Anna as 'the prodigal daughter.'"

"Perhaps she was jealous of their bond," said Grania.

"I'm sure that was in there somewhere, yes. But at least they were reconciled before Mary died. And after what she'd done to help Anna in the early days, my grandmother deserved that, so she did. And I can tell you, Grania, that fresh flowers appeared without fail on Mary's grave up at Dunworley church every week, and only stopped the very day after Anna herself died. 'Twas her way of saying sorry and that she loved the woman she'd always called 'Mother.'"

The thought of this gesture brought a sudden, unbidden lump to Grania's throat and warmed her a little toward Anna.

"Sebastian decided not to take action against Mary for stealing Anna away from his brother all those years ago?" she asked.

"Whatever Anna told him about the situation was enough. And besides, Lawrence Lisle was long dead and the past was the past. As far as Sebastian was concerned, Mary had cared for the love of his life and that was all that mattered. I swear, Grania, I've never seen a man so blinded by love for a woman."

Grania struggled to take it all in. "Then Lily was born?"

"Yes, Lily was born. God save us all," Kathleen muttered.

"And the three of them lived up at Dunworley House happily ever after?"

"Hardly," Kathleen snorted. "Do you really think Anna Langdon was going to be content to play mammy to a baby and a three-year-old stepson, shut away in a crumbling house on the edge of the world?" Kathleen shook her head. "No. A nursemaid was engaged for the baby, and Aunt Anna took off a few months later. She'd say she had to go for one of her ballet performances, and disappear for weeks. My mammy was sure there were other men she saw too."

"So Lily grew up virtually motherless, and Sebastian Lisle a lonely cuckold?"

"That's about the size of it, yes. And you've never seen a man more miserable than Sebastian. He used to come down to see us here with Lily. He'd sit at the table, and ask my mother if she'd heard from her sister. I was only five at the time, but I still remember his face . . . 'twas a picture of despair. It was as if he was enchanted by her, the poor, deluded old man. And when Aunt Anna turned up from wherever she'd been—sometimes after months away—he'd always forgive her."

"And what about Lily? What kind of life must she have had—an aging father and an absent mother?"

Kathleen's face closed suddenly. "Enough of this talk now! I don't want to discuss it anymore. What about you, Grania? What about your future?" she retaliated. "Aurora's father will be home here soon enough and you'll not be needed there when he comes back."

"Like you don't want to discuss the past, I'm not that keen on discussing the future." Grania stood up as mother and daughter reached deadlock in the conversation. "I'll be off up to my room to collect a couple of bits and pieces to take up to Dunworley House before Aurora comes back with Shane."

"As you want," said Kathleen to Grania's disappearing figure. She sighed, feeling drained by thoughts of the past, and knowing that the telling of the story wasn't yet over. But she'd told enough for now, and besides . . . she didn't feel strong enough to talk of the rest. And maybe she never would.

"Ah now, darlin'." John entered the kitchen and put his arms around her. "Where's that brew?"

Aurora

I feel I must intervene here . . . things were going well until I realized that if I was reading this, I would be utterly confused. It is complicated. So, for your comfort, I shall resort to a family tree.

Well! That took me longer to work out than writing the three chapters before it. I hope it helps explain things.

I'm worried you may feel it's all too coincidental. But actually, it isn't at all. We—the Ryans and the Lisles—lived in a tiny, isolated community on the edge of the world. We've been neighbors for hundreds of years, so I don't think it's surprising our lives and our subsequent histories became entwined.

I admit to finding the compiling of the tree difficult. I know that soon, I too will have the second date entered and become part of the past, not the present. It also struck me that we humans behave as though we are immortal, taking decisions as though we will live forever, with no acceptance of the inevitable, which comes to us all. Of course, it is the only way we can survive.

I feel it's time to move away from Ireland and the past now, and look to the future, to America. The land of hope, where dreams can come true, where anything is possible.

Reader, this is my kind of country!

They believe in magic, like I do, because they are a young race, still to learn the wisdom and cynicism that comes with experience.

So, let us find out how Matt is getting on . . .

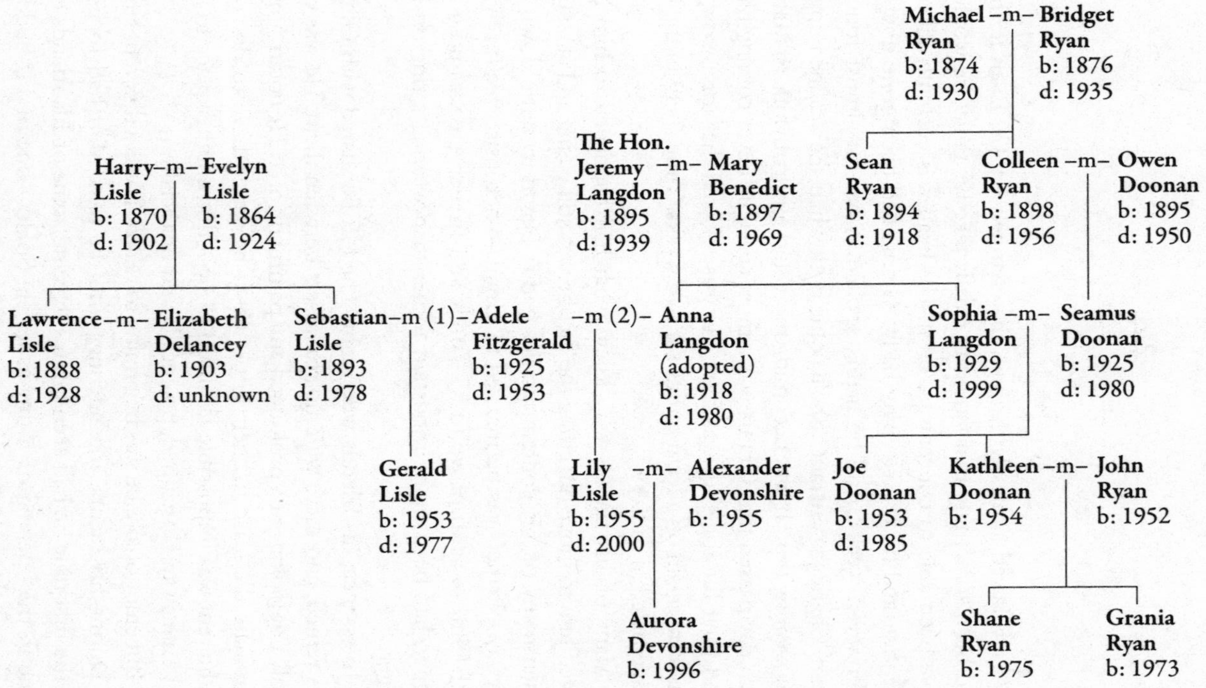
Michael –m– Bridget
Ryan b: 1874 d: 1930
Ryan b: 1876 d: 1935
The Hon. Jeremy Langdon b: 1895 d: 1939
–m– Mary Benedict b: 1897 d: 1969
Sean Ryan b: 1894 d: 1918
Colleen –m– Owen
Ryan b: 1898 d: 1956
Doonan b: 1895 d: 1950
Harry–m– Evelyn
Lisle b: 1870 d: 1902
Lisle b: 1864 d: 1924
Lawrence–m– Elizabeth
Lisle b: 1888 d: 1928
Delancey b: 1903 d: unknown
Sebastian–m (1)– Adele –m (2)– Anna
Lisle b: 1893 d: 1978
Fitzgerald b: 1925 d: 1953
Langdon (adopted) b: 1918 d: 1980
Sophia –m– Seamus
Langdon b: 1929 d: 1999
Doonan b: 1925 d: 1980
Gerald Lisle b: 1953 d: 1977
Lily –m– Alexander
Lisle b: 1955 d: 2000
Devonshire b: 1955
Joe Doonan b: 1953 d: 1985
Kathleen –m– John
Doonan b: 1954
Ryan b: 1952
Aurora Devonshire b: 1996
Shane Ryan b: 1975
Grania Ryan b: 1973

24

Matt flicked aimlessly through the channels on TV. Even if there had been something that would normally take his fancy, he wouldn't have been able to concentrate on it. His head was currently all over the joint and he was sleeping badly. Grania had been gone now for over seven weeks. And he hadn't spoken to her for almost four of them. Charley's constant "She'll come back when she's calmed down" was wearing thin. It was becoming more and more obvious to Matt as each day passed that Grania was almost certainly never coming back. And their life together was over. He was relieved that tomorrow, he was away again on a lecture tour for two weeks. Time spent in the loft exacerbated his misery.

Many of his friends who knew what had happened to him had urged him to move on, citing the fact he was still young and at a stage when many of his contemporaries hadn't begun to settle down yet anyway. Neither was he married to Grania—her insistence on living with him, so as to prove to his family and friends she was no gold-digger, had been more important to her than wearing a ring on her finger.

In essence, his friends were right. The loft he shared with Grania was rented, and there were no real assets between them. He was certainly not looking at a prolonged and painful divorce. He could simply terminate the lease to their loft—which he would have to do soon as the rent was impossible to afford alone—find another place to live and walk away. Unscathed, practically and financially.

But emotionally, he was beginning to realize, it was a different story.

During his mental meanderings into the past, Matt had focused on the first time he had seen Grania. He and some of his friends had gone to the opening of a tiny gallery in SoHo—one of his buddies knew the owner of the gallery and the plan had been to pass by and show their faces, then move uptown for dinner. His crowd had arrived, the girls with them, immaculate as always in their designer jeans and freshly blow-dried hair.

The gallery was crowded and Matt had glanced cursorily at the modern art displayed on its walls; strange daubs that looked as if they'd been painted by toddlers were not really his thing. Then his eyes fell on a small sculpture standing on a plinth in the corner of the room. He moved nearer to inspect it and saw it was a beautifully fashioned swan. His hands were drawn to trace the elegant neck, and the impression of the softness of the swansdown wings the sculptor had managed to create. It appealed to him. It was a beautiful thing. He checked the price and saw it was within his budget. He'd looked for someone who could tell him how to go ahead and purchase it. Having found the gallery owner talking to Al, a buddy of his, he was led over to a desk, where he produced his credit card.

"You have good taste, sir. It's one of my favorite pieces too. I've a hunch its creator is going to go far." The gallery owner had pointed across the room. "That's her right there. Want to meet her?"

Matt's gaze had fallen on the small figure, dressed in a pair of old jeans and a red checked shirt. Her curly blond hair was hanging—possibly unwashed—in an unkempt mass around her shoulders. As the gallery owner called her name, she'd turned around. Matt took in the big turquoise eyes, the retroussé nose with a dash of freckles upon it and the pale pink lips. With her face devoid of makeup, she looked like a child, and her naturalness could not have been in greater contrast to the sophisticated women he'd arrived with.

As the girl acknowledged the gallery owner's signal to come over, Matt had taken in her slim body, her small hips and long legs. This girl was not a beauty, but she had a prettiness and a sparkle in her eyes that Matt instinctively reacted to. As he'd stared at her, he hadn't known whether he wanted to throw his arms around her and protect her, or strip her naked and make love to her.

"Grania, this is Mr. Matt Connelly. He's just bought your swan."

"Hello, Mr. Connelly," she said with a smile, and her cute nose had wrinkled in pleasure. "I'm happy you have. Sure, I can be eating now for the next few weeks!"

Looking back, perhaps it was that soft Irish accent, so much pleasanter on the ear, *and* sexier, than the harsh tones of New Yorkers.

Whatever it was, fifteen minutes later Matt found himself asking Grania if he could take her out to dinner. She'd declined, saying she'd already arranged to go out with the gallery owner and the other artists exhibiting that night. But he had been able to inveigle her cell phone number, using the excuse of wanting to view other pieces of work she had in her studio.

Matt, so handsome, friendly and attractive, had never before had a problem getting a girl to go out on a date with him. Grania Ryan proved to be different. He'd called her up next day and left a message on her voice mail, but did not receive a call in return. He'd tried her again a few days later, and this time she'd answered, but it seemed she was busy most nights.

The more she seemed to avoid him, the more Matt was determined to gain an audience. Eventually, she'd agreed to meet him for a drink in a bar she knew in SoHo. Matt had duly turned up dressed in his blazer, chinos and brogues, to find himself in a bohemian establishment where he was the odd one out. Grania seemed to have put little thought into what she was going to wear for the occasion—still in the same pair of jeans, but this time in an old blue shirt. She'd asked for a half pint of Guinness and drank it down thirstily.

"I can't stay long, I'm afraid."

She'd offered no explanation as to why.

Matt, having finally got her in captivity, had struggled manfully to make conversation. Grania had seemed completely uninterested in most things he had to say, her attention elsewhere. Eventually she'd stood up, apologized and said she had to leave.

"Can I see you again?" Matt had asked as he'd hurriedly paid the bill and followed her out of the bar.

She'd turned to him on the sidewalk outside, and asked, "Why?"

"I want to. Is that a good enough reason?"

"Speaking honestly now, Matt, I saw all your smart friends come into the gallery the other night. I don't think I'm your type, and you're not mine."

Matt was taken aback. As she turned on her heel, he followed her. "Hey, what do you think my 'type' is, Grania?"

"Oh, you know . . . born in Connecticut, some smart private school, then Harvard to finish you off, before you go and make your bucks on Wall Street."

"Yeah, well, some of that is true." Matt had reddened. "But I sure have no intention of following my pop into his investment business. As a matter of fact, I'm studying for my Ph.D. in psychology at Columbia. Once I've completed that, I hope to become a lecturer."

At that, Grania had stopped and turned around, a flicker of interest in her eyes. "Really?" She'd folded her arms. "I'm surprised. You don't give the impression of being a poor student, do you now?" She'd swept her hands up and down his body. "So, what's with the uniform?"

"Uniform?"

"The whole preppy look," she'd giggled. "You look as though you've walked straight out of an advert for Ralph Lauren."

"Well, hey, some girls seem to like it, Grania."

"Well, some girls aren't me. I'm sorry, Matt. I'm just not one to be played with by some rich kid that thinks he can buy his way into people's affections."

Matt's emotions had veered between anger, laughter and fascination. This pint-sized, feisty Irish girl who, on the outside, resembled Alice in Wonderland, but obviously had a core of steel and a tongue that could whip the hide of the toughest customer, enthralled him.

"Whoa there!" he'd shouted at her as she proceeded along the sidewalk. "That sculpture I bought of yours? I spent every penny of a legacy from my aunt to buy it. I've been looking real hard for months for something that appealed to me. It was stipulated in my aunt's will that I buy something of beauty with the money." Matt had realized he was shouting at the petite figure fifty yards from him, and people were staring. For the first time in his life, he didn't care. "I bought your swan because I thought it *was* beautiful. And, for the record, my parents are pissed with me because I'm not following in Daddy's footsteps! *And* the 'uptown prince' has no penthouse on Park Avenue, ma'am. He lives in student accommodation on campus, which comprises a studio, shared kitchen and restroom!"

Grania had stopped again and turned around, silently raising an eyebrow.

"You wanna see it? None of my uptown buddies will come there. It's on the wrong side of town."

At that, Grania had smiled.

"And"—Matt knew he was letting rip, but somehow it was imperative this girl knew who he really was—"there's every chance I'm not in line to inherit a penny from my rich folks unless I do as they ask. So if you're looking for that kind of guy, yeah, I suggest we call it quits."

They'd stared at each other for a good twenty seconds. As had the onlookers, enthralled by the street drama.

Then it was Matt's turn to walk away. He'd walked fast, not understanding his unusual outburst of a few seconds ago. A minute later, Grania was keeping pace with him.

"Did you really use your legacy to buy my swan?" she'd asked quietly.

"Sure I did. My aunt was a great collector of art. She told me only to buy stuff which gave me a gut feeling. And that's what your sculpture did."

They'd walked on in silence for a while, neither of them knowing where they were heading. Finally, Grania had spoken. "I'm sorry. I judged you and I shouldn't have done."

"Hey, that's OK, but what's the big deal anyway, about where I came from and how I dress?" He'd looked at her. "I'd say that's as much your issue as it is mine."

"Don't pull that psychology malarkey on me, Mr. Connelly. I might still be thinking you're trying to impress me."

"And I might be thinking you'd had a rough ride with one of my type in the past."

Grania had reddened. "I'm thinking you might be right." She'd stopped walking suddenly, turned and looked up at him. "How did you know?"

"Hey, Grania"—Matt had shrugged—"no one can be that set against Ralph Lauren. He makes some real nice stuff."

"Fair play. Yep, my guy was an eejit to end all eejits. So, there we are." Grania had seemed suddenly unsure of herself. "Well, I suppose . . ."

"Listen, instead of having this conversation on the move, why don't we go someplace and eat?" Matt had winked at her. "And I swear there'll be no blazers in sight!"

That night, and the few weeks afterward, Matt remembered as some of the best times in his life. Grania had blown him away with her lack of guile, freshness and honesty. Used to the uptight, uptown women who hid their true thoughts and feelings behind a veil of sophistication, which meant that a guy had to use guesswork to know where he stood, Grania was a breath of fresh air. If she was happy, he'd know about it, and if she was angry, or frustrated over her current sculpture, then he'd know about that too. She'd also treated his future career, and the work he put in to gain it, with respect. Did not assume, like so many of his friends, that this was a game for him, a little time-out until he capitulated and followed his father into the world to which he'd been born.

Although not educated to the same level as Matt, Grania's mind was bright and inquiring, and she'd soaked up information like a sponge. Then leaked it out again, using her instinctive wisdom to make sense of what she'd heard. The only fly in the ointment was that he'd had to tell Charley their relationship was over. For him, it had been a casual fling that couldn't lead to anything permanent. She'd taken it well, or had at least seemed to, and as the months passed, Matt had seen less of her and his old friends anyway. Matt had understood where Grania was coming from and, through her eyes, had seen further how shallow some of the people who inhabited his world *were*. But the point was, it *was* his world and even though he had cast off his friends, his family was not so easy.

He'd taken her home to meet his folks one weekend. Grania had spent the few days before trying on numerous possible outfits, until, with hours to go, she'd burst into tears of frustration. Matt had hugged her. "Listen, honey, what you wear is unimportant. They'll love you because you're you."

"Hmph," had been the answer. "I doubt it. I just don't want to let you down or embarrass you, Matt."

"You won't, I swear."

The weekend had passed as well as it could have done, Matt had thought. Yes, his mom, Elaine, could be overpowering at times, but anything she did or said was usually out of best intentions for her son. His father was less approachable. Bob Connelly had been brought up in a generation where men were men and were not expected to intrude in either domestic affairs or the emotional dilemmas of their women. Grania had done her best, but his dad was not a man with whom one could have an open heart-to-heart on anything.

Grania had been quiet on the way home, and Matt spent plenty of time in the week afterward reassuring her how much his folks had liked her. Perhaps, he'd thought, if he could give her the security she needed, show Grania this wasn't some mere dalliance for him, it might help her. Six months later, on a holiday to Florence, after they had made love in the shuttered room not far from the Duomo, Matt had asked Grania to be his wife. She had looked up at him, her eyes wide with surprise.

"Marry you? Matt, are you serious?"

Matt had tickled her. "No, I thought I'd say it for a joke. Grania, of course I'm serious!"

"I see . . ." she'd breathed. "Well now, that's a shocker, to be sure."

"Why the hell is it so shocking?" Matt had raised an eyebrow. "We're way past the age of consent; I love you, and I think you love me. It's a natural progression, isn't it? What normal human beings *do,* under these circumstances?"

Grania's eyes had darkened, and she'd seemed close to tears. It was not the reaction Matt had either expected or wanted.

"Honey, I didn't mean to upset you. What have I done wrong?"

"Nothing," she'd whispered. "It's just, that I can't . . . no, I can't ever marry you, Matt."

"I see. Can I ask you why?"

Grania had buried her face in her pillow and had shaken her head. "It's not that I don't love you, because I do," she'd said in a muffled voice. "But I can't play at being Mrs. Matthew Connelly. Your parents and friends would be horrified, Matt, whatever you think. I know they would. And I'd spend the rest of my life feeling guilty, with everyone looking at me as though I was some kind of gold-digger. Besides, I'd lose my own identity."

"Grania, honey," Matt had sighed, "I don't get why you care so much about what other people think! This isn't about them, it's about us! And what makes *us* happy. And it would make me real happy if you would say yes to being my wife. Unless, of course, all this is just an excuse to try and hide the fact you don't love me."

"Don't be an eejit, Matt! You know it's not that." Grania had sat up and swept a hand through her tangled hair. "It's my pride, Matt. It's big in me and it always has been. I couldn't bear for even one person to look at me and think I was marrying you for the wrong reasons."

"And that's more important than doing the right thing for us?"

"You know me, sweetheart, when I've got one on me; nothing can shift me. Listen"—Grania had reached for his hands and held them—"if you're saying you want to spend the rest of your life with me, and live with me, then yes. It's what I'd be wanting too. Can't we do that bit, Matt? Without the ring and the surname and everything?"

"You mean, live together?"

"Yes." Grania had smiled at Matt's shocked expression. "People do these days, you know. Besides, I don't know the legalities here, but after a few years I'd probably be regarded as your common-law wife anyway. Matt." She'd squeezed his hands and looked at him earnestly. "Do you think we really need a piece of paper to show the world we love each other? Wouldn't it say more about us if we were together and we didn't need it?"

Despite Matt's serious efforts to turn the conventions of his upbringing on their head to be with the woman he loved, this had been a tough one for him. He'd never considered the possibility of living with someone, always assumed he'd follow his parents and his friends into a traditional marriage.

"I . . ." He shook his head. "I need to figure it out for a while."

"I understand." Grania lowered her eyes. "I mean, I'd be happy to wear your ring if you wanted to buy me one, that is. Or we could go to Tiffany's, like Audrey Hepburn does in *Breakfast at Tiffany's,* and get them to inscribe a can-pull!"

"And what about when the kids come along?" he asked nervously.

"Jaysus!" Grania smiled. "We've just begun to think about merging our few sticks of furniture. I don't think I can look that far ahead."

"Yeah, sure. But if I'm even gonna consider this, Grania, I'd have to know that it would be something we talked about when the time came. I'm doing my best here, honey, but the thought of my kids being technically illegitimate and not even legally taking my name is one too far for me just now."

"Well now, I'm up for a compromise. If you're prepared to live in sin with me to begin with, then I'm prepared to talk about marriage if and when the babies come along."

Matt was silent for a moment, then he chuckled and kissed her nose affectionately. "Lady, you are a romantic poet's dream! OK, if that's the way you want it, we have a deal. And no"—he eyed her—"I'm not shaking on it. I know a far better way to seal it than that."

So, in order to safeguard his relationship with his fiercely proud, independent, frustrating yet exhilarating, and always surprising love, Matt had compromised all his principles and moved in with Grania. He'd bought her a ring from Tiffany's, as requested, and she'd worn it proudly. When they saw the ring, his parents had only one question. And that was when the two of them would name the day.

That day had never come.

Now, here Matt was, eight years on, with nothing more on paper than he'd had that day in Florence. He'd found himself almost wishing for the pain of a messy divorce; at least it would give credence to the magnitude of what was ending. The two of them had never even shared a bank account. There was almost nothing to separate. All that had held the two of them together had been a mutual wish to be so. Matt went to the window and stared out. Perhaps he should just accept what Grania had made so very clear to him and move on. However, not knowing exactly what it was he'd *done* made that difficult. But if she wasn't prepared to tell him, or even discuss it, what could he do?

"Hi, hon, good day?" Charley closed the door behind her, walked over and gave him a hug from behind.

"Hey, you know . . ." Matt shrugged.

"Feeling blue? Oh, Matty, it's been weeks now, and it's real hard to see you put yourself through this."

"Yeah, well, just the way things are, I guess." He moved out of her embrace and went to the kitchen to find himself a beer. "You'll be shot of me tomorrow. I'm off to California to lecture for a couple of weeks. Drink?"

"Why not?" Charley flopped on to the sofa. "I'm bushed."

"Hard day at the office?" Matt asked conversationally as he pulled the cap off his beer and poured her a glass of chardonnay.

"Yeah." She smiled. "This girl could sure use a party." Charley took a sip of her wine. "Hey, Matty, why don't we do just that and go out and get ourselves one! I could call round some of the old gang—they'd all be real pleased to see you. What about it?"

"Thinking about it, I don't know whether I'm in a party mood tonight." Matt shrugged. "I have to be up early tomorrow."

"Well, no harm in finding out, is there?" Charley had whipped her cell phone out and was already calling. "If you can't do it for you, do it for your flatmate, whose ears you've chewed off with your misery for the past few weeks. Hey, Al!" she said into the phone. "Got any plans for tonight?"

An hour and a half later, Matt was sitting in a smart bar uptown, which he hadn't frequented for years, with a bunch of his old friends. Charley had bullied him into pulling out his blazer and chinos. His life with Grania was spent in jeans and a T-shirt, and an old tweed jacket Grania had found him at a flea market, which she'd said made him look "professor-like," for work.

Champagne was ordered and Matt was gratified that the guys seemed so pleased to see him. As he sipped the champagne, Matt realized he hadn't been out on his own with them for eight years. None of them had so far settled down, and their lives as glossy, successful people had remained unchanged. As he set to on his second glass of champagne, he felt as though he was in a time warp, but it wasn't an unpleasant one. Grania's presence in his life had forced him to back away, and he'd been happy to do so because of his love for her. But Grania was no longer here . . .

After three bottles of champagne, the six of them went on to a newly opened Japanese restaurant and had an uproarious dinner, consuming far more wine than they should and talking of times past. After the solitariness and misery of the last few weeks, Matt felt light-headed with alcohol and the pleasure of being with old friends he had known since childhood.

It was two in the morning before they left the restaurant. Unsteadily, Matt hailed a cab to take him and Charley home.

"Great to see you, old pal." Al slapped him on the back. "Guess we might be seeing more of you in the future."

"Maybe," acknowledged Matt, following Charley into the back of the cab.

"Come up to Nantucket for a few days at Easter. Mom and Pop would love to see ya, kiddo."

"Sure, Al. You take care of yourself real well," Matt slurred happily. As the cab pulled off from the sidewalk, he closed his eyes. His head was doing that thing it used to do in sophomore year; spinning like a plate on a stick inside his skull. He lolled it to one side to see if it might feel better and found it on Charley's shoulder. He felt fingers brush against his hair, threading it gently. The space felt familiar and comforting.

"Did you have a good time, hon?"

"Yeah," Matt muttered, feeling sick.

"Told you it would do you good to see the gang. We still love you."

Matt felt the fluttering of soft lips against his scalp.

The following morning, Matt woke with a blinding headache. He lay and stared at the ceiling. He couldn't remember paying for the taxi, coming up in the elevator, or getting into bed. Matt shifted his position to find some comfort for his thumping headache.

As his vision cleared and he saw with horror that he wasn't alone, he also could not remember how Charley had ended up in bed next to him.

25

Grania was trying to coax Aurora into eating a fresh mackerel Shane had caught and given to her to cook for their supper, when the phone rang. "Hello?" she asked, licking her fingers clean from the fresh, salty taste of the fish she'd been prising into Aurora's mouth.

"Is that Grania?"

"Yes."

"It's Alexander Devonshire here."

"Hello, Alexander." Grania put the receiver between cheek and chin, and responded to Aurora's mouthed "Is that Daddy?" with a mouthed "Yes" in return.

"How is Aurora?"

"Extremely well, I'd say."

"Good. I'd obviously like to speak to her, but I also wanted to let you know I'll be home on Saturday."

"I'm sure she'll be thrilled. She's missed you."

Aurora nodded vehemently in response.

"And I've missed her. Everything else OK?"

"We're doing just fine, I promise."

"Good, good."

The conversation felt as if it was dwindling, so Grania said, "Would you like to speak to her now? I'm sure she's got lots to tell you."

"I'd love to. I'll see you on Saturday, Grania."

"Yes. Here's Aurora."

Grania passed the phone to Aurora and discreetly left the room. She knew stories of puppies and ballet lessons would be forthcoming, and she went upstairs to run a bath for Aurora.

As she sat on the edge of the bath watching it fill, she realized Alexander's imminent return was a call to arms to make some decisions.

• • •

Aurora and Grania spent much of their last few days before Alexander returned down at Dunworley Farmhouse. A relationship had sprung up between Aurora and the Ryan family. As her father had said, she was a grand little girl. Kathleen, so eager to dislike, was now asking Grania if she could bring Aurora down to the farm before breakfast, so the child could collect the fresh eggs with her. Aurora had subsequently named every chicken in the coop, and been inconsolable when a fox had run riot and eaten Beauty and Giselle.

"For all the sophisticated Lisle ways, that small one's a natural with animals. She'd make a wonderful farmer's wife one day," Shane had said one night while Aurora was busy saying good night to each of the cows in the shed.

"And that's not something you can manufacture," added John.

Grania made sure Aurora had a good scrub in the tub on the morning of Alexander's arrival home. She didn't want the child smelling of the animals she'd spent so much time with. She thought proudly that Aurora looked as pink and pretty and healthy as it was possible to be. They waited on the window seat in Aurora's bedroom. When they glimpsed Alexander's taxi snaking up the hill toward the house, Grania stayed upstairs as Aurora ran down to greet her father.

Eventually, Grania heard her name being called, and walked downstairs to join them. Aurora was standing in the entrance hall, her face a mixture of pleasure and consternation.

"Oh, Grania! It's so wonderful to have Daddy home. But I think he's been working too hard. He looks very thin and sort of gray. We need to take him on to the beach to give him plenty of fresh air." Aurora reached for Grania's hand as she pulled her toward the kitchen. "Come and say hello. I'm trying to make him a cup of tea, but I'm not doing very well."

As Grania entered the kitchen, she tried not to let shock feature on her face. When Aurora had described her father as thin and gray, to Grania's eyes, that was a subtle understatement. Alexander looked dreadful. She asked him how his trip had been and finished making the tea that Aurora had begun.

"I must say," said Alexander, "Aurora looks healthier than I've ever seen her."

"Yes, Daddy. I told you London didn't suit me. I like the countryside. Fresh air is very good for you." Aurora turned to Grania. "Daddy says I can have Lily when she's ready to leave her mummy. Isn't that wonderful?"

"Yes." Grania nodded, turning to Alexander. "I'm sorry if it's not what you want. My family have said that Aurora can come and visit the puppy anytime down at their farmhouse, if she would cause too many problems for you living here."

"No. I'm sure that somehow we can accommodate, in this very spacious house, one small puppy. Especially if it makes Aurora happy." Alexander looked at his daughter, affection shining out of his eyes.

"Well now, why don't I take myself off home?"

Both father and daughter's faces filled with anxiety at Grania's suggestion.

"Don't go, Grania!" said Aurora.

"No, please don't go yet," added Alexander. "At least, stay tonight. And perhaps you'd like to take Aurora down to the farm this afternoon. It's been a long journey home."

"Of course," agreed Grania, seeing Alexander's weary expression. "Aurora, why don't we go down there for tea, so that Daddy can have some peace and quiet until later?"

"That would be most kind, Grania." Alexander opened his arms to Aurora. "Come here and give your daddy a hug. I missed you, darling."

"Me too, Daddy. But I do love it at the farmhouse. Grania's family are grand, as they say round here!"

"Good. And I'm looking forward to seeing that pup."

Grania tried not to notice the tears in Alexander's eyes. Neither did she want Aurora to notice them.

"Let's get your coat and wellies and we'll be off to leave Daddy in peace." Grania forced a smile. "See you later."

"Alexander looked . . ." Grania sighed. "Dreadful. He's lost weight, and there's something in his eyes . . ." She shook her head. "I know there's something wrong."

Kathleen had returned to her usual brusque self now that Alexander was back. "Well, you've done all you can to look after Aurora while Himself has been away. Whatever he needs to sort out, it's not your worry or your business."

"How can you say that, Mam?" Grania retorted angrily. "Whatever is wrong with Alexander will almost certainly affect Aurora. And whether you like it or not, I care about her."

"Sorry," Kathleen sighed, "You're right. But you can understand, after what you've read in those letters and what I've told you, it's history repeating itself? There always seems to be a Lisle child in need of our love and under our roof."

"Mam, please stop it," Grania said wearily.

"I will feel as I feel. It's as if our two families are linked and there's no getting away from it."

"Well, if there's no getting away from it, I might as well accept it." Grania stood up, not in the mood for any more of her mother's nonsense. "I'll go and call Aurora in for tea."

When Grania and Aurora arrived back at Dunworley House later, all was quiet.

"Looks like Daddy was so exhausted he took himself off to bed," said Grania as she led Aurora up the stairs to her own bedroom. "Best we don't wake him. America's a long way away."

Aurora accepted this and let Grania tuck her into bed.

"Night, sweetheart," Grania kissed her on the forehead. "Sleep tight."

"Grania, do you think Daddy's all right?"

"Yes, I'm sure he is. Why?"

"He didn't look very well, did he?"

"He's probably just tired."

Grania did not sleep well that night. Alexander's presence in the house made her edgy. She noticed he slept at the other end of the corridor from the bedroom that had once been Lily's, and wondered if they'd always had separate rooms. She'd checked the handle on Lily's door earlier, and it was still locked.

Alexander did not emerge for breakfast, so Grania and Aurora carried on with their usual morning routine. Grania continued to coax the clay into the shape of Aurora's face as her subject frowned over her sums, thumb automatically stuck in her mouth. By lunchtime, Grania was genuinely worried about Alexander. Aurora didn't mention his absence, too excited about the prospect of her ballet lesson that afternoon in Clonakilty. Just before they were about to leave for town, Alexander appeared in the kitchen. He smiled wanly. "Are you two off somewhere?"

"Yes, Daddy, I'm going to my ballet lesson."

"Are you now?" Alexander forced another smile.

"You don't mind, do you?" asked Grania nervously.

"Mind? Of course I don't mind. Enjoy it, darling."

"I will." Aurora was heading for the door, eager to leave.

"Grania?" he said suddenly.

"Yes?"

"I was wondering if you would join me for something to eat tonight? I'm not sure what we have available, so perhaps I should be asking if I can join you?"

"I'm sure I can manage to knock up something simple. I wasn't sure whether I was to continue the shopping once you came back."

"Why don't we talk about it tonight?"

While Aurora was in her ballet lesson, Grania went to the butcher's and the greengrocer's to buy ingredients with which to cook supper. When they arrived home, she put the lamb to slow roast in the oven, bathed Aurora and allowed her to sit for an hour in front of the television. Humming to herself as she basted the potatoes in oil, adding fresh rosemary for flavor, she saw Alexander appear in the kitchen.

"Something smells good," he said with pleasure.

Grania was pleased to see he looked better tonight. Freshly washed and shaved, he was wearing a deep-blue linen shirt and a pair of immaculately pressed chinos.

"Where's Aurora?"

"In the drawing room, watching TV. I hope you don't mind, but I bought her one."

"Grania, would you please stop asking me if I mind! My child looks happier than perhaps she ever has. If it's taken some ballet lessons and television to achieve that, I can only say I'm very grateful. Why don't you open this?" Alexander handed Grania a bottle of red wine. "I'll go and put Aurora to bed."

As Grania set the table and poured the wine in readiness for Alexander's reappearance, she worried at how comfortable this domestic scene felt to her. And at her eagerness to be sharing dinner with him alone. The adrenaline she could feel pumping through her was not in anticipation of the lamb.

"All tucked up and settled," said Alexander as he rejoined Grania in the kitchen. "She really does look the picture of health. And seems far calmer than I've seen her for years." He picked up his wineglass and clinked it against hers. "Thank you, Grania. You've obviously been a tonic for her."

"Really, it's been a pleasure. And, yes, I think she has blossomed. Although at the beginning . . ."

"Yes?"

"She sleepwalked. I found her one night on the balcony at the end of the landing. I thought"—Grania stopped carving the lamb and turned to look at Alexander. "For a few seconds, I thought she was about to jump."

Alexander sighed and sat down. He was silent for a while before he spoke. "She tells me she sees her mother out there on the cliffs."

"I know," Grania said quietly. "I . . . took the liberty of locking the bedroom door. If you'd like to reopen it, I have the key."

"A very sensible idea. And I think it should stay locked. You may well have guessed it was my late wife's bedroom."

"Yes."

Alexander took a sip of his wine. "I've obviously taken Aurora to see a number of psychologists about her nightmares and her sleepwalking. They've told me it's a condition called posttraumatic stress disorder. That one day she'll grow out of it. You say she hasn't had either nightmares or sleepwalked for two or three weeks now?"

"No, she hasn't."

"Then maybe that day has come."

"Let's hope so. Was Aurora close to her mother?"

"It's hard to say," Alexander sighed. "Whether Lily was capable of being close to anyone, I really don't know. Although there's no doubt she loved her daughter, and Aurora worshipped her."

"Oh." It was all Grania could think of in reply. She continued to drain the fresh peas and added them to the potatoes and the lamb on the plate. "There now," she said as she carried the plates over. "I don't know whether you're keen on gravy, but there's some in the jug, and some fresh mint sauce too." She indicated another jug.

"My, what a treat. After weeks of plastic American food, I've been dreaming about this. Thank you, Grania," said Alexander gratefully.

"Well, it's a treat for me too. I love your daughter dearly, but it's nice to have some adult company for a change." She smiled.

"Yes, you must have felt quite isolated up here, especially after living in New York."

"At least I've had my parents close by. And they've become very attached to Aurora too. Please"—Grania picked up her knife and fork—"eat it before it gets cold."

They both chewed in silence for a while, Alexander only pausing to comment how tender the lamb was. "So, Grania," he said eventually as he placed his knife and fork together, even though his plate was still half full, "What are your future plans? Have you made any decisions yet?"

"I've been far too busy with your daughter to do that," Grania chuckled. "I was just thinking yesterday that this last month was probably exactly what I needed."

"A time of reflection, you mean?"

"Exactly."

"Will you go back to New York?"

"As I said, I haven't made any firm decisions."

"Grania, I need to ask you something."

She looked up at him, noting the sudden urgency in his voice. "What is it?"

"Would you be averse to staying up here with Aurora and me for longer? I'm going to be very busy and just won't have the time to give her the attention she needs."

Grania paused. "I . . . don't know," she replied truthfully.

"No." Alexander looked down at the knife and fork sitting on his plate. "Of course you don't. Why would a young and beautiful girl like you want to be stuck up here with a small child for any longer than she needed to be? Sorry, I feel like a heel for asking. Obviously, you're my first port of call, considering how happy and well Aurora looks under your care."

"How long would it be for?" Grania eyed him.

"The truth is, I don't know." Alexander shook his head. "I really don't know."

"Do you have a business problem?"

"No . . . It's hard to explain," he said. "Forgive me for being vague. I was thinking that, if by any chance you would consider it, there's a barn which I converted into a studio when Lily decided she wanted to try her hand at painting. Not that she ever used it, but it's certainly a very pleasant space in which to work. With a wonderful view out over the bay."

"Alexander, that's very kind of you to offer, but there's hardly time to work while I have Aurora full-time."

"Well, I was also thinking, now she seems so much better, about your idea of Aurora's joining the local school. That would mean, if she did, you'd have all day to work."

"Well, I certainly think it would do Aurora good to be with children of her own age," Grania agreed. "She spends far too much time either by herself or in adult company. But whether—"

Alexander laid a hand on hers. "I understand, Grania. I'm being selfish. You have a life far away from here, and a talent. I certainly don't want to stand in the way of those things. What I would ask, unless you have anything immediately pressing, is that you stay here with us for the next couple of weeks. I'm under considerable pressure and won't have the time Aurora deserves to spend with her. Or the energy," he sighed.

"All right, I'll stay for a couple more weeks." Grania knew she was responding far more to the touch of his hand on hers than to any logical thought process. "I have to finish Aurora's sculpture anyway."

"Thank you."

"And if you're happy to go ahead, the headmistress at the school is a cousin of my mother's," said Grania. "I'm sure that she could speak to her about Aurora and see if it was possible for her to start immediately."

"Wonderful! And, of course, I must pay your family for this puppy that Aurora is so set on having."

"Really, Alexander, that won't be necessary." Grania stood up and began to clear the plates. "Coffee?"

"No, thank you. It seems to make my headaches worse. You know,"

Alexander commented as he watched her moving around the kitchen, "my late wife always believed in angels."

"Did she?" said Grania as she piled everything into the sink.

"Yes. She said that all you had to do was call them." Alexander smiled sadly, surveying Grania. "Maybe she was right after all."

That night, alone in bed, Grania found herself in turmoil. She had just agreed to share another two weeks of the Devonshires' life, and possibly longer. But this time it was not simply about Aurora, it was about Alexander. Perhaps it was her maternal nature—Alexander seemed just as vulnerable as his daughter—or perhaps it was some kind of displacement technique, as any New York therapist would call it. Maybe she was attaching her thwarted emotions and feelings for Matt to another man. The situation with Matt was still unresolved. Yet here she was, fantasizing about the cozy domestic setup Alexander and Aurora presented. A proper home and a family, with a ready-made child to boot.

Grania sighed and turned over. Perhaps the years of living with a man who had a Ph.D. in psychology and could psychoanalyze a sausage if he so wished, had affected her more than she'd thought. Or perhaps it was simply that her life had taken an unexpected turn, and Alexander and Aurora were providing the temporary solace she needed.

Besides, another couple of weeks here, while Alexander attended to whatever business he had that was so pressing, plus settling Aurora into her new school, was hardly making a lifetime's decision. And Grania knew only too well that even lifetime decisions could go horribly wrong.

26

The following two weeks did nothing to help Grania move forward with thoughts of the future. On the morning, three days later, that Grania arrived home from dropping Aurora at the local school, Alexander was waiting for her in the kitchen with a set of keys.

"For the studio in the barn," he said as he handed them to her. "Go and take a look and see if you feel it's suitable."

"Thank you."

"I don't think Lily ever touched it, so just move whatever you want out of the way and use it as if it's yours." Alexander nodded at her and left the kitchen.

Grania made her way across the courtyard and opened the door to the studio. She gasped as she saw the vista from the floor-to-ceiling window that let in buckets of the natural light an artist needed, and encapsulated a magnificent view of Dunworley Bay. Grania looked around at the immaculate, untouched easel, the tubes of paint and a selection of expensive mink brushes, still sheathed in their covering of protective film.

The cupboards were stocked with canvases and fresh white pads of artist's paper, yet there was not a sign of a paint splatter anywhere. Grania stood by the window, staring out at the cliffs, wondering why Lily had never taken advantage of such a wonderful space. Any professional artist would give a couple of their best paintings—or sculptures, for that matter—to have a studio like this. There was even a small anteroom, containing a toilet and a large butler's sink in which to wash and clean the brushes.

It was all Grania had ever dreamed of.

That afternoon, she moved the half-finished sculpture of Aurora into the studio and placed it on the workbench in front of the window. The only downside, thought Grania as she sat down and gazed dreamily out of the window, was that she might spend her days mooning over the view rather than concentrating on her work.

When she collected Aurora from school, the little girl was full of stories about her new friends, and announced proudly that she seemed to be the best reader in the class. That evening, over supper, Alexander and Grania listened like proud parents as Aurora told her father of her achievements.

"So you see, Daddy, I wasn't as badly educated as you thought I was. Actually, I'm quite clever."

Alexander ruffled her hair. "I know you're clever, darling."

"Who do you think I take after? You or Mummy?"

"Oh, Mummy, definitely. I was always a dunce at school."

"Was Mummy clever?" questioned Aurora.

"Very."

"Oh." Aurora continued eating then said, "She seemed to spend an awful lot of time in bed, or away, like you."

"Yes, she did, but Mummy was often tired."

"Time for your bath, madam." Grania had seen Alexander's expression tightening. "We have to be up early again tomorrow to get you to school on time."

When Grania arrived back downstairs, Alexander was in the kitchen doing the washing-up. "Leave that," she said, embarrassed. "It's my job."

"Hardly," said Alexander. "You're not here to skivvy, but to look after Aurora."

"I don't mind at all," said Grania, grabbing a tea towel and standing companionably next to him at the sink as he passed her the wet dishes. "It's ingrained in me, being the daughter in a household of men."

"It's a good role model for Aurora to see. You really are a natural mother, Grania. Have you ever thought of having children of your own?"

"I . . ."

Alexander heard the catch in Grania's voice. "Sorry, did I say the wrong thing?"

"No." Grania could feel the wave of unshed tears threatening to break. "I lost a baby a few weeks ago."

"I see." Alexander continued to rhythmically wash the plates. "I'm terribly sorry. It must have been—must *be*—difficult for you."

"Yes, I . . ." Grania sighed. "It was."

"Is that why you left New York?"

"Yes." Grania could feel Alexander's navy blue eyes boring into her. "That and other things. Anyway . . ."

"There'll be another, I'm sure."

"Yes. I'll put these away in the dresser, shall I?"

Alexander watched her silently as she moved away from him, understanding that her reticence to discuss it further came out of pain. He changed the subject.

"Well, as I said a few minutes ago, you're a good influence on Aurora. Her mother was not what one would call domestic."

"Well, maybe she had talents in other directions."

"But so do you."

"Thank you." Grania reddened under his gaze.

"I hope you don't mind, but when you were out collecting Aurora from school, I popped into the studio. Your sculpture of her is absolutely exquisite."

"It's nowhere near finished yet. I'm struggling with her nose at present," Grania added.

"It's a Lisle nose, all the women in the family have inherited it. I imagine it is difficult to reproduce in clay."

"Your late wife was very beautiful."

"Yes, she was, but"—Alexander sighed—"she had a lot of problems."

"Did she?"

"Mental problems," he added.

"Oh." Grania struggled to know how to reply. "I'm sorry."

"It's amazing how beauty can mask so many flaws. I'm not saying it was Lily's *fault,* of course, but when I first met her, I didn't think for a moment that a woman who looked like she did could possibly be . . . who she was. Anyway . . ." Alexander stared off into the distance.

Silence hung over the kitchen. Grania dried the rest of the plates quietly and stowed them in the dresser. When she turned back, she saw Alexander was watching her.

"Anyway," he repeated, "it's a pleasure for both myself and Aurora to have a normal woman living in the house. Aurora was somewhat lacking in a role model. Although Lily did her best of course," he added hastily.

"Many would say that I was hardly normal," Grania grinned. "Ask my parents, or some of my friends in New York. I'm sure they'd be telling you differently."

"Grania, to me you seem like everything a woman should be. And a mother, for that matter. I'm truly sorry about your loss."

Alexander was still staring at her. "Thank you," she managed.

"Now I've embarrassed you. I'm sorry. I'm . . . not myself at present."

"Well, I'll be off upstairs for a bath. And thank you for the use of that beautiful studio. It's a dream, it really is." Grania smiled weakly at Alexander and left the kitchen.

Upstairs in bed later, Grania berated herself for allowing her emotional cracks to open up. Yet something about Alexander's obvious vulnerability underneath the stoic façade mirrored her own. He touched her because she recognized herself in him.

For the first time, Grania allowed the tears to fall properly. She wept for the tiny, fragile life that had been lost. And when she lay down to try and sleep a couple of hours later, she felt calmer, as though something had been both broken then mended inside her.

As the days passed, Alexander began to appear downstairs more often. Sometimes he'd wander into her studio and watch her working. He began to join her at lunchtimes, and when she mentioned she liked listening to music while she worked, a smart Bose music system appeared in her studio. And, as time went on, Alexander opened up more and more about Lily.

"At first, I used to love the way her mind flitted like quicksilver from one subject to the next. She was enchanting," Alexander sighed. "She always seemed happy, as though life was simply an exciting adventure, and nothing could bring her down. Anything Lily wanted, she had a way of getting, because she charmed those around her so completely. And I fell under her spell. If there was the odd black mood when the world turned full circle for her, and she'd sit and sob over a dead rabbit she'd found in the garden, or the fact that the moon had waned and it would be another month before it shone full again, I presumed it was simply part of her sensitive nature. It was only when the black moods began to become more protracted, with the moments of happiness becoming less and less visible, that I realized something wasn't right. A couple of years after we were married, Lily began to spend whole days in bed, saying she felt too exhausted and low to get up. And then suddenly she'd appear, in one of her most beautiful dresses, her hair freshly washed, and insist that we did something exciting. She was almost manic in her need to chase happiness. When she was in one of those phases, it was frenetic, but wonderful. We had quite a few adventures, I can tell you. Lily had no boundaries and her exuberance was infectious."

"I bet it was," Grania answered quietly.

"And, of course, every time she was like that, I wished and believed and wanted the dark side never to return. But it always did. She swung up and down like a pendulum for the next few years, with me always chasing her coattails, trying to keep up with her abruptly changing moods. And then . . ." Alexander exhaled and shook his head sadly. "She went down and didn't come back up for months. She point-blank refused to see a doctor. Would go into a mad, hysterical rage if I even suggested it. In the end, after she'd refused to eat or drink for almost a week, I did call a doctor. She was tranquilized and hospitalized. Manic depression was diagnosed."

"Alexander, I'm so sorry. It must have been so hard for you."

"Well, it wasn't her fault she was ill," emphasized Alexander, "but it was made worse by the fact that Lily had a childish quality about her. She didn't seem to understand what was happening to her. And, of course, when I had to put her for her own protection into an institution that specialized in Lily's problem, it broke my heart. She screamed and clawed and clung on to me, begging me not to leave her, as she put it, in the madhouse. But she was a danger to herself by that time, and had tried suicide on a number of occasions. She was also violent and came at me a couple of times with kitchen implements. She could have seriously injured me if I hadn't defended myself."

"Oh God, Alexander. How awful. I'm surprised you had Aurora," said Grania, genuinely shocked by what he was telling her.

"Aurora was a surprise to both of us. Lily was almost forty when she discovered she was pregnant. But the doctors thought it was possible that having a child to care for might help Lily, as long as she was under constant supervision. And you must remember, Grania," explained Alexander, "that there were large portions of Lily's life, while she was taking her medicine, when she was stable. Although I always lived with the fear of deterioration. And I could never trust her to take her medications. She hated taking her "zombie pills," as she called them. Although they stopped the dark times, she felt they prevented the high times also. Which, of course, they did. The pills calmed her, evened her out, but she said it was like living life from behind a curtain of mist. Nothing seemed as real or joyful or painful as it did when she was off them."

"Poor thing," said Grania. "And did she improve when Aurora came along?"

"Yes, she did. For the first three years of Aurora's life, Lily was the perfect mother. Not domestically, like you, Grania." Alexander smiled. "Lily always commanded a large team of servants to do her bidding, but her focus was solely on her little girl, and I really felt then there might be hope for the future. It didn't last." Alexander swept a hand through his hair. "And, unfortunately, Aurora took the brunt of it. Once, I came home here to find Lily asleep in bed, and no sign of Aurora. I woke her up to ask where Aurora was, and Lily looked at me and said she honestly couldn't remember. I found Aurora, cold and very frightened, wandering out on the cliff by herself. The two of them had gone out for a walk together and Lily had simply forgotten about her daughter."

"Oh, Alexander, how dreadful." Tears sprang unbidden into Grania's eyes at the thought of Aurora's abandonment.

"After that, I realized I could never leave Aurora alone with Lily again for even a few minutes. But I needn't have worried as Lily deteriorated and was institutionalized again. And really, from then on, Aurora only saw her mother sporadically. We moved back to London so that I could work and be near Lily's hospital. Aurora had a stream of unsuccessful governesses, as you've heard. Then, when Lily was stable again, she insisted on coming back to Dunworley House. I should never have agreed, but she loved it so much here. She said the beauty of the surroundings helped her."

"My mother said she took her own life," Grania said quietly.

"Yes. Your mother was right." Alexander put his head in his hands and sighed. "And I'm sure Aurora saw her do it. I heard screaming from Lily's bedroom and found Aurora standing on the balcony in her nightdress, pointing down at the cliffs below. Two days later, they found her mother's body washed up on Inchydoney beach. I can never know what effect that has had on Aurora. Let alone having a mother who, through no fault of her own, turned the taps of love for her daughter on and off so abruptly."

Grania did her best not to allow her own emotion to show on her face. The thought of Aurora watching her mother jump to her death was horrific to contemplate. She put a comforting hand on Alexander's. "Well, all I can say is, considering what Aurora's been through, I think she's extremely well balanced."

"Do you?" Alexander looked at Grania, desperation in his eyes. "The problem was, Aurora's reaction to her mother's death has naturally worried the doctors. It's been suggested that Aurora has inherited her mother's mental instability. Aurora's delusions about seeing her mother on the cliffs, hearing her calling to her, her nightmares . . . they could all be taken as the seeds that will grow into Lily's condition."

"Or, as you first said, it could simply be a traumatized little girl trying to deal with what she may have seen and the loss of her mother."

"Yes, let's hope so." Alexander smiled wanly. "And she certainly seems to have made great progress since she's been with you. I'm so very grateful, Grania. I can't tell you what that little girl means to me."

"Do you happen to know if Lily suffered any trauma in her early life?" asked Grania. "Sometimes that can trigger all sorts of problems."

Alexander raised an eyebrow. "For a sculptor, you seem rather knowledgeable on the subject."

"My . . . ex-boyfriend was a professor of psychology. His pet subject was childhood trauma. I probably learned the little I know by osmosis," Grania confessed.

"I see." Alexander nodded. "Well, getting back to your question,

I know very little of Lily's early life. When I met her, she was living in London. She was always reluctant to talk about her past, although I did know she'd been born here in this house and spent a lot of her childhood in it."

"I think my mother knows something about Lily's time here," Grania said slowly.

"She does? Would she be able to tell me?"

"I'm not sure"—Grania shrugged—"she's very cagey about it. But I'm pretty sure something did happen, because every time I mention Lily's name, it produces a negative reaction."

"Oh dear. That doesn't sound good. But any information that helps me understand the puzzle of Lily would be gratefully received."

"I'll see what I can extricate," agreed Grania, "but don't hold your breath. My mam's as stubborn as a mule. You could be waiting a long time."

"And time is something I just don't have," Alexander muttered. "I must leave again in ten days. Have you thought any more of what you're going to do?"

"No," said Grania abruptly, knowing she was swimming against an ever-growing tide.

"All right. I don't want to pressure you, but obviously I must sort out some arrangements for Aurora if you don't wish to stay on."

"Do you know how long it'll be?"

"Maybe a month, possibly two."

"OK." Grania nodded. "You'll have your answer by tomorrow." She stood up and began to clear their lunch things away.

"Grania." Alexander was by her side, taking the plates from her hands and setting them back on the table. He placed her hands in his own. "I want to say that whether you stay or leave, it's been a pleasure knowing you. I think you're a very special woman."

He kissed her very gently on the lips, then turned and walked away into the garden.

In typical female fashion, Grania spent the next few hours analyzing, agonizing and antagonizing herself over the motive for Alexander's unexpected kiss. It had been over so abruptly, she could hardly believe it had happened. Which probably meant that it *meant* nothing. It hadn't seemed as if he'd wanted more. On the other hand, was it not inappropriate to kiss your daughter's nanny directly on the lips?

There was no doubt that Alexander, his behavior and feelings, were an enigma. Yet she could feel her emotional walls slowly crumbling as the unfathomable empathy of two people who both understood the pain of loss drew them ever closer.

All Grania knew was that she was sinking slowly into the quicksand of infatuation. And it had to be halted in its tracks.

"I've decided, Alexander," she said to him as she arrived back in the kitchen from taking Aurora to school the following morning.

"And your answer is?"

"I can't stay. I'm so sorry. I have some . . . problems that I really need to go and sort out in New York. You know how much I love Aurora, but . . ."

"You don't need to say any more." Alexander held his hands out, almost in self-defense. "Thank you for telling me. I shall now go full steam ahead to find a replacement for you." He turned on his heel and walked directly out of the kitchen.

Grania crept out of the kitchen and crossed the courtyard to the studio guiltily, feeling like a charlatan for having declined to stay on. The sculpture of Aurora was almost ready, and all it needed now was to be cast out and dipped in bronze. She sighed. The sooner she got away from this house, the better.

She spent the morning clearing up every trace of herself from the studio. And pondering that perhaps her mother was right; that the Lisle effect on the Ryans was insidious and unstoppable—it had certainly addled *her* brain. Even for Aurora, she could not become emotionally involved with a man she hardly knew. Who might feel fondly toward her because she had cared for his child . . . who might have tried to bribe her with a kiss, and then more . . .

Every instinct in Grania told her to leave.

Collecting Aurora from school that afternoon proved hard. Aurora was full of plans for a future that included her. Knowing she had only a few more days until Aurora would be in the care of someone else was almost more than Grania could bear.

"What do you mean, you're leaving?"

"Oh, Aurora, sweetheart, you knew my being here was only temporary. That I couldn't stay here at Dunworley House forever."

It was the following morning and since Alexander had turned tail and walked out of the kitchen, Grania had not seen him. But she knew she must tell Aurora she was leaving and allow the child to prepare herself for what she knew the little girl would see as yet another adult deserting her.

"But, Grania, you can't leave!" Aurora's big eyes filled with tears. "I love you and I thought you loved me! We're friends, we have fun, Daddy loves you and—"

Aurora burst into great, heaving sobs.

"Darling, please don't cry. Please don't. Of course I love you, but you know that I live in New York. I have a life and a career which is very important to me."

"You're going back to America and you're leaving me!"

"Not immediately, sweetheart, I'm going back to live with my mammy and daddy at the farmhouse first. I'll be just down the lane."

"You are?" She looked up at Grania with desperate eyes. "Then can I come and live there with you? Your family like me, don't they? I promise I'll help milk the cows, and look after the sheep and—"

"Aurora, you can come and visit as often as you want." Grania's reserve was slowly cracking.

"Please let me come with you! Don't leave me here! The nightmares will come back, Mummy will come back!" Aurora threw her arms around Grania and hugged her so tightly and desperately she could hardly breathe.

The quicksand was closing over Grania's head now and she had to escape. "Darling, I'm going to talk to you woman to woman." Grania lifted Aurora's chin and looked her in the eyes. "Just because someone isn't in the same room as you, or isn't with you at that moment, doesn't mean that person's not loving you. Truthfully, I wish you *were* my daughter, and that I could take you with me." Grania gulped back the tears to enable her to continue. "But you can't come with me, Aurora. Because you can't leave Daddy here by himself. He needs you, sweetheart. You know he does. And sometimes in life, we have to do things that are really hard."

"Yes." Aurora stared back at her, understanding in her eyes. "You're right," she sighed. "I know I need to be here for Daddy. And that you can't stay with me. You have your own life, and that's very important." Aurora suddenly took her hands away and turned her back on Grania. "Everybody's lives are more important than mine. That's what grown-ups *do*."

"One day you'll be an adult, Aurora. And you'll understand."

"Oh, I understand." Aurora turned back to Grania. "I understand what it is to be an adult." After a pause, she took a deep breath and walked back toward Grania. "I understand you need to go, Grania, but I hope I will see you again."

"I promise you, sweetheart, you will. Anytime you need me, all you have to do is to call me. I promise I will always be there for you."

"Yes." Aurora nodded. "Well, it's time we went to school, isn't it?"

Aurora was quiet on the journey, but Grania understood. Understood, as Aurora got out of the car and went to join her friends in the playground without a backward glance, that the hurt and the pain of rejection she was feeling ran deep.

Grania set her chin and thought of Mary, who had given up everything to protect a child who wasn't even her own. And who, in the end, had turned her back on Mary when it suited her. Whatever her feelings for Aurora, the child could not be her responsibility. And she could not allow history to repeat itself.

"I can't bear it, Mam; her face, so broken, yet so proud and so brave . . . you have no idea what that child has been through." Grania had dropped in at the farmhouse on her way back from taking Aurora to school. She sat at the kitchen table with her mother, tears streaming down her cheeks.

"I'm sure I haven't now, pet," Kathleen comforted. "But what you've done, however hard, is right. As you say, she isn't your responsibility. She's her daddy's."

"I don't know what she'll do without me. Everyone's left her, Mam." Grania sighed. "Everyone. And she thought I loved her, and cared for her and—"

"I know. But the bond between the two of you will never be broken. And I promise, you can tell Aurora from me, there's always a welcome for her in this house. We all love her, so we do. Come here now and let your mammy give you a hug."

Grania did so. For all that Kathleen sometimes irritated her, at this moment she felt blessed to have her.

The next three days up at Dunworley House were surprisingly calm. Aurora seemed to have accepted the situation completely. She did not distance herself from Grania, but in fact asked if they could spend the remaining time they had together doing her favorite things. Grania complied, and they went for long walks along the cliffs, spent a sticky and successful afternoon indulging in papier-mâché and then, on the last evening, had tea at Grania's parents' house.

When it was time for them to return to Dunworley House so Aurora could go to bed, Grania watched her mother hug Aurora as if she were her own.

"I can come and visit you and my puppy lots and lots, can't I, Kathleen?"

"'Course you can, pet. And Grania's not going anywhere for a while, and our door's always open, promise," comforted Kathleen, giving Grania a look of despair. "Bye now, pet."

Alexander was waiting for them in the kitchen when they arrived home.

"Aurora, go up and get ready for bed, please. I need to speak to Grania."

"Yes, Daddy," said Aurora obediently, and left the kitchen.

There were some envelopes waiting on the kitchen table for Grania.

"That's everything, paid in full."

"Thank you." Grania wondered why she felt so embarrassed and uncomfortable, when it was she who had originally given the favor in *his* hour of need.

"I have a very nice local girl arriving at ten tomorrow morning. If you would be so kind as to take Aurora to school, then spend a couple of hours with Lindsay, showing her the ropes, she will go and pick Aurora up at home-time."

"Of course. Now," Grania collected the envelopes from the table, "I want to go and put Aurora to bed."

"Yes." Alexander nodded.

Grania walked toward the door and pulled it open.

"Grania . . ."

She turned around and looked at him, took in the sorrow in his eyes.

"One day, I hope you will understand why I—" He shook his head. "If I don't see you tomorrow, good luck for the future. As I said the other night, you're very special. Thank you for everything, and I hope your life goes well from here on in."

Grania nodded, left the kitchen and climbed the stairs to say good night to Aurora for the last time.

27

Aurora had shown no signs of despair, nor had she tried to plead for Grania to stay when she'd dropped her off at school the next morning. "I'm going to meet your new nanny now," Grania explained. "Her name is Lindsay and she sounds lovely. You know Daddy wouldn't employ someone to look after you who wasn't."

Aurora nodded. "I know."

"And you also know that I'll be down the road in the farmhouse. And you can come and visit us all as many times as you want?"

"Yes."

"Good-bye, darling. Come and see me as soon as you can."

"Yes. Good-bye, Grania." Aurora smiled, turned on her heel and walked into the school.

Lindsay, the local nanny Alexander had employed, seemed to be kind, experienced and up-to-date with the situation. "I'm used to sole charge, so it's really no problem, Grania," she said.

"Yes, I'm sure you'll do a much better job than me. I'm only an amateur who's been filling in."

Nevertheless, Grania had needed to tell Lindsay all about Aurora's particular needs and wants. Where the teddy should be placed on the pillow, how she liked being tucked in, that she was ticklish on the right side of her neck . . .

Grania had asked Shane to come and collect her. She was driven away from Dunworley House experiencing relief and foreboding in equal measure.

It had been three days now since Grania had left and the entire family had been on tenterhooks waiting for the sight of Aurora's small, graceful body tripping down the lane toward them. So far, she had not appeared.

"It must mean she is settled and happy with the new girl," Kathleen commented.

"Yes," Grania answered weakly.

"She'll be down in her own time, so, and you're not to worry. Children are survivors, and Aurora has got strength."

"Yes," repeated Grania.

But both of them knew they didn't believe a word of it.

Later that evening, Grania's cell phone rang. It was Lindsay.

"Hi," said Grania, closing the kitchen door behind her and wandering into the sitting room for some peace. "How are the two of you getting on?"

"I thought we'd been getting on fine. Up until this afternoon, when I went to collect her from school. And she wasn't there."

"What do you mean, she wasn't *there*?"

"She'd vanished. Her teacher said that one minute she was in the playground and the next she'd disappeared."

"Jaysus," Grania muttered as her heart rate increased. She glanced down at her watch. It was ten to six. That meant Aurora had been gone for over two hours. "Where have you looked?"

"Everywhere. I—" Grania heard the desperation in Lindsay's voice. "I was calling you to find out if you knew any special places she liked to go to, or someone she might run to. I thought—that is, I hoped—she might be with you."

"No, although I will check around the house and in the barns. She could have come in over the fields without us noticing. Is Alexander there?"

"He went off to Cork city this afternoon and he hasn't returned yet. I've tried his cell phone several times, but he's not answering."

"You've checked by the cliffs?"

"Yes, but no sign."

Grania stopped herself from asking whether Lindsay had looked down on to the rocks below.

"Right, why don't you go round the house and gardens again and I'll check our farm this end? If there's no sign, just sit tight in case Aurora comes back. I'll call you if there's any sign of her, or if I have any ideas. We'll speak soon."

Grania sent Shane out to comb the barns, while John took off in the Land Rover to check the fields around the farmhouse. Kathleen stood in the garden, uselessly shouting Aurora's name for want of something better to do.

Shane met Grania in the courtyard. "No sign, I'm afraid," he reported. "But that pup she was so keen on seems to be missing too."

"Really?"

"Perhaps it's coincidence, but do you think Aurora's been here and taken her?"

"If Lily's gone, then yes," agreed Grania, comforted that at least there was some possible knowledge of Aurora's recent whereabouts. It gave her hope that the child was heading somewhere with the dog, not lying dead and broken on the rocks at the bottom of the cliffs. "I'm taking the bicycle up the cliff path. Why don't you go in the opposite direction, toward Clon?" Grania suggested, pulling a rusty specimen away from the barn wall.

"Right," said Shane, pulling another out and climbing on. "I have my phone with me, as has Dad. Mam can stay here just in case she turns up."

Two hours later, the Ryans reconvened in the kitchen. None of them had found any trace of Aurora.

"I've been racking my brains to try and think of hidey-holes where she might be," said Kathleen, pacing the kitchen. "Jesus, Mary and Joseph! If anything has happened to that poor little mite, then . . ."

"Should we be after calling the guards?" suggested John.

"Lindsay says she's managed to get in contact with Alexander, who's on his way home from Cork. If anyone's going to make that decision, it should be him." Grania warmed her hands against the range.

"Anyone for a brew?" asked Kathleen.

"Yes please, pet," said John. "Without transport, an eight-year-old girl and a puppy aren't going to get far, are they now? Someone's bound to spot them. I doubt she'd have any money on her. Perhaps she'll come back when she's hungry," he said rationally.

"Well now, that pup won't be too happy at not having its mammy's milk," added Shane.

Grania was hardly listening. Her mind was speeding across the past ten weeks, trying to identify any place to which Aurora would go. She heard the crunch of gravel under tires and saw it was Alexander's car.

He jumped out and walked toward the kitchen door. When he entered, the entire family saw the gray tinge of fear on his gaunt face.

"Sorry to barge in like this, but Lindsay said you'd all been out looking for Aurora. Any news?"

"No, Alexander, not so far. We've scoured everywhere. This is my mother, by the way, my father, and my brother, Shane," Grania added.

"Good to meet you." Alexander offered the polite response automatically. "Has anyone got any ideas?"

"Well, we're thinking maybe she took that pup she loved with her, so at least she's not alone," offered Shane.

"There, pet." Kathleen handed Alexander a hot cup of tea. "Drink that, it's got plenty of sugar in, good for shock."

"Thank you. You say she's taken the puppy? Which means . . . ?"

"That she was around these parts earlier, sir," said John.

A flicker of relief appeared in Alexander's eyes. "Well, at least that's something. How far can a small girl with a puppy get in a few hours?"

"Not far, I'd say," said Kathleen.

"We were wondering, sir, if it was time to call the guards?" said Shane.

"Not yet," said Alexander quickly, "but if there's no sign of her in the next couple of hours, I suppose we'll have to."

"If you'll excuse me now, and if it's all right with you, I'm going to put the word out to my farming friends," said John. "They can at least have a quick scout of their barns and their land for us, while we still have some light left."

"Good idea, pet," Kathleen agreed as John got up and left the room. She stared into her teacup. "You know, this might only be a feeling, but I'd be thinking that little girl is somewhere close."

"Your instincts are usually right, Mam." Shane gave an encouraging nod in the direction of Alexander. "The question is, where?"

After further fruitless forays up and down the cliffs, in surrounding barns and the fields, Alexander capitulated and said it was time to call the guards.

Grania took herself outside and stood in the field in front of the farmhouse. The sky was a deep black now, with no moon or stars to help shed light on Aurora's whereabouts.

"Where are you, sweetheart?" she whispered into the darkness. She paced up and down. There was something nagging in the back of her mind which would not surface. Suddenly, she knew what it was. She turned on her heel and ran back to the kitchen. Alexander had just put the phone down to the guards.

"They'll be up to Dunworley House in the next ten minutes to take some details. I'd better be on my way so I'm there to greet them."

"Alexander, where was Lily buried?"

Alexander turned slowly to Grania. "In Dunworley church. You don't think—"

"Can we take your car?"

"Yes." He needed no second bidding. The two of them left the house, climbed into Alexander's car and sped off up the road to where Dunworley church sat, nestled on its own in a side of the hill.

Alexander broke the silence as they drove. "Lily always said it was where she wanted to be laid to rest. She said she'd have the best view in the world for all of eternity."

They parked the car on the roadside and, using a torch Alexander had produced from a pocket in his car, passed through the creaking wrought-iron gate and into the churchyard.

"She's just to the left, right at the end." Alexander led as they picked their way carefully around the graves.

Grania held her breath as they drew near enough to shine the torch on Lily's headstone. And there, nestled in the wildflowers and weeds that had sprung up on top of the grave, lay Aurora. In her arms, fast asleep, was Lily the puppy.

"Thank God," gulped Alexander.

Grania could see relief had brought him close to tears.

He turned and put a hand on Grania's shoulder. "Thank you, Grania, for knowing my daughter better than I do."

Alexander tiptoed toward Aurora then bent down and gently scooped her up in his arms. Aurora's eyes half opened at the motion, and she smiled up at her father.

"Hello, Daddy," she said sleepily.

"Hello, darling. We're going to take you home to tuck you up in bed, safe and warm."

Grania followed behind as Alexander carried his child and placed her on Grania's lap in the back of the car.

"Hello, Grania." Aurora smiled up at her. "I've missed you."

"And I've missed you too."

"How did you find me, Daddy?" she asked.

"It wasn't me, darling," Alexander said as he drove up the hill toward Dunworley House. "It was Grania who guessed where you'd be."

"Yes. I knew she would." Aurora sounded almost smug. "She's just like a real mother. I love you, Grania," she said. "You won't leave me again, will you?"

Grania looked down at the desperation in Aurora's eyes, took a deep swallow and said, "No, darling, I'll never leave you again."

Later, when Aurora was safely in bed with a hot-water bottle to warm her up, the puppy had been taken by Shane back down to its mother, and Alexander had called the guards to say Aurora had been found, he offered Grania a brandy in the kitchen.

"Thank you." Grania sat down wearily and nursed the glass in her hands.

"I've sent Lindsay home to her mother's in Skibbereen," said Alexander. "She was pretty shaken." He sat down next to Grania looking exhausted. "My God, what a relief. At least Aurora seems relatively unscathed. Chilled, but unscathed," he repeated.

"Yes. The worst thing was that I thought . . ." Grania stared at Alexander, and he nodded, his face turning in the direction of the cliffs too.

"So did I." He reached out a hand to Grania. "I can't say how thankful I am that you found her for me. If I'd lost Aurora . . ." Alexander shook his head. "I think that would just about have ended it."

"Yes. I'm sure."

"But, Grania, listen to me," Alexander's tone was urgent, "Aurora is a beautiful, sweet-natured and bright little girl. But she's also manipulative, like her mother. Tonight was a cry for help, and I don't think it was a cry for me. It was you she wanted. Please, you mustn't give in to what amounts to emotional blackmail."

"I don't think she means it that way, Alexander, really."

"I'm sure she doesn't," he agreed. "It's her childish way of trying to get you to come back. The fact she loves you the way that she does is testament to how you've cared for her. *And* the fact she feels safe with you. But, and I underline the 'but,' you mustn't be swayed by her. You have no obligation to my daughter whatsoever. And I would hate to think that, in any way, she was curtailing the plans you must have made by now."

What plans? thought Grania to herself, only able to focus on Alexander's physical presence so close to her and his hand touching hers.

"I hear what you're saying, Alexander, and I appreciate it. The problem is," Grania sighed, "I love her too."

"I reiterate, she is not your responsibility. She's mine."

"What are your plans, Alexander?" Grania looked at him square in the eyes, wanting to know, for all of their sakes.

"I . . ." Alexander withdrew his hand from hers, sighed heavily, and stroked his fingers through his hair. "Grania, I need to tell you something."

"Tell me then," she said softly.

He turned to her, and took both her hands in his. He searched her face before he shook his head. "I can't."

The brandy had softened Grania's normal reserve. It was her turn now to squeeze his hands. "Please, Alexander, tell me."

He leaned toward her, their knees now touching, and planted a soft kiss on her lips. "Oh God." He kissed her again. "I . . . you're wonderful." With that, he drew her into his arms and kissed her properly. She smelled the scent of him closing around her, powerful and so wanted. Her own arms reached around him as she clung to him and kissed him with equal fervor. Then, suddenly, he broke away.

"Forgive me! I can't . . . *mustn't* do this. None of this is fair on you. Whatever my feelings for you, I—" He stood up suddenly, anger on his perfect features. He picked up his brandy glass and threw it at a wall, where it smashed elegantly to the floor.

Grania watched his action in amazement and horror.

"Oh God! Sorry . . ." He sat back down and folded her in his arms again. Then he gently pushed her away from him and looked into her eyes. "You have no idea how difficult this is for me."

"Perhaps you could try explaining." Grania managed a rational response.

"Yes. But I *can't*." He took her fingers, molded them around his own and reached forward to kiss her face gently. "If you only knew the thoughts I've had . . . how beautiful I think you are . . . how kind, how gentle, how loving, how *alive*. And what you've given to Aurora, well, I can never repay that. I'd give anything to sweep you into my arms right now and carry you upstairs." He was tracing the contours of her face with his fingertips. "But believe me, Grania, you're best to get out of this doomed house. Go back to your life and live it elsewhere. Forget about me and Aurora, and—"

"Alexander," Grania said weakly, "You're sounding like a scene out of a bad movie. Please stop. It's not getting us anywhere."

"Yes, you're right. Lily always said I had a dramatic side to my nature. I apologize. It's been a pretty dramatic night." He smiled grimly.

"Yes, it has."

Alexander looked away from her. "I'm meant to be leaving tomorrow. I think I should delay it, for Aurora's sake."

"How long will you be away? Will it be longer than two months?"

"If the worst comes to the worst, it may be a good deal longer than that."

"Look, I've got a suggestion," said Grania.

"What?"

"You might have noticed tonight how fond my family is of Aurora. Why don't I take her down there to live with me while you're away? If I decide, at any point, I need to return to my life in New York, she will at least have the continuity of my family there for her. And then, when you're back, you can make some decisions."

"You think your parents would mind?"

"After tonight's performance?" Grania raised her eyebrows. "I think it's pretty obvious they wouldn't. I haven't managed to produce any grandchildren for them yet, so they seem to have adopted Aurora."

"Well . . . that sounds like a dream scenario to me." His drawn face relaxed a little. "Thinking of Aurora being cared for in a proper family. I would, of course, pay for everything she costs you and your parents."

"Right. I'll give my mother a quick call in the morning to check if it's OK, but I'm sure it will be." Grania was still reeling from the gamut of emotions she'd experienced that evening. And Alexander's mercurial changes of behavior had exhausted her. "If you don't mind," she said, standing up, "I'm going to go to bed now. I'm very tired."

"Of course. It's been one hell of a night. Of which, I might add, you're the heroine."

"Thank you." Grania stood up. "Good night, Alexander."

He watched her put her brandy glass into the sink, wash it out and then walk across the kitchen toward the door. "Grania?"

"Yes?"

"Please forgive me. Under any other circumstances . . ."

She turned to him then and nodded. "I understand," she lied.

Aurora

Before you ask, I'm not proud of myself. My father was right, of course—I was manipulative. But I was also desperate. And besides, I'd already been told Grania would be coming to look after me for a long, long time, so I wasn't happy it seemed to be going wrong and she had left me.

And it took a lot of thinking about to decide where to go and hide. Somewhere I knew, if she loved me, she'd find me, but not too obvious, like in a barn with the puppy, or up on the cliffs.

Even though I'm not scared of ghosts, knowing and understanding them the way I do, I didn't like it much up there in the graveyard alone. I felt like the odd one out, being alive when they were all dead. Besides, I was only eight, and human . . .

Poor old Grania. There really wasn't a lot she could do about it, being the kindhearted soul she is. And, of course, she loved me. Which, as I said earlier, often saves the day.

And I think she could have loved Daddy too, if things had been different . . .

I must stop wishing I could rewrite this story. I'm sure that the Master Storyteller, who weaves the subtle threads of fate in and out of our lives, is far better at it than I can ever be. Even though it's sometimes hard to understand why *one must trust that He is. That He knows the reasons for the things that happen to us, and will provide us all with a Happy Ending. Even though it may well be beyond the gossamer curtain we call death and means we can't see it while we live.*

As you may have noticed, I'm not much of an Evolutionary Theory fan, although I have read Darwin's Origin of Species.

Actually, I lie. I read two chapters and gave up in favor of War and Peace, *which made for far lighter reading.*

I am a Creationist.

But perhaps, when one is nearing the end of one's life, I suspect one needs to be.

Apologies for the self-indulgence, Reader. I've had a bad few days. And War and Peace *isn't exactly a fairy tale either.*

Some Austen for me next, to cheer me up. I like her endings, more than I currently like mine.

So, we move on with the story . . .

28

Grania didn't understand. As she drove down the hill toward her parents' farmhouse, Aurora and all her most precious possessions stowed in the back of the Range Rover, she had no conception of what was going on in Alexander's head.

"We're here!" called Aurora as she exploded from the car and ran across to open the kitchen door. She launched herself into Kathleen's arms. "Thank you so much for having me to stay, and can Lily sleep on my bed? I promise I'll give her straight back to her mummy in the morning when she needs more milk."

"Now then, we don't take pups away from their mammys until they're ready. Neither do we allow dogs upstairs in this house. Except on very special occasions, like maybe your first night here." Kathleen touched Aurora's cheek, and over Aurora's beautiful Titian curls exchanged a look of resignation with her daughter.

Before teatime, Shane took Aurora off to the top field, where the sheep were beginning to lamb.

"'Tis amazing," said Kathleen. "I told you that having a Lisle child in the Ryan family's care was predestined."

"Oh, Mam, enough of your tea leaves! And talk of the past," added Grania. "It's obvious you adore her."

"Yes." Kathleen was big enough to admit it. "Somehow that child has wound her way into my affection, despite my best intentions. Your daddy, now he's a lost cause. I think he's reliving the past when you were a small one. He's painted that spare bedroom of ours pink, and even went into Clon to find some dolls for her. You've never seen the like of their ugly faces, Grania," Kathleen chuckled. "But he's doing his bit. And your brother, he's smitten too," she added.

"You know it's only temporary, Mam, until Alexander comes back home."

"There's nothing in the Ryan household that's temporary about

Lisle children inhabiting it, you mark my words." Kathleen wagged a finger at her daughter. "But I will admit, young Aurora has brought new life to all of us." Kathleen put the kettle on the range to boil. "And I'd probably fight for her tooth and nail if I felt it was in her best interests. So now, I've admitted I'm just as bad as the rest of the women in the family when it comes to a Lisle child. But who can knock it, when she makes me smile?" She turned to face her daughter and crossed her arms. "The bigger question is, Grania, what *you* do now. With Aurora here, and safe and happy, at least you're free to make your own decisions."

"Yes, Mam. And I'm grateful for that. I'd like to say I've made some, but I'd be lying. Perhaps a few days' space after all the drama will help."

"Yes," sighed Kathleen. "And that Alexander, even I can see he's the size of a good-looking fella. The eyes on him . . ."

"Mam! Behave yourself." Grania smiled.

"I always have, and that's to my loss," she grinned. "A woman can dream, can't she? Now then, we'll be having a grand dinner tonight. I thought I'd lay on something special for our little princess."

The evening, with Aurora added to the table, took on a life of its own. After supper, John, horrified that Aurora seemed to know none of the old songs of her birthland, took out his banjo and played for all of them. Shane, breaking the habit of a lifetime, did not go to the pub. The five of them danced Irish jigs until Aurora yawned and Grania saw the exhaustion in her eyes.

"Time to go up to bed now, sweetheart."

"Yes," she said, almost gratefully.

Grania led Aurora up the narrow staircase and into the newly decorated spare room, put her into her nightdress and tucked her up in bed.

"I love your family, Grania. I hope I don't ever have to leave." Aurora yawned, her eyes half-closed in contentment.

Before Grania had left the room, Aurora was asleep.

• • •

Matt arrived home and put his hold-all of clothes in the utility room to launder later. He went into the kitchen to fix himself something to eat. He hadn't been back here since the morning after the night he'd gotten hammered with Charley and the guys two weeks ago. He wandered into the sitting room, relieved that the loft was currently empty, and threw himself on to the sofa. Of course, Charley might well have moved out anyway. Surely, by now, her own apartment must have been redesigned to within an inch of its existence?

Matt blushed at the thought of that last morning he'd spent here, horrified when he'd seen Charley and realized she was naked next to him. He'd showered and packed his bag with all he'd need for the next couple of weeks, then crept out of his home like an unwanted lover. And the worst part was he'd had no recollection of what he may or may not have done the night before.

Charley hadn't contacted him since anyway, none of the coy or maybe buddy-buddy conversations that one would expect after they'd spent the night together. He hadn't contacted her either; what the hell could he say? He needed her to give him a clue first, so he could react appropriately.

Matt heard the key turn in the lock. Charley walked through the door and looked at Matt in surprise.

"Hi, wasn't expecting you home."

"Really?" Matt commented nervously. "Strangely, I do live here."

"Yeah, sure you do," she said as she made her way through to the kitchen and got herself a glass of water. She passed back through the sitting room, heading in the direction of her bedroom.

"You OK?" Matt called. She was being uncharacteristically silent.

"Yeah, I'm OK. Just real tired."

That was the last he saw of her that evening or, in fact, any evening in the following week. When they were at home together, Charley would offer monosyllabic answers to his questions, then disappear into her room and not emerge until the following morning. Matt knew she was avoiding him, and understood why, but it was beyond him to know how to fix the problem.

Finally, Matt decided the only thing to do was to tackle Charley head-on. That evening, she came home and walked to the fridge to pour herself a glass of milk.

"Charley, honey, I really think we should talk."

Charley paused in her journey across the sitting room toward her bedroom. "What about?"

"I think you know 'what about.'"

Charley studied him for a while. "What's there to say? It happened, it was a mistake, it's obvious you regret it . . ."

"Whoa!" Matt instinctively put his arms out in front of him. "Stop right there. I suggest we go catch a bite to eat and talk this through."

"OK." Charley shrugged. "If that's what you want. I'll go take a shower."

An hour later, they were sitting across a table in an Italian restaurant a couple of blocks away. Matt was drinking beer, but Charley had refused alcohol and was on water.

"You feeling OK? Physically, I mean. Not like you to refuse a glass of wine, Charley." Matt smiled, trying to break the tension.

"I'm not feeling that great just now."

"You should go to the doctor and get yourself checked out," Matt encouraged.

"Yup." Charley's eyes were downcast; she was fiddling with her napkin, refusing to make eye contact.

"Hey, Charley, it's Matt you're talking to. I hate it that I've obviously done something to upset you."

Charley remained silent. Matt manfully continued.

"The problem is, honey, I was out of it that night. This guy must be getting old, he can't handle the drink the way he used to."

The weak joke did not elicit a response.

"Look," he tried again, "I'll be honest and tell you that my mind is fuzzy on what actually happened that night, after we got back from the restaurant. I mean, did we . . . ? Did I . . . ?"

Matt came to a grinding halt. There was no more he could say until Charley answered him. She raised her eyes to him slowly. He wasn't sure if they were full of sadness or anger.

"You don't . . . *remember*?"

"No." Matt blushed. "I don't. I'm real sorry, but it's better that I'm truthful."

"Jeez," Charley sighed, "Well, that just about caps the whole thing."

"What can I say? I'm embarrassed and horrified. I suppose . . . it's not as if we haven't . . . I mean . . . been there before."

"Oh—" Charley's eyes glazed over. "So that makes it all right, does it? The fact you jumped me is made 'OK' because we'd done it before. Is that what you're saying to me, Matt?"

"No, I—shit, Charley!" Matt ran a hand through his hair distractedly then looked at her. "Are you serious?! You say I 'jumped' you that night?"

"Yes, Matt, you did. Or are you accusing me of lying?"

"Of course not. Goddammit! I can't believe I could behave like that. I'm sorry, Charley. Real sorry," he emphasized.

"Yeah, well"—Charley shrugged—"not as sorry as I am. Don't worry, I got with the program pretty soon after. Whether you remembered or you didn't, the fact that I heard nothing from you in the two weeks afterward told me all I needed to know. It's the gentleman's job to call the lady, in case you've forgotten," she added. "You used me, Matt. And I don't think I deserved that."

"No, you didn't," Matt agreed, squirming under her cold gaze. "I feel like a total jerk, and if I were you, I doubt I'd want to have anything to do with me again."

"The thought has crossed my mind," agreed Charley as their pizzas arrived. "I mean, if nothing else, I thought we were friends. And you sure shouldn't treat your worst enemy the way you've treated me."

"No." Matt was struggling to deal with a scenario he could hardly believe he had created. The behavior Charley described was completely out of character for him, therefore he had few tools at his disposal to defend himself. "Charley, I don't know what to say. Jesus! I hardly know who I am at the moment. Having prided myself on being Mr. Nice Guy, maybe one way or another I have to come to terms with the fact I'm not."

"No." Charley put a tiny piece of pizza in her mouth and chewed it, obviously reluctant to let him off the hook. "Just maybe, you're not. And there's me listening to you pour out your heart day after day, night after night, about Grania. Trying to be there when you needed me. And how do you treat me in return?"

"Hey, Charley, I understand why," Matt breathed, dazed from her verbal assault, "but you sure know how to make a guy feel bad."

"I'm sorry, Matt," she agreed. "But that night, before you jumped me, you were very persuasive."

"Was I?"

"Yeah. For example, you told me you loved me."

Matt felt he was drowning in a sea of accusations. And yet, they must be true. Why would Charley lie? She simply wasn't that kind of girl. They'd grown up together—he knew her better than any other female with the exception of Grania. Matt had run out of words to say. He sat silently, regarding her across the table.

"Look, Matt . . ." Charley let out a heavy sigh. "I really get that you're not in a good space at the moment. You were drunk that night and I accept you said and did things you didn't mean. And I was available and believed what you said, when I shouldn't have done. So I guess it's my fault too."

"Hell, Charley, it sure isn't your fault. It's mine, and I don't want you to take one iota of blame. If I could press the rewind button, I would. And you're right, I'm not in a good space right now. But that's not your problem and I'll never forgive myself for hurting you. I'm surprised you haven't moved out, decided never to speak to me again."

"I would have done if I could, but the apartment's taking far longer to get fixed than I thought. Don't worry, Matt," she added sadly, "When it's habitable, I'll be out of there."

"Is this the end of our friendship?" he asked slowly.

"I don't know, Matt," she sighed. "Now we've talked, I need some time to think things through."

"Sure."

"I need to ask you, Matty, to be real honest with me. When you said . . . what you said that night before we made love, you didn't mean it, did you?"

"You mean that I loved you?" questioned Matt.

"Yeah."

"I *do* love you, Charley," he struggled, "You know I do. I wasn't lying. As I've said before, we've known each other forever, you're the sis I've never had. But . . ." Matt sighed, simply not knowing how to phrase the words he needed to use next.

"It's not *that* kind of love," Charley prompted.

Matt paused before he spoke. "No."

"Because you're still in love with Grania?"

"Yeah. I guess I am."

Matt watched as Charley cut another tiny piece of pizza, placed it on her fork and chewed it thoroughly. She swallowed, then immediately stood up. "Sorry, Matt, I gotta use the restroom."

Matt watched as Charley walked as swiftly across the restaurant as her upbringing would allow and disappeared down some steps. He put the pizza to one side, rested his elbows on the table and grazed his cheeks roughly with the palms of his hands. This was a nightmare . . . How *could* he have done what Charley had reported to him? *He,* a psychologist, aware of the failings of human nature, had himself fallen victim to its weaknesses.

Matt wondered just what was up with him; his entire self-image during his thirty-six years had been built around the knowledge that he was a "good guy." He'd believed he had always treated women with respect, never abused them or taken advantage of them. Valued their strengths and qualities and stayed within the parameters of the background and education he'd been given. Above all, Matt had always tried to act with integrity, and the thought that he hadn't done so on the night with Charley—one of his closest friends, for Christ's sake—filled him with self-loathing.

Matt looked toward the steps, but there was still no sign of Charley. At least he'd had the guts to be honest with her and make it clear that there wasn't a future for them. However much it hurt her, and even if what had happened that night had made their friendship irreparable, Matt knew it had been the right thing to do.

Because . . .

Whether Matt liked it, or wished it, or wanted it, the painful truth was that he was still in love with Grania.

A pale Charley emerged from the restroom and sat down opposite Matt.

"You OK?" Matt frowned. "You look real sick."

Charley shook her head. "No, I'm not 'OK.' I'm not OK at all."

"Is this me? Have I done this to you?"

"Yup, I suppose in a way you have." Charley looked up at him, tears in her eyes, limpid against the canvas of her pale skin. "Because the problem is, Matt, that I'm pregnant."

29

Grania had woken up one morning and seen the first buds of wild fuchsia that would eventually turn the hedgerows along the lane into a riot of purple. The sight of them not only heralded the fact that spring was here, with summer hot on its heels, but that she had been in Ireland for almost four months. As she dressed and went down for a hurried breakfast, before driving Aurora to school then heading up to Dunworley House, Grania felt unnerved at the ease with which she had slipped into a routine. And how her everyday life here felt as normal as her previous life in New York. As she unlocked the door to her studio, Grania wondered whether this was partly to do with the fact she was involved in a new project. The feeling was reminiscent of the times she'd spent in her studio in the loft in TriBeCa; those moments when a sculpture had consumed her every waking thought.

As she took off her jacket and went over to her workbench, Grania mused on the fact that, recently, obtaining a creative thrill from her work had been rare. Producing sculptures of children and animals for the well-heeled of the East Coast had become her bread and butter. It had been a way of earning a living, and allowed her the head space to pursue the "project" closest to her heart; that of having a baby.

Grania studied the two sculptures that currently sat on her workbench. And felt a tinge of excitement run through her. Both of them were as yet unfinished and imperfect, but she was enough of a professional to know they had the makings of the best work she had ever produced. And the reason, she thought to herself, was simply because she had been inspired, not forced, to create them. The feeling she had as she sat down at the bench and concentrated on molding the clay into a delicately arched foot was that which had taken her into sculpting in the first place. Creating an image, a likeness of something beautiful—holding on to the moment she'd seen it and transferring it into a material object which captured it forever—was invigorating.

She'd had the inspiration one afternoon as she and Aurora had walked up the cliff path with Lily the puppy. She'd watched as Aurora danced ahead of her, her effortless grace exquisite to behold. Grania had been beset then by a sudden urge to capture it. Whipping out her phone, she'd taken some fast photos of the child in various positions of physical exuberance. And, the next morning, had begun work on a series of sculptures.

Since then, she'd experienced a sense of peace—working in her wonderful studio all day, classical music on the sound system, the view in front of her a magnificent window to the subtlety of the changing season.

This afternoon, having asked permission from Miss Elva, Grania was going down to the studio to watch and take photos of Aurora dancing.

Having lost herself in her work all morning, Grania glanced at her watch and realized it was past three o'clock. She would only just make it in time to collect Aurora from school and take her down to Clonakilty for her class.

The subject of her enthusiasm sat next to her happily as they drove into town, chattering about her new best friend at school, who was coming around for tea at the farm tomorrow to see the puppy. As she parked the car, Grania thought how the simple things many children took for granted were those that gave Aurora the most pleasure. She was living a normal life for the first time *in* her life.

Grania sat in a corner of the studio, having resorted to her sketchbook as a less intrusive means of capturing Aurora as she danced. Even in the past two months, Aurora had improved beyond all recognition. The natural ability she possessed was slowly being honed into the technical positions ballet required. And, Grania thought as Aurora executed a perfect pirouette, while her life at the farmhouse might verge on the normal, Aurora's talent was extraordinary.

At the end of the class, Miss Elva shooed Aurora out of the studio and told her to change out of her leotard. She turned to Grania. "Well now, what do you think?"

"She's exquisite to watch."

"Yes, she is." Miss Elva spoke in reverential tones. "She's by far the most talented pupil I've had the good fortune to teach. I was worried that her late start would cause a problem, and she's still a way to go on her technique. But I think she has every chance of being accepted into the Royal Ballet School. Did you manage to speak to her father?"

"He knows Aurora's taking lessons, but I haven't mentioned the idea of a full-time ballet school. And I'm not sure whether it would be right for her. She's settled, for the first time in her life. When would she have to audition?"

"At the latest, in eighteen months' time. She should be training full-time when she's eleven."

"Right. Well, why don't we see how she goes? And maybe next year we can think again." Grania handed over the money for the lesson, thanked Miss Elva and went to collect Aurora.

"So," she said lightly to Aurora on the way home, "do you think that one day you'd like to go away to a ballet school and learn to dance full-time?"

"Well, I love ballet, you know that, Grania," Aurora confirmed. "But the problem is, who would look after Lily or help Shane milk the cows if I did?"

"Good point," agreed Grania.

"And I wouldn't want to leave behind all my new friends from school," continued Aurora. "Perhaps when I'm older."

"Yes, perhaps when you're older."

Later that night, just as Grania was preparing to go upstairs to bed, her cell phone rang.

"Hello?"

"Is that Grania?"

"Yes."

"It's Alexander here."

It was probably a bad line, but his voice sounded muffled and weak.

"Hello, Alexander. How are you?"

"I'm . . ." there was a pause before Alexander said, "OK. How's Aurora?"

"She's very happy and settled here with us at the farm. School seems to be going really well and she's made lots of new friends. And I was speaking to her ballet teacher today and—"

"Grania," Alexander halted her, "I need to see you. Urgently," he added.

"Right, when will you be home?"

"*That* is the problem. I'm afraid that I can't come home just now. I have to ask you to come here to me."

"And where would that be?" Having not heard from him for over a month, Grania had no idea where he was.

"Switzerland. I'm in Switzerland."

"I see. Well, if it's urgent, then . . ."

"It is," Alexander underlined. "Forgive me for asking you to make the journey, Grania, but really, I have little choice."

"OK. Well now, it's Wednesday today . . . we've got the sheep-shearing on the farm this weekend, so how about next Tuesday?"

"Grania, I need you to come tomorrow."

"Tomorrow!"

"Yes. I've already booked you a flight. You leave Cork airport at two forty-five, land in London at four, then take the British Airways flight to Geneva, which leaves at six. My driver will collect you from the airport and bring you here to me."

"Right," Grania said uncertainly. "Do you want me to bring Aurora?"

"No. Definitely not . . ." Alexander's voice trailed off. "Oh, and remember to bring your birth certificate. Swiss passport control can be notoriously difficult, and it's best to be prepared."

"Right."

"I'll see you tomorrow evening. And Grania?"

"Yes?"

"Thank you."

Grania pressed the button to end the call and sat at the kitchen table, dazed. She wondered what Alexander would have said if she'd refused to go. As far as she could see, it had been a done deal before he'd even picked up the receiver to call her.

"What is it that you're thinking, Grania?"

Her mother's voice broke into her thoughts. She was standing by the door, staring at her daughter.

"I . . . I just had a very strange call from Alexander," Grania said slowly. "He wants me to fly to Switzerland to see him tomorrow. He's already booked the flight for me to go."

"Really?" Kathleen folded her arms and raised an eyebrow. "And are you?"

"I don't feel as though I have any choice."

"Well now, you could always say no."

"Yes, I could, Mam, but there was just something in his voice that"—Grania shrugged—"something's not right. I know it isn't."

"I'd say that if Himself has got a problem, it would be up to him to come back here and tell you about it. Not have you chasing across the world to see him."

"I agree, but there's not a lot I can do about it, is there? He's also asked me to take my birth certificate, says the authorities can be difficult. Could you dig it out for me, Mam?"

"I could, yes, but something doesn't smell right to me."

"To me neither," Grania said. "But the best thing to do is to go and see what he wants."

"Grania." Kathleen walked toward her. "Please understand that I don't want to interfere, but is there . . . has there been anything between you and Alexander?"

"I just don't know." Grania's need to open up to *someone* overrode her normal reticence to divulge information to her mother. "I really don't know."

"Has he . . ." Kathleen cleared her throat. "When you were up there . . . ?"

"We've kissed, Mam," she confessed, "and yes, if truth be told, I do feel something for him. But then . . ." Grania shook her head in confusion. "He said—well, he said he couldn't take the relationship any further."

"Did he tell you why?"

"No. Perhaps he's still in love with Lily, perhaps there's someone else . . . who knows? One thing's for sure, I certainly don't," Grania sighed.

"Well, for what it's worth, I watched Himself that night when Aurora had taken it in her head to run away. I watched him watching *you*. Whether the fondness that was there in his eyes as he looked at you was because of the love you've shown his daughter, or whether it's more than that, I wouldn't be knowing. Either way, Grania, you mean something to him. The question is, does he mean anything to you?"

"Yes, Mam, he does. But how, or why, or where it's going, I can't say. Besides, I . . ."

"Yes?"

"I'm not over Matt," she admitted.

"I know you're not, pet. And maybe you never will be. But you've made it mighty clear to me that's all in the past," said Kathleen. "Just don't rush into a future now, will you?"

"No." Grania stood up. "I'd better be off to bed if I'm to travel to Switzerland tomorrow." She walked over to her mother and gave her a hug. "Thanks, Mam. As you always say, it'll probably all come out in the wash."

"Let's hope so. Good night."

Kathleen watched her daughter as she left the kitchen then put the kettle on the range to boil. The sixth sense her children and husband teased her about, yet trusted when it suited them to do so, was on red alert.

"That family," she muttered as she pulled her cardigan tighter around her and paced up and down the kitchen, waiting for the kettle to boil. She sat down with a mug of hot cocoa, trying to rationalize why something inside her was telling her that Grania needed to know the rest of the story now . . . *now,* before she left the safety of this house for Switzerland tomorrow.

"I'm after being a silly old woman, why should Grania need to know any more of the past?" she muttered to herself. Having drunk her cocoa, she sighed heavily. "I surrender," she said to the heavens, then stood up from the table. She climbed the stairs wearily and knocked on Grania's bedroom door. "'Tis me, Mam," she whispered. "Can I come in?"

"Of course, Mam," said Grania, who was sitting cross-legged on her bed, a half-packed suitcase in front of her. "I'm not sleepy either. I'm wondering what on earth I'm going to face tomorrow." She raised an eyebrow.

"Yes, well—" Kathleen sat down on the bed. "That's why I've come to see you. That voice in my head, well now, that voice is telling me I need to tell you the rest of the story before you go. About Lily." Kathleen reached for her daughter's hand and squeezed it. "It's quite a story, and it'll be some time in the telling, so it might be a late night for both of us."

"I don't mind, Mam," Grania encouraged, "I can do with something to take my mind off tomorrow. I'm all ears."

"Right, so." Kathleen swallowed hard. "'Tis not a story I've ever told before on my own tongue. And I might shed a few tears in the telling of it too."

"Oh, Mam." Grania held her mother's hand tightly. "You take your time. We've got all night, there's no rush."

"Right." Kathleen steeled herself to begin. "This part of the story starts when I was sixteen years old and Lily Lisle was fifteen."

"Were you friends, Mam?" Grania was surprised.

"Yes, we were." Kathleen nodded. "You have to remember, Lily spent so much time down here at the farmhouse that I regarded her like my little sister. And my big brother—"

"Your *brother*?!" Grania stared at her mother in surprise. "I didn't know you had a brother, Mam. You've never spoken about him."

"No . . ." Kathleen shook her head slowly. "Now then, where shall I begin . . . ?"

30

Dunworley, West Cork, Ireland, 1970

Sixteen-year-old Kathleen Ryan woke up and jumped out of bed to pull the curtains back and see what the weather was doing today. If it was fair, she, Joe and Lily were taking a picnic down on to the sands of Dunworley beach. If it was raining—which it often did, even in high summer in these parts—it was another dull day inside playing cards or board games. Lily would want to make up a play, in which she would have the leading part. She had her mother's trunk of old evening clothes up at the big house and liked nothing better than preening in dresses that were too big for her in front of the mirror.

"When I'm properly grown up, I'll be beautiful and a handsome prince will carry me away from here," she would say as she struck a pose.

There was no doubt that Lily *would* be beautiful—she was already a stunner at fifteen. "There'll be boys knocking down her door to take her out, that's for certain," Kathleen's mother had once said to Seamus, her husband.

Kathleen had miserably regarded her own solid body in the mirror—her mouse-colored hair and pale face with its annoying sprinkling of freckles across the bridge of her nose.

"It takes more than beauty to win a man, sweetheart, and they'll love you for your other qualities," her mammy had comforted her when she'd complained. Kathleen wasn't sure what these other "qualities" were exactly, but she didn't really mind being the plain one. Or that Lily seemed to simply demand being the center of attention wherever she went.

Or that Joe, her brother, worshipped the ground Lily walked on. Kathleen understood that Lily, with her exotic looks, her glamorous mother and her rich daddy up at the Big House, was an entity she could never begin to compete with.

And she didn't envy her; in fact, she felt sorry for her. Aunt Anna, Lily's mother—who was a famous ballerina—was rarely at home. Sebastian Lisle, her daddy, was a distant, elderly figure whom Kathleen rarely saw. And from the sound of things, neither did Lily. She was left in the care of a succession of governesses, whom she spent her life trying to evade, and usually succeeding.

As Kathleen dressed hastily to begin her morning tasks of collecting the eggs and bringing in a pail of fresh milk from the cowsheds, she thought of Lily, probably still lying asleep in her pretty bedroom in the big house on top of the cliffs. Lily didn't have tasks to do. She had a maid to serve her breakfast, lunch and supper, wash her clothes and provide her with everything she needed. Sometimes Kathleen would grumble about this to her mother when the day was freezing and she had to go outside.

"But, Kathleen, you have the one thing Lily doesn't, and that's a family," her mammy would reply.

To Kathleen's mind, Lily had that as well—she more or less lived under their roof. And yet no one would ever ask *her* to lift a finger.

Still, despite Lily's privilege, and her sometimes irritating airs and graces, Kathleen felt very protective of her. Even though Lily was about a year younger, she had a childlike quality, a vulnerability that brought out Kathleen's latent maternal instincts. And she didn't seem to have an ounce of common sense on her. Lily was always the one to suggest adventures—climbing down precarious rocks, sneaking out at night to go to the beach and swim in the sea—and she seemed to have little fear. Often, these ideas would go horribly wrong, and Kathleen would not only find herself rescuing Lily from danger, but taking the punishment from her mam and dad as though it had been her idea in the first place.

And of course, Joe, bless him, would follow Lily to the ends of the earth if she asked him to.

If Kathleen felt protective of Lily, it was nothing to what she felt for her big, gentle brother. Three years ago, Kathleen had arrived home wretched, having found Joe in the lane. He'd been used by the boys in the village as target practice after the recent conker harvest.

"They called him names, Mam, terrible names! They said he was the village idiot, that he had no wits, that he should be in a home for spastics. Why do they do this to him, Mam? He just wants to be friends."

After Sophia had bathed her son's bruises with witch hazel, then sent him off outside to help his daddy bring in the cows, she shut the kitchen door and explained to Kathleen why her big brother was different from other boys.

"It was a difficult birth," Sophia had said, "and the doctors think that Joe was starved of oxygen for a while before he was born. It did something to his brain."

"But Joe's not stupid, Mam, is he? He can write his name and count a bit?"

"No, darling, Joe's not stupid. He's just what the doctors would call 'slow.'"

"And the animals love him, Mam. He talks to them so gently and they trust him."

"Yes, Kathleen, they do. But then, animals are kinder than human beings," Sophia had replied with a sigh.

"Those boys at school are always getting him into trouble, Mam. And just because he's bigger than they are, the teachers always believe 'tis Joe that started it. And, Mam, he just takes it!" Kathleen had buried her head in her hands. "I can't bear to watch how they bully him. And he never fights back, just smiles and accepts his punishment. It's not fair, Mam, it's not fair. Joe wouldn't hurt a fly, you know he wouldn't."

Shortly after that, her mother and father had taken Joe out of school. "I'd say he's learned all he ever will and he'll be happier on the farm with me and his animals," Seamus had said.

And her daddy had been right. Joe now helped full-time on the farm, his way with animals and his astonishing physical strength an asset to the family business.

As Kathleen collected the eggs, she pondered Joe's existence. He was always happy, never seemed to be getting down or cross. He'd rise early in the morning, eat his breakfast and be out on the land until the night. He'd come in, eat the supper prepared for him and go to bed. Joe had no friends outside his family, yet he didn't seem lonely. And at seventeen, he had none of the normal teenage interests of other boys his age. The only moment Joe's eyes really lit up was when Lily Lisle came to the house. He would watch her silently as she pranced around the kitchen, flicking her mane of red-gold hair back over her shoulder.

"Tiger," Joe had once said suddenly when the three of them were out on a walk together.

"Where's the tiger, Joe?" Lily looked around.

"You, tiger."

"Tiger-Lily!" Kathleen and Lily had exclaimed together.

"Hair," Joe had pointed at Lily. "Tiger color."

"Joe, that's a very clever name for me," Lily had said, tucking her small, pale arm into his big one. "It's a character from a book called *Peter Pan,* and she's an Indian Princess."

"You are princess." Joe had looked down at Lily, love shining from his eyes.

Despite Lily's inherent selfishness, she was very good with Joe. She'd take time to listen as he formed his words, and feign interest in the thrush with the damaged wing that Joe had rescued and was nursing back to health. This, above everything, made Kathleen forgive Lily her many failings. Spoiled and self-obsessed she might be, but she was kind and caring to Joe.

Kathleen placed the fresh eggs in the pantry and went into the kitchen for breakfast. Joe was already sitting at the table eating, his big hand curled around his cereal spoon.

"Morning," Kathleen offered as she sliced some bread and buttered it. "The day's fine, Joe, will we go to the beach?"

"Yes. And Lily."

"She said she'd be down here about eleven. She promised to bring some food, but she's always after saying that and forgetting," said Kathleen. "I'll make enough sandwiches for the three of us."

"Hello, everyone, I'm here!" Lily appeared in the kitchen later with her usual dramatic flourish. "Guess who's home?" she said, rolling her eyes as she plucked an apple from the fruit bowl and bit into it.

"Who?" asked Kathleen, stowing the sandwiches into the picnic basket.

"Gerald! My ghastly half brother, Gerald." Lily flopped daintily into a chair. "I haven't seen him for over a year—last hols he went to stay with his mother's relatives up in Clare."

Both Kathleen and Joe sent Lily sympathetic glances. Gerald, Sebastian Lisle's only son by his first wife, Adele, had been the bane of their lives. An arrogant little boy who regarded Kathleen and Joe as though they were a nasty smell under his nose, he'd still want to join the three of them in their games, but spent most of his time ruining them. He'd sulk if he didn't win every time, accuse them of cheating, and often lash out aggressively, especially at Joe, whom, being the same age, he teased mercilessly.

"He isn't coming to the beach, is he?" Kathleen asked anxiously.

"No, he told me this morning that he's nearly eighteen now and practically an adult. Luckily, I don't think he wants anything to do with us. He's grown up a lot, really. I hardly recognized him. He looks like a man and he's almost as tall as Daddy. If he wasn't Ghastly Gerald, I'd actually think he was rather handsome," Lily giggled.

"Not with that personality on him." Kathleen shuddered. "Well now, it sounds grand that he's too above himself to join us. Are you ready, Joe?"

Joe, as always, was staring adoringly at Lily. "Ready," he answered.

The three of them made their way to the beach, Lily hitching a piggyback on Joe's strong, broad shoulders, clinging like a baby monkey and screaming in pretend fear as he clambered down the rocks.

"There now," said Kathleen, panting as she set down the heavy picnic basket on the soft sand, "let Lily down, Joe, and she can help me unpack the basket."

"Oh, but it's so hot and I want a dip in the sea immediately!" answered Lily, removing her dress to reveal a bathing costume, and the soft white contours of a body burgeoning into womanhood. "Race you, Joe!" Lily screamed excitedly as she charged off across the sand toward the sea.

Kathleen watched as Joe lumbered behind Lily, throwing off his shirt on the way and plunging into the sea in his shorts a few seconds later. Kathleen set the blankets on the sand and placed the picnic she'd made earlier on one of them. She looked at Lily, in all her lithe-limbed beauty, screaming and splashing in the waves with Joe, then down at her own dumpy body, and wished she could be as unself-conscious as her cousin.

Ten minutes later, Joe plodded back toward her and pointed to the towel. "Lily cold," he said.

Kathleen nodded, handed over the towel and watched Joe return to the shoreline to shroud the shivering Lily in its warmth. She thought it was a good job she was not the jealous type. Even though she'd looked out for Joe all of his life, protected him fiercely because he was incapable of protecting himself, loved him and defended him, Kathleen knew where Joe's heart lay. If it were a choice between saving his sister or his cousin from drowning, Lily would win hands down. Joe's adoration of Lily lit him up; any crumb from her table would be worth a year of practical and domestic care from herself. And if Lily made Joe happy, then what harm? Kathleen only hoped that when Lily grew up and moved on—there was no doubt she was so beautiful she'd have the pick of any man she chose—that Joe would survive it.

Kathleen already understood how beauty helped you; even at school, the pretty girls got away with more than the plain ones. It didn't seem to matter who you were inside—good or bad—but if your packaging was more appealing, it seemed you had an immediate advantage. People were in awe of beauty, especially men. They said it was only skin deep, but Kathleen disagreed. All the film stars were beautiful, the ladies who lived in the big houses were beautiful, and you rarely found a beautiful girl languishing as a skivvy in a kitchen. Unless you were Cinderella, but then your prince came along and knew you were the one because you had a pair of tiny, feminine feet on you.

"Oh, Kathleen! I'm starving! Can I have a sandwich?" Lily was back, Joe following a few paces behind her.

"There now, we've potted meat and jam." Kathleen handed Lily a paper napkin with the sandwiches placed on them.

Joe picked up the spare blanket and wrapped it around Lily's shoulders. Then he sat himself on the sand in his wet shorts next to his sister.

"Here, Joe, you need to eat too." Kathleen indicated his share of the sandwiches.

"Joe, can I swap my potted meats for your jam?" said Lily. "I hate potted meat."

Kathleen watched Joe hand over his jam sandwiches silently. Lily chewed them, tossing the crusts into the sand, then lay back and stretched her long, slim legs in the direction of the sun.

"Why did I have to be born with such pale Irish skin?" Lily groaned. "I look like a white moon on a dark night."

"No. Beautiful." Joe smiled.

"Thank you, Joe. Do you know what, Kathleen?" Lily pulled herself up on her elbows. "Joe asked me to marry him when we were in the sea." She giggled. "Isn't that sweet?"

"Well now, I should say it was," said Kathleen, not liking the patronizing look in Lily's eyes.

"Look after you," Joe nodded as he chewed his way through another potted meat sandwich.

"Thank you, Joe. I know you always look after me. And I promise you I'll think about the offer." Lily, eyes full of amusement, lay back down on the sand to sunbathe.

31

I hope you don't mind, but Gerald wants to come along."

Kathleen stared at the tall, handsome figure standing behind Lily on the doorstep of the kitchen. She tried to equate the "new," manly Gerald with the Gerald of old, and was comforted to notice the familiar sneer on his thin lips. "Hello, Gerald," she offered.

"Hello . . ." Gerald scratched his head. "Sorry, can't remember your name."

"Kathleen, 'tis Kathleen Doonan. And this is my brother, Joe."

"Of course, excuse me. How are you both?"

"Grand altogether," said Kathleen. "Well now, are we off?"

"Hello, Lily," Joe said, waiting for his usual hug.

"Hi, Joe," Lily replied, not moving from Gerald's side. "We've stolen Daddy's fishing rods, haven't we, Gerald?" Lily smiled up at him.

"Yes, a little better than a wooden pole and string with a piece of bacon on the end of it," he smirked, glancing at Kathleen's and Joe's tools for the job in hand.

The four of them left the house and walked down toward the stream. There was an uncomfortable silence, Kathleen unnerved by Gerald's presence. Lily walked by her half brother's side, chatting to him comfortably, while Joe brought up the rear. They reached the stream, Gerald producing a smart folding stool, which he immediately handed to Lily with a flourish. "Can't have that *derrière* of yours getting soiled, now can we?" he commented.

"Thank you, Gerald, it's very kind of you," said Lily, sitting down.

The other three settled themselves on the bank, Gerald taking care to show Lily how to use the rod. They sat in silence, their normal banter quieted by Gerald's presence. Every sentence Kathleen thought of stuck on her lips. She glanced to her left and saw Joe gazing morosely into the river, nose out of joint that he was not sitting next to his beloved Lily.

Of course, Gerald was the first to get a catch. There was a lot of excitable praise from Lily as Gerald reeled in a very respectable trout.

"Well done." She smiled at him. "You obviously have the knack."

"It helps that these rivers are still well stocked. Father's always looked after our lands well."

"Beg pardon, Gerald, but 'tis our stream now. My mammy and daddy bought this land last year." Kathleen's pride couldn't stop her from mentioning it. "We hope to buy the rest of the land we rent and the farmhouse too, when your daddy has a mind to sell it to us."

"Well, well, landowners after all these years," Gerald sneered. "I presume Lil's mother had something to do with that, eh? Wanted to give her sister a gift, perhaps?"

"No, sir, I mean, Gerald." Kathleen reddened with anger. "My mammy and daddy bought it outright fair and square, so they did."

"I see." Gerald raised an eyebrow, the news not pleasing him.

"Really," sighed Lily, "What does it matter who owns it? That poor fish will still end up on someone's dinner plate tonight. I shouldn't think he cares. Take my rod, Joe, I'm hot and I want to go for a swim."

Joe did so as Lily walked down the bank to find an easy place to enter the river. Pulling off her dress, she plunged into the icy water. Kathleen glanced from Joe to Gerald, watching two sets of male eyes pinned to Lily as she swam.

"I must admit," said Gerald, after they'd eaten their picnic, "this part of the world is rather beautiful when the sun shines on it. Pity your mother isn't here more often to enjoy it, Lil. Where is she at the moment, by the way?"

"Oh, in London, you know how she hates the country," replied Lily casually.

"I'm amazed Pa puts up with it. Having an errant wife must be awfully hard," said Gerald.

"You know Mummy; she's a bird of paradise and needs to be free," Lily said equably. "She'll fly home when she's ready."

"Whenever that may be," Gerald muttered under his breath. "Well, I won't be around much in the future, I'm off to Sandhurst to learn how to be an army officer," he announced, glancing at Joe and Kathleen. "I envy you two in some ways. Everything the same, day after day; counting the sheep, milking the cows . . ."

"I'd say 'twas more to our life than that," Kathleen said defensively, loathing the way he constantly patronized them.

"And what about his?" Gerald indicated Joe.

"Joe's happy. Aren't you, Joe?" Kathleen said softly.

"Am." Joe nodded. "Love Lily. Lily fine, Joe fine."

"Really?" Gerald raised an eyebrow. "'Love,' is it? Do you think that one day Lil'll marry you, Joe?"

"Yes. Marry Lily. Look after her."

"Goodness!" Gerald laughed. "Did you hear that, Lil? Joe thinks you're going to marry him."

"Don't tease him, Gerald, he doesn't understand," countered Lily.

"Well, he will soon, when you're packed off to boarding school in a few weeks' time and you're no longer here."

Lily pulled her knees up to her chest. "They can't make me go if I don't want to, Joe. And I don't want to, so there," Lily pouted.

Kathleen glanced at Joe's face, which had horror written all over it.

"Lily go?" he asked slowly.

Lily stood up, walked to Joe and sat beside him, patting his hand. "Don't worry, Joe, I promise I won't be leaving here, whatever Mother and Father say."

"I doubt you have any choice, little sister," said Gerald.

"Lily stay." Joe glanced at Gerald and put a protective arm around Lily's shoulders.

"You see?" Lily smiled. "Joe won't let me go, will you?"

"No." Joe stood up suddenly and walked toward Gerald, bearing down on him. "Lily stay here."

"There's no need to get upset with me, Joe, it's the parents that are in charge, not me. Although I'd say that for Lil's sake, it's about time she learned a few more manners and how to be more ladylike."

"Lily *lady*!" The punch was thrown by Joe in a second, striking Gerald squarely on the jaw.

Gerald was knocked backward by the force of the blow. "I say! No need for that, old chap!"

Kathleen felt paralyzed, stunned by Joe's aggressive reaction. Never had she seen him lash out with violence before. And he could not have inflicted his uncharacteristic behavior on to a more malicious victim.

"Joe!" She came to her senses. "Now you apologize immediately to Gerald for punching him. Sure, Gerald, he didn't mean it, he's just very protective of his Lily." Kathleen tugged at Joe's arm. "Come on, say sorry, Joe."

Joe looked at his feet, took a deep breath and said, "Sorry."

"Well, no harm done, eh?" Gerald stood up, brushing himself down, and turned to Lily. "Taken worse punches than that in my time and lived to tell the tale."

Kathleen could see his ego was more bruised than his jaw. Especially in front of Lily.

"Well, let's be hoping we can forget all about it and not let it spoil the rest of the day," Kathleen said desperately.

"Of course," said Gerald. "Let's forget it. Shake, Joe?"

Reluctantly, Joe offered his hand.

"There, all forgotten," said Gerald.

Somehow, Kathleen knew Gerald Lisle would neither forgive nor forget.

The summer wore on and Joe and Kathleen saw less of Lily than they normally would. Joe spent hours staring out of his bedroom window at the lane, waiting for Lily to appear. When she did, she seemed distracted, different somehow. Kathleen thought that perhaps it was the looming specter of boarding school in her thoughts.

"I shan't stay if I don't like it, you know," Lily said to Kathleen and Joe one hot August night as they strolled along the cliff path. "I shall simply run away."

"Ah, now, I'm sure 'twill be better than you think, Lily." Kathleen looked at Joe's sad, earnest face. "And remember, you'll be back for the Christmas holidays in the blink of an eye. Won't she, Joe?"

"Lily stay. Lily stay here."

"I promise I'll be back, Joe." Lily threw her arms around Joe's shoulders. "But I have to leave for London in a week's time to buy all my clothes for school. Mummy's arriving here to take me to England. Father's all of a quiver because he knows she's coming." Lily raised her eyebrows. "Honestly, I don't know how he puts up with her. She plays that rotten ballet music over and over again in the house. It's so depressing. I can't understand why anyone enjoys watching lots of people standing on one leg and not saying a word for a whole two hours! It's so boring."

Kathleen had heard her mother saying that Lily had an aversion to ballet because it represented the passion that was the center of her mother's world, and took her away from her daughter. She, however, was inclined to agree with Lily. Having been taken by her aunt to see a ballet in Dublin once, she'd fallen asleep halfway through.

"Now, I must dash. Gerald's teaching me to play bridge. And I'm getting to be rather an expert." Lily kissed both Joe and Kathleen and skipped off in the direction of Dunworley House.

Joe watched her until she was a mere dot in the distance. Then he sat down heavily and stared out to sea. Kathleen knelt next to him, putting her arm around his broad shoulders.

"She will be back, Joe, you know she will, so."

Tears appeared in Joe's eyes. "Love her, Kathleen. Love her."

Kathleen always knew when Aunt Anna had come down to visit as soon as she entered their farmhouse. The pungent smell of perfume and cigarette smoke drifted into the kitchen from the sitting room. And she could hear her aunt's throaty laugh and the tinkle of china cups—only ever brought out of the cabinet by her mother when Aunt Anna graced them with her presence.

"Kathleen, my darling! How are you, p-precious?" Aunt Anna said as Kathleen bent to kiss her. "My," she cast an appraising eye over her niece, "You've filled out since I last saw you."

"Thank you," said Kathleen automatically, not at all sure it was a compliment.

"Come." Aunt Anna patted the seat next to her on the sofa. "Sit down and tell me what you've b-been up to."

Kathleen sat, feeling—as she always did—like a carthorse next to the whisper-thin elegance of her aunt. Aunt Anna's jet-black hair, which her mammy said came out of a bottle, was held sleekly in a coil at the nape of her neck. Her huge eyes were rimmed with kohl, her lips a fiery red. Which, set against the backdrop of her perfect white skin, gave her a dramatic and arresting look.

As usual, Kathleen was tongue-tied by the sheer presence of the woman she knew was world-famous in the ballet community. The contrast between the sisters, who may not have been connected by blood—her mammy had told her Anna had been adopted by her parents—but had grown up together in the same household nevertheless, could not have been greater. Sitting in this small room, filled with drab, dark furniture, Aunt Anna looked like an exotic bloom growing by mistake in an Irish bog.

"So come now, Kathleen, talk to your aunt and tell her all your news," Anna encouraged.

"I . . ." Kathleen's mind was a blank; she could not think of one thing she could possibly say that would be interesting to someone like her aunt. "Well . . . I've had the holidays, and I go back to school in a week's time," Kathleen managed.

"Any thoughts on a future c-career yet?" Anna probed.

Kathleen hadn't a clue in her head. To say she wanted to be a wife and mother and not much more seemed the wrong answer to give. "I don't know, Aunt."

"And how about boys?" Anna nudged her conspiratorially. "Surely there must be some young man beating a p-path to your door?"

Kathleen thought of the young man she'd met recently from Skibbereen, at a local hop. John Ryan had danced with her four times and they'd worked out that they were distantly related through her grandmother, Coleen Ryan. But then, around these parts, everybody was related somehow.

"I can see there's someone, my d-darling. You're blushing!"

"Really, Kathleen?" said her mother from the armchair opposite her. "You have a young man, do you? Well, she's never mentioned anything to me about it, Anna."

"Well, all girls like to have their secrets. Don't they, Kathleen?" Aunt Anna smiled.

"I've no secrets," she faltered, but could feel herself blushing.

"There's nothing wrong with a few secrets anyway, is there, Sophia?" Aunt Anna smiled. "I'm sure your mother has t-told you, Kathleen, that in order to keep me safe, Mary, my adoptive mother, told Lawrence Lisle, my guardian, that I'd died at boarding school of influenza! Can you imagine it?" Anna gave her signature throaty laugh. "And then I t-turned up in Ireland as bold as brass, and married the brother of a man who'd been told I was dead years before. Now that's what I call k-keeping a secret."

"Personally, Anna, I don't think it's a laughing matter." Sophia's eyes were full of thunder. "You know as well as I do that our mother did everything she could to protect you and keep you safe. Through great cost to herself, I might add. She could have ended up in prison."

"I know all that, little sister, and I'm awfully g-grateful to her for doing it. You know I am."

"That's why you didn't talk to her for fifteen years, and broke her heart, is it?" countered Sophia.

As she sat between them, Kathleen wished the ground would swallow her up.

"Honestly, Sophia! Please don't lecture me." Anna rolled her eyes. "All I did was what any normal young girl would d-do, and flew the nest. Please remember, at the time I had no idea of what Mary had done to help me. I can't be held responsible for that, can I? Now then, let's move on to the future. You know I'm t-taking Lily to London next week to fit her out for boarding school?"

"Yes, I do."

Kathleen watched her mother struggle to compose herself and realized there was a lot she still didn't know about the history between the two sisters.

"I just can't believe that I've got to leave on Monday," Lily sighed as she and Kathleen lay on the sand gazing up at the stars. "How can I live without *this*? All the space and freedom . . . the smell of the sea that comes through my bedroom window on the breeze in the morning . . . the storms that hurl the waves so angrily against the cliffs. And most of all," Lily sighed heavily, "no people. I'm not sure I like people. Do you, Kathleen?"

Kathleen was used to Lily's bizarre thoughts. "Well now, I can't say I've ever thought about whether I liked people or not. They're sort of *there,* aren't they? You have to live with them, don't you?"

"But can you imagine sharing your bedroom with seven strangers? That's what I'll be doing in a week's time. I don't think you even get to have a wash privately. Oh, Kathleen, can you imagine?"

To be fair, Kathleen could not. It suddenly made her own life seem very comfortable. She didn't understand why a girl who had been brought up to be as privileged as Lily was going to be taken and put into an establishment that, from what Lily described, was little better than what she had read of in Charles Dickens's *Oliver Twist*.

"Anyway," continued Lily, "as I said to you before, if I don't like it, I'll run away. I've stolen some money from Daddy to make sure I have enough to pay my fare back to Ireland. And, if needs be, I can sleep in one of your barns and you can bring me food."

"Ah now, Lily," Kathleen comforted, "it's got to be better than that. You said there are lots of well-to-do families sending their girls to the school you're going to. You'll make lots of friends, to be sure."

"But I *hate* rules, Kathleen. You know I do," Lily moaned. "I'm not good at them, really I'm not."

Kathleen wondered to herself whether this was because Lily didn't have many rules to begin with, or if it was simply her personality. Sophia always called her niece a free spirit and Kathleen supposed that was what she was.

"I'm sure it won't be as bad as you're thinking it will be. It's the thing young ladies have to do, isn't it?"

"Gerald says he loved Eton," sighed Lily. She turned suddenly on her front and put her elbows beneath her cheeks, gazing up at Kathleen. "I actually think Gerald's rather handsome now, don't you?"

"He wouldn't be my type," answered Kathleen, physically shuddering at the thought.

"Well, he's definitely improved from the arrogant, spotty toe-rag he used to be. By the way, he suggested that on my last night in Ireland, the four of us come down to the beach in the evening, build a fire and have a picnic as a sort of celebration good-bye to me. Are you on, Kathleen? You and Joe?"

"I am, to be sure, but as for Joe . . ." Kathleen sighed. "I wouldn't have thought Gerald wanted him anywhere near him."

"Oh, Gerald's forgotten all about that." Lily flicked Kathleen's worry away with a wave of her hand. "Just tell Joe I'll be there and I'm sure he'll want to come along. It wouldn't be the same without him, would it?"

"No," Kathleen agreed, "it wouldn't."

32

Sure enough, Joe's face lit up at the thought of an evening on the beach with Lily. Even if it did mean they had to tolerate Ghastly Gerald. As the sky became laden with the weight of night, Kathleen and Joe walked down to the cove.

"Now, Joe, remember, 'tis Lily's last night and a party. Whatever that Gerald says to you, promise me you won't let him rile you?"

"No, Kathleen."

"You promise, Joe?"

Joe nodded. "Promise. Have something. For Lily." Out of his pocket, Joe produced a tiny, exquisitely carved angel. "Lily is Angel," he stated.

Kathleen stopped walking and studied the object in the palm of Joe's hand. She had no idea how long it must have taken Joe to carve the wood or how his huge hands had found the delicacy to do so.

"Joe," Kathleen said with genuine admiration, "it's beautiful, it really is. I'd say you have a real talent for sculpting wood." She put her own hand on top of his palm. "And she'll be thrilled with it, so, I know she will."

Gerald and Lily had already set up camp by the time Kathleen and Joe arrived. A small fire was blazing on the sand and Gerald had begun to toast sausages on the flames.

"Hello, you two," said Lily excitedly. "Hope you've brought lots of food, I'm starving! Isn't this wonderful?"

The three of them watched as Lily suddenly careered across the beach, leaping and twirling with happiness.

"Even though she hates ballet, she's definitely inherited her mother's grace, wouldn't you say, Kathleen?" commented Gerald, his eyes never leaving Lily's dancing figure.

"Yes, she has." Kathleen cast a glance at Joe, who was staring at

Lily in wonder. Kathleen took up the blankets she'd brought with her and spread them on the ground. "Sit down there now, Joe."

Joe did so, without taking his eyes from Lily.

Lily arrived back panting and threw herself to the ground to catch her breath. "Oh! When hateful boarding school is over I shall come back here and live at Dunworley forever. Anyone for a swim before supper?"

Kathleen shook her head. "Too cold for me, Lily."

"What a yellow-belly you are. Where's your sense of adventure? It's my last night!"

"Oh, go on then," Kathleen replied reluctantly. "You be taking care of those sausages now, won't you, boys?"

The two boys watched the girls run off toward the waves. Gerald pulled a bottle out of the knapsack he'd brought with him. "And while they go for a swim, I thought you and I could take a taste of this to keep out the cold."

Joe's gaze turned slowly from Lily's disappearing figure toward Gerald. He surveyed the bottle in Gerald's hand.

"It's poteen. Homemade at that. One of my father's tenants gave it to him. Have you ever tried it, Joe?"

Joe shook his head slowly.

"Well, let's both have a little snifter. Cheers!" Gerald knocked back a healthy gulp and passed the bottle to Joe.

Joe sniffed the contents and wrinkled his nose.

"What are you? Man or mouse? Every Irishman should try their national drink. We wouldn't want Lily thinking you were a coward, Joe, would we?"

At this, Joe put the bottle tentatively to his lips and took a swig. Choking and coughing, he handed the bottle back to Gerald.

"The first gulp is always the worst, promise it tastes better after a few more." Gerald took another swig.

When the girls arrived back, the sausages were cooked, and Joe and Gerald seemed to be laughing at some unknown joke. Shivering, Kathleen wrapped a blanket around herself, glad to see there was no tension between the two boys.

"Have some elderflower juice." Gerald winked at Joe and handed both girls a glass. They both downed it thirstily.

"Yuck!" spluttered Lily. "It's got a very strange taste."

"It has, so." Kathleen eyed Gerald. "What's in it?"

"Just a little something to keep out the chill, eh, Joe? Like some more?"

Kathleen watched through the firelight as Gerald passed Joe a bottle.

"Now, who would like a sausage?" he asked.

Forty minutes later, Kathleen was lying on her back looking at the stars, wondering why they were spinning. She'd never seen them do that before. She could hear Gerald and Joe giggling uproariously at something and the shadowy image of Lily dancing in the firelight.

Kathleen smiled, feeling very warm and content. She closed her eyes and went to sleep.

When she awoke, she felt disorientated and very, very sick.

"Jesus, Mary and Joseph!" she said as her stomach heaved and the contents landed on the sand next to her. Twice more she was ill, but at least when she was done her head had stopped spinning. When she'd buried her mess, she felt a raging thirst on her and turned toward the fire to find the bottle of water she'd brought with her.

The blankets next to her were empty and the fire had gone out.

She drank thirstily from the bottle then stood up to see if the other three had gone swimming. Her legs feeling strangely shaky, she walked toward the shore, but could neither hear the normal shouts of exhilarated laughter nor make out figures splashing in the waves. Turning back toward the camp, Kathleen shouted for them again. "Come on now, you three, I know you're hiding from me. Come out, wherever you are!"

There was no answer. Only the sound of the waves breaking evenly on the sand. "Surely they wouldn't have gone home and left me?" Kathleen said to herself. "There's no way I'll be carrying this lot up the cliffs by myself."

Having shouted until she was hoarse, Kathleen sat back down on the blanket. And noticed an empty bottle lying on the sand. She picked it up, smelled it and groaned, understanding now why she'd been so ill. Gerald must have laced their elderflower juice with poteen. Made out of potatoes by many around these parts, she knew how lethal it could be.

"You eejit, Gerald! What were you doing feeding us this?"

An ominous feeling of dread assailed Kathleen as she imagined the other three drunk, wandering into the waves, not in their right senses. She tried to work out what she should do. If she went for help, her daddy would flay her alive if he thought she'd been drinking, and would doubtless not believe how Gerald had laced the elderflower with it. And just how much had Joe drunk? He'd never tasted a drop of alcohol in his life. The saints only knew what kind of effect it would have on him.

Having spent another ten minutes searching the beach and calling their names, Kathleen realized with a thumping heart she had no choice but to go and raise the alarm. She had no idea of the time and, as she stood up, decided her only hope was that the three of them had left her sleeping where she was and headed home. Not caring about leaving their belongings on the beach, Kathleen turned miserably and began to walk toward the cliff path.

Suddenly she heard a shout coming from the corner of the beach, which led on over rocks to the next cove.

She turned and looked back, but could not make out the figure.

"Kathleen, is that you?"

"Yes!" she shouted back.

"It's me! Gerald!" He began running toward her. When he reached her, he was panting with effort and bent over to catch his breath. Looking up at her, he asked, "Have you seen them? Lily and Joe? They said they were going for a swim an hour or so ago. I said I'd mind the camp, because you were sleeping. When they didn't return, I went to try and find them. But there's no sign of them down on the shore. Have they been back here? Have I missed them?"

"No, I've been here the whole time and I haven't seen the hide of either of them."

"God," groaned Gerald, standing upright. "Joe especially was pretty merry. I hope something awful hasn't happened to them."

"Well now," Kathleen put her hands on her hips, "What did you think you were doing, feeding him drink?"

"Joe is a grown man. And he wasn't saying no."

"And what about Lily? And me?" Kathleen's anger and fear rose to the surface. "You put poteen in our juice, you eejit! What possessed you? What if Lily's drowned out there in the sea? It'll be *your fault*! And how will you live with that, Mr. Lisle!" she shouted hysterically.

"Look here, Kathleen, I've done nothing except spice up a rather dull party. And no one can prove it anyway. Besides, who do you think they're likely to believe, eh? You or me? Anyway"—he shrugged—"that's irrelevant. We need to find Lily and Joe as soon as possible. I've looked for them everywhere, and there is literally no sign."

Kathleen's eyes were drawn to a murky patch of blood on Gerald's shorts.

"What's that, there?" she pointed.

Gerald looked down. "Must have cut myself clambering over the rocks and it's seeped through. Never mind that, do we search again or go for help?"

"I'd say we go for help."

"Right. And I'm warning you now." Gerald bore down on her and she shrank back in fear. "You might own a few acres of useless bog down by the stream, but you're still a tenant on my father's land. You say one word about the bottle I brought down to the beach tonight and I'll have my father throw you and your family out of your house and off our land faster than you can possibly imagine. Understand?"

"Yes." Kathleen nodded tearfully. "I understand."

An hour later, the small community of Dunworley had been alerted to the emergency and was down on the beach, searching the coves and the sea for signs of either Lily or Joe.

As dawn broke, a local farmer called everyone to a small cave in which Lily lay, unconscious. Her dress was ripped and she'd been brutally beaten. The farmer carried her up the rocks to a waiting car. She was placed gently in the back, and driven off to the hospital in Cork city.

Twenty minutes later, Joe was found fast asleep behind an outcrop of rocks, not twenty yards from where Lily had been lying.

When they woke him, he was disoriented.

"Lily," he murmured, "Where Lily?"

33

There was a knock on the door of the farmhouse later that afternoon. Two guards were standing on the doorstep when Sophia opened it.

"Mrs. Doonan?"

"Yes?"

"We'd like to speak to your son and daughter about last night," said the guard.

"They're not in trouble, are they?" Sophia said nervously as she let them in. "They're both good children, never done anything wrong."

"We'll be speaking to your daughter first, Mrs. Doonan," said one of the guards as Sophia led them into the sitting room.

"How's Lily? She must have fallen down the rocks. Kathleen, my daughter, said. I—"

"That's what we're here to talk to her about," interrupted the other guard.

"I'll go and get her," said Sophia.

Kathleen entered the room a few minutes later, her knees shaking with fear.

"Kathleen Doonan?"

"Yes, sir."

"Sit yourself down, Kathleen. There's nothing to be nervous about, we're just wanting to ask you some questions about what happened last night."

"Lily is all right, isn't she?" Kathleen asked anxiously.

"She's going to be fine, don't you be worrying," said one of the guards. "Now, Kathleen, can you talk us through the events of last night? From when the four of you went on to the beach."

"Well now"—she swallowed—"We went down to have a picnic to celebrate Lily's leaving before she went away to boarding school. The boys minded the fire and cooked the sausages while Lily and I went in for a swim," Kathleen stated, watching the other policeman take notes.

"And then?" he prompted.

"We came back, ate our picnic, and then I . . . well now, I fell asleep."

"Were you tired?"

"I must have been, sir."

"What time did you wake up?"

"I don't know, but when I did, Lily, Joe and Gerald had gone. I went looking for them everywhere but I couldn't find them. Then I saw Gerald, coming from the cove where Lily was found. He said he'd been looking for them too. Then we went to raise the alarm. And that," shrugged Kathleen, "is all I can be telling you that you won't already know."

"Kathleen, I'd like you to answer me honestly," said the guard gently. "Would you four have been taking any drink last night with your picnic?"

"I . . . no, sir. Why would you be thinking that?"

"Because there was a fair amount of alcohol found in your cousin Lily's blood when they tested her at the hospital. Are you saying she was the only one partaking of it?"

"Sir . . ." Kathleen remembered what Gerald had said to her last night about throwing her family off their land if she ever told the truth. "Yes," she admitted, shamefaced. "We all had a drink, so. But not very much, sir. And I couldn't be saying about Gerald," she added hastily.

"What about your brother, Joe?"

"I'd be thinking he'd had a swig or two," Kathleen answered honestly.

"Well now, when we interviewed Master Gerald before we came here, he told us your Joe was mighty drunk."

"I don't think so, sir. Joe never drinks, so maybe even a little would go to his head."

"Something went to his head," muttered the other guard under his breath.

"Master Gerald said your brother was very fond of Lily. Is that true?"

"Oh yes, sir, he adores her," Kathleen agreed.

"Master Gerald said he heard Joe say he wanted to marry Lily. Was he hearing right?"

"Ah, now . . ." Kathleen struggled to think of the right answer. "We've always known each other since we were kids. We're family. Joe's always loved Lily."

"Yes, miss, but you're not kids anymore, are you? Or, at least, your brother isn't," the other guard said grimly. "Would you say your brother is an aggressive character, Miss Doonan?"

"Joe? No! Never! I'd be thinking he was one of the gentlest souls to walk the earth. He wouldn't hurt a fly, so."

"That's not what Master Gerald told us, Kathleen. He said Joe punched him in the face a few weeks back. He said you saw it. Did you?"

"I . . ." Kathleen could feel herself sweating with the stress of the situation. "Yes, I saw Joe hit Gerald, sir, but Joe only did it because Gerald had said something Joe wasn't liking about Lily. As I said, he's very protective of her. I'm promising you, ask anyone, Joe is harmless," Kathleen added desperately. "He's kind and loving and he didn't mean it, honestly he didn't."

"Would you say he was obsessed with his cousin Lily?" asked the guard.

"No." Kathleen shook her head, feeling she was being led down a path and made to say things that sounded all wrong. "He just adored her," she shrugged.

"Kathleen, did you ever see your brother touch Lily?"

"Of course! All the time! He'd give her piggybacks, pick her up and throw her into the sea . . . they'd play together . . ."

"Thank you, Kathleen. We'll be having a short word with your mammy now, and then we'll be talking to Joe."

"I don't understand, sir. Please, Joe's in no trouble, is he? He may have had a bit to drink, and hit Gerald that time, but you have to believe me, he'd never harm a hair on anyone's head, especially not Lily's," she urged desperately.

"That's all for now, Kathleen. We may need to speak to you again."

Kathleen stood up disconsolately and walked out of the sitting room, her eyes stinging with tears. Her mother was waiting in the kitchen. She glanced up as Kathleen came in, her own eyes full of anxiety.

"What did they want, Kathleen?"

"I don't know, Mam, I don't know. They asked me lots of questions about Joe, but they wouldn't be telling me why. I know Lily was hurt, but that was from falling down the rocks, wasn't it? Not because someone—" Kathleen put her hand to her mouth.—"Oh, Mam, you don't think the guards think that Joe—"

"We'll be seeing you now, Mrs. Doonan."

One of the guards stood on the threshold of the kitchen.

"Right then," Sophia sighed. She stood up and followed them.

Kathleen climbed the stairs to her bedroom and paced wretchedly around the confined space, knowing something was dreadfully, horribly wrong. Leaving her bedroom, she knocked on Joe's door. Receiving no reply, she pushed it open, and found Joe lying on his bed, hands under his head, staring at the ceiling.

"Joe." She walked across to the bed and sat down on the edge of it. "How are you?"

Joe did not reply. He continued to stare at the ceiling, his eyes full of misery.

Kathleen put her hand on his thick arm. "Are you after knowing what happened to Lily last night? And why the guards are here?"

Eventually Joe shook his head.

"Did you see her fall and hurt herself, Joe? That *is* what happened, isn't it?"

Finally, he turned his eyes to Kathleen and shook his head slowly. "Can't remember. Asleep."

"Oh, Joe, I'm scared. You have to remember. Did you see Lily fall and hurt herself?" she repeated.

"No," Joe again shook his head. "Asleep."

"Joe, please, it's important you listen to me," Kathleen said urgently. "And try and understand what I'm saying to you. I don't know for certain, but the guards might have taken it into their heads that you hurt Lily."

At this, Joe sat bolt upright. "No! Never hurt Lily! Never!"

"I know that, Joe, but they don't. And whatever's happened to Lily has sent them here. To find out about last night. And I'm thinking they might be trying to pin the blame on you."

"No! Never hurt Lily!" he shouted, thumping the bed.

Kathleen could see the betrayal and anger in Joe's eyes. "You don't have to be telling me. I know how you love Lily. But maybe those guards downstairs don't, and might be seeing what happened to Lily through a different set of eyes. Will you be promising me that you won't get angry if they ask you questions you don't like? Please, Joe, try and keep calm, even if they ask you if you hurt Lily," Kathleen entreated him.

"Never hurt Lily, love Lily!" Joe repeated again.

Kathleen bit her lip in despair, understanding there was nothing she could say or do to protect her beautiful, gentle brother from himself. "Ah, Joe, maybe I'm looking on the black side. Maybe Lily will be able to tell her own story." Kathleen knelt on the bed and put her arms around Joe tightly. "You just be yourself, and tell them that you were asleep."

"Will." Joe nodded vehemently.

Kathleen was still hugging him when her mother came in a few minutes later, her face pale, to say that Joe was wanted downstairs. She watched him heave himself to standing and leave the room, the feeling of dread in her heart overwhelming.

The guards took Joe away that afternoon for further questioning. Two days later, another guard came to the house and told the three of them that Joe was to be charged with the rape and assault of Lily Lisle. He was to be kept in Cork jail until the trial.

When he'd left, Sophia sat down in a chair at the table. She put her head on her arms and wept silently. Seamus went to put his own arms around her, tears in his eyes too.

Kathleen watched her parents, the despair etched on their faces, and knew they were broken.

Eventually, Sophia looked up, clasping her husband's hand. "He didn't do it, did he?"

"No, pet, we know he didn't." Seamus shook his head slowly. "But what we can do to put this wrong right, I just don't know." Seamus turned to Kathleen. "Surely someone in this house must remember what happened that night? What possessed you, girl, to drink poteen? You know what it does to a mind, especially one as slow as Joe's!"

"Pa, I'm sorry, I'm so, so sorry." Kathleen wrung her hands, desperate to tell him the truth about how Gerald had deceived them all into drinking it.

"And the guards are taking the word of the Englishman, as always. Maybe I could go and speak to him, go and speak to Gerald?" Seamus paced around the kitchen.

"And will he be telling you the truth? Someone did this to Lily, and we know it wasn't our Joe. But what can we do?" Sophia shook her head in anguish. "If it was Gerald, will he ever admit it? Never!"

"What about Lily?" asked Kathleen. "Could I go and see her? You know how close we've always been, Mam."

Sophia looked questioningly at her husband. "What do you think, Seamus? Should Kathleen go and visit Lily?"

"I'd say anything was worth a go at this stage," agreed her father.

The following day saw Kathleen on the bus up to Cork city. Lily was being cared for at the Bons Secours Hospital.

When Kathleen walked into her room, Lily's eyes were closed. Kathleen studied her, the black and purple circle around her left eye, the cut to her lip and the bruises on her lower jaw. She swallowed hard, knowing that it was impossible even to consider that Joe could have done this to his beloved Lily. She sat down in the chair by the bed, knowing that when Lily woke up and they spoke, she must keep calm, and not become hysterical at the dreadful injustice that was happening to her brother.

Eventually, Lily opened her eyes, blinked, then noticed Kathleen sitting next to her. Kathleen reached for her hand. "How are you?"

"Sleepy," answered Lily, "very sleepy."

"Will they be giving you something to help with the pain? Maybe it's making you drowsy."

"Yes." Lily licked her lips. "Could you pass me some water?"

Kathleen helped Lily sit up to drink some. When she'd finished and Kathleen had replaced the glass on the table next to her, she asked gently, "What happened to you, Lily?"

"I really don't know." Lily closed her eyes again. "I can't remember."

"You must remember something," Kathleen urged. "You don't

think . . . I mean, you know that Joe could never have done this to you. Don't you, Lily?"

"The police keep asking me the same questions and I can't answer them."

"They've arrested him, Lily. They've arrested Joe," Kathleen whispered. "They're blaming him for what's happened to you. You will tell them, won't you? Tell them that Joe loved you, would never hurt you . . . you know he wouldn't. Please, Lily, tell them that."

Lily's eyes remained closed. "I don't think he would, no, but I can't tell them what I don't remember."

"What about Gerald? Did he try and . . . ?" Kathleen couldn't voice the words. "Did you have to fight him off . . ."

Lily's eyes shot open. "Kathleen! He's my half brother. I can hardly accuse him of doing this, can I? Besides"—her eyes began to close again—"as I said, I can't remember. Now, please, I'm very tired and I don't want to talk about this anymore."

Kathleen fought back her tears "Lily. If you don't speak up for Joe, they might send him to prison! *Please,* I'm begging you, I—"

"That's enough of that," said a voice from behind her.

Aunt Anna was standing by the door, arms folded. "I think it's t-time for you to leave, Kathleen. As Lily has asked you to."

"Please, Aunt Anna," said Kathleen in desperation, "they think our Joe did this to Lily and you know how he's always adored her, wanted to protect her."

"Enough!" Her aunt's voice was harsh. "You're becoming hysterical and that's not g-good for Lily. I suggest you allow the police to complete their investigation. No one has any idea what Joe might d-do when drunk, and I hardly think you're in a position to comment either, young lady. You apparently p-passed out from drink and saw and heard nothing."

"No, but I did see Gerald and he had blood—"

"I said enough! I wish you to leave my daughter's room *now,* or I will have you removed. And let me tell you, Sebastian and I are in full agreement that the man who has assaulted our d-daughter deserves everything he gets! And we shall see to it that he does!"

Kathleen ran from the room, tears blurring her vision. She left the hospital and sat down on a bench in the pretty gardens outside. It was useless, useless . . . and Joe, because he was Joe, was not equipped to protect or defend himself from what was happening to him. If Lily wouldn't speak up for him, or Aunt Anna, she knew all hope was gone.

Three months later, Kathleen sat with her parents and watched Joe sentenced to life imprisonment for the rape and assault of Lily Lisle. Joe's solicitor had managed to plead for Joe, due to his limited mental capacity, to be placed in a secure institution up in the Midlands.

Kathleen knew she would never forget the look of confusion and fear on Joe's drawn face, pointing to his family sitting at the back of the courtroom as he was taken roughly by the elbows, a guard on either side of him.

"Joe!" Sophia screamed across the room. "Don't take him, please! He's my son, he doesn't understand! Please . . . he's my baby, he needs me . . . Joe! Joe!"

As Joe was led out of the dock and disappeared from view down the steps, Sophia slumped in her chair and cried pitifully. "He'll die in there, locked up with the mad ones, and none of his precious animals around him. Oh God . . . oh God . . ."

Kathleen sat next to her mother, with her father, equally heartbroken, trying to calm her, and stared straight ahead.

She knew then that she would never forgive the Lisles for what they had done to her family for the rest of her life.

Dunworley Farmhouse
The Present

"Oh, Mam," Grania said softly as she watched Kathleen's shoulders heaving as she wept. She moved to put her arms around them. "Oh, Mam."

"Sorry, pet, it's the telling of it that's so painful."

"Mam, I just don't know what to say. Here, have a tissue." Grania pulled one from the box by her bed and patted her mother's eyes gently.

"I know you'll be thinking this was a long time ago," said Kathleen, trying to pull herself together, "but, Grania, I see Joe's innocent, trusting eyes every day of my life. He didn't understand, you see, what was happening to him. They put him in that place, that *terrible* place full of mad people who would scream and shout at the top of their voices, bang on locked doors to be let out." Kathleen shuddered. "Ah, Grania, you have no idea."

"No, I'm sure I don't," said Grania quietly. "So, did you try appealing?"

"Would you be surprised to know the solicitor we saw advised us we'd be wasting our money to try?" Kathleen chuckled sadly. "Besides, Joe went into that place and deteriorated. He'd always struggled with his speech, but when he got there, he gave up completely. I'd doubt he uttered a word for the next ten years of his life. He'd sit by a window, staring out, and even when we went to visit him, he didn't seem to understand who we were. I think they must have put him on drugs, like they did all of them. Something to keep them quiet, make the nurses' lives easier."

"Is he still there now, Mam?"

"No." Kathleen shook her head. "He died of a heart attack when you were twelve. That's what they told us anyway. Joe always had a heart murmur, but I'd reckon it wasn't the technical workings that went wrong, but the fact it snapped in two." Kathleen sighed. "What did that poor boy have to live for? He'd been accused of hurting the person he'd loved more than his own life. And ended up losing his freedom because of it. Joe didn't start out with many brains, so I'm sure that working out what had happened to him was impossible. So he coped by disappearing inside himself. At least, that's what the psychiatrist told us."

"Oh, Mam"—Grania shook her head—"it's a terrible story. Did Lily ever talk to you about it again? Did she remember what happened?"

"That day at the hospital was the last time I ever spoke to Lily Lisle," said Kathleen. "Aunt Anna swept her off to London as soon as she was home and we didn't see hide nor hair of her again. Until she arrived back at Dunworley House with her husband in tow, many years later."

"And what about Gerald?" Grania asked. "From what you've just said, I gather he must have been the real perpetrator of the crime?"

"That's what I'll believe until my dying day," reiterated Kathleen adamantly. "It had to be one of them, and it could not have been my gentle Joe. But at least there's some comfort there. I heard from someone who used to work up at Dunworley for Mr. Sebastian Lisle"—she spat the name out—"that Gerald got himself killed while he was overseas. Not, I might add, because he was serving his country in combat, but at a drunken brawl outside a bar in Cyprus. He died before Joe did, at the age of twenty-four. Which is how Lily came to inherit Dunworley House."

"Do you think what happened to her that night affected Lily? I mean . . ." Grania trod carefully, knowing it was painful for her mother, "Alexander has told me that Lily suffered serious mental instability."

"I wouldn't be able to say, because Lily was always an odd child and a strange teenager," mused Kathleen, "and she never let on whether she remembered what had happened that night. But you'd be thinking, wouldn't you, if she'd remembered any of it, that it would affect her?"

"Yes, of course it must have done," Grania agreed. "It also explains why you've been so worried about my association with the Lisles. I really understand now." Grania grasped her mother's hand. "And I'm sorry if my connection with them has upset you and brought back the past."

"Well, as your daddy has said to me over and over, the past has nothing to do with you. But it destroyed my family, to be sure. Mam and Dad were never the same again. And, of course, it wasn't just Lily, but Mam's sister, Anna, who refused to speak up for her nephew. Even though my mammy begged her to tell the guards how harmless Joe was, Anna refused. If she had spoken, Grania, they might have listened. After all, she was the squire's wife and would have been heard."

"But, Mam," Grania sighed, "how could she be expected to do that? Gerald was Anna's stepson. She was married to his father. God, what a terrible mess."

"Yes," Kathleen agreed, "and, of course, you're right. Aunt Anna always knew which side her bread was buttered. Sebastian provided her with a comfortable life, and as much freedom as she wanted. After the incident, Aunt Anna rarely came back to Ireland, spending most of her time in London at the house she had grown up in. The two sisters never spoke again."

Grania was silent for a bit, taking time to make sense of what her mother had told her. "I understand you must hate Lily for what she did to Joe, but actually, Mam, was it really her fault? She had to suffer that terrible attack, *whoever* was the perpetrator of it. Perhaps she really couldn't remember, but even if she could, would she ever have been likely to blame her half brother?" pondered Grania. "And who knows? Gerald threatened you; he may well have done the same to Lily to make sure she kept her mouth shut. I'm not trying to make excuses for her," she added hastily, "but I don't see how she could have won."

"You're right, so," said Kathleen. "That's what your daddy has said to me for years. And, to be fair, when Sebastian Lisle died just after Gerald, and Lily inherited the Dunworley Estate from her father, my daddy wrote to her in London asking if he could finally purchase our farm. She agreed and was very fair about the price."

"Being cynical, perhaps it was to minimize any kind of contact between your family and hers?"

"Yes. It probably was," Kathleen agreed. "That, and maybe guilt too."

"Obviously, Alexander knows none of this," said Grania.

"I'd hardly think his wife would be telling him."

"No, but perhaps it would help him if Alexander did know. He's always said he's been uncomfortable living in Dunworley. And I think"—Grania scratched her head—"that even though you are not responsible for your partner's problems, you still feel guilty that you didn't do enough to help. And I know, from what Alexander has told me, that he did everything he possibly could to support Lily."

"I'm sure he did. And if it makes any difference to you, Grania, I've stopped blaming Lily for what happened. But the pain in my heart over my Joe will never go away."

"No . . . and Lily sounds as though she paid the price too. Poor thing. Would you mind if I did tell Alexander when the moment is right?"

"No. I was feeling suddenly it was important to tell you before you left to see him tomorrow. The sad thing is," Kathleen sighed, "I'm the only survivor left out of that night on the beach. It's almost as if the world turned wrong for all of us that evening."

"Mam! I'm here and Shane and Dad," Grania teased, "so something continued to go a little bit right."

"Yes, pet." Kathleen reached out a hand and stroked her daughter's cheek. "Of course it did. And your daddy, Grania, well now, if it hadn't been for him being there for me after it all happened, I'd have gone mad altogether. He was wonderful, so he was. And he still is, for all his irritating habits," she chuckled. "And now, I'd better let you get some sleep before you leave tomorrow. Promise me you'll take care of yourself?"

"Of course I will, Mam, I'm a big girl now."

"Never too big for a hiding from your mammy." Kathleen smiled wearily.

"I know." Grania watched as Kathleen heaved herself off the bed and walked toward the door. "Good night, Mam. I love you."

"And I love you too, Grania."

Kathleen left her daughter's room and walked next door to her own. John was fast asleep, the light still on. Dropping a tender kiss on her husband's forehead, she wandered over to her dressing table. And picked up the small, exquisitely carved wooden angel Joe had fashioned with such love for Lily. She'd spotted it, lying in the sand, just outside the cave where Lily had been found, a few weeks after Joe had been sentenced. Holding it to her breast, Kathleen looked up.

"Sleep tight now, Joe," she murmured.

Aurora

Oh, Reader! Poor Kathleen! Under the circumstances, I'm surprised she ever let me darken her doorstep, given the black cloud of family history I brought with me.

And poor Joe . . . one of life's vulnerable humans, unable to protect or defend himself; a "victim" through fate's lottery, and no fault of his own. I can only hope that his gentle spirit came back as a much-loved family pet, a cat for example; and that Ghastly Gerald was the mouse the Joe-cat stalked, played with and finally killed, just for fun.

The worst thing is, as I learn more about my past I worry for the genes I have inherited. Ghastly Gerald was my uncle! Not to mention my granny Anna, whose inherent selfishness meant Lily grew up without what I believe to be perhaps the most important element of a human being's life: the love of a mother. And, subsequently, so did I, until Grania came along and saved me.

At least this part of the story has helped me understand Lily. I've been musing that, just as Joe was a victim through a lack of the normal portion of gifts we are given at birth, it was Lily's "gift"—her beauty—that made her so vulnerable. Perhaps too much of any quality is as bad as too little. And she was so fragile—just as fragile as Joe, yet in a different way. Perhaps that's what he recognized in her, even if others could only see her from the outside. To most people, like the young Kathleen, beauty and wealth are associated with power and strength. Yet Joe saw her vulnerability and simply wanted to protect her.

Among other things, I've been reading a lot of religious philosophy recently. (If I sound more serious than usual, these books are the reason.) Science has now identified the genetic physical link we hand down, but I prefer to think that each little baby born is its "own" spirit, and that, whatever their upbringing, they will become who they are despite it. This makes me feel better personally, given my own gene pool.

I said earlier on that the world doesn't learn its lessons. Reader, I think I'm wrong. In the space of fifty years, people like Joe, who have for centuries been either drowned at birth or shut away because of their imperfections, are now cared for by society. Of course, there's a flip side to that. In the Western world anyway, children are no longer put up chimneys, they are treated with kindness and consideration. But from being an often unwanted by-product of a man and a woman playing the most enjoyed human game (you know the one I mean!), they have now become the center of the family universe. I have met some very spoiled little people recently, and I struggle to imagine a world in which they can think of others and not themselves. Which may mean the human race turns another full, selfish circle again when their generation begins to run things, because we humans never stand still.

I am only happy I lived this life when I did. In the past, I'm sure I would have been drowned as a witch. Along with Kathleen, who sees and feels the things I do and understands.

Perhaps this is longer than usual because I am putting off writing the next bit of the story. It is not going to be easy for me . . .

34

A liveried chauffeur was holding up Grania's name as she emerged through Arrivals at Geneva Airport.

"Follow me, madam."

Outside, a black Mercedes was waiting. She climbed in and the driver set off silently.

As she drove through Geneva to an unknown destination, Grania wondered if she'd been naive. Should she have trusted Alexander? She knew so little about him. He could be involved in all sorts of things that were illegal: gun-running, drugs . . .

"Get hold of yourself, woman, and stop letting your imagination run away with you," Grania admonished herself. Still, she fished in her handbag for her cell phone and tucked it safely in the pocket of her jacket.

After a journey which took them out of the city and upward into the mountains behind, the car drew to a halt in front of a brightly lit modern building. The chauffeur opened the passenger door for her and she stepped out.

"I will be waiting for you here. Mr. Devonshire is on the second floor. Ask at the desk and the nurses will tell you where to find him."

It was then Grania looked up above her and saw she was standing outside the entrance to the Clinique de Genolier. Instinctively, her hand went to her mouth. "Oh God, oh God . . ." she whispered to herself.

Numbly, she took the elevator to the second floor as the chauffeur had directed, and walked to the nurses' station to make herself known.

"Your name?" asked the nurse.

"Grania Ryan."

"Yes." The nurse gave a smile of recognition. "Mr. Devonshire's been expecting you. Follow me, please."

Heart in her mouth, Grania walked down the corridor and waited as the nurse knocked on the door. A weak voice said, "Come."

The nurse indicated for Grania to push the door open.

Alexander, or at least what Grania could only describe as a vague shadow of the man she'd said good-bye to a few weeks ago, was lying in the bed. He was completely bald, his skin a sallow gray, his body hooked up to tubes, with monitors beeping monotonously around him. With effort, he lifted a thin arm in recognition of her arrival.

"I'll leave you alone for a while," the nurse nodded as she closed the door behind them.

"Grania, thank you . . . for coming."

Grania was rooted to the spot, her shock, she knew, visible on her face. But there was little she could do to control it.

"I know," croaked Alexander. "I know. You weren't expecting"—he indicated himself—"*this*."

Grania shook her head silently, willing herself not to break down. He made a small movement with his hand to indicate she should come closer. When she drew next to him, she saw that his navy blue eyes were full of tears. Instinctively, she leaned forward and placed a kiss on his cold forehead.

"Alexander," she whispered, "What's happened to you? I don't understand."

He motioned her to pull up a chair and sit down next to him. Once she had done so, he moved his hand toward hers and she took it in her own.

"Brain tumor. I knew a year ago. Times I was away was for treatment." He smiled sadly. "You can see. Didn't work. I'm dying, Grania. Thought I'd have longer, but"—he licked his dry lips to aid his speech—"haven't."

"I . . ." the tears were rolling unchecked down Grania's cheeks now. "I'm so sorry, Alexander. Why didn't you tell me? I knew something was wrong; you looked terrible the last time you came home. And all those headaches . . . it makes sense now. Excuse me." She rooted in her handbag to find a tissue to stem her running nose. "Why didn't you say something?" she repeated.

"While there was still hope, didn't want Aurora to know. Or you," he added.

"Is there . . . nothing the doctors can do?" Grania knew, looking at him, she was grasping at straws.

"Nothing. Tried everything. Done for, I'm afraid."

"How long—?" Grania could not finish the sentence.

Alexander helped her. "Two weeks, maybe three . . . way I feel, I think sooner. Grania"—she felt sudden pressure on her hand from his—"need your help."

"Whatever I can do, Alexander, tell me."

"It's Aurora. Worried for her, no one to take care of her when I'm gone."

"You mustn't worry about that. I and my family will look after her. You know we will, Alexander." Grania could see that both the effort of speaking and the emotion were draining him.

"My poor little girl . . . what suffering she's known." It was Alexander's turn to cry now. "Grania, why is life so cruel?"

"I don't know, Alexander, I really don't. All I can promise you is that Aurora will be safe and well and *loved*."

"Excuse me . . . so tired, the drugs, you know."

Grania sat there as Alexander's eyes closed and he slept. She felt giddy, faint with shock. Of all the things she'd expected, sitting at the bedside of a dying Alexander had not been one of them. She tried to think rationally about what this meant, but her brain was numb. She sat there holding his hand as tightly as she could, as if she and her own health and energy were his conduit to life itself.

Eventually, his eyes fluttered open, and he turned his head to focus on her. "I trust you, Grania. Seen your love for Aurora. And your family . . . good people. Want Aurora to be with you and . . . them."

"I've said, Alexander, she can be. She *will* be."

"No." Alexander made an effort to shake his head. "Not good enough. Can't take any chances. Grania, need to ask you a favor."

"Anything, Alexander, you know that."

"Will you marry me?"

After an evening of shocks, this was the largest so far. Grania wondered seriously if Alexander was mentally sound.

"*Marry* you? But . . . ?"

"Hardly a dream proposal, know that." Alexander's lips turned up in a sad facsimile of a smile. "Wish could be asking you under different circumstances."

"I don't understand, Alexander. Can you try and explain?"

"My solicitor will do that tomorrow. Then I can die knowing . . ." Alexander took a deep breath to try and curb his emotion, "my little girl is safe."

"Oh, Alexander—" Grania's voice cracked.

"Will you? Do this? For me?" he managed.

"I . . ." Grania put her fingers to her forehead, "this is such a shock, I—I need some time to think about it."

"Haven't got 'time.' Please, Grania, I'm begging you. Promise, I will leave you financially secure for the rest of your life."

"I don't want your money, Alexander."

"Please, Grania. Need to do this before it's . . . too late."

She looked at his anguished face and knew she had no choice.

"Yes," she answered slowly, "I'll do it."

The following morning, having spent an entirely sleepless night—albeit in a beautiful suite at a hotel in Geneva—Grania met Alexander's chauffeur in the lobby at ten o'clock and was taken back to the hospital.

Alexander managed a weak smile as she walked through the door. Sitting in the chair next to his bed was an older man, graying hair combed neatly, dressed immaculately in a suit.

He stood up, towering over Grania, and offered his hand.

"Hello, Miss Ryan, my name is Hans Schneider. I am Mr. Devonshire's solicitor, old friend and godfather to Aurora," he added.

"Hans is here to talk to you about what we discussed last night," said Alexander. "You . . . haven't had second thoughts?"

"To be frank, I haven't had any thoughts at all. I think I'm still in shock," Grania replied.

"Of course," said Hans. "What I suggest is that you and I take ourselves off downstairs to the restaurant and I will talk you through everything that Alexander has suggested."

Grania nodded silently, feeling she was a pawn in a complex game of chess she didn't understand.

Downstairs in the pleasant restaurant, Hans ordered coffee for both of them. He drew out some thick files. "Now, Miss Ryan," he said in his clipped German accent, "may I call you Grania?"

"Of course," she replied.

"First of all, it is important you understand that everything we are doing is to safeguard Aurora when Alexander is no longer able to do so himself."

"Yes, but what I don't understand, Hans, is that surely all Alexander would need to do is to state in his will, or maybe on a separate legal document of some kind, that he wishes myself and my family to adopt Aurora?"

"Under normal circumstances, that would almost certainly be enough. But the problem is, Grania, these are extraordinary circumstances," explained Hans. "I have asked Alexander if I may speak for him—he is too weak now to be able to elucidate his thoughts properly to you, and of course, it is important that you know. His concern is purely for Aurora's well-being and safety. He wishes to know that when he dies, he has left her future watertight. By marrying him, you become Aurora's stepmother, and if we start the adoption process now, it is unlikely it can be overturned."

"But why would anyone wish to overturn it?"

"Grania, Alexander is an extremely wealthy man. The fortune he leaves will go to Aurora. Not only that, but Aurora will inherit Dunworley House and other valuable property from her mother, Lily, when her father dies. Even though most of it is already tied up in trusts until Aurora reaches the age of twenty-one, there is obviously a large lump sum that must be entrusted to the person or persons who will bring her up. At present, Mr. Devonshire has a number of relatives who might be eager to lay their hands on such an amount. For example, his sister—his closest blood relative—who might well have a case in court which overturns Alexander's wishes. He has not spoken to her for ten years. Trust me, Grania, having met her"—Hans raised his eyebrows—"I can understand why Alexander does not wish Aurora and her fortune to end up in his sister's hands."

"I see."

"Perhaps you think Alexander is being overcautious, but having been a solicitor for thirty-five years, I will guarantee that once Alexander dies, the vultures will descend," Hans remarked. "And he wishes to take no chances."

"I understand that," said Grania.

"Now, not only as Alexander's solicitor, but his good friend and godfather to Aurora, I must ask you whether you are prepared to take on the responsibility of adopting her?"

"Yes, if that's what is necessary. I love her," Grania replied simply.

"And that is the most important thing of all." Hans smiled. "The only worry Alexander has is that adopting Aurora should not curtail your own future in any way. He wants you to know that, if you wish to return to New York, he would be happy for Aurora to stay living in Ireland with your parents. May I ask, how does your family feel about Aurora?"

"They adore her and she adores them. She's with them now in Ireland and as happy as I've ever seen her. But, Hans," Grania shook her head despairingly, "how am I to break it to Aurora that her father . . ." Tears sprang spontaneously to Grania's eyes at the mere thought of the conversation.

"I know." Hans reached across the table and patted her hand. "This is the other reason Alexander believes it is a good idea if you marry him. Yes, Aurora will lose her father, *but*—at the same time—she will have gained a mother. He thinks it might lessen the blow for her. He said that was how she regarded you, anyway."

"It was kind of him to say so," Grania answered, trying not to let emotion get the better of her. "I certainly love her like my own. There's been a bond between us since the beginning."

"I do believe that God works in mysterious ways sometimes," said Hans quietly. "And at least if you are prepared to accept Alexander's proposal, he can die knowing his beloved daughter is safe and loved. I cannot tell you how highly he regards you, Grania. I should also say that time is very short, shorter perhaps than even Alexander realizes. We should arrange the marriage ceremony for as soon as tomorrow. I will contact the local registrar who will come to the hospital and perform it. Sadly, Grania, tomorrow will be your wedding day."

She nodded silently, the bitter irony of refusing to marry Matt for all those years, set against this tragic act she seemed to have no choice but to make, bringing a lump to her throat.

"I believe Alexander asked you to bring your birth certificate. If I could take that and your passport with me, and you could sign this, which I have already taken the liberty of filling in, I will make the arrangements."

Numbly, Grania scribbled her signature at the bottom of the form, then took her birth certificate and passport from her handbag and handed them to him.

"Thank you. Now, these are the papers to start the formal adoption process."

Grania signed form after form mindlessly and passed them back to Hans.

"So . . ." Having stacked his papers together and stowed them in his briefcase, Hans looked at her. "You know nothing of the settlement Alexander is proposing for you, as his wife. Yet you have signed all these forms?"

"It's hardly the money that matters in this, surely? I'm doing it simply because I love Aurora and I'm very fond of her father."

"Yes." Hans gave her a sudden warm smile. "I now understand why Alexander wishes you to bring up his daughter. He said you would not be interested in the financial arrangements and"—Hans winked at her—"he has just been proved right."

"Good," said Grania defensively, realizing he had tested her. "Please remember, I haven't asked to be involved in any of this. And I earn my own living, thank you. I don't need Alexander's money."

"My apologies. Knowing what Alexander is entrusting to you, I had to make sure for myself, given he is so ill, that he was sound of mind, if not body. I can now categorically sign the papers to say he is. I will be executor of his will and handle his financial affairs for you and Aurora in the future. I will be helping you as much as I can. And I will tell you now that in his will, he has left you—"

"Enough!" Grania was exhausted and couldn't take any more. "Could we leave it there, Hans? We can talk about that another day. I'd like to go back and see Alexander now."

"Alexander," whispered Grania as she sat down next to him. He opened his eyes and looked at her.

"Hello, Grania."

"I wanted to tell you that Hans and I have sorted everything out.

I've signed the adoption papers, and you and I are getting married tomorrow."

With great effort, Alexander twisted his head to look at her and lifted a hand out to be held. "Thank you, Grania. Will you buy yourself something beautiful to wear? And, of course, there's the ring." Alexander indicated the drawer in the bedside table next to him. "Open it."

Grania did so and inside found a red leather Cartier box. Alexander held out his hand to receive it from her. With much effort, he propped himself up, opened the box and took out an exquisite diamond solitaire ring.

"Grania Ryan, will you marry me?"

Her eyes blinded by tears, Grania nodded. "Yes, Alexander."

With all the strength he possessed, Alexander placed the ring on her finger. "Just one more thing, Grania." The pressure on Grania's fingers increased. "Will you . . . stay with me until . . . the end? Like . . . my wife would." He smiled sadly.

"Of course I will. But . . . what do we tell Aurora?"

"That we are on honeymoon. She'll be pleased."

"Oh, but, Alexander, what do I—*how* do I tell her?"

"I trust you to say the right thing. And at least now she has a new mother she loves."

Alexander's eyes drooped. Grania sat at his bedside as he slept, gazing out of the window at the magnificent view of Mont Blanc in the distance.

Even though tomorrow would be her wedding day, she had never felt more alone in her life.

After Kathleen had dropped Aurora off at school, she came back to feed the chickens and collect the eggs. It had been four days now since Grania had left. And not a word from her. Kathleen had tried that phone of hers on numerous occasions. It was permanently switched off.

"That girl needs a good leathering," she grumbled as she stomped back into the house with the eggs. "Taking off and not letting her mammy know how or where she is, and having her worry half out of her mind."

Later that day, the telephone rang and Kathleen picked it up.

"Mam? It's me, Grania."

"I know 'tis you! Jesus, Mary and Joseph! I've been imagining all sorts of things."

"Sorry, Mam. I can only say that whatever you're imagining won't come anywhere near the truth, but I can't talk now. Is Aurora there?"

"No, it's Monday, if you've forgotten. She's at school."

"Of course," said Grania distractedly. "Listen, I'll try to talk to her later, but it's difficult at the moment. Mam, I need you to tell her something for me."

"And what might that be?"

"Tell her . . . that her daddy and I have got married. And that I'm to be her new mummy."

Kathleen felt as though all her breath had been knocked out of her body. "*What?!* You're telling me that you and Alexander have got wed?"

"Yes, but Mam, it's a very long story. I can't explain now, but I promise you, it's not what it seems."

"I'd say it is," said Kathleen, "and there was you the night before you left, telling me you were still hankering after your Matt. What possessed you, girl? Are you out of your mind?"

"Mam, for once in your life, please trust me. I need you to tell Aurora that her daddy and I are taking a honeymoon. We're not sure"— there was a sudden catch in Grania's throat—"how long for."

"I see. And can you be telling *me* how long for?"

"I wish I knew, Mam."

"Grania Ryan . . . or in fact, Grania *who*? These days—"

"Devonshire. I'm Mrs. Devonshire."

"Well, at least it's not a Lisle name you'll be taking."

"Look, Mam, I really have to go. I promise I'll explain everything when I get home. Send a big kiss to Aurora, and tell her that both her daddy and I love her very much. I'll speak to you soon."

The line went dead in Kathleen's hand.

It wasn't often Kathleen took to the drink, but she walked into the sitting room and poured herself a glass of sherry from the tray. Swigging it down in one, she went back to the phone, looked up her husband's rarely used mobile number and dialed it.

35

Matt felt as though he was living in a miasma of misery and confusion. For someone who spent his life lecturing others on the workings of the human mind, wrote papers on the subject regularly and had a book published by Harvard Press, he seemed to have screwed up his own life well and truly.

When Charley had told him her news, Matt had been lost for words—and, in fact, thoughts. He still was. He knew he'd reacted badly. Charley had left the restaurant that night in floods of tears. After he'd paid the bill and followed her home a few minutes later, Charley had already disappeared into her bedroom. He'd knocked on the door and received no reply.

"Can I come in?" he'd asked.

Again there had been no reply, so he'd walked in anyway. Charley was lying huddled under her covers, her face streaked with tears.

"May I sit down?"

"Yup," had come the muffled response.

"Charley, honey. I am so, so sorry."

"Thanks," she'd replied miserably.

"Have you . . . thought about what you wanna do? I mean . . . do you want it?"

At this, the covers had been thrown back and Charley had sat upright, anger blazing from her eyes. "Are you asking me to have a termination?"

"*No.* Shit! I haven't even begun to think what *I* want. This is about *you.*"

"What?! Hey, Matty boy, you were there too, you know. This isn't just about me, it's about us."

What "us"? Matt had thought, but didn't say, not wishing to incur Charley's wrath any further. "I know, honey, but I thought I should get your thoughts first."

Charley had drawn her long legs up to her chin and put her arms around them protectively. "As on the night in question you swore you loved me, then right now I suppose I would be looking forward to the prospect of you, me and 'it.' But as that's not the case, and you've sure made that clear to me tonight, I just don't know what I want."

"Then maybe we both need some time to think."

"Yeah, well, I don't have the luxury of too much time. This is growing inside me and I don't wanna get attached to it if I have to . . ."

The words had hung in the air.

"No," Matt had agreed. "You are . . . real sure, aren't you?"

"What? Are you doubting me? Next thing, you'll be asking me for DNA tests to prove the goddamned baby is yours!"

Matt had moved to put his arms around her shoulders. "Of course I won't, Charley, I know you'd never do that. We've been buddies forever and you're no liar. Don't cry, honey. We'll sort this out, I promise. I gotta go away tomorrow, which maybe is a good thing. We both need some space and some time to think. Why don't we talk when I'm back? When both of us are calmer?"

"OK," Charley had agreed tearfully.

Matt had kissed her on the top of her head, then stood up. "Try to get some sleep." He'd walked toward the door.

"Matty?"

"Yep?" He'd paused.

"Do you want this baby?"

Matt had turned around to face her slowly. "I'm so sorry, but if I'm honest, Charley, I just don't know."

That had been a week ago. And now Matt was back home, just as uncertain as he'd been when he'd left. Actually, he thought, as he turned the key in the lock to open the door to his apartment, who the hell was he kidding? He was *completely* certain he didn't love Charley *or* want a baby by her. If he went through with it, he would be doing it simply because he was a gentleman and had made an irreversible mistake. But then, how many guys had been caught out in exactly the same circumstances and had to do the "decent" thing? Charley was a childhood friend, whose parents saw his own on a regular social basis. He shuddered at the thought of the raised eyebrows at the country club if word got around that Charley was pregnant by him and he'd refused to stand by her.

The point was, thought Matt as he took his hold-all to the bedroom, she held all the cards. If she decided she wanted to go ahead and keep the baby, Matt reckoned he'd have no choice but to at least make the effort to give their relationship a go. He supposed it could be worse—at least he knew her well, they got on, shared the same social background and friends . . .

Perhaps he should look at it like an arranged marriage. The concept was a tried and tested one. After all, it hadn't worked out with Grania. Matt glanced at the photo sitting on his bedside table and swallowed hard. Grania looked scarcely older than a teenager in the picture. It had been taken when they were on holiday in Florence, in front of the Duomo, and Grania was giggling as the sea of pigeons she was feeding flocked around her.

Matt sat down heavily on the bed they had once shared—the bed in which he had unknowingly betrayed her with Charley. Maybe all he could do was wait and see what Charley had to say. But, Jesus, he missed Grania right now. What had shocked him was the need to speak to her about what had happened to him; apart from being his lover, she'd been his best friend. Her down-to-earth Irish wisdom had always helped clear his head. On a sudden, desperate whim, Matt reached inside his hold-all and drew out his cell phone. Not stopping to process what he was doing, he dialed Grania's number, not even knowing what he would say to her if she answered, but simply needing to hear her voice. Her cell phone was off, so he dialed her parents' number.

It was answered on the second ring.

"Hello?" It was a young voice, one that wasn't familiar to Matt.

"Hello," he replied. "Who am I speaking to?"

"You're speaking to Aurora Devonshire," answered the voice in its clipped English accent. "And who may this be?"

"It's Matt Connelly here. Do I have the right number? I'm looking for Grania Ryan."

"You do, Mr. Connelly. But I'm afraid Grania isn't here."

"Would you happen to know where she is?"

"Yes, she's in Switzerland. On her honeymoon with my father."

"I'm sorry?" Matt struggled to make sense of the words he'd just heard. "Could you repeat that for me please, miss?"

"Certainly. I said that Grania married my father a week ago, and is on her honeymoon in Switzerland. May I take a message? She's due back any day."

"No . . . I mean . . ." Matt had to make sure what the child was telling him was the truth. "Is Kathleen, her mother, at home?"

"Yes. Would you like me to get her for you, Mr. Connelly?"

"I'd sure appreciate that." Matt waited in an agony of suspense, praying that Kathleen would be able to denounce what the child had just told him.

"Hello?"

"Kathleen, it's Matt here."

"Oh . . ." Kathleen paused before she said, "Hello, Matt. How are you keeping?"

"I'm good," he answered automatically. "I'm real sorry to bother you, but the kid I just spoke to told me that Grania is on her honeymoon. That she has gotten herself married. Is this true?"

Silence ensued at the other end of the line. Matt heard Kathleen sigh heavily. "To be sure, Matt, apparently it is."

"Grania is—*married*?" Matt had a need to repeat the word over and over, to help his brain make sense of it.

"Yes, Matt. She is. I'm . . . sorry."

"I gotta go now, Kathleen. Thanks for . . . er . . . telling me. Good-bye."

"You take care now, Matt," Kathleen said, but the line was already dead.

Matt stood where he was, shell-shocked. Grania . . . *married*? After all those years of refusing to do the same with him. She'd upped and left him without explanation, then only a few months later was married to someone else. Matt's heart was pounding and he could feel the blood rushing around his body, rendering him dizzy. He didn't know whether he should laugh or cry. It was surreal, bizarre . . .

Matt decided to take the third option and get angry. He took her photo from his bedside table and hurled it against the wall, where the glass smashed into a hundred pieces. Panting with emotion, he heard the sound of the front door opening.

"Jesus." Matt swept a hand through his hair. "Give a guy a break for a few seconds, will you?" he threatened the skies. Inhaling deeply, he tried to control his immediate physical reaction to the news. It would take far longer to come to terms with the emotional ramifications.

Five minutes later, there was a tap on his bedroom door. He stood up and opened it. "Hi, Charley." To his relief, she looked far more like herself, her usual immaculate exterior back in place.

She smiled brightly at him. "Hi, Matty, how's it hanging?"

"Oh, you know . . ." he managed.

"Hey, honey, you look rough."

"Thanks, Charley, I feel it."

"Hard week at the office?" she said.

"You could say that, yes."

"You on for dinner tonight?"

"Yeah, that was the plan, wasn't it?"

"Sure was. I'll go take a shower and we can be out of here in fifteen."

"Fine."

As Charley went to take a shower, Matt wandered into the sitting room and mindlessly pulled a beer out of the fridge. He switched on the TV, flicking channels, and found some baseball—mind-numbing enough to focus his attention away from the pain he was feeling. The intercom buzzed and Matt stood up to answer. "Hello?" he said into the intercom.

"Hi, Matt, it's Roger here. Grania lent me a book which I promised to drop by when I'd finished it."

Roger was a friend of Grania's whom she'd once shared an apartment with when she'd first arrived in New York. Matt liked him. "Come on up." He pressed the button and three minutes later he was offering Roger a beer. "How come you're passing the neighborhood?" he asked.

"I just visited a room to rent in a loft a couple of blocks down. Think I'm gonna take it. I like the area. Grania not around?"

"No," said Matt, slamming the fridge door harder than he needed to.

"Right. So, how's the career going? Grania told me you were getting quite a name for yourself."

"Did she? Yeah, well, we all gotta make a living. You're an intern, aren't you?"

"Yeah, and with the hours I'm putting in at the hospital, I'm beginning to wonder whether I should plump for an easier life." Roger raised his eyebrows and took a swig of his beer.

"Rather you than me," agreed Matt.

"So, how's Grania?"

"I . . ." Matt sighed. "The truth is, old buddy, I don't really know."

"Right."

There ensued an embarrassed silence as both men took another gulp of their beer.

"I'm ready." Charley walked out of her bedroom, then stopped as she saw Roger. "Who's this?" she asked.

"Roger Sissens, hi there," he said, extending his hand. "And you are?"

"Charley Cunningham. Good to meet you."

"You too," Roger said as he stared at Charley for a little too long. "Say, haven't we met before?"

"No," said Charley categorically, "I always remember faces. I'm real sorry, but I don't remember yours. Are we off, Matty?"

"Yeah, sure." Matt was squirming in discomfort. He knew exactly what Roger was thinking and it was all wrong. Or, more painfully, right.

"Don't want to hold you guys up," said Roger, gulping down his beer as fast as he could. "I'll come down with you."

They left the loft and waited for the elevator in silence.

"Well, good to meet you, Charley," said Roger, who had reclaimed Grania's book, having guessed the lay of the land. "See you around, Matt," he said.

"And you, Roger."

Charley took hold of Matt's arm and tucked her own inside it, walking him swiftly off along the sidewalk. "Strange guy," she commented. "I've never set eyes on him in my life."

Over dinner, Charley seemed intent on making small talk. They'd reached the coffee stage before Matt had the courage to bring up the subject they were there to discuss.

"So, what are your thoughts?"

"On the baby, you mean?"

"Yeah, on the baby."

"Oh, I'm going ahead with it, of course. I mean, I'm thirty-five years old, I've always wanted kids. It's a no-brainer, isn't it?"

"Is it? If you say so," added Matt quickly.

"And I wanna say that I'm sorry for the dramatics of a week ago. I'd just heard the news and I guess I was in shock. I behaved like the kind of needy female I've always despised. Hey, I'm a big girl, with a good job and a home of my own. Which," Charley added, "Will be ready for me to move into next week. So, one way and the other, I'll be out of your hair sooner than you know it."

"So are you saying," Matt tried to choose his words carefully, "that you're gonna have this baby whether or not I'm by your side?"

"Yup." Charley nodded. "This is the new millennium, after all. Women don't need a man around any more to have a kid. OK, it'll cause a few raised eyebrows at the country club, and Mom and Dad won't like it much, but they're just gonna have to live with it."

"Right."

"Hey, Matty." Charley reached out her hand toward him. "Don't look so shocked. I really got you last week, and I understand. I'm not interested in trapping you. You made it obvious to me that it had all been a mistake, a misunderstanding . . . really, I'm so over it now. We're both grown-ups, and we can make this work, I'm sure. At whatever level," she added pointedly.

"What do you mean?"

"Well, I guess it's your turn to say how you feel. If you've decided you're not ready to be a father, that's fine by me. On the other hand, I'll be happy if you want visitation rights to the baby, want to be involved in its upbringing. But those are all things we can work out as we go along." Charley smiled brightly at him.

"Sure." Matt nodded. "So, I guess you've ruled out the thought of our bringing up the child together? As a real Mom and Dad?"

"Yeah, of course I have." Charley raised an eyebrow. "From everything you said, and everything you didn't say," she added. "Last week you made it real clear that a relationship with the baby's Mom wasn't in the picture."

Matt looked at her. And experienced a sudden rush of blood to his head. Whether it was the heartbreak of what he'd just discovered, or a gut instinct to hurt Grania as much as she'd hurt him, Matt didn't know. But Grania was gone, and the woman sitting at the table opposite him, whom he'd known for most of his life, was having his child. What had he got to lose by giving it a go?

"I've changed my mind," he announced.

"You have?"

"I told you I needed some space to think. And I think that you and I could be good together."

"Really?" said Charley dubiously.

"Yup."

"And what about Grania?"

The name hung in the air like a black cloud.

"It's over."

"You sure?" Charley looked suspicious. "It didn't seem to be this time last week. What's happened to change your mind?"

"I suppose I just got to thinking that you and me . . . we've always been close, even had a relationship way back when. And now this"—he indicated Charley's stomach—"has happened, it feels like maybe fate is giving us a prod in the right direction."

"I see." She continued to eye him. "You sure about this, Matty? As I said, I'd come to terms with having this baby alone. There's no pressure from me at all. And I want you to know that."

"I do know that, Charley, and it's appreciated. But I've just said I'm prepared to give it a try. How about you?"

"This turnaround of yours is a real shock. I . . ." Charley was flustered. "I just don't wanna get hurt by you again."

"I know you don't. And I give you my word, on our baby's life, that I won't hurt you, Charley."

"I've been so sure that you didn't feel for me the way I've always felt for you." Charley lowered her eyes, embarrassed. "You know, Matty, that I've always loved you, don't you?"

"And I've always loved you," Matt heard himself lie with surprising ease. Something had snapped inside him.

"As a friend?"

"We've been friends for a long time, Charley. And I think it's a real good basis to take it further."

"OK," Charley said slowly. "So, what are you suggesting?"

"That, first of all, you don't move out, but stay in the loft with me."

"In my bedroom?" Charley queried.

"No." Matt took a deep breath, and reached for her hand. "In mine."

"Wow, you sure know how to shock a girl. This was *so* the last thing I was expecting you to say tonight."

"Hey, you know me, full of surprises," Matt replied, an edge of bitterness to his voice.

Charley didn't notice. Instead, she took his proffered hand. "Here's to us," she said softly, "and the little guy or girl we've created together."

"Yes." Matt felt sick. "Here's to us."

36

Two weeks after Grania had left Dunworley to travel to Switzerland, she appeared in the kitchen unannounced just after lunchtime. Kathleen walked downstairs and found her daughter slumped at the table, her head resting on her elbows. She surveyed her for a full few minutes before she announced her presence.

"Hello, Grania."

"Hello, Mam," came the muffled reply. Grania did not raise her head.

"I'll be putting the kettle on for a brew, shall I?" said Kathleen.

There was no answer from her daughter. Kathleen filled the kettle slowly and placed it to boil on the range. Then she sat down on the chair next to her and put a gentle hand on her shoulder. "What's happened, Grania?"

"Oh, Mam . . . oh, Mam . . ."

"Come here, pet. I don't know what it is that's upset you, but come to Mam for a cuddle."

Grania raised her weary head and her mother glimpsed her pale, pinched face. Kathleen closed her arms around her daughter and Grania began to sob pitifully. The kettle whistled for a full two minutes before Kathleen stirred. "I'll be turning that kettle off now and making us both a cup of tea." Silently, she made the tea, then brought it back and placed a cup in front of Grania, who was sitting upright now, but catatonic, staring straight ahead.

"Grania, I don't want to interfere, but God help me, the look of you is awful. Can you be telling your mammy what's happened?"

Grania opened her mouth to try to form words, but failed on the first few attempts. Finally, she managed to utter: "He's dead, Mam. Alexander's dead."

Kathleen's hand flew to her mouth and she crossed herself with the other. "Oh no, oh no, no, no . . . *how?*"

Grania licked her lips. "He had—*has* had—a brain tumor. He was having treatment all the times he's been away. He died . . . four days ago. As his wife, I had to stay and arrange his funeral. And sign all the papers." Her words were robotic.

"Sweetheart, pet, can you be managing to drink your tea? I think you're needing some sugar. And I'm going to get something else that will help both of us." Kathleen searched in a cupboard for the brandy she used to cook with. She poured a healthy amount into each of their mugs. Then she lifted the mug to her daughter's mouth. "Drink, Grania."

Grania took three sips before she coughed and refused a fourth.

"Grania, I know there is a story you've got to tell me, but"—she glanced up and checked the time on the kitchen clock—"Aurora will be home in less than an hour. Shall I call Jennifer, the mammy of Aurora's best friend, and ask her to collect her from school and keep her for her tea? I'm thinking she shouldn't see you like this."

"Please," Grania agreed. "I'm not up to . . . I can't . . . no." A silent tear rolled down one cheek.

Kathleen brushed it away with a gentle finger. "You look like you haven't slept for a week. How about you getting into bed and your mammy bringing you a hot bottle?"

"I don't think I can sleep," said Grania as her mother helped her to stand and led her up the stairs.

"No, but where's the harm in trying?" Kathleen removed Grania's jacket and then her shoes and jeans, and tucked her up into the bed. She sat on the edge of it, as she used to do when Grania was small, and stroked her daughter's forehead. "You try and sleep now, sweetheart. I'll be downstairs if you need me." As she rose, she could see Grania's eyes were already closing. Kathleen paused on the landing, tears filling her own eyes. For all that her family laughed at her sixth sense, and her worry about her beloved daughter becoming involved with the Lisles, it seemed that her premonition had been proved right.

Two hours later, Grania reappeared in the kitchen, looking disoriented.

"How long have I been asleep? It's almost dark."

"Just as long as you needed to be," said Kathleen. "Now, so, I've arranged with Jennifer that Aurora sleep over with them. Your daddy popped an overnight bag round there half an hour ago, and he's taken himself off to the pub with your brother. So you needn't be worrying about anyone coming in."

"Thanks, Mam." Grania sat down at the table wearily.

"I've made you some lamb stew. It was always your favorite. And you look to me as though that tummy of yours hasn't seen a square meal since you left."

"Thanks, Mam," Grania repeated as Kathleen put a bowl of stew in front of her.

"There now, eat what you can. An empty stomach doesn't help a painful heart."

"Oh, Mam . . ."

"Eat, Grania, don't talk."

Grania shoveled the food into her mouth, chewed and swallowed automatically. "I can't eat any more, Mam, really." She pushed the bowl away.

"Well now, at least there's a little more color in those cheeks of yours." Kathleen removed the bowl and put it in the sink. "Grania, I'll not be pushing you to talk, but you know I'll be listening if you want me to."

"I—I don't know . . . where to begin."

"I'm sure you don't. While you were sleeping, I've been putting two and two together. When Alexander came here that night when Aurora was lost, the color on him, well . . . that told me then something wasn't right inside him. I'd say he knew a long time ago how ill he was."

"Yes, he did. But by the time the doctors discovered the problem, they couldn't operate because of the size of the tumor and the position in his brain. All he could hope for was that chemotherapy would help. But it didn't."

"No."

"He realized he had to accept the inevitable a few weeks ago, when he started to deteriorate. And that was when he began to make plans for Aurora. I . . ."

"No rush, pet." Kathleen sat down next to her at the table and put her hand over Grania's. "You just take your time."

Haltingly at first, Grania began to tell her mother the story. Kathleen listened quietly, taking in and understanding all Grania was telling her. And inwardly berating herself for criticizing what she had initially seen as Grania's capriciousness in marrying Alexander.

"Hans, his solicitor, will be coming over to see me here in the next two weeks, and bringing Alexander's ashes with him. He said he wanted them spread on Lily's grave." Grania paused and gave a long, deep sigh. "Oh, Mam, watching him die . . . it was dreadful. *Dreadful*," she emphasized.

"From what you say, pet, it sounds like a merciful release."

"Yes. He was in so much pain." She looked up at her mother suddenly and gave a weak smile. "You know, Mam, your instinct that you needed to tell me the story of Lily before I left for Switzerland was right. I was able to tell Alexander what had happened to Lily when she was younger before he died. He said it had helped him and I think it did. He loved her so very much."

"Well, let's hope they're together now, somewhere up there, and the pain of living is over for both of them," said Kathleen somberly. "And that they can look down and know that their precious daughter is safe here with us."

"Oh God, Mam," Grania shook her head despairingly. "How on earth do I tell her?"

"Grania, that is something I don't have the answer to. And I'm thinking it's a terrible thing her daddy's left you to do."

"It is," agreed Grania, "but if you'd have seen the state he was in . . . he looked like his own ghost. And even though he was desperate to see Aurora just one last time, he was adamant that it would make it worse for her if he did. He wants—wanted—Aurora to remember him as he was. We all know how unstable Aurora had been after her mother died. I think he did the right thing."

"Have you an idea of what you should tell her?" asked Kathleen.

"I've thought of nothing else for the past few days," Grania replied desolately. "Do you have any suggestions, Mam?"

"I'd say it's better not to lie if you can avoid it. Tell her the truth, as gently as you can."

"Yes," agreed Grania, "but I don't want her to know that he suffered so much."

"Well, it's an awful burden he's given you, but all I can say is that we'll be here for her when you have told her, and we'll give her, *and* you, as much love and support as we can. You know, Grania, that whatever you decide to do with your life, Aurora will always have a home here with us."

"Yes, Mam, thank you. It was the one thing that worried Alexander; he didn't want my adoption of Aurora to affect my future plans."

"And your mammy will be making sure it doesn't," said Kathleen firmly.

"Well," Grania sighed, "I doubt I'm off anywhere soon. I have nowhere else to go." She shrugged, then yawned and rose from the table. "Oh, Mam, I'm so tired. If I'm to tell Aurora tomorrow, I think I should try and get some more sleep."

"Yes." Kathleen put her arms around Grania and hugged her. "Sleep tight, pet. And I just want to tell you how proud your mammy is of her daughter," she whispered.

"Thanks, Mam. Night-night," Grania answered, and left the kitchen.

John and Shane came home half an hour later. Kathleen told them the dreadful tale Grania had related to her.

"That poor little pet," said John, surreptitiously wiping a tear from his eye. "Well now, at least Aurora has us."

"She does that," added Shane. "We all love her like she's our own."

"And she's going to need to feel every ounce of it," Kathleen underlined. "And Grania too. She's been put through a terrible time, through no fault of her own."

"Well now, seems your sixth sense was right again, sweetheart," said John. "You said you had a bad feeling right from the start."

"There's no doubt you're a witch, Mam," Shane agreed and patted his mother's arm affectionately. He stood up. "I'm for my bed now, Mam, but you be telling Grania and that small one I love them both."

Later, as husband and wife climbed into bed, John asked, "When is Grania going to tell Aurora?"

"I'd be thinking when she comes back from school tomorrow afternoon. It'll give Grania another day to collect herself."

"Come here, darlin'." John reached out his strong arms and encircled his wife inside them. "Try not to worry. I'd be looking on the bright side and say that, although Aurora's in for a terrible shock tomorrow, at least there's no future uncertainty for her. She'll know she has a home here with us for the rest of her life. And for all it's put our Grania through, I admire Alexander for having the foresight to make sure it would be the case."

"Yes. Night, pet."

"Night."

It was only then, as Kathleen closed her eyes to try to sleep, that she remembered the phone call from Matt.

Grania woke the following morning feeling at least physically refreshed. She lay and tried to take on board what had happened to her, not just in the past two weeks, but in the past four months. Aurora had arrived like a whirlwind in her life and changed it irrevocably. To the point where she was now officially Mrs. Devonshire, stepmother to a child who would soon become officially her daughter. *And* a widow . . .

Just like Mary before her.

Grania tried to focus on the words she would choose to tell Aurora about her father then decided it was pointless. She couldn't plan, because she had no idea of how Aurora would react. She'd have to play it by ear. And the sooner it was over, the better.

Grania felt a sudden urge to leave the house and breathe some fresh air into her lungs. Being cooped up in a stuffy hospital for the past two weeks had been an ordeal. She threw on her tracksuit bottoms, hoodie and trainers, and went downstairs. Kathleen was nowhere to be seen, so she jogged off down the lane and turned right up the cliff path toward Dunworley House. It was a beautiful day and the sea was mill-pond still.

Panting, Grania sat down on the grassy rock where she'd first seen the little girl standing alone on the cliff's edge. She looked up at the house above her—a house that was now in trust for Aurora to live in if she so wished.

Hans had eventually outlined the amount Alexander had left Grania in his will; enough to ensure that, if she chose not to, she'd never have to do another day's work for the rest of her life. She was a wealthy woman.

"Oh, Matt." Grania suddenly choked out his name. Her mother

had been wonderful, but right now she was in desperate need of the warmth, understanding and love of the man she'd always considered her soul mate. The pain of his loss was physical. And the fact that it was over and she would never know the comfort he had offered her again was palpable.

Grania stood and continued up the hill toward Dunworley House. She could not dwell . . . life had happened and there was no turning back. She pushed open the gate and walked through the front garden. Alexander had stipulated in his will that the house would become Aurora's on her twenty-first birthday. It was then up to his daughter to decide whether she wished to keep it or sell it. He had set aside a healthy sum to renovate it, but she would discuss all that with Hans when he arrived over here.

Walking into the courtyard at the back, Grania rooted under the boulder for the key to her studio. Once inside, she studied the sculptures sitting on her workbench. And for the first time in two weeks, felt a tiny surge of pleasure. They were as good as she'd remembered they were, but they could be better.

"Jesus, Mary and Joseph, Grania! Where have you been?" exclaimed Kathleen as Grania entered the kitchen.

"Sorry, Mam, I went up to my studio and must have lost track of time. Is there anything to eat? I'm starving."

"I'll make you a quick sandwich." Kathleen glanced at the clock nervously. "You know Aurora will be home in half an hour?"

"Yes." Grania's stomach turned over at the thought. "When she gets here, I'm taking her off for a walk."

"Grania!" Aurora catapulted herself into Grania's arms and hugged her tightly. Mother and daughter shared a glance of sorrow over the top of her head.

"It's wonderful to see you, sweetheart," Grania responded. "How have you been?"

"I've been very well, thank you," said Aurora. "Did Shane tell you that Maisie, the sheepdog, is having pups? He said I can be there when she gives birth *even* if it's the middle of the night," she added, throwing a surreptitious glance at Kathleen. "And I've been telling all my friends at school that you are my real mother now." Aurora let go of Grania and began to pirouette around the kitchen. "I'm so happy!" She paused in mid-twirl and suddenly asked, "Where's Daddy?"

"Aurora, why don't you fetch Lily and we'll take her up the cliff path for a walk?" suggested Grania.

"All right," she agreed. "Be back in a minute."

"I wait for you outside," Grania called to Aurora's retreating back.

Kathleen walked over to her daughter and placed a comforting hand on her arm. "Good luck, Grania. We'll be here for you both when you get back."

Grania nodded silently and left the kitchen.

Aurora was full of chatter on the way up the hill as the puppy chased flies and darted in and out of her young mistress's legs.

"You know, I was thinking the other day," Aurora said in her quaint, adult way, "how much more I like my life now. I was so lonely before I met you and Kathleen and John and Shane. And I love living on the farm. And now you've married Daddy, they are my real family too, aren't they?"

"I'm going to sit down for a bit now, Aurora," said Grania as they reached the grassy rock overlooking the sea. "Will you come and sit with me?"

"Yes." Aurora sank gracefully to the ground and Lily came to snuggle into her lap. She looked up at Grania's solemn face. "What is it? You have something to tell me, don't you?"

"Yes, I do, Aurora." Grania reached for the child's hand.

"Is it about Daddy?" Aurora asked earnestly.

"Yes. It is. How did you know?"

"I don't know, I just . . . *did*."

"Aurora, darling, I'm not really sure how to tell you this, so I'm going to say it very quickly . . ."

"Daddy's gone, hasn't he?"

"Aurora . . . yes, he has."

"Up to heaven?"

"Yes. He was very ill just after we got married and . . . he died. I'm so, so sorry."

"I see." Aurora's eyes concentrated intensely on stroking the puppy on her lap.

"But I just want to tell you, my darling, my darling Aurora, that you're going to have all of us—your new family—to look after you. And," emphasized Grania, "not only am I your stepmother, but Daddy and I signed the papers which mean I will legally adopt you as soon as possible. You will be my daughter and no one will ever be able to take you away from me."

So far, Aurora was showing no visible signs of distress. Grania's own vision was blurred by tears. "You know I love you like my own child. I always have . . . somehow," Grania continued, wishing she could show the same amount of strength as the little girl in front of her. "Aurora, do you understand what I'm telling you?"

Aurora raised her eyes from the puppy and looked over the cliff top, out to sea. "Yes, I understand. I knew that he would be going soon. I just didn't know when."

"Aurora, how did you know?"

"Mummy"—Aurora checked herself—"my *old* mummy told me."

"Did she?"

"Yes. She said the angels would be coming to take him to heaven, to be with her." Aurora turned and looked at Grania. "I told you she was lonely."

"You did."

Aurora sat in silence for a long time before she said, "I'll miss him. Very much. I would have liked to say good-bye." She bit her lip, and Grania saw the first glimmer of tears.

"Darling, I know I can't replace your mummy and daddy, but I promise you, I'll do my best."

Aurora was looking out to sea again. "I understand Mummy wanted him with her, but why does everyone I love leave me?"

Then she cried, great sobs that racked her body. Grania pulled Aurora into her arms and sat her on her knee, rocking her like a baby.

"I won't leave you, darling, I promise," she murmured over and over again. "And Daddy didn't want to, believe me. He loved you so very much. He loved you enough to make sure that you'd be safe with me and my family. That's why we got married."

Aurora looked up at her. "I think he loved you a little bit too."

She wiped her tears away with her forearm and asked, "Are you sad, Grania? That he's gone?"

"Oh, yes," said Grania, "I'm terribly, terribly sad."

"Did you love Daddy?" asked Aurora.

"Yes, I think I did. I'm just sad I didn't have very much time with him."

Aurora reached for Grania's fingers and clasped them tightly. "So, we both loved him. And we'll both miss him, won't we?"

"Yes."

"Then we can help cheer each other up when one of us feels sad about it, can't we?"

Aurora's bravery and strength was far more poignant than her tears. "Yes," Grania said as she held Aurora tightly to her, "We can."

"Where's Aurora?" Kathleen asked as Grania walked back into the kitchen.

"She's putting Lily to bed and she says she wants to go with Shane and check on the sheep."

"Really?" Kathleen raised an eyebrow. "You did tell her? Didn't you?"

"Yes, I did."

"And how did she take it?"

"Mam"—Grania shook her head in confusion and amazement—"she said she already knew."

Aurora

Yes. I did know.

Though to explain "how," exactly, is almost impossible. If I say I heard voices telling me, you will almost certainly, and with good reason, think I'm as mentally unstable as my poor mother, Lily. Let's just say I had a "premonition." Lots of people have those, don't they?

Still, it was an awful shock, just as everything was going so perfectly. Grania married to my father . . . what I had wanted, and yes, I admit, had helped to engineer.

The change between joy and sadness happened in the blink of an eye. There was no time to "tread water," to savor the moment for a few months, or even weeks.

Daddy had done all he could to protect me by marrying Grania and making it easy for her to adopt me. He showed his love for me in practical ways, as many men do. But I would have liked to have said good-bye in person, however awful he looked.

I wouldn't have minded, because I'd known he was ill all along. And if you love someone, it's not at all about how they look . . . it's feeling their "essence," one last time.

In retrospect, it was probably just as hard for Grania. Her life had been tossed into the maelstrom of our family's storm, forced to adapt by a father desperate to protect his beloved child.

I read a book recently that explained how spirits travel in "groups" through time. They change roles, but are endlessly drawn to each other through an invisible connection.

Perhaps that could explain why Kathleen felt history was repeating itself with Grania and me. After all, she was kindhearted and needy for a child to love when she met me, and I was the "orphan" she took under her wing. Oh dear, Reader, I hope I've never behaved as callously as my grandmother Anna did to Mary. The Buddhists say we must come back to earth until we've learned our lessons and I hope that I've always treated Grania with gratitude and love. As, actually, I would quite like to move on to the next level after this. Nirvana sounds very pleasant. Perhaps I have some way to go yet, but I've always tried to be a good person. And I could certainly do with a new, stronger body . . .

I'm going to return to New York now, to the mess Matt is currently making of his life.

At this stage, I feel I can categorically say it's all going horribly wrong. The question is, can Matt make it right . . . ?

37

Charley had moved into Matt's bedroom the night they'd agreed to give their relationship a shot. She had, however, vetoed any form of physical contact due to her pregnant state. Matt had been relieved at this—at least it had provided him with a stay of execution. As he couldn't remember the last time they'd made love due to his drunkenness, his mind could only flit back to when they'd previously been an item. He remembered their couplings as uninspiring and, for him, mechanical. Unlike the exquisite lovemaking he'd experienced with Grania, when he'd literally felt as if their souls were joined . . .

Matt checked himself from that train of thought, climbed out of bed and went into the bathroom to take a shower, thinking that Charley's new status had other, annoying, consequences. For a start, her vast array of cosmetics—lotions and potions that could stock a beauty counter at Saks cluttering up the sink and shelves. Grania's low-maintenance beauty regime—a pot of face cream had been her nod to it—not to mention that his clothes now inhabited an eighth of the wardrobe due to Charley's vast array of designer garments, only underlined the differences between the two women.

As Matt searched out his razor, managing to knock a makeup bag into the sink at the same time, he tried to stem his irritation. He was the one, after all, who had said they should give it a try. Charley had not pressured him or even made him feel guilty. He mustn't blame her.

However, she had already made noises about moving—suggested buying a house in Greenwich near to their parents. Matt was not enthusiastic about the idea. Yet, the fact that he and Grania—faced with similar issues only a few months ago—hadn't given a thought to moving out of the city, didn't make Charley's wish to have her child breathe fresher air abnormal. When Matt had mentioned there was no way he had the money to provide that kind of home for them, Charley had dismissed his objections with a flick of her wrist.

"Mom and Dad will help us, Matty. You know they will."

Matt understood a little of what Grania must have felt when his own parents had offered to provide some help. He didn't want Charley's folks to give him anything. Charley had also turned to him the other night and asked him whether he really was set against going into his dad's business.

"I'm gonna have to stop work when this one comes along, even if only for a few months. And maybe"—Charley had shrugged—"forever. I hate to say it, Matty, but what you earn will just about buy us a Filipino maid three times a week, not the kind of live-in support I'm gonna need."

Matt dressed swiftly, glad that Charley had taken herself off to her apartment uptown to pay the final check to her interior designer. She'd taken Matt to see it last week, and Matt had goggled at the über-chic interior. Full of glass, chrome and white, its starkness was as welcoming as an operating theater. Matt wondered how Charley could bear to slum it here with him in the loft. He fixed himself a coffee and found an out-of-date bagel in the fridge. Charley was no cook—they'd eaten take-out solidly in the past two weeks—and Matt felt his juices flowing as he remembered the delicious ham and colcannon Grania had cooked for him regularly.

"Shit!" Matt checked himself. He could not continue comparing the two women. They were different, that was all. The real problem was that, to him, Charley measured up unfavorably every time. Matt sat himself down at his desk and switched on his laptop. He was writing a paper that should have been finished three weeks ago—what with everything going on, his concentration was all over the place. He read through what he had written and knew it wasn't up to scratch. He sat back in his chair and sighed. He could see very clearly where his life was heading. After all the years of avoiding an existence similar to his parents, he was already on his way toward it. He wished he had somebody to talk to . . . he was desperate. And the only person available to him since Grania was gone was his mom.

He grabbed his cell phone and pressed her home number. "Mom? It's Matt here."

"Matt, it's a pleasure to hear from you. How are you?"

"Look, Mom, I was thinking I could do with a few hours out of the city. You got a busy weekend?"

"We have some friends over for a barbecue tomorrow, but today your father's playing golf and I'm here alone. Want to stop by and have some lunch?"

"You're on, Mom. I'll leave now."

The West Side Highway was clear and Matt arrived in his parents' Belle Haven drive within forty-five minutes.

"Hi, sweetheart." Elaine was on the doorstep to greet him with a warm hug. "What a lovely surprise. Not often I get my boy to myself any more. Come in."

Matt followed his mom through the spacious entrance hall and into the large kitchen, stuffed with every conceivable appliance. His father, Bob, loved gadgets. He bought them for his wife every Christmas and birthday. Elaine would open them with a resigned smile, say thank you, then hide them away with the rest in one of the capacious kitchen units.

"Can I fix you a drink, sweetie?"

"A beer will do just fine." Matt stood uncertainly in the kitchen; now he was here, he wasn't sure what to say. His mom knew Grania was gone, but nothing more.

"So how's life in the city?"

"I . . . shit, Mom!" Matt shook his head. "I'm not gonna lie to you, I'm in a real mess."

"Well, then." Elaine put the beer in front of her son, her eyes full of motherly sympathy. "You tell your mom all about it."

Matt did so, and was as honest as he could be about the situation, though he avoided mentioning the fact he couldn't even remember the night in question. He didn't think Elaine's sensibilities would cope.

"So," Elaine recounted, "let me catch up. Grania disappears soon after she arrives home from the hospital. She takes off to Ireland and won't tell you what it is you've done. There's silence between you for months. And then you hear she's married to someone else?"

"Yup, that's the bare bones of it," Matt agreed with a sigh.

"Next, Charley moves into your apartment to keep you company, while hers is under renovation. You two become close and start a relationship." Elaine scratched her head. "And what you're saying is you're not sure of your feelings for her?"

"Yes," agreed Matt. "Can I have another beer?"

Elaine went to fetch it for him. "So, you think you might be on the rebound?"

"Yup. And," Matt took a deep breath, "there's something else."

"You'd better fess up, honey."

"Charley's pregnant."

Elaine gave him an odd look before she said, "Really? You sure?"

"Of course I'm sure, Mom. She's booked in for a scan in a couple of weeks' time. I'm going with her."

"OK," Elaine said slowly. "I've prepared a salad for lunch. Let's go eat it on the terrace."

Matt helped transfer the salad, plates and cutlery outside. As they sat down, Matt could see his mother was shaken.

"I'm real sorry, Mom."

"Don't be, Matt. I'm a big girl, I can take it. It's not that, it's just . . ." something that doesn't make sense. She frowned, "But let's put that to one side. The question is, do you love Charley?"

"Yes, I love her as a friend, maybe as a partner . . . I don't know yet, Mom, I really don't. I mean, sure, we grew up in the same place, know the same people . . . you're friendly with her folks . . . what's not to like? It's easy," he sighed.

"Marrying someone in the same world as you is always easier. Of course it is, Matt. It's what I did." Elaine smiled as she served the salad. "It's comfortable, and familiarity can breed love. But it's not"—Elaine searched for the right word—"exhilarating. It's a 'safe' ride."

Matt was surprised at his mother's empathy. "Yeah, spot on, Mom."

"Don't think I don't understand, Matt, because I do. Grania was your walk on the wild side and I admired you for breaking out. She was your passion. She brought the world alive for you."

"Yep, she did." Matt swallowed hard. He knew he was close to tears. "And it's only since she's been gone that I realize how much I loved her . . . *do* love her."

"I loved someone once . . . before your father. My parents didn't think he was suitable—he was a musician. I broke it off, sent him away . . ."

"I didn't know." Matt was taken aback by his mom's revelation. "Do you regret it?"

"What's the point of regrets?" Elaine asked bitterly. "I did what I thought was the right thing to keep everyone happy. But there's never a day goes by when I don't think of him, wonder where he is . . ." Her voice trailed off, then she checked herself. "Sorry, Matt, this isn't for you to hear. And your pop and I have always had a good life together. And I got you. So, no, I don't regret anything."

"The difference is, I didn't send Grania away."

"No. And now she's married," said Elaine.

"That's what her mom said when I called her up."

"Well, I'm real surprised at that. I know she felt uncomfortable in our world, Matt, probably thought we didn't like her. But I have such respect for her and her talent. And," Elaine underlined, "I knew she loved my boy. For that, I could forgive her anything."

"Well, Mom, Grania's gone. And she's not coming back anytime soon. I gotta get on with my life. The question is, do I continue to try and make a go of it with Charley?"

"It's a tough call. Charley's beautiful, bright and from your world. And, besides, it's complicated by the baby. You are sure she's pregnant?" Elaine asked again.

"Yes, Mom!"

"Well," Elaine sighed, "looks like you've got yourself a done deal. And I know you were heartbroken over losing the child with Grania. Although I . . ."

"What, Mom?"

"Nothing, nothing," Elaine answered quickly. "If everything is as you say, I don't think you have much choice."

"No," Matt agreed morosely, "seems like I don't. And I gotta pay for the lifestyle. She's already mentioned me going into Dad's business. An uptown girl like Charley won't be satisfied with a psychology lecturer's income."

"You know it's your father's dream for you to take over. But, Matt, if it's not what you want—"

"Mom, *nothing* is what I 'want' just now." Matt put his knife and fork together and looked at his watch. "I'd better be getting back. Charley will be wondering where I am." He raised his eyebrows.

"I wish there was something more I could say, but if Grania is married . . ."

"Somehow, and I don't even know how, I managed to screw it up."

"You know, honey, I do understand. You will grow to love Charley. I sure had to learn to love your dad," Elaine offered with a wry smile.

"I'm sure you're right," he agreed with a sigh. "Anyway, thanks for lunch and listening. Bye, Mom."

Elaine watched her son as he pulled his car out of the drive. She shut the door and walked back to the terrace. Breaking the habit of a lifetime, she did not immediately clear the plates from the table. Instead, she sat down and began to process what her son had told her.

Half an hour later, Elaine had come to the conclusion that she had a choice to make: she could toe the party line and keep quiet about what she knew. Which would not only preserve the status quo, but also her own selfish wish for closeness in terms of proximity to her son and forthcoming grandchild. There wasn't a doubt in Elaine's mind that Charley would drag Matt back to Greenwich when the baby was born. Or she could investigate her suspicions further . . .

Elaine heard her husband's Jeep pull up in their drive.

And decided to sleep on it.

38

The occupants of the farm were on red alert for signs of emotional stress from Aurora. She was certainly quieter than usual, her normal joie de vivre muted.

"Well, that surely is to be expected," commented John to Kathleen one evening.

Kathleen had asked her if she wished to take some time off school, but Aurora had been adamant she wanted to go.

"Daddy always wanted me to concentrate on my lessons, and besides, Emily might find a new best friend if I'm not there," Aurora had replied.

"I take my hat off to that small one," Kathleen said as she arrived back in the kitchen having kissed Aurora good night. "I can only hope she's not too good to be true now and heading for a crash later."

"Yes," agreed Grania, having just returned from her studio. "There's no sign of it so far—it's almost as if she was prepared."

"I'd agree there." Kathleen glanced at her daughter. "But I've always said she's been here before. There's an old soul inside her. She understands things that maybe we don't. There's sausages for you keeping warm in the range."

"Thanks, Mam, I lost track of time."

"What is it you're doing in that studio of yours?" asked Kathleen.

"What I always do," said Grania, in a tone that brokered no further discussion. She'd never been one for discussing her work until it was finished. And this project was so close to her heart—as if she had poured her soul into the clay itself—she couldn't release it just yet. "Hans is arriving tomorrow."

"Is he now?" Kathleen withdrew the sausages and mash from the range and placed the plate in front of Grania.

"He's sleeping up at Dunworley House. I prepared a bedroom there for him today."

"Right." Kathleen sat down next to Grania and watched her as she picked at her food. "And how are you feeling, pet?"

"I'm all right. A little tired, but I've been working hard." Grania shook her head. "I think I've left it too late to eat." She put her knife and fork together.

"Not like you to be off your food."

Grania stood up and put her plate in the sink. "I'll be off to bed now, Mam."

"Sleep well."

"Thanks, Mam."

"And there was me thinking it was Aurora that would be affected by all this. It seems she's taken it better than our daughter," commented Kathleen.

"Well now." John reached for the light switch as his wife settled herself down next to him for the night. "I'd say Aurora's lost a daddy, but found a life, whereas Grania's *lost* her life."

In the dark, Kathleen raised an eyebrow at her husband's profundity. "I'm worried about her, John. This is the time of her life, right now. The time when she should be in her prime, at her peak. And she's lost, John, she really is."

"Give her some time, pet. She's been through a lot, through no fault of her own, I'd say."

"What did I tell you? It's the curse of that Lisle family. I—"

"Enough, Kathleen. You can't be blaming others. Grania did what she did with her own free will. Night, pet."

Kathleen said no more—she knew better than to continue a conversation her husband did not wish to be part of. But she lay in the dark, sleep eluding her, worrying for her precious daughter.

Grania felt oddly relieved and comforted to see the sturdy figure of Hans Schneider pulling his car into the courtyard of Dunworley House. Wiping her clay-spattered hands on her apron, she opened the door of her studio and went outside to greet him.

"How are you, Grania?" He kissed her on both cheeks.

The shared trauma of watching Alexander die had brought them close and negated a need for formality between solicitor and client.

"I'm all right, thanks, Hans. Did you have a good journey?"

"Yes." Hans turned around to survey Dunworley House. "It looks as if it is in need of a new roof."

"It probably is. Shall we go inside?"

An hour later, they were eating a lunch of fresh oysters that Grania had bought from the quayside at Ring earlier that morning. Grania had also plundered the wine cellar, asking for advice from Hans on which one she should open.

"So, how is Aurora?" Hans asked.

"Amazing," replied Grania. "Perhaps too amazing, but we shall see. Sadly," Grania sighed, "losing someone she loves isn't a new experience for her. And her life is so busy; between school, her ballet lessons and living on the farm, luckily she doesn't have a lot of time to brood."

"And you?" asked Hans.

"To be honest, I'm still struggling to get those last few days at the hospital out of my head."

"Yes. I know what you mean. It was . . . difficult. I have brought the ashes, by the way."

"Right," Grania acknowledged soberly. "Another oyster?"

They ate in silence for a while, until Grania said, "Should I ask Aurora if she wants to help me spread them on Lily's grave?"

"Will it disturb her, do you think?"

"I don't know, but she was very upset she didn't have a chance to say good-bye to her daddy in person. Perhaps it might help. Having said that, seeing him reduced to a few grains of ash may not be the right thing to do."

"Well, from what you have told me, you have handled the situation very well so far. Perhaps you should again trust your instincts."

"Thank you, Hans. It's actually Aurora who's handled it well. And my parents and my brother have been wonderful. They adore her."

"In some ways, even though it is a tragedy Alexander and Lily have both gone, perhaps the life Aurora is leading now, the stability she has within a normal family, is healthy for her," Hans mused. "She has had a very difficult childhood."

"Yes. And listening to the stories of the Lisle history, it seems her mother didn't fare much better either. Perhaps it's this house . . ." Grania shuddered suddenly. "It has a very strange atmosphere."

"I am sure that once the renovation is completed, it will help. Has Aurora said if she wishes to live here?" asked Hans. "Or does she prefer to stay at the farm with you?"

"At present, wild horses couldn't drag her away from her precious animals." Grania smiled. "But she may change her mind."

"In the week I am here, I intend to make inquiries to find a surveyor who can tell me what is needed structurally," said Hans. "Perhaps he may be able to suggest a reliable firm of builders to carry out the work the house needs. All I would ask is that when it comes to choosing new paint colors for the walls, I may borrow your artist's eye." Hans smiled.

"Of course," Grania agreed.

"Whether or not Aurora wishes to keep the house when she is older, at least it will be in a good state of repair for her to sell it," Hans continued. "I will also travel to Cork city to talk to my Irish contact and see how far we have got with the adoption process. But neither he nor I are expecting any problems. Alexander has been as efficient in death as in life. Which, as he knew it would be, is imperative under the circumstances. His sister has already made contact with me, wishing to know the contents of Alexander's will." Hans gave a grim smile. "As I have said to you before, when there is a death, the vultures descend. And what of you, Grania?" He studied her. "Have you had time yet to think of your future?"

"No," she replied shortly. "I'm simply focusing on making sure Aurora is all right, and doing some work. It's helped."

"I find work is always a balm for the soul. And I would love to see some of your sculptures, Grania. Alexander told me you were exceptionally talented."

"He was very kind . . ." Grania blushed. "I feel as though the only thing left to me after the past few months *is* my work. I'll show you later. And I was thinking that I might bring Aurora up to see you. It's Saturday tomorrow, so she has no school."

"I would be delighted to see her. It has been at least a couple of years since I did."

Grania cleared the plates and put them in the sink. "Will you be all right up here at the house alone?"

"Of course," Hans smiled. "Why do you ask?"

"No reason. If you need anything, just call me. There's milk in the fridge, bread, bacon and eggs for breakfast."

"Thank you, Grania. I look forward to seeing you and Aurora up here tomorrow."

"Good-bye, Hans," Grania said as she left the house.

"Good-bye," he called in reply. Hans poured himself another glass of wine and thought how sad it was that Alexander had been unable to enjoy for longer the lovely woman he had taken as his wife.

Grania drove Aurora up to Dunworley House the following morning.

"Uncle Hans!" Aurora threw herself into his arms. "I haven't seen you for years! Where have you been?"

Hans grinned. "Where I always am, Aurora, working hard in Switzerland."

"Why do men spend their whole life working?" asked Aurora. "No wonder they get sick."

"I think," said Hans, his eyes twinkling over Aurora's head at Grania, "You have a very good point, *liebchen*."

"I hope you're going to take a holiday today, Uncle Hans, so I can show you my animals. Maisie's new puppies are only two days old. They haven't even opened their eyes yet."

"I think that sounds like a very good idea," interjected Grania. "Aurora, why don't you take Hans off to the farm while I do some work? Then come up here at lunchtime and maybe we can go to the beach for a picnic?"

"Grania," Aurora pouted, "now it's *you* that's working! All right, I'll look after Uncle Hans, and come up and collect you later."

When they had left to walk down the hill to the farm, Grania went into her studio. She glanced through her window at Aurora, dancing by Hans's side. She looked at the sculpture in front of her and only hoped she had captured Aurora's ethereal, effortless grace.

The morning flew by and all too soon there was a knock on her door.

"Can we come in? I've shown Uncle Hans everything and I'm starving!" Aurora burst into the studio and put her arms around Grania's shoulders, planting a kiss on her cheek as she sat at her bench. Her eyes fell on the sculptures on the table in front of Grania. She looked and then looked again.

"Is that me?"

Grania hadn't wanted to show Aurora the figures until they were finished. "Yes."

"Uncle Hans, come and see! Grania's turned me into a statue!"

Hans walked toward the bench and stared at the sculptures.

"Mein Gott!" He bent to study them more closely. "Grania, they are"—he struggled to find the words—"unbelievable! I only wish that . . ." Hans glanced at Grania, new respect in his eyes, and she knew instantly what he was thinking. "Alexander would have bought them all. You have captured Aurora's energy in clay."

"Thank you," said Grania. "It's been cathartic."

"Yes. And out of that, you have created something very beautiful."

"Can you stop talking about my statues and tell me what's for lunch?" Aurora pleaded.

The three of them spent a pleasant afternoon on Inchydoney Beach. Aurora leaped, skipped and twirled in the shallow waves and Hans and Grania sat in the dunes enjoying the warmth of the sun.

"You are right when you say she does not seem outwardly to have been badly affected," commented Hans. "She looks . . . happy. Perhaps it is that she had little attention as a child. Now, she has much."

"And she likes an audience," Grania smiled as Aurora executed an effortless *jeté*. "Her ballet teacher thinks she has extraordinary potential as a dancer," she added. "And, of course, her grandmother was a famous ballerina."

"Then, if she wishes to pursue it, she must. As you must pursue your sculpture," Hans said. "Where do you exhibit?"

"There's a gallery in New York that shows my work, but in recent years I've been working on more and more private commissions. It's not what I've wanted to do, but at least I've known I can eat," replied Grania honestly.

"It seems then that there is one positive thing to come out of this difficult time for you, Grania. And you know that you are a wealthy woman now."

"And you know, Hans, that I don't wish to take it." Grania's tone changed immediately at the mention of money.

Hans eyed her. "Grania, if I may speak plainly, it seems to me that your pride sometimes overtakes your common sense."

"I . . ." Grania was taken aback by Hans's assessment. "What do you mean?"

"Why is it wrong to accept a gift from someone who wishes to give it to you?"

"It isn't, Hans. It's just that—"

"What, Grania? Tell me," he challenged.

"Well . . ."

Suddenly, Grania thought back to all those times with Matt. Staunchly refusing any help his parents wanted to give them *and,* even worse, refusing to marry him. Those decisions had been taken purely out of pride. Not because it was necessarily what she wanted. Or, in retrospect, the right thing to do. After all, perhaps if she *had* married Matt, they wouldn't be where they were now. And there was no doubt that some help from Matt's parents, who, as Hans had just pointed out, simply wanted to give them a gift, would have made their life easier.

"Maybe you're right," Grania agreed eventually, feeling disturbed by her sudden inner revelation. "But I can't help it, I've always been that way."

Hans watched her silently before he said, "Perhaps it is simply your personality or, more likely, it is borne out of a sense of insecurity. You should ask yourself why do you not wish people to help you? Perhaps you believe inside that you are not worth their help."

"I . . . don't know," answered Grania truthfully. "But you're right, I think that in some ways my pride has blighted my life. Anyway, enough of me. But thank you, Hans, for being honest. It's helped me, it really has."

The following morning, as her family made their normal Sunday pilgrimage to mass, Grania stayed behind to mind Aurora.

"Would you like to walk up to Dunworley church later? Uncle Hans has brought a pot back with him from Switzerland, which contains"—

Grania chose her words carefully—"I suppose what you might call Daddy's magic dust."

"You mean his ashes?" said Aurora, taking another bite of toast.

"Yes. I was wondering whether you wanted to help me spread them."

"Of course I do," agreed Aurora. "Can I choose where?"

"Yes, although Daddy did suggest he might be sprinkled on Mummy's grave."

"No," Aurora swallowed her toast and shook her head. "That's not where I want to put him."

"Right."

"That's just Mummy's old bones. It's not where she *lives*."

"All right, Aurora, you just show me."

As dusk was falling, Aurora announced she wished to go with Grania and spread her father's ashes.

With Alexander's urn held in a carrier bag, Grania followed Aurora outside and up the lane. Aurora led her up the cliff path toward Dunworley House. When they reached the grassy rock, Aurora stopped.

"Now, Grania, you sit here in your usual place." Aurora opened the carrier bag and took out the urn. She took the lid off and looked inside in fascination.

"It's like gritty sand, isn't it?"

"Yes."

Aurora turned and walked over to the cliff, stopping only inches away from the edge. Suddenly, she paused and turned back, seeming nervous. "Grania, will you come and help me?"

"Of course." Grania walked a few paces forward and stood next to Aurora.

"This is where Mummy fell. I see her here, sometimes. Mummy!" she shouted. "I'm giving Daddy to you." Aurora looked down into the pot, her eyes glazed with tears. "Bye-bye, Daddy, go to Mummy, she needs you." Aurora threw the ashes over the cliff, where they were caught by the wind and carried away across the sea. "I love you, Daddy. And you, Mummy. See you both in heaven soon."

Aurora's stoicism and bravery brought a lump to Grania's throat. Eventually, she walked back to her rock to let Aurora be. She watched as Aurora knelt, perhaps in silent prayer—she didn't know—as night began to fall.

Finally, Aurora stood up slowly. She turned to Grania. "I'm ready to go home now. They want to go."

"Do they?"

"Yes."

Aurora reached out her hand and Grania took it in her own. They turned in the direction of the farmhouse and began to walk slowly down the hill.

Suddenly, Aurora turned back. "Look, look!" She pointed. "Can you see them?"

"See who?"

"Look . . ."

Grania forced herself to turn her head and looked out over the bay in the direction Aurora was pointing.

"They're flying," Aurora said in awe. "She came to collect him and they're going off to heaven together."

Grania studied the skyline and could see nothing but clouds caught by the breeze, scudding across the sky. Grania gave Aurora a gentle tug and walked her down the hill to begin a new future.

39

Matt blinked at the shadowy, moving image. There, on the screen, was living proof of the night he couldn't remember.

"You want to see it in 3-D?" asked the scanner operator.

"Sure," agreed Charley as the technician moved across her belly.

"There's the head, and the arm . . . if it stops wriggling, we should be able to get a good picture . . ."

"Wow," Matt breathed as he watched the screen. Full color, back, front, all singing and dancing. This was what you paid for at a top private clinic. The scan he'd seen of Grania's baby at the local hospital down the road from their loft was like a 1940s black-and-white movie compared to a James Cameron epic.

Afterward, clutching the pictures in her hand, Charley reached with her other for Matt's. "You want to take in some lunch? I seem to be hungry suddenly," she chuckled.

"Sure, whatever you say."

Over lunch, Charley talked enough for both of them. Matt understood. Whatever his feelings, this was Charley's first child and she had every right to be excited. Tomorrow, Charley's parents were having a barbecue at their house to announce their daughter's state of togetherness with him. *And* their forthcoming baby. He sighed. Even the dates the scanning technician had given them were right on target. And he had to finally accept that this was *his* life. The one he'd created, whether he wanted it or not. It was how it was.

As Charley talked about tomorrow, how excited she was about telling all their friends, their *mutual* friends, Matt surrendered. He looked across the table at Charley. There was no doubt she was the most beautiful woman in the restaurant. A "catch." Surely, as his mother had suggested, he would grow to love her, grow to love their life together? And grow to love the baby they'd created.

Grania was gone . . .

Matt signaled for the waiter and whispered in his ear.

Five minutes later, a bottle of champagne appeared on the table. Charley raised an eyebrow. "What's this about?"

"I thought we should celebrate."

"Really?"

"Yeah."

"You mean, the baby?"

"That, and . . ." The waiter poured champagne into two glasses. Matt lifted his. "Us."

"You think so?"

"I do. And before tomorrow, I want to ask you, whether you, Charley, will do me the honor of marrying me?"

"Really, *really*?" Charley repeated. "Is this a proposal?"

"It is."

"You sure?" She furrowed her eyebrows.

"I'm sure, honey. So what do you say? Shall we give this baby my surname? Make it legal? Announce our forthcoming marriage at the barbecue tomorrow?"

"Oh, Matty . . . you don't know how I've . . ." Charley shook her head as her eyes filled with tears. "Hey, ignore me. It's the hormones. I just wanna make sure you're doing this for the right reasons. That it's about 'us,' not the baby. Because if it isn't, you know it won't work."

"I guess . . ." Matt scratched his head, "We're destined to be together."

"That's what I've always thought, but been too afraid to say," she answered quietly.

"So?" Matt lifted his glass. "Will you say yes?"

"Oh, Matty, of course I will. Yes!"

"Then we'd better go out shopping now and choose an engagement ring that you can produce tomorrow."

Matt arrived back at the loft with Charley three hours later. He was wrecked. He'd taken her to Cartier, Tiffany and then back to Cartier again as she'd tried on every ring in the goddamned shop. It seemed to him the only difference between what she'd originally liked and the one she'd finally chosen was the increased size of the exorbitant price.

The end result had cost him almost six months' salary—he'd charged it to a credit card—and which she seemed to be delighted with.

You will grow to love her . . .

As Matt put his head on the pillow that night, his mother's words were the only comfort he could find.

The setting of the barbecue to celebrate their good news, the atmosphere and the people were what Matt had always known. He drank far more than he should have—they were staying the night at his folks anyway—and when he announced their engagement and forthcoming marriage, his eyes filled with tears. There wasn't a person watching, given his obvious emotion, who would have doubted how much Matt loved the woman he was to marry. Charley looked radiant in a new dress from Chanel, bought for the occasion. Matt's back was sore from the slapping it had received. Later, when the guests had drifted off and it was the two sets of parents and their children, Charley's father spoke a few words.

"I sure can't express the joy I feel at this moment. And I know your parents, Matt—our dear friends, Bob and Elaine—would join me in that. And we have decided, the four of us, that we want to give you kids a wedding present. There's a house not far from here in Oakwood Lane that would be real perfect for you; big space inside and a great garden for the kid to play in . . . Matt, your pop and I are gonna talk to the real estate agent tomorrow. And we're gonna buy it for you."

"Oh my, Matty!" Charley turned to Matt in delight and grasped his hand. "Isn't that awesome? Just think, we'll have both sets of grandparents on the doorstep to babysit!"

Everyone laughed, except Matt, who poured himself some more champagne.

Later that night, when they'd driven the ten minutes to his parents' house, Matt's mother found him outside on the terrace alone.

"You happy, sweetheart?"

"Yes, Mom," Matt said, hearing a morose timbre to his voice. He checked himself. "'Course I am, why wouldn't I be?"

"No reason." She placed a hand on Matt's shoulder. "I just want my boy to be happy."

Elaine walked on across the terrace. She turned back and looked at Matt. Everything about his body language spoke the opposite of his words. Elaine sighed. She guessed it was simply the way life was. Later, she lay sleepless in bed next to her husband and pondered the past thirty-nine years of a life that, on the outside, was as perfect as it could be. Yet, inside, her heart sang a different song, because her marriage was a sham of conformity.

And her son was right on target to suffer the same.

The summer passed gently in Dunworley Bay; days when it was warm enough for Grania to take Aurora to the beach and swim in the sea, and others of light rain that misted rather than soaked its recipients. Aurora seemed settled and content, spending time out on the farm with John and Shane, going to Cork city to shop for new clothes with Kathleen, and enjoying explorative trips with Grania to beauty spots along the coast. When she wasn't with Aurora, Grania was locked away in her studio perfecting the six studies of her subject in different, graceful positions.

One day in August, Grania stretched and stood up from her workbench. There was no more she could do to them now without harming them. They were finished. Grania experienced a short burst of exhilaration as she wrapped each one carefully, ready to take to Cork to have them dipped in bronze. Once she had done that, she sat at her workbench feeling empty and desolate. The project had allowed her a focus with which to avoid the odd numbness she currently felt. It was as if she couldn't quite connect with the rest of the world, as though she were looking on from behind a veil, her usual passionate emotions muted. Just now, Grania felt like a black-and-white facsimile of her former colorful self.

Of course, the fact Aurora would soon become her daughter—Grania had already been interviewed by the Irish authorities with Aurora—was a wonderful and positive addition to her life. She tried to focus on that, rather than other, more difficult aspects of it. For, however much she loved her parents, she did not wish to remain under their roof forever. Dunworley House was in the full throes of renovation, but even when it was finished, Grania was not sure she would be comfortable living in it. Besides, Aurora was blissfully happy on the farm and wouldn't take kindly to any suggestion of moving. And while she was still adjusting to the loss of her father it would probably be detrimental too.

So, for now, it looked as if she was stuck where she was.

In September, Hans flew back to Ireland and the three of them went to the family court in Cork city to complete the formal adoption process.

"Well, Aurora," said Hans afterward over lunch, "You officially have a new mother. How does that feel?"

"Wonderful!" Aurora hugged Grania tightly then added, "*And* a new grandmother and grandfather and," she scratched her nose, "I think Shane is now my uncle. Isn't that right?"

Grania smiled. "Yes, it is."

"Do you think they'll mind if I start calling them Granny and Grandpa . . . and Uncle Shane?" Aurora giggled.

"I don't think they'd mind at all," said Grania.

"And you, Grania?" Aurora was suddenly shy. "Can I call you Mummy?"

Grania was moved. "Darling Aurora, if that's what you'd like to call me, I'd be honored."

"Now I am feeling left out," Hans pouted. "It seems I am the only one who is not officially related to you, Aurora!"

"Don't be silly, Uncle Hans! You're my godfather! And you can always be my honorary uncle."

"Thank you, Aurora." Hans's eyes twinkled at Grania. "I appreciate it."

Hans joined the celebration supper Kathleen had prepared in honor of Aurora's legally becoming part of their family. He stood up after supper was over and said he must be getting off to his hotel in Cork city in preparation to fly back to Switzerland early the next morning. He kissed Aurora good-bye, thanked Kathleen and John, and Grania accompanied him outside to his car.

"It is good to see that child so happy. And she is a lucky girl to be part of such a close-knit, loving home."

"Well, as my mother says, Aurora's brought new life to them too."

"And what of you, Grania?" Hans paused before he climbed into the car. "What about your plans?"

"I have none, really." She shrugged.

"Please, you must remember Alexander's wish that Aurora's presence in your life does not inhibit your future," Hans reminded her. "I have seen for myself how happy Aurora is living here. If you ever wished to make a different life for yourself, I doubt it would hurt her."

"Thank you, Hans, but I have no 'different' life any more. This *is* my life."

"Then you must find yourself one. Perhaps take a trip back to New York sometime soon? Grania"—Hans put a hand on her shoulder—"You are too young and talented to bury yourself here. And do not use Aurora as an excuse to give up. It is down to all of us to make our own destinies."

"I know, Hans," Grania agreed.

"Forgive me, I am lecturing you. But I think you are suffering. And that the past few months have been harder on you than you think. I worry you are now in a rut and you must climb out. And to do that, one must sometimes swallow one's pride, which I understand is particularly difficult for you, Grania." He smiled and kissed her on both cheeks, then climbed into his car. "Take care, and remember I am just a phone call away. Any help I can give you, either personally or professionally, I will."

"Thank you." Grania waved Hans off, sad to see him go. The two of them had grown close over the past few months and Grania respected his opinion. He was a wise man, and seemed to have an unerring knack of pinpointing and voicing Grania's innermost thoughts and fears.

Perhaps she *should* go back to New York . . .

Grania yawned. As Scarlett O'Hara had famously said, she'd think about that tomorrow. It had been a long day.

• • •

As the cold winds of the Atlantic began to blow once more across the West Cork coastline and fires were lit again in the hearths of its residents' homes, Grania started a new series of sculptures. This time, she used Aurora's grandmother, Anna, as her study, taking the painting of *The Dying Swan* that hung in the dining room at Dunworley House and giving it physical form. She remembered how it had been her original "swan" sculpture that had allowed her path to cross with Matt's. There was a sad irony in the title of her current work-in-progress. But, if nothing else, she had found out of adversity her particular metier. The elegance and grace of dancers inspired her and suited her particular abilities as a sculptor.

Aurora's ninth birthday fell at the end of November, and when Grania heard that the English National Ballet was coming to perform in Dublin, she secretly booked tickets. As she'd known Aurora would be, the little girl was beside herself with excitement.

"Grania! This is the best present I've ever had! And it's *Sleeping Beauty*—*my* ballet!"

Grania had booked the two of them into the Jurys Inn Hotel in Dublin for the night, thinking they could enjoy some shopping while they were in the city. Observing Aurora's enraptured face as she watched the ballet was more pleasurable than the ballet itself.

"Oh, Grania," Aurora said dreamily as they left the theater, "I've decided now: even though I love the animals on the farm, I think I need to be a ballerina. One day, I want to dance the part of Princess Aurora."

"I'm sure you will, sweetheart."

Back in their hotel room, Grania kissed Aurora good night and climbed into the twin bed next to her. As she switched off the light, a voice came out of the darkness.

"Grania?"

"Yes?"

"I know Lily always said she hated ballet, but if she did, why did she call me after the famous princess in one?"

"That's a very good question, Aurora. Perhaps she didn't hate it, really."

"No . . ."

There was silence for a while. And then, "Grania?"

"Yes, Aurora?"

"Are you happy?"

"Yes. Why do you ask?"

"Because . . . sometimes, I see you looking very sad."

"Do you?" Grania was shocked. "Of course I'm happy, sweetheart. I have you, and my work, and my family."

There was another pause. "Yes, I know. But you don't have a husband."

"No, I don't."

"Well, you should. I don't think Daddy would be very happy if he thought you were by yourself. And lonely," Aurora admonished.

"That's kind of you to say so, sweetheart. But I'm fine, really."

"Grania?"

"Yes, Aurora?" Grania sighed, weary now.

"Did you love anyone before Daddy?"

"Yes, I did."

"And what happened?"

"Well, it's a long story, and the truth is . . . I don't really know."

"Oh. Well, shouldn't you find out?"

"Aurora, you really should be going to sleep now." Grania wished to end the conversation. It was far too uncomfortable. "It's late."

"Sorry. Just two more questions. Where did he live?"

"In New York."

"And what was his name?"

"Matt, his name is Matt."

"Oh."

"Good night, Aurora."

"Good night, Mummy."

40

Charley was now six months into her pregnancy. She was blooming with health, her wardrobe of designer maternity clothes equally expansive. The purchase of the house, three leafy streets away from both his own and Charley's parents, had been completed. Charley was hard at work giving the house a complete overhaul, even though Matt thought it was just fine as it was. She had already taken maternity leave, and spent most of her time at her parents' house so she could oversee the renovations. Matt was grateful; it gave him some breathing space and some time to concentrate on work. They'd had heated discussions on Matt's refusal to join his father in his investment business, but he felt he must at least salvage something of who he had been—the identity he had worked so hard to create seemed to be dwindling by the day.

He was losing himself . . .

He'd also begun to sift through his belongings in preparation for the move to the new house. Grania's stuff was still here in the loft. Matt had no idea what he was meant to do with it. Perhaps he should simply box it up, put it into storage and write to Grania at her parents' address to let her know where it was. If she hadn't wanted it by now, it was doubtful she ever would. Besides, Matt thought coldly, he was sure her new husband had helped her replace everything she'd needed.

He only wished the love and the pain of missing her could turn into anger. There was the odd moment when this happened—when he got real mad at her—but it didn't last long.

Matt decided to go out and get himself some breakfast. He sat in a small café, drinking a latte and chewing on a bagel.

"Hi there, Matt, how's it hanging?" Matt looked up and saw Roger, Grania's friend, standing by him.

"It's good, good." He nodded, with as much enthusiasm as he could muster. "You're a local now, Roger?"

"Yup, love the neighborhood. How's your girl?" Roger asked.

"You mean Charley?"

"Yeah, Charley."

"She's good. We're"—Matt blushed—"getting married."

"You are? Congratulations."

"After Charley's had the baby." Matt thought he might as well go for broke. There was no point in lying.

"That's great news!" Roger smiled. "To be honest, I knew you guys had been trying. After I saw Charley in your loft that night, I remembered where it was I'd seen her before. I work in the fertility clinic and she came in. You can tell her from me, she's a lucky lady. Despite the progress of medical science, it's only a small percentage who manage to conceive, even with the best treatment."

Matt shook his head in confusion. "You saw Charley at the fertility clinic?"

"Yeah, it was definitely her, I helped her get into her gown. But I understand that a lot of couples don't want it broadcast. Anyway, good luck with it all in the future."

"Thanks."

"See you around, Matt."

"Yup, see you." Roger turned to walk out of the café.

"Roger? Can you remember when this would have been?"

Roger scratched his head. "Mid-May, I guess."

"You sure?"

"Yeah, pretty sure, but . . . is there a problem?" Roger looked confused.

"No, I—hey, it doesn't matter."

Matt walked back home to the loft. Surely Roger must have made a mistake? Why would Charley have been in the fertility clinic in mid-May? Unless . . .

His cell phone rang and Matt answered it automatically.

"Hey, Matt, Mom here. How's the daddy to be?"

"Um . . ."

"You OK, son?"

"You know what, Mom? Right now, I don't know. I just heard something . . ."

"What is it, what's happened, Matt?"

"Jesus, Mom, I . . . don't think I can tell you."

"Matty, you know you can tell me anything."

"OK, Mom, but I wanna tell you I have no proof it's true. I just met an intern guy I know who told me Charley went for treatment in the fertility clinic he was working in. He recognized her when he came to the loft to drop something off. He says it was around May—the time when . . . shit, Mom! He's probably made a mistake, I guess, but . . . I feel real confused. He was pretty certain it was her. Do you think—?"

It was some time before Elaine answered. Finally she sighed, and said, "No, I don't 'think.' Listen, Matt, there's something I've known but I haven't told you. You wanna come here?"

"I'm on my way."

"Charley had a problem when she was a teenager and started her—woman thing." A faint color came to Elaine's cheeks at the mention of it. "She was in a lot of pain every month—to the point where she missed a lot of high school. In the end, her mom took her to see a specialist uptown. He diagnosed her with something called endometriosis—which means you have cysts on your ovaries. Charley was told then she would probably never conceive naturally, if at all. I only know this because her mom came to see me. She was distraught that her daughter might not be able to have kids. They didn't tell anyone else—it's not the kind of thing you broadcast round the country club, especially if you're hoping your daughter will make a good marriage. Charley was put on the pill, which helped control the pain. And I've never heard her mom mention it since."

Matt whistled. "I see."

"Please understand, honey, that I'm breaking a confidence to tell you this, and perhaps losing a friendship too. But, maybe, if you decide to talk to Charley about it, you keep my name out of it. Will you, Matt?" Elaine begged. "Because the chances are that your intern friend is telling the truth. And even though it will make my life difficult if Charley's mom finds out I told you, I won't have my boy deceived over something as important as this."

A rare anger had appeared in Elaine's eyes. Matt patted her hand. "Don't worry, Mom, I won't say a word. And I need to think about what I should do. If Charley did . . . if she has—Christ, Mom! I just don't get it, I really don't. I need some time to think before she comes home." Matt stood up and hugged his mother. "I really appreciate your telling me. I'll call you in the next couple of days."

Matt drove back to the city, his brain a whirling mass of confusion. He didn't know what to think, what to feel . . . At best, it had been an unfortunate coincidence that Charley had decided to have a baby and he had gotten drunk that night. Hell! He couldn't even remember if he *had* screwed her, after all . . . Had she prepared her body in some way to maximize her chances? Had she engineered the whole thing and he had been simply an innocent victim of Charley's desire for a child . . . ?

The options were endless, and endlessly confusing. Matt knew, as he opened the door to the loft, that these were questions which could be answered by only one person. And even then, whether he'd get the truth or not, he really didn't know.

Charley arrived home later that night, buzzing with excitement that she and the interior designer she'd chosen had bonded and had some great ideas for the new house.

Matt could hardly speak to her. He needed to get his thoughts in some kind of order before he confronted her. Anger, he knew, was not the best way to approach this. Charley would become defensive and less likely to be honest with him. And even though there was damning evidence against her, she was innocent until proven guilty.

Matt managed to get through the evening, nodding and smiling at the appropriate moments. They climbed into bed and Charley reached over to kiss him.

"Night, honey. I'm so excited about our future." She turned to switch off the light.

It was then that Matt cracked. He switched the light back on.

"Charley, we gotta talk."

"Hey, OK, hon." She sat up in bed and took his hand. "You feeling nervous about being a daddy? Don't worry, Matty, the doc said it's perfectly normal to feel like that. He said—"

"Charley, I need to ask you something. And I need you to tell me the truth." Matt looked at her intently. "Whatever the consequences, I need you to do that for me, OK?"

"Sure, honey, I'd never lie to you."

"OK . . ." Matt took a deep breath. "Did you go to a fertility clinic in May to have treatment to help you conceive a baby?"

Matt did not let his gaze move from her face. He knew that in those first few seconds, before the brain had moved into gear to concoct a story, the truth would appear in her eyes.

"I—Christ, honey!" She gave a nervous smile.

And in that moment, Matt knew she'd deceived him.

"Jesus, Charley! I'm not sure of how, or why, but you did go for treatment, didn't you? You need to be honest with me, because I have to know what the story is." Matt was still holding her stare. Charley wavered uncertainly for a few seconds before she burst into tears.

"Oh, Matty . . . how did you find out?"

"I saw that guy Roger in a coffee shop yesterday. He congratulated us on a successful conclusion to our project. But 'how' is irrelevant, I—"

"OK! Yes, I did go for treatment, but I wasn't trying to dupe you or trap you. I was prepared from the start to have this baby alone. Remember?" she urged desperately. "When we talked about it? I told you then I was going to have the baby whatever you decided. It was a miracle, Matty, after all those years of thinking I'd never have a child of my own. To find myself pregnant . . . Oh, Matty, can you forgive me? Please, I love you!"

"Look at me, Charley." Matt took her hands in his. "Was it a coincidence, you getting pregnant when we spent the night together? Or preempted?"

"Oh, I know what I did was wrong, but—"

"I need to ask you now—" he knew he wasn't giving her a chance to explain, but there was one vital question he needed the answer to—"is that baby in there mine?"Again he held her eyes but she looked away. "Did we?" he urged. "I mean, that night . . . ? Goddammit, Charley! I need a straight answer. *Am* I the father of your baby?"

Charley's crying halted. She sat in silence, staring at the wall. Matt got out of bed and paced around the room. "I have to know *now,* I really do." He turned back to look at her. "And I have to trust that you will give me the truth."

All the energy seemed to drain away from Charley. She shook her head slowly. "No, Matt, you're not the father."

"Shit!" It was all he could do in that moment to stop himself hitting her. He took some deep breaths to calm himself. "So if I'm not, who is?"

"I don't know his name." She shrugged. "But it's not what you think, Matty."

"Hell! How can it not be what I *think,* Charley? You've screwed some other guy and you were going to pass this baby off as mine?"

"*No!* That's not how it was," Charley keened in pain. "The reason I don't know the guy's name is because the sperm that was put inside me only had a DNA profile. And nothing more."

"What?" Matt shook his head. "Call me naive, but goddammit! I haven't a clue what you're talking about."

"OK." Charley nodded, visibly trying to collect herself. "The baby's father is a twenty-eight-year-old Ph.D. student living in California. Whose coloring is dark, with brown eyes, and he measures five foot nine inches in height. He's never had a serious illness and has a higher than average IQ. That's his genetic profile, and that's all I know."

"So." Matt sat down on the bed, understanding beginning to dawn. "You're telling me that you went to a sperm bank and chose an anonymous DNA profile to be the father of your child? And you were inseminated with that sperm?"

"Yup."

"Right."

They both sat in silence for a while, Matt struggling to comprehend what she had told him. "So where the hell did I come in? Was I part of the plan from the beginning?"

"Matty." Charley was drained of tears now, her face pale. "I need you to know that I'd decided to do this way back. Months ago, before I moved in here with you."

"So, let's get this straight: I was just a convenient guy in situ, a schmuck who you could pass off as the daddy?" Matt interrupted bitterly.

"No! I loved you, Matty, and I still do!" Charley wrung her hands.

"And that night, a day after I'd had the treatment—yeah, you could say it was coincidence. You were drunk and affectionate, and you said some real nice things to me. And I thought—"

"Charley, did we actually make love that night, because I sure as hell can't remember doing so. And no matter how drunk I've been, that's never happened to me before."

"No. At least, not in a way that could ever produce a child," Charley confessed. "We kissed and played around some, but there was no way you were in a fit state to—"

"Screw you?"

"Yeah, 'screw' me," she said bitterly.

"Jesus! So why the hell did you say I did? And why that guilt trip . . . why the lies? Godammit, Charley! That was so cruel."

"Enough, Matt!" Charley's eyes blazed with sudden anger. "I'll take the rap up to a point, but what I told you happened that night wasn't a complete lie. You were affectionate, friendly . . . you kissed me and touched me . . . told me I was beautiful, that you loved me—" She choked suddenly, paused, then began again. "Even if you couldn't . . . get it up, I was at least expecting a call or a text from you afterward. I thought that perhaps, just maybe, you did care for me in the way I cared for you. And I heard . . . nothing. I felt like some cheap hooker you'd used for the night."

"You're right." Matt was cowed. "I behaved like a jerk, Charley. And I apologize. But does that honestly give you an excuse to lie to me about"—Matt pointed a finger at her stomach—"*that*?"

"I swear to you, I didn't know I was pregnant, that the IVF process had actually worked, until just before you came back from your lecture tour and then we went out to dinner. Maybe it was the hormones that night, maybe it was the shock, but perhaps it was the combination of knowing I was going to be a mom, at the same time as realizing I'd been no more to you that night than any female you could pick up off the street. That you've never loved me like I've loved you. And never would. I was so hurt, Matt, at the way you'd treated me. And . . . I suppose I wanted to punish you."

Matt, calmer now he knew the facts, listened silently.

"And then, as I realized you would always love Grania, not me, I started making decisions for myself. I was going to have the baby anyway, as I told you when we met up a week later. I'd resigned myself to going it alone, like I'd done originally. And then you said, why didn't we give it a go? Not just with the baby, but with you and me. Gee, Matt, I was beside myself with happiness. It was all my dreams come true. Suddenly, it all seemed so right. All those years of loving you . . ." Charley sighed. "And then you asked me to marry you and I really started to believe that we could make it work." She moved toward him suddenly, enveloping him tightly in her arms. "And we still can, can't we, Matty? Please, I know I lied to you but—"

Matt moved out of Charley's grasp. "I need to get outta here, get some fresh air."

"Please, Matty . . ." She watched him as he threw on some clothes. "You won't leave me now, will you? We've told everyone, the house is bought, and the baby . . ."

Matt slammed the door behind him and took the stairs to the ground floor. Outside, he jogged along the sidewalk, pounding the streets until he wound up at Battery Park. He leaned against the railing, looking at the lights twinkling on the Hudson. A throng of humans—those who enjoyed the cover of darkness—shadowy figures of drunks, lovers and restless teenage boys milled around him. He slowed his breathing and tried to process the series of events that had brought him to this point.

It wasn't just what Charley had *done,* but what her motives were for doing so. Had she set out to trap him from the beginning? *Was* her decision to try IVF *really* little to do with him? She'd been under his roof while going through the process . . . she'd admitted she loved him . . . could he really believe the timing was *coincidence*?

Even if it was, it did not vindicate Charley from having told him categorically that the baby was his. She had blatantly lied. Not only that, but she'd been prepared to accuse him of an act he hadn't even *committed.*

The psychologist in Matt understood that anyone in the wrong would do what they could to finesse their actions. There was always a perfectly valid excuse, a reason the perpetrator themselves *believed,* which justified their behavior. But, whichever way he looked at what Charley had done to him, there were few excuses. What made it worse was that she had been prepared to live that lie for the rest of their lives together. He might never have known that the child he would surely have loved as his own wasn't his.

Matt felt physically sick at the thought.

He walked along the river for a while, still trying to take in the facts.

He realized he also had to accept his part in it; his hurt at hearing Grania was married, which had led to his knee-jerk reaction that night at the restaurant. His sudden willingness to stand by Charley had exacerbated the situation and led, in part, to where they were right now.

She *had* told him she was prepared to go it alone with the baby that night. It had been *he* who had refuted it and suggested they try to make it work. And he realized now that he'd had no idea how Charley had always felt about him. When he'd met Grania, he'd been blinded by his feelings for her, sparing little thought for Charley when he told her their relationship was over.

Matt shuddered at the mess the two of them had created. But were the whys and wherefores relevant anyway? Surely what he needed to do now was to decide where they went from here?

He considered the options.

It was possible to continue as they were—as Charley said, he knew the truth now. He didn't love her—he never had—and in that sense, he was already *living* the lie. What had changed, however, was the fact that the baby inside her was not his.

Matt sighed as he remembered how protective he'd felt when Grania was in the early stages of pregnancy; every time he'd thought of their baby and its impending arrival, his stomach had turned over in anticipation. He'd wanted to protect Grania with every fiber of his body while she was at her most vulnerable. There had been nothing vaguely reminiscent of those feelings for either Charley or the growing baby inside her. Just resignation. Could he learn to love the baby he would bring up as his own? Matt bit his lip. Or would he look on it with resentment? He lectured all too regularly on the sins of the fathers impacting on the child. He knew the effect it could have and he sure as hell didn't want to fall into the same trap.

Eventually, as a lazy sun was beginning to rise over the New Jersey skyline, Matt walked slowly back home. He was still no further on and had little idea of what he would say to Charley. But at least he was calmer.

The loft was deserted. Propped up on his desk was an envelope addressed to him.

Matt,

I've left. I'm so sorry I deceived you, but you played your part in this mess too. I'm making it easy for both of us, and the baby. We all deserve more.

See you around,
Charley

Matt sighed in relief. Charley had taken the decision for him. And for that, at least, he was grateful.

41

Winter rolled on. In front of Grania's studio window, scudding clouds painted the raw palette of Dunworley Bay different hues of blue and gray. Her collection of sculptures grew as she worked relentlessly, sometimes until late in the evening.

"Will you not be doing something with these sculptures, Grania?" said Kathleen one afternoon when she brought Aurora up to the studio to see her. "I'm no expert in art, pet, but even I'd be saying these are something special." Kathleen turned to her daughter, awe and pride in her eyes. "And the best work you've ever done."

"They're beautiful, Mummy." Aurora's fingers traced the lines of her figurines. "But Granny's right. It's no good them sitting here with only us to look at them. You should put them into a gallery where people can buy them. I want people to see me!" she giggled.

Grania, immersed in a new sculpture, nodded distractedly. "Yes, maybe I will."

"Are you coming down home for some tea now, Grania?" asked Kathleen.

"In a while, Mam, I just want to finish this arm."

"Well now, don't you go being too long," Kathleen clucked. "We're missing the shape of you at our table, aren't we so, Aurora?"

"Yes, we are," Aurora agreed. "You look pale, Mummy. Doesn't she, Granny?"

"That she does."

"I've said I'll be down in a bit," Grania chuckled. "Jaysus! It's bad enough having a mother nagging at me, but now I've got a daughter as well."

"We'll be seeing you." Kathleen nodded and ushered Aurora out of the studio.

There was a chill wind blowing up as Aurora and Kathleen walked down the cliff path.

"Granny?"

"Yes, Aurora?"

"I'm worried about Mummy."

"So am I, pet."

"What do you think is wrong with her?"

"Well, now." Kathleen had learned it was pointless patronizing Aurora with platitudes. "If you want me to be honest, I'd be saying she's missing a man. "It isn't healthy for a woman of Grania's age to be alone."

"The man she loved before she met Daddy—Matt, Mummy said he's called—do you know what happened? Why Mummy left him behind in New York and came to Ireland?"

"Ah now, Aurora, if I did, I'd be a happier woman. But when my daughter's got one on her, nothing will shift her. And she won't say a word."

"Was he a nice man?"

"He was a true gentleman," Kathleen said softly. "And he loved Grania like his two eyes."

"Do you think he still does?"

"Well, I'd say from the amount he called our house when she ran away from New York, that he did, yes. As for now . . ." Kathleen sighed, "Who knows? 'Tis a pity Grania refused to talk to him at the time about whatever it was that had happened. Many's the thing that can be sorted over a brew and a good chat."

"But Mummy's very proud, isn't she?"

"She is that, pet. Now, let's be getting a move on." Kathleen shivered as the wind grew stronger. "This isn't a night to be outside."

Hans called Grania a few days later to check in and find out how the renovation work was progressing at Dunworley House.

"I also wondered whether you would be able to meet me in London next week. There is an art dealer friend of mine who has a gallery on Cork Street. I have told him about you and the new work you are doing and he is eager to meet you. Besides," added Hans, "it might do you good to have a few days away. At the same time, I can show you the property in London that is part of Aurora's trust from her mother."

"That's kind of you, Hans, but—"

"But what, Grania? You are not going to tell me you cannot fit it into your busy schedule, are you?"

"Are you bullying me, Hans?" Grania allowed herself a wry smile.

"Perhaps a little. But, as any good solicitor should, I am simply following the instructions in my client's will. I shall book you a flight to London for next Wednesday, along with a hotel, and e-mail you the details."

"If you say so, Hans," Grania sighed, surrendering.

"I do. Good-bye, Grania, I will be in touch."

A few days later, Grania went on to the house computer to retrieve her e-mails and the details of the flight to London that Hans had booked for her.

Aurora came up behind her and put her arms around Grania's shoulders.

"Where are you going, Mummy?"

"To London, to see Hans."

"That'll be nice for you, it's about time you had a break." Aurora was studying the computer screen as Grania typed in the number of her passport to check in online.

"Can I do it for you?"

"Do you know how?"

"Of course I do. I used to help Daddy all the time."

Grania moved from the seat and let her sit down. Aurora giggled at the photo in Grania's passport as she typed in the details proficiently. "You look so funny!"

"Excuse me"—Grania smiled—"I don't think yours is much better."

"Do you have my passport?"

"Yes, it's here in the file, with mine."

"There, it's finished. Shall I press 'print'?" asked Aurora.

"Yes, please." Grania replaced her passport in the wallet along with Aurora's and stowed it back in the desk. "Time for bed, young lady."

Reluctantly, Aurora climbed the stairs, brushed her teeth and got into bed. "I didn't mean it about your passport photo," Aurora said. "I think you're very beautiful, Mummy."

"Thank you, sweetheart. I think you're beautiful too."

"But I'm worried if you don't have a boyfriend soon, you might get too old and men won't like you anymore. Ouch!" Aurora giggled as Grania tickled her.

"Charmed, I'm sure. The problem is, Aurora, that there's nobody I want."

"What about Matt? The man you told me about who lives in America? You loved him, didn't you?"

"Yes, I did."

"I think you still love him."

"Maybe I do," sighed Grania. "But it's no good crying over spilled milk, is it?" She kissed Aurora. "Night-night, darling, sweet dreams."

"Night-night, Mummy."

On Wednesday morning, Grania drove herself to Cork airport and flew to London. Hans met her at Arrivals and they took a taxi to Claridge's.

"My goodness me," exclaimed Grania as she walked into the beautiful suite Hans had booked for her, "this must have cost a fortune! You're spoiling me."

"You deserved a treat, and besides, you are a rich woman with a very wealthy daughter, whose joint estate earns me my fees. Now, I will leave you to do whatever women must before dinner, and see you downstairs in the bar at eight o'clock. Robert, the gallery owner, is joining us at a quarter past."

Grania luxuriated in the bath, wrapped herself in the soft terry robe and had a glass of complimentary champagne in the beautifully appointed sitting room. And decided, despite her antipathy to overt luxury, that this was all rather pleasant. Putting on the short, black cocktail dress she'd found in a boutique in Cork city last week—what she'd brought with her from New York had not included anything smart—she added some mascara and a smudge of lipstick. Then she picked up the sculpture of Aurora she'd brought with her to show the gallery owner, and went downstairs to join Hans in the bar.

The evening passed pleasantly. Robert Sampson, the gallery owner, was good company and excited about Grania's work. She'd also brought photographs of the rest of the series of sculptures she'd recently completed.

"I think, Grania," Robert said over coffee and Armagnac, "that if you could complete another six sculptures in the next few months, we'd have enough for an exhibition. You're unknown at present in London, and I'd like to give you a big initial push. We'd send out invitations to the great, good and rich collectors I deal with on my database, and launch you as the Next Big Thing. What is exciting is that you've found your metier. The fluidity shown in your sculpture is exquisite. And rare," he added.

"You really think my work warrants that?" Grania was flattered by his enthusiasm.

"Yes, I do. Obviously, I'd like to take a trip over to Cork and see the series for myself, but based on what I've seen so far, I'd be very happy to take you on."

"And it probably helps that Grania is young and relatively photogenic too." Hans winked at Grania.

"Of course," agreed Robert, "as long as you're not averse to doing some publicity."

"If it helps, of course not," agreed Grania.

"Excellent." Robert rose and kissed Grania on both cheeks. "It's been a pleasure to meet you, Grania. Have a think over what I've said and, if you're interested, e-mail me and I'll fly to Cork so we can discuss things further."

"Thank you, Robert."

When Robert had left, Hans said, "So, a successful evening?"

"Yes, thank you for introducing me to him," said Grania, wondering why she wasn't feeling quite as thrilled as she should. Robert Sampson was a serious mover and shaker in the art world. Gaining his approval for her new work was an enormous compliment.

Hans noticed immediately. "Is there a problem?"

"No, I . . . well, I suppose that, mentally, I hadn't quite closed the door on New York and my career there."

"Well"—Hans patted her hand as they headed for the elevator—"perhaps it is time to move on."

"Yes."

"Now, tomorrow, I suggest a little light shopping for you in the morning. Bond Street, which is awash with boutiques, is a stone's throw away. Then we can meet for lunch, over which I need to run through some boring paperwork with you. And tomorrow afternoon I will take you to see Aurora's London house. Good night, Grania." Hans kissed her affectionately on the cheek.

"Good night, Hans, and thank you again."

Grania was mindlessly looking through the racks of exquisite clothes in Chanel the following morning, pondering the fact that anything she wished to buy could be hers, when her cell phone rang.

"Hello, Mam," she said distractedly, "everything all right?"

"No, Grania, it isn't."

Grania could hear the panic in her mother's voice. "What's happened?"

"It's Aurora. She's disappeared again."

"Oh no, Mam!" Grania's heart sank. She checked her watch. It was half past eleven. "How long has she been gone?"

"We're not sure. You know she said she was staying over at Emily's house last night?"

"Of course I do! I dropped her off yesterday morning at school with her overnight bag, remember?"

"Well now, she wasn't staying over. The school rang me about twenty minutes ago to ask if she was ill, as she hadn't arrived this morning. I called Emily's mammy straight away, and she said there'd been no plan for Aurora to sleep over last night."

"Oh God, Mam! So when was the last time anyone saw her?"

"Emily said Aurora left the school yesterday at home time, saying she was walking back up to the farm by herself, because you were in London."

"And no one's seen her since?"

"No. She's been missing all night. Oh, Grania"—there was a catch in Kathleen's voice—"Where is she after going this time?"

"Listen, Mam," Grania left Chanel and began walking swiftly along the street, "I can't hear for the traffic. I'm going back to the hotel and

I'll call you in ten minutes when I've had a think. It's me that's at fault; I shouldn't have left her. Look what happened last time. I'll speak to you in a bit."

Two hours later, Grania was pacing around her suite, Hans trying and failing to keep her calm. John, Shane and Kathleen had scoured the surrounding areas and all the places Grania had suggested Aurora might be, but had come up with a blank.

"Dad's calling the guards," Grania said, her heart beating like an unsteady tom-tom. "Oh God, Hans, why has she gone? I thought she was so happy at the farm with Mam and Dad. I shouldn't have left her . . . I shouldn't have left her . . ."

Grania collapsed onto the sofa and Hans put his arms around her. "Please, my dear, you must not blame yourself."

"I do, because I've obviously underestimated the effect Alexander's death has had on Aurora."

"Well, I for one do not understand it," sighed Hans. "She seemed so settled."

"The problem is, Hans, that Aurora is very difficult to read. She's so self-contained, seems so grown up in many ways . . . but maybe a lot of her pain has been hidden. What if . . . what if she thought I'd left her, and she took it in her head to join her parents? I said I'd never leave her, Hans, I promised her . . . I . . ." Grania cried on his shoulder.

"Grania, please, you must try and keep calm. I have never seen a less suicidal child than Aurora. Besides, she was the one who encouraged you to come to London, was she not?" added Hans.

"Yes," agreed Grania, blowing her nose, "she did."

"And I have a strong feeling that this is nothing to do with Aurora's unstable state of mind," he added.

"Well, if it's not that, what could have happened to her?" Grania put a hand suddenly to her mouth. "Oh my God, Hans! What if she's been kidnapped?"

"I am afraid to say that the thought has crossed my mind. As you know, Aurora is an exceptionally wealthy young lady. If there has been no sign of her in the next hour, I will speak to my contact at Interpol and have them investigate, just in case."

"And I think I should be getting myself on the flight back home immediately."

"Of course."

"If anything has happened to that child, Hans, I will never be able to forgive myself." Grania wrung her hands. "Her cell phone rang and she answered it immediately. "Any news, Mam?"

"Yes. Thank the heavens! Aurora's safe."

"Oh, Mam, thank God . . . thank God! Where was she found?"

"Ah, well now, that's the interesting part. She's in New York."

"New York?! But how . . . why . . . *where*?"

"She's with Matt."

It took a few seconds for her mother's words to sink in. "She's with *Matt*? *My* Matt?" Grania repeated.

"Yes, Grania, your Matt. He rang here about ten minutes ago. He said he'd had a call from the airline to ask him why he wasn't at the airport to collect a child by the name of Aurora Devonshire, as arranged."

"What?" Grania exclaimed. "How on earth did she—?"

"Grania, don't be asking me any more questions. I don't know the answers. Matt's calling me back in a bit, but I wanted to tell you immediately that Aurora was safe. Whatever the child has taken into her head to do, we'll find out in good time."

"Yes, Mam, you're right." Grania let out a long sigh of relief and confusion. "At least she's safe."

42

Matt had indeed had a call from Aer Lingus at ten o'clock that morning. He'd listened to the representative asking him why he hadn't been at JFK as arranged, to meet a girl called Aurora Devonshire, traveling as an unaccompanied child from Dublin, Ireland.

At first, Matt had been at a loss, wondering if someone was playing a practical joke on him. The airline seemed to have his name, his telephone number and address, but who the child was, he had no idea. As he refuted any knowledge of the arrangement, he could hear the representative becoming nervous.

"Are you saying you don't know this child, sir?" she'd asked.

"I . . ." Matt knew the name rang a bell but he could not put it in context.

"Excuse me, sir." He'd heard a muffled voice at the other end of the line, before the representative came back and said, "Miss Devonshire says that a Miss Grania Ryan made all the arrangements with you."

"Did she?" Matt was flummoxed.

"That's what the little girl says, sir. If you are unable to collect Miss Devonshire, then we have a problem."

"No . . . it's OK. I'll be down in forty."

As Matt made the journey to the airport, he still had no concept of what the hell was going on. However, the name Grania at least was familiar, so Matt had to presume that there was a connection, however vague. And at the very least he needed to investigate.

Arriving at JFK, Matt duly went to the appointed meeting place, where he found a small, beautiful child with flame-red ringlets, eating Ben & Jerry's ice cream. She was flanked by an airline representative and an airport security guard.

"Hi, I'm Matt Connelly," he announced uncertainly.

The little girl immediately put down her tub of ice cream and threw herself into his arms. "Uncle Matt! How could you have forgotten I was coming? Grania promised me you'd be here. Really"—She turned to the airline representative and the security guard and sighed—"Uncle Matt is so absentminded. He's a professor of psychology, you know."

The guard and the representative smiled indulgently, won over by the child's charm. She turned back to him, and he saw the glint of warning in her eyes. "Can we go home now to your loft, Uncle Matt? I can't wait to see Grania's sculptures. But"—Aurora yawned—"I'm very tired."

There was that look in her eyes again. It said: "Play along and get me out of here."

"OK . . . Aurora," Matt agreed. "Sorry to put you guys to any trouble. As she says, I guess I'm a little forgetful. Where's your luggage, honey?" he asked her.

"Just this." She indicated a small backpack. "You know I never bring much, Uncle Matt, I like it when you take me shopping." Aurora put her small hand in his and smiled up at him sweetly. "Shall we go?"

"Sure. Bye, guys, and my apologies for being late. Thanks for taking care of her."

"Bye, Aurora." The security guard waved as Matt led Aurora away. "You take good care now."

"I will."

As soon as they were out of sight and earshot, Aurora said, "Sorry about this, Matt. I'll explain everything when we get to your home."

As they arrived at his car, Matt turned to Aurora. "Sorry, honey, we're going no further until you tell me who you are and what you're doing here. I've gotta be certain this isn't some elaborate hoax, in which I end up accused of kidnapping a child. You better start talking real fast."

"OK, I understand, Matt, but it's long story."

"The bare bones will do." Matt folded his arms as he eyed her. "Shoot."

"Well, you see," began Aurora, "it's like this. I met Grania up on the cliffs at my house near Dunworley and then, because Daddy had to go away, he asked Grania to look after me while he did. And then he found out he was dying and asked Grania if she'd marry him, so she'd become my stepmother and be able to adopt me easily. So they did get married, and he did die and so Grania is my new mummy and . . ."

"Whoa, Aurora!" Matt was completely confused by the child's story. "Let me get one thing straight: Grania Ryan has adopted you, right?"

"Yes. I have proof if you want it." Aurora shrugged her backpack off her back, delved into it and produced a photo of herself and Grania. "There." She handed it to Matt, who studied it.

"Thanks. Now, second question: What are you doing here in New York?"

"Well, Matt, do you remember when you called Granny and Grandpa's house to speak to Grania? And I answered the phone?"

That was why her name had rung a bell. "Yeah, I do," agreed Matt.

"And I said that Grania was away with my daddy on their honeymoon. Of course, I didn't know at the time that Daddy was so ill. And that Grania had only married him so she could adopt me and I could live with her family."

Matt nodded, taken aback by Aurora's adult way of expressing herself. "Yup, I'm with you so far."

"Well, Grania looked so sad after Daddy died, and she still does. I didn't like her being lonely. So I asked her if she loved somebody. And she said it was you. And then I realized I'd told you that she'd married my daddy and was on her honeymoon. And that you might have thought she didn't love you anymore. Which, of course, isn't true," Aurora added. "So I thought I'd better come and tell you in person that she isn't married any longer and that she does still love you."

"I see," Matt wanted to believe her but needed more facts. "OK, third question: Does Grania know you're here?"

"Umm . . . no, she doesn't. I knew she wouldn't let me come, so I had to plan it in secret."

"Aurora, does *anyone* know where you are right now?"

"No." Aurora shook her head.

"Christ! They'll all be out of their minds with worry." Matt took his cell phone from his jacket pocket. "I'll call Grania right now. And you can speak to her, so I know you're telling me the truth."

"Grania's in London at the moment," Aurora said, nervous for the first time. "Why don't you call Kathleen? She's always at home."

"OK." Matt did so and heard the huge relief in Kathleen's voice. Then he put Aurora on the line to her.

"Hello, Granny . . . yes, I'm fine. What? Oh, getting here was easy-peasy. I have done it before, you know. Daddy was always putting me on planes as an unaccompanied child. Granny, now I'm here, can I at least go to Matt's loft for a bit before I come home? I'm very tired, you see."

It was agreed that Matt should take Aurora home with him. And that plans for her return to Ireland would be made later, when she'd had some sleep. On the journey back to the city, Aurora looked out of the window at the huge buildings. "I've never been to New York, but Grania has told me all about it."

"Now, honey," Matt said as he drove, "can we please go back to the beginning when you said you met Grania on the cliffs?"

Aurora told the story again, this time with Matt asking questions if he didn't understand something.

"And Grania's so good and pretty, and I felt awful that I might have stopped you two ever getting back together again," Aurora explained as the two of them called the elevator to take them up to the loft. "She's been so kind to me, and I wouldn't want to see her spending the rest of her life lonely. Or growing into an old maid because of something I had said. Do you understand, Matt?"

"Yup." As he put the key in the lock, Matt gazed in wonder at this extraordinary child. "I think I'm getting the picture, sweetheart."

"Oh, Matt." Aurora gazed around the airy sitting room. "This is lovely, and just how I imagined it would be."

"Thanks, honey. I like it. Can I get you anything? A glass of milk, maybe?"

"Yes, please." Aurora sat down as Matt poured her some milk and handed it to her. She drank it, then rested her small elbows on her knees, leaned forward and eyed him. "Now, I have to ask you something very important, Matt. Do you still love Grania? Because if you don't, actually"—she seemed suddenly flustered—"I don't know what I'll do."

"Aurora, I've always loved Grania, right from the very first moment I set eyes on her. You have to remember it was she that ran away to Ireland and left me. Not the other way around." Matt sighed. "Sometimes, adult things can get very complicated."

"But if you love each other, then I don't see what the problem is," said Aurora logically.

"No . . . ain't that the truth," breathed Matt. He'd already given up trying to treat Aurora like a child, so he spoke to her as an adult. "If you could tell that new mom of yours that she needs to explain to me what it was I did wrong all those months ago, and just why she ran off to Ireland, then maybe we could get somewhere."

"I will," Aurora agreed, then yawned. "Oh, Matt, I'm very tired. It's a long journey from Ireland to New York."

"It sure is, honey. Let's get you a lie-down and some sleep."

"OK." Aurora stood up.

"And I still haven't got a clue how you managed to make the journey from Ireland alone."

"When I wake up, I'll tell you," said Aurora as Matt led her into his study/spare bedroom and she lay down.

"OK, sweetheart." Matt pulled the curtains to. "You have a real good rest now and we'll talk later."

"OK," answered Aurora sleepily. "Matt?"

"Yeah?"

"I know why Mummy loves you. You're nice."

"Apparently, Aurora took your credit card details and managed to book and pay for a flight to Dublin, then to New York, on the computer." Hans repeated what Kathleen had just told him over the telephone. "She took a bus to Clonakilty and, from there, a taxi to Cork Airport. She presented herself as an unaccompanied child, which she says she had done many times before with Alexander, then changed planes at Dublin. On arrival in New York, she managed to coerce this Matt into collecting her."

"I see."

Grania, persuaded by Hans, had taken a short lie-down to recover from the morning's tension. She'd lain sleepless, trying to come to terms with where and, more to the point, *who* Aurora was currently with.

"You have got to hand it to her," Hans continued, "she is certainly a resourceful child. The question is why she felt she needed to make the journey?" He eyed Grania, waiting for some answers.

Grania was unforthcoming. "Who knows?" she said.

"Obviously, Aurora thought she had a very good reason. I am presuming Matt was the man you shared your life with in New York?"

"Yes, he was." At this moment, Grania felt she could strangle Aurora with her own bare hands.

"Why did it end?" probed Hans.

"If you'll excuse me, I'd prefer not to go through the grand inquisition," Grania answered defensively. "I just want to think about the best way to get Aurora home. And whether I should fly out to New York immediately to collect her."

"Well, I think Aurora herself will have some thoughts on that. She seems to be in a safe pair of hands. Your mother said Matt was a reliable man. And if *she* says that, I will believe her," Hans smiled, trying to lighten the atmosphere.

"Yes, he is," Grania agreed grudgingly.

"And I am sure that Aurora will want to speak to you, so why don't you call her? Check for yourself she is OK."

"I . . . " That would mean speaking to Matt. I'll wait until she calls me. She might be sleeping."

"All right, Grania, I will leave you alone." Hans knew when he was beaten. "But I am as much in the dark as I ever was. I have some work to do. Put a call through to my room if you want to join me for some supper later."

"I will."

Hans patted Grania on the shoulder and left the suite. Once the door was closed, Grania stood up and started to pace. Now the shock had worn off, Grania felt cross . . . yes, furious that Aurora had seen fit to interfere in her life. This was not a fairy tale, not a childhood game where everybody found their prince and lived happily ever after. It was *reality*. And some things that were wrong could never be put right, however much Aurora wished them to be. She simply wanted Aurora home and out of Matt's clutches as soon as possible. The thought of the two of them together, discussing her, was more than she could bear. And now, just when she was trying so hard—and it *was* hard—to move on, as Hans had suggested she must, she was being dragged back into the past. One way or another, there would have to be contact with Matt. Matt, who was almost certainly still shacked up at the loft with *her* . . .

Grania let out a groan of despair. She knew she should speak to Aurora as soon as possible, check she was all right for her own peace of mind. She picked up the receiver and dialed the number, then ended the call before it had a chance to ring. No. She couldn't face it. So she dialed her mother's number instead.

"To be sure, we are all mighty relieved here!" Kathleen's voice was euphoric. "Fancy our little pet making it all the way to New York!"

"Yes, isn't she clever?" Grania said flatly. "Mam, I'd like you to call Matt and make arrangements for Aurora to be put on a plane home as soon as possible. Would you do that for me?"

"If that's what you want, Grania. When I spoke to Aurora earlier, she was talking about spending a couple more days with Matt. As she's got herself there, bless her, she might as well be seeing the sights of New York. Matt sounds very taken with her, so he does."

"Well, from my point of view, I'd like her home as soon as possible. She's missing school, Mam."

"And what harm?" asked Kathleen. "I'd say she'll be having an experience worth any lesson she can learn in class. And a native to show her around too."

"Well, I'll leave it to you to arrange," Grania replied tersely. "I'll send you an e-mail with my credit card details, to pay for Aurora's ticket home."

"All right," agreed Kathleen. "I'll be getting Shane to book it, mind. Computers are not my thing. Grania?"

"Yes?"

"Are you all right?"

"Yes, of course I am, Mam," she said brusquely. "Speak soon."

Grania slammed the receiver into its cradle and went into the bedroom. Flinging herself down on the bed, she put a pillow over her head to try and block out her frustration and pain.

Aurora and Matt spent the following forty-eight hours seeing all there was to see in New York City. Matt found himself bewitched by her. She was a mixture of naïveté and intelligence, innocence and maturity . . . he could understand why Grania had fallen in love with her.

On Aurora's last night, Matt took her to a diner for a hamburger as she'd requested. He was due to put her back on a plane the following morning. Up until now, the subject of Grania had been carefully avoided by both of them.

"Matt, have you come up with a plan yet to win back Grania's love?" Aurora asked as she bit into her burger.

"No." He shrugged. "I think she's made it clear that she doesn't want to speak to me. It's her mother that's been contacting me about the arrangements for you."

"Grania's very stubborn," said Aurora. "That's what Granny says, anyway."

"I know she is, honey." Matt smiled at the idea of being counseled by a nine-year-old girl.

"*And* proud," she added.

"Yup, you're sure right there."

"But we know she still loves you."

"Do we?" Matt raised an eyebrow. "You know what, Aurora? I just don't know that anymore."

"Well, *I* do." Aurora reached across the table toward him conspiratorially. "And I have a plan . . ."

Grania had spent the past two days skulking in her hotel suite at Claridge's. Now that she knew Aurora was safe, she'd decided not to fly back home, unable to face the pressure she'd be under from her mother to make direct contact with Aurora. And hear what a wonderful time she was having with Matt. And perhaps Charley . . .

When Aurora was safely on the plane tomorrow, she could return home.

She and Hans shared a quiet dinner that night. He was also leaving London for Switzerland the following day.

"I hope next time you're in London, I can show you Aurora's house," said Hans. "It is very beautiful."

"Next time, yes," said Grania distractedly.

"Grania." Hans looked at her. "Why are you so angry?"

"Angry? I'm not angry. Well, perhaps a little with Aurora, for giving us all such a fright. *And* for interfering in my life," she added honestly.

"I can see why you might feel that," comforted Hans, "but we've talked before about your problem with receiving gifts from others. Don't you see that, in her way, Aurora was trying to give you a gift? Trying to help you?"

"Yes, but she doesn't understand—"

"Grania, it is not my place to interfere," Hans cut in, "and certainly not in the affairs of your heart. But your anger betrays the strong sense of emotion this man stirs in you. In simple terms, you must either love him or hate him. But only you can decide which."

Grania sighed. "I love him," she admitted sadly. "But it all went wrong months ago. And he's with someone else now."

"You know this for sure?"

"Yes." Grania nodded.

"But maybe he doesn't love this other person?"

"Hans, you're very sweet, but really, I don't want to talk about it any further. And I'm only embarrassed that my love life has caused all this upset."

"Well, perhaps Aurora was simply trying to return a little of the love and care you have shown to her. Do not blame her or chastise her when you see her, Grania, will you?"

"Of course not. Believe me, Hans," breathed Grania with feeling, "I want to forget this whole episode ever happened."

43

When Grania arrived home in Dunworley the following day around lunchtime, she drove straight up to her studio, knowing that Aurora wouldn't be home for a few hours yet and not wishing to be interrogated by her mother. She sat down at her workbench and began to sketch the outline of a new sculpture. At teatime, Grania reluctantly drove herself back down to the farmhouse.

"Mummy!" A small thunderbolt emerged from inside it and threw itself into her arms. "I've missed you."

"And I've missed you." Grania smiled as she hugged Aurora tightly.

"New York was wonderful! I bought you lots of presents. But I'm very glad to be home now and see you," Aurora said as she pulled her toward the house. "And you'll never guess who's decided to come back with me for a visit."

"Hi there, Grania."

Grania halted on the threshold of the kitchen when she saw who was sitting at the table. Her heart began to bang against her chest. Finally, she found her voice. "What are *you* doing here?"

"I came to see you, honey."

Grania glanced at her mother, who seemed to be set on "pause," the teapot suspended above Matt's cup as she stared at her daughter and watched for her reaction.

Aurora shrugged. "He wanted to see you." Her voice echoed into the silence. "You don't mind, do you, Mummy?"

Grania was too shocked to answer. She watched Aurora walk toward Matt and hug him.

"Don't worry, Matt, I said she'd be surprised, but I'm sure underneath it she's happy. Aren't you, Mummy?"

Aurora, Kathleen and Matt stared at her for a reply. Grania felt like a cornered animal. And had her usual instinct to bolt.

"Well now . . ." Kathleen did her best to break the tension. "I'm sure 'tis a shock for Grania to see her . . . old friend sitting at our kitchen table," she said to Aurora.

"Mummy, please don't be cross," begged Aurora. "I had to go to see Matt in New York, really I did. He telephoned here, you see, when you were away with Daddy on your honeymoon. And I told him you'd got married. Which you aren't anymore, are you, Mummy? And I didn't want Matt to think you were, when you weren't, if you see what I mean. I told Matt that underneath, you really did want to see him, and so I—"

"Aurora, *please*!" Grania couldn't take any more.

"Grania's tired, like we are, honey," interjected Matt gently. "And I'm sure we have some talking to do, don't we, Grania?"

"Let's be getting you upstairs and into a bath, miss. Scrub off that dirt from those planes, and then it's an early night." Kathleen grabbed Aurora's hand and pulled her out of the kitchen, closing the door firmly behind them.

Grania gave a deep sigh and took a step further into the kitchen. "So, what *are* you doing here?" she asked Matt coldly.

"It was Aurora's suggestion at first," Matt admitted, "but she's right, Grania. I needed to come and see you, so at least we could talk, and I could understand why you left me."

In slow motion, Grania took a mug out of the cupboard and poured herself some tea from the pot.

Matt surveyed her. "Well?"

"Well, what?" she asked, taking a sip of lukewarm tea.

"Can we talk?"

"Matt, I have nothing to say to you."

"OK." Matt knew how stubborn Grania could be when she'd dug herself in. He had to tread carefully. "Well, perhaps, as I've just flown across the world to see you, you could cut a guy a break and listen to what *he* has to say."

"Go ahead." Grania shrugged, putting her tea down and crossing her arms defensively. "I'm all ears."

"How about we go out and walk? I get the feeling that in this house you're not the only one with ears."

Grania offered a cursory nod, then turned and headed out of the kitchen door. Matt followed her outside and caught up with her.

"I need to tell you, if you're expecting any great revelations, you're not going to get them," he began. "I still don't know what got you so pissed that you left me. And I won't unless you give me a clue." Matt glanced at her, but saw Grania's chin was set hard, betraying no emotion. "Right," he sighed, "then I'll have to tell you how it is from my point of view. Is that OK?"

Still silence, so Matt began.

"I was in shock at first, when you upped and left. I thought it most probably had something to do with the miscarriage. That maybe your hormones were all over the place. That, just maybe, this didn't have as much to do with me as with losing the baby, that you just needed to get away. I understood that. And then, when I called and you were so cold, I began to realize it must be something to do with me. I asked you time and again what it was, and you wouldn't tell me. And then you refused to talk to me at all." Matt sighed. "Jeez, I didn't know what to think. Weeks pass and I don't hear from you and you don't return. So I tie myself in knots going over and over what it is I might have done. And more than that, realizing how much I love you. And miss you. Hell, Grania! My life's been a mess since you left. A train crash, baby, in ways you wouldn't believe possible."

"Ditto," Grania offered grudgingly.

"When Aurora suggested this, I decided she was right," Matt continued. "That if the mountain wouldn't come to Mahomet, I needed to get my ass on a plane and come to you. If for nothing more than an explanation, so I can stop tearing myself apart and sleep at night."

Matt fell silent as he followed Grania up the cliff path. He had nothing else to say. Finally, they reached the top of the cliffs, and Grania sat down on her favorite rock, then rested her elbows on her knees and stared out to sea.

"Hey, honey, please, I need to know." Matt crouched next to her and tipped her face up to his own. "Please," he said gently, "put me out of my misery."

Her eyes were like flint as she stared at him. "You mean, you can still look me in the eyes and tell me you don't know?"

"You always said I was a crap actor, honey, and I couldn't put on a performance like this if I did."

"All right then." Grania took a deep breath. "Why didn't you tell me you'd had a relationship with Charley before we met? That you were actually seeing her *when* we met? And how long was it going on for after we *did* meet? And what's going on *now*?"

"Grania, baby, I . . ." Matt looked at her in astonishment. "Is that what this has all been about? The fact I was seeing Charley when we first met and I didn't tell you?"

"Don't trivialize it, Matt, I hate liars. I hate liars more than anything."

"But I didn't lie, Grania. I just—" Matt shrugged.

"Forgot to mention it," Grania interrupted. "Omitted it from your biography, even though it was current at the time."

"But, Grania, don't you see?" Matt was deeply shocked that apparently this was the reason for Grania's exit from his life. "I didn't even feel it was important. It wasn't love or anything, just a casual relationship that—"

"—Went on for eighteen months, from what I heard from your mother and father."

Matt looked at her oddly. "You heard that from my mom and dad? When? Where?"

"When they came to see me at the hospital after the miscarriage, I was in the bathroom when they arrived. They didn't know I was in there. Your mom talked about how sad it was I'd lost the baby, then your dad commented how much easier it would have been for you if you'd stuck with Charley and not dumped her for me." Grania's eyes were sparkling with tears. "I suppose what they were suggesting was that my genes, coming as they do from the bogs of Ireland, weren't up to scratch for upstate royalty such as yourself."

"You left me because of what you overheard my *dad* say?" Matt sat down on the grass and put his head in his hands. "Hell, Grania, I accept it wasn't a conversation that you should ever have heard, but I think you overreacted. You know what my dad's like: as warm and sensitive as a fridge."

"I know," answered Grania with vehemence, "and as for overreacting, maybe I wouldn't have done if I'd had the slightest inkling that you and Charley had once been an item. But, of course, I didn't. Anyway, you're welcome to continue to pursue your blue-blooded princess now I'm out of the way," she added bitterly.

"Goddamn it, Grania! I don't know what the hell you've cooked up in that mind of yours, but I can honestly swear to you I'm not interested in Charley. And the point is, I never was!"

"Then why did she answer our home phone when I called you a few weeks after I'd left?" Grania spat the words out.

"Oh, Jesus, baby . . ." He sighed heavily. "It's a long story." It was Matt's turn to fall silent and stare out to sea. Eventually, he said, "All I can promise you is that Charley is out of my life for good."

"So, you're admitting that something was going on recently?"

Matt shook his head despairingly. "Grania, a bit like me hearing you'd gotten yourself married, my life has been . . . complicated too. And sure, I can tell you the story, but it's so bizarre, I doubt you'd believe it."

"Well, I suppose that's one thing we share," said Grania quietly. "I doubt you could get more complex than the past year of my life here."

"No." Matt looked up at her. "And what about Aurora's father? Did you . . . were you . . . ?"

"Oh, Matt," Grania sighed, "so much water has flowed under the bridge since I left New York."

"Well, just maybe, if you had trusted in my love for you in the first place, and believed that if I'd have wanted my 'blue-blooded princess,' as you call her, I could have had her, then none of this would have happened."

"But it has happened, Matt," said Grania, "and yes, I accept that when I heard what your dad said, I was in a state of high emotion. Yes, I was irrational. Losing the baby brought out every insecurity I had. I was hurting so much at the time, and I bolted. Hans says"—she bit her lip—"that my pride makes me do stupid things. And he's probably right," Grania admitted.

"Hey, I don't know who this Hans is, but I'd sure like to meet him," Matt commented wryly.

"But don't you see? When I *did* calm down and realized I was probably overreacting, a couple of weeks after I left, I called you at home to try and sort it out. But Charley answered the phone and I flipped. It was confirmation of my worst fear."

"Yeah, I can see how it would have been." Matt reached out a tentative hand to Grania. "Well, baby, I've sure got some stuff to tell you.

But I'm nearing hypothermia out here. Is there anyplace we can go where we can talk, over some food perhaps? I could use a bite to eat."

Grania took Matt to a pub in nearby Ring that served fresh seafood straight from the day's catch. She sat opposite him, feeling uncomfortable. Gone was the unconscious touch of the hand, the easy familiarity which came out of years of love. Matt felt both familiar and yet unknown.

"So," he asked across the table, "Who's gonna tell their story first?"

"Well, as I'd begun, I might as well continue." Grania looked at him. "And I want us both to be truthful. After all, we have nothing to lose, and maybe we owe it to each other."

"Agreed," said Matt. "There's a lot you're not gonna like. But, I swear, what I say, you can believe."

"Me too," said Grania quietly. "OK, so Aurora's obviously told you how we met. What you want to know is about my relationship with Alexander?"

"Yup." Matt steeled himself to hear it. And as he listened to Grania explaining the dramatic events of the past few months, Matt noticed that she was different, more mature and softer, somehow. And even as she told him of the closeness of the relationship she'd forged with Alexander, Matt found he loved her more. For her goodness, her generosity and the strength she had shown in what sounded like dreadful circumstances.

". . . and that brings us up to date, really," Grania shrugged.

"Wow, that's quite a story," Matt sighed. "Thanks, baby, for being so honest. Listen," he said reluctantly, needing to clear up one point so he didn't fret later. "Please understand I'm just a guy, and I really wanna believe that your physical relationship with him didn't go any further. But if it did, please tell me."

"Matt, we kissed and that was all. I swear. He was so ill." Grania reddened. "But if I'm honest, I can't say it wouldn't have happened if he'd been well. I was attracted to him."

"Right." Matt shuddered at the thought, but knew he must handle it. "OK, so . . . your name is now Grania Devonshire, you're a widow with a nine-year-old child. *And* rich to boot. My, that takes some doing in the space of a few months!" he grimaced.

"Yes, I know, but I promise I've told you the truth. And Aurora and my parents can verify almost every word of it. Now, Matt, I think we both need another drink. And after that, I'd like you to tell me about Charley."

Matt went to the bar and, while he ordered, realized with a heavy heart that every word which would fall from his mouth would only underline all Grania's preconceptions and insecurities.

Grania watched him as he stood there, chatting in his naturally easy way to the barmaid. He looked older than she'd remembered him. Perhaps it was the stress of the past few months which had imprinted the contours of maturity on his boyish face. Whatever it was, she thought with a sigh, it had only made him more attractive.

He placed the drinks in front of them. "Thought I'd try the local brew," he smiled, taking a sip of Murphy's. "Now, I told you earlier it wasn't gonna be pleasant, but here goes . . ."

Matt spoke as realistically and honestly as he could. He didn't spare himself, because he knew that if this woman—the woman he loved—and he were going to have a shot at any kind of future together, he had to be truthful. He looked at her occasionally as he talked, trying to gauge what she was thinking or feeling, but her face was a blank canvas.

"And that's about it," Matt breathed, his relief at telling his story now palpable. "I'm sorry, baby, I told you it wasn't pretty."

Grania shook her head slowly. "No, it isn't. Where is Charley now?"

"My mom says she's living in our house in Greenwich. And dating my old friend Al, who's practically moved in, apparently. He's always had a thing for her." Matt gave a grim smile. "The baby's due in a few weeks. My name is dirt at the country club, but hey, who cares?"

"What about your mother and father? Surely the situation makes it hard for them?"

Matt managed a weak smile. "Well, seems what's happened to me meant my mom has kinda got with her own program. And as from next week, I have a new roommate."

"What do you mean?" Grania frowned.

"Apparently, Mom's not been happy for years with my dad. You can imagine he didn't take kindly to Charley and me splitting, said I should still stand by her for the sake of 'form.' It was the proverbial last straw for my mom. So she's leaving him." Matt shook his head. "Ironic really, but she says she's had enough of toeing the party line. She wants to live a bit while she still can. You know, Grania, despite the impression you had of her, she thought you were just great. She even told me you were an inspiration to her."

"Really?" Grania was genuinely surprised. "But you must be sad, Matt. They've been married such a long time."

"Yeah, well, my hunch is that she'll go back eventually, but it won't do Dad any harm to be without her for a while. Maybe he'll start appreciating her and soften that rod up his ass in order to have a proper relationship with her. And his son too." Matt raised an eyebrow. "Anyway, my parents' marriage is not what we're here to discuss. It's you and me who are important. How are you feeling, baby?" he asked quietly.

"I honestly don't know, Matt." Grania stared into the distance then finally said, "There's been a lot to take on board tonight."

"But isn't it a real good thing we had the chance to talk? We should have done this months ago, Grania," Matt said with feeling.

"I know," she answered softly.

"And that little kid of yours, she did everything to give us the opportunity," added Matt. "She acted like our fairy godmother."

"She did," Grania agreed, "but . . ."

"But what?"

"It still can't make the wrong things right. Or erase the past."

"What exactly are the 'wrong' things?" Matt stared at her. "Unlike you, I've only ever seen the 'right' things about you and me."

"I'm tired, Matt," Grania sighed. "Can we go home, please?"

"Sure."

They drove back to the farmhouse in silence, Grania staring out of the window at the blackness of the night.

They walked into the kitchen and Matt said, "Where do I sleep?"

"I'm afraid it's the sofa. I'll get you a pillow and some blankets."

"Grania . . . please, baby, at least give me a hug. I love you . . . I—" He reached for her hand as she walked past him, but she ignored it, went upstairs and retrieved what Matt needed.

"There." She dumped the pile on the kitchen table. "Sorry the accommodation isn't up to much."

"It'll do just fine," he said, suddenly cold. "And don't worry—I'm out of your hair tomorrow. I have a lecture tour starting on Wednesday."

"Right. Good night, Matt."

Matt watched her leave the room. He understood her shock, that the stuff he'd had to tell her tonight was difficult to hear, but listening to Grania's story had hardly been a walk in the park for him either. Yet he was still prepared to reach out to her, to accept and understand and put the past behind them. Simply because the need to be with the woman he loved overrode everything else.

Whereas she was as cold as ice, and refusing to give him an inch. He'd made the effort, encouraged by Aurora, to fly across the world to see her, to try one last time to salvage their relationship. As he threw himself and the blanket disconsolately on to the sofa, Matt sighed heavily. Maybe he was tired from the journey, but tonight he was all out of hope for the future.

Grania lay upstairs, unable to sleep. Even though she believed Matt's story, the unpalatable bit of it kept going around in her head. Whether Matt had been drunk or not, Charley had still ended up in his bed. And subsequently stayed there for five months. Her stuff had been hung in the closet where her clothes used to hang, they currently owned a house together and had announced their engagement. The scenario was her ultimate nemesis. Grania shuddered as she thought of how smug Matt's dad would have been at his son's reunion with a more suitable female.

But she knew also that many couples managed to combine their different backgrounds. And most women seemed to relish being carried off by their prince. Grania sighed. So why couldn't she? Besides, Matt was hardly a prince. The fact that his dad was a pompous, arrogant, narrow-minded ass who'd always made her feel inadequate—and, from the sound of it, his wife too—was not his son's fault. The thought of Elaine's leaving her husband was the one thing that made Grania smile.

And the fact Matt had come across the world to see her must mean he hadn't given up. That he still loved her . . .

As the endless hours of the night wore on and Grania sat upright, her legs drawn to her chin, the truth began to dawn on her. She began to look back and realize it had been Matt's choice to be with *her,* whatever his dad had thought. In fact, Matt was the one who'd pursued their relationship from the start. She'd never coerced him, or forced him to live the life they'd forged together. It was what he'd wanted. In fact, *he* was the one who'd bent over backward to accommodate her hang-ups. He'd accepted her stubbornness at refusing to take handouts even when they were desperate, he'd understood she found his friends difficult so steered clear, and he'd agreed to live together, rather than marry.

"Oh God . . ."

Grania saw clearly now that it wasn't Matt who had the problem, it was *her.*

Her stupid, stubborn, ridiculous, destructive pride. *And* insecurity, which had blinded her to his love. And that conversation she'd overheard in the hospital, when she'd been feeling so weak and vulnerable, combined with her "blind spot," had tipped her over the edge. She'd felt like a failure as a woman, a partner and a human being.

Grania sighed, thinking of Hans and his assessment of her. She'd learned a lot about herself in the past few months: what she had misguidedly seen as her strengths, she realized now, were also her weaknesses. So what if Matt had had a relationship with Charley before he'd met her? He hadn't mentioned it before simply because he hadn't deemed it important. And *not* because he was harboring some deep, secret love.

In fact, she realized now, Matt had done absolutely nothing wrong.

As a weary dawn began to break, she drifted off to sleep. She was awoken not long afterward by a soft tapping at her door. "Come in," she said drowsily.

Aurora, dressed in her school uniform, peeped shyly around the door. "It's me."

Grania hauled herself upright and smiled. "I know it's you."

Aurora walked hesitantly to Grania's bed and sat down on it. "I just wanted to say I'm sorry."

"Sorry for what?"

"Granny said last night that it really wasn't a good idea to interfere in other people's lives. I thought I was doing something good for you, Mummy, but I wasn't, was I?"

"Oh, sweetheart, come here and give me a cuddle."

Aurora went into Grania's open arms and sobbed on her shoulder. "I thought that you looked so lonely and sad. And I wanted you to be happy, the way you've made me happy . . . I wanted to do something for *you*."

"Darling, what you did was wonderful. And brave, and a little bit dangerous," Grania added.

"And you're cross with me, aren't you?" Aurora looked up at her through tear-filled eyes.

"No, I'm not cross at all, I just . . ." Grania sighed. "Sometimes even fairy godmothers can't make it all right."

"Oh," said Aurora, "I thought you loved each other."

"I know, darling."

"And Matt is so lovely, and very handsome, though not as handsome as Daddy," she added quickly. "And you did talk for a long time last night, didn't you?"

"Yes, we did."

"Well," Aurora extricated herself from Grania's arms and stood up, "I have to go to school now. I promise I won't say another word. As Granny says, it has to be your decision."

"Yes, it does, sweetheart, but thank you for trying to help."

Aurora paused at the door. "I do think you go together very well, though. See you later."

Grania lay wearily back on her pillows, wanting to gather her thoughts before she went downstairs.

Even if she and Matt managed to get over all the water that had passed under their mutual bridge, how could they combine their now disparate lives? Matt's was on the other side of the Atlantic, whereas she was rooted here with Aurora. She'd become a mother—ironically, under the circumstances—since she'd last seen Matt. She had no idea whether he would want or be able to take that on board.

Grania showered, dressed and went downstairs. Aurora had already left for school with Kathleen. Matt was sitting at the table in the kitchen, making his way through the full cooked breakfast Kathleen had made for him.

"Your mom sure knows how to spoil a guy," Matt commented as he finished. "I've missed your home cooking as well, baby."

"Well, I'm sure Charley kept you fully supplied with takeout from Dean & Deluca," Grania commented, then kicked herself. It had fallen out of her mouth before she could stop it.

"Grania," Matt sighed, "don't go there, please."

A tense silence hung over the kitchen, neither of them knowing what to say. She made herself a cup of tea, while Matt finished his coffee. Then he stood up and headed for the back door, pausing as his hand clutched the handle. "Look, honey, I've tried, but it's obvious that you're not gonna be able to put the past where it belongs. And perhaps you don't even want to make a fresh start." Matt shrugged. "To be honest, I'm tired of fighting a one-way battle. And this morning, that's what our relationship feels like."

"Matt . . ."

"It's OK, baby, you don't need to explain. And maybe all this stuff about our different backgrounds and Charley, and not wanting to marry me, says something more; maybe, Grania, it says you've just never loved me enough to want to make it work. You know, everyone has shit to deal with in their lives. That's what makes a relationship strong. That and compromise. You've never been prepared to do that—it's all been *your* way. And at the first sign of trouble, you turn tail and leave me. I'm all in." He checked his watch. "I gotta go. See you around."

Matt left the kitchen, banging the door shut behind him. Grania heard his rental car drive off down the lane as tears of shock stung in her eyes. Why had Matt turned on her like that? Yes, a caustic comment had slipped out of her mouth, but what did he mean by "not loving him enough" to make it work?

And now he'd left.

And it was over. He'd reached his limit. He'd made that very clear.

Grania left the house and drove numbly up to the studio, her stomach churning. As she sat at her workbench, tears continued to blur her vision. She wasn't used to Matt fighting back. He was so gentle, easygoing and reasonable. It was she who was the feisty, volatile one. And after all her good thoughts and intentions during the night, a single sentence had slipped out and ruined it all.

"You stupid, stubborn eejit, Grania! You love him," she moaned as the tears dripped on to her new sculpture, soaking the clay. "Matt tried so hard to fight for you and now he's gone! And it's *you* that has pushed him away!" She stood up, wiping the tears away with the back of her hand, and paced up and down the studio.

What should she do?

Part of her, the old, proud Grania, felt she should let him go.

But the new part, that Hans and the events of the past few months had helped her recognize, told her she should swallow her pride and go after him. And beg him to give them another try.

There was so much to lose if she didn't. Of course there were problems to be worked out, such as where they should live, and whether Matt was prepared to take on Aurora and be a father to her. But as Matt said, if you loved someone enough, surely it was worth a try?

"*But I thought you loved each other . . .*"

Aurora's sad face earlier came to Grania's mind. Could she break the habit of a lifetime, swallow her pride and go after the man she loved?

Go . . . go . . . go . . .

Maybe it was the wind howling around the studio, or perhaps Lily, her presence urging her to trust in love.

Grania grabbed her car keys and sped off in the direction of Cork airport.

On the journey, she tried Matt's cell phone number on numerous occasions, but it was switched off. She drove far faster than was safe, yet when she arrived at Departures, she saw the flight to Dublin was already boarding. She ran to the Aer Lingus information desk and stood impatiently in the queue.

"My—er—boyfriend is about to board the flight to Dublin. I have something I must tell him. Is there any way of contacting him?" she asked the young girl desperately.

"Have you tried his mobile?" the girl replied sensibly.

"Of course I have! It's switched off, presumably because he's about to get on the plane. Can you not put a message out on the PA for him?"

"Well now, it depends on the level of urgency," said the girl slowly. "Is it urgent?"

"Of course it's urgent!" Grania replied irritably. "Incredibly urgent.

Could you put out a message for Matt Connelly, telling him Grania Ryan . . . is waiting for him by the Information Desk. And could he please call her before he boards the plane."

And that she loves him and needs him and she's so, so sorry . . .

Grania thought this, but didn't say it, as the girl took forever to speak to her superior, leaving her with tears of frustration in her eyes.

Finally, the call went out, loud and clear across the small airport. Grania waited in an agony of tension, staring at the cell phone in the palm of her hand. It lay there, an unresponsive, silent testament to the terrible mistake she knew she'd made.

"Miss, the plane's just taken off," said the girl behind the desk. "I don't think he'll be calling you now," she added unnecessarily.

Grania turned and looked out of the window. She managed a mumbled "thank you" and staggered off in the direction of her car.

She drove home slowly, knowing she had reaped the future she deserved. Matt wanted nothing more to do with her and she wasn't surprised. It was as if, up to today, she'd been incarcerated in a bubble of numbness, the walls plastered with a thick veneer of insecurity and pride. All that had now fallen away, and Grania could only see what she had lost. And why.

Pulling her car to a halt outside the farmhouse, she wandered disconsolately toward the kitchen door, intending to head directly upstairs to her bedroom.

"Where on earth have you been, Grania Ryan? We've been worried half out of our minds all this time!" Kathleen stood up from the kitchen table where the rest of the family were gathered nursing cups of tea, a communal expression of relief at Grania's appearance visible on their faces.

"We have, Mummy," Aurora added, "and now I know how you must have felt when I went missing."

"Come and sit down, darlin', and have a brew," encouraged John, patting the seat next to him.

Grania did so, her reluctance tempered by the genuine warmth of her family who so obviously loved her, despite her many failings. "Thanks, Dad," she muttered as John poured her a cup of tea and placed it in front of her. She took a sip as the rest of the family continued to stare at her silently, gauging her state of mind.

"The price of a calf has risen by ten percent," John announced suddenly to no one in particular, trying to break the tension. "When I was at market today in Cork, the other fellas were complaining that their herds will be smaller next year if the price rise continues."

The door from the stairs opened behind Grania, but she didn't turn around.

"Feeling fresher now?" John looked up. "Those cattle markets can leave you with the smell of them on you for days."

"Yeah, thanks," said the voice behind Grania. "I appreciate you taking me along, John. It was real interesting to see how the auction works."

A hand touched Grania's shoulder. "Hi, baby, you're back. Me and your folks were worried about you."

She turned around and looked up into Matt's eyes. "I . . . thought you'd left."

"Your pop offered to show me the cattle auction in Cork," he replied, pulling out the chair next to Grania and sitting down. "Thought I should see a little local Irish color before I left, and I sure saw that," chuckled Matt.

"But . . . your flight . . . I thought you were leaving today. You said you were last night."

"Your pop suggested I go with him to Cork at breakfast this morning, so I moved it." Matt reached under the table and squeezed her hand. "And besides, me and your folks thought maybe me staying a little longer might be a good idea, under the circumstances. They figured you needed some time to think, have some space, so I got out of your hair for the day. Do you mind that I'm still here, Grania?"

The family gaze turned upon her yet again, waiting for her response. Her throat was constricted, a huge lump of emotion lodged in it. With the support of everyone around the table, Matt had loved her enough to give her one final chance.

"Oh, do say you don't mind, Mummy!" Aurora rolled her eyes. "We all know you love Matt to bits, and the cows need to be shut away for the night."

Grania turned to Matt, her eyes shining with tears, and smiled at him.

"No, Matt. I don't mind one bit."

Aurora

Reader, I did it!

Yes, I know my disappearing act caused a lot of trouble and stress, for Grania in particular, but you know how desperate I've been during stages of this book to rewrite the plot and engineer a different ending. Well, that was my moment to step in, to do what any fairy godmother always does, and pop up in a puff of smoke to make things better.

And they always fly. Just like I did, all the way to America.

I wasn't frightened at all.

People have often asked me why I seem to have no fear. It's apparently that which stops so many people doing what they need to make their life happier. Well, I really don't have the answer, but maybe if one isn't afraid of ghosts or, in fact, death itself, which is the worst thing that can happen to a human being, there isn't much else left to be frightened of.

Except pain . . .

Spending so much of my childhood with grown-ups, it's always surprised me the way they couldn't quite seem to say what they meant. How communication would break down, even though I could see in their heart they were hurting, that they loved the other person. How pride, anger and insecurity so easily kills the chance of possible happiness.

Yes, it could have all gone horribly wrong, but sometimes one has to take the leap of faith and trust in the fact it might not. At the very worst, at least I had tried and, really, I believe that is all one can do in life. Because it's so short and, as I know, looking back when one has little time left, it's best to have as few regrets as possible.

And, of course, Grania helped me. I've talked earlier about having to learn lessons in life, and Grania saw and accepted her failings, just in the nick of time. It was a close-run thing, but hopefully, now she's done that, not only will her current life be easier, it might also mean she comes back as something lovely next time. Personally, I quite fancy being a bird—perhaps a seagull. I want to know what it feels like to take wing, fly off the cliffs and circle high above the ocean.

And Matt is just the kind of man I wish I could have married. And I knew he would make a very good stand-in daddy to replace the one I'd lost. These days, I know that many women wouldn't agree that they need a male in their life but, Reader, were we humans not born to find a mate? Do we all not chase after and wish for the magic of love for most of our lives?

Having watched a lot of films recently, I've realized there are only three main topics: war, money and love. And normally, even in the former, the latter sneaks in somewhere.

And they are certainly all in this story.

We are nearing the end now, in all sorts of ways.

I'd better hurry up . . .

44

London, One Year Later

Grania and Aurora stood in front of the elegant white house and looked up.

"It's beautiful," breathed Aurora. She turned to Hans. "Is it really mine?"

"All yours, Aurora. You inherited this and Dunworley House from your mother." Hans smiled. "Shall we take a look inside?"

"Yes, please," said Aurora.

Grania paused on the step and put her hand on Hans's arm. "What is the address of this house?"

Hans consulted the details. "Cadogan House, Cadogan Place."

"Oh, my goodness!" Grania's hand went to her mouth. "This is the house where my great-grandmother, Mary, worked as a servant. And where Anna Langdon, Aurora's grandmother, was brought to by Lawrence Lisle when she was a baby."

"How interesting. One day, perhaps, you can tell Aurora what you know about her past heritage." They stood in the darkened entrance hall and Hans sniffed. "Damp," he surmised. "This house has been empty for many years."

"I know Lily lived here with her mother after the problems in Ireland," confirmed Grania, trying to put the pieces together. "When Lawrence Lisle died, Sebastian, her father, inherited this from his brother."

"Well, Alexander, Lily and Aurora did not live here when they were in London. Alexander had a very pleasant house of his own just up the road in Kensington. Not on this scale, it must be said," commented Hans, "but certainly more welcoming."

"It's huge!" Aurora said in awe as she walked into the elegant drawing room and Hans opened the shutters to let in some light.

"It is, young lady," Hans agreed, "but I think, like Dunworley House, it will need some funds to restore it to its former glory."

As Grania followed Hans and Aurora through the many rooms, and then upstairs, she felt as if the house had been dipped in aspic and preserved as a relic from another era. Aurora had huge fun with the bellpulls, and they could hear a faint tinkling beneath them in the kitchen.

"My great-grandmother Mary would have been one of the servants to answer that bell," commented Grania as they made their way back down the stairs.

Hans shivered as they arrived back in the entrance hall. "Well, Aurora, in my opinion, we had better consider your father's house as your London residence," he said, his Swiss liking for order and cleanliness coming to the fore. "And perhaps sell this?"

"Oh no, Uncle Hans, I love it here!" She danced back into the drawing room and pointed to something sitting on top of a desk. "What is that?"

"That, my dear Aurora, is a very old gramophone." Hans and Grania exchanged a smile. "It is what we relics from the past used to play our music on."

Aurora glanced at the dusty piece of vinyl that lay upon the spindle. "It's *Swan Lake*! Look, Grania, it's *Swan Lake*! Perhaps it was my grandmother, Anna, who last played it. She was a famous ballerina, Uncle Hans."

"Perhaps it was. Now, I think we have seen all there is to see." Hans was heading for the front door. "I am sure there are many developers who would be eager to get their hands on this. It would be perfect to convert into three or four apartments. It is in a prime location too. It will sell for many millions."

"But, Uncle Hans, if I decide I want us all to live here while I'm at ballet school, would it cost a lot of my money to make it a bit brighter?"

"Yes, my dear Aurora, it would. A lot of money," he confirmed.

Aurora, arms crossed, eyed him. "And do I have enough to make this house into a nice place for us to live?"

"Yes, you do," confirmed Hans, "but I would not advise it. Especially as you have a perfectly comfortable house a few miles down the road in Kensington."

"No. I've decided that this is where I want to live." She turned to Grania on the doorstep as Hans locked up behind them. "What about you, Mummy? After all, you'd have to live here too."

"It's a beautiful old house, Aurora, and of course I'd be happy to live here with you. But as Uncle Hans says, it might be more sensible to sell it."

"No," said Aurora adamantly. "This is where I want to be."

The three of them left Cadogan House and took a taxi back to Claridge's. Over tea and cakes, Aurora imperiously ordered Hans to make the necessary arrangements to begin the process of renovating her house. "We can live in Daddy's house in Kensington while all the things are put right. Can't we, Grania?"

"If you're sure that's what you want, Aurora, then yes." Grania's cell phone rang. "Excuse me." Grania left the lounge and went into the lobby to take the call in private.

"Hi, baby, how's it hanging? Have you seen the house?"

"Yes, I have. It's beautiful and absolutely huge, and needs just about everything doing to it to make it habitable. But Aurora has decided that's where she wants to live."

"And the audition at the Royal Ballet School yesterday?"

"Aurora said it went well, but we won't know for certain for a week or so."

"And you, honey?"

"I'm fine, Matt. Missing you."

"Me too. Only a few days now, though, and I'll be there with you."

"You are sure this is what you want, Matt?"

"Never surer. In fact, I can't wait to get out of New York and start my new life with my two girls. On that note, give my other girl a hug from me."

"I will."

"Oh, and Grania?"

"Yes?"

"You're not going to welch on the deal at the last moment, are you? I mean, I don't wanna throw up everything this end and then, when my UK visa runs out in three months' time, find you've changed your mind about marrying me."

"I won't change my mind, Matt," Grania promised. "I have no choice really, do I? You'll be thrown out of the country if I do."

"Exactly. I'm making damned sure that, this time, there's no get-out clause. I love you, baby, and I'll be there with you both real soon."

"I love you too, Matt." Grania smiled as she replaced her cell phone in her handbag and walked back to the lounge. It had taken a year of commuting between New York and Ireland to settle on the best plan to combine their three lives and forge a future. The decision had been made when Aurora had announced that she wanted to try for a place at the Royal Ballet School, situated in leafy Richmond Park, just on the outskirts of London.

Grania's exhibition, three months ago now, had been a big success, and she'd been spending more and more time in London too. All that had remained was for Matt to find a job as a psychology lecturer, which he'd achieved at King's College three weeks ago. In the long holidays both Matt and Aurora would have from their respective university and ballet school, they planned to return to Dunworley and take advantage of the beautifully renovated house. It would also mean Grania could work in her studio, and Aurora could spend time with her adopted Irish family and her beloved animals.

Grania knew what Matt was sacrificing to leave New York, but as he'd said himself, maybe London was the perfect compromise; they'd both be on neutral territory—neither of them a native—and would forge a new future together.

"I've just been telling Uncle Hans that I think we should sell Daddy's house in Kensington once Cadogan House has been made beautiful. That will help pay for the cost of it," said Aurora.

"Her father's daughter," Hans raised his eyebrows, "showing financial acumen at the age of ten. Well, Aurora, as you are my client, and therefore my boss, I must adhere to your wishes. And yes, as your trustee, I believe they are sensible."

"I'm going to powder my nose, as Granny says," said Aurora.

When she'd skipped off, Hans asked, "How is Matt?"

"He's good, thanks, Hans. Busy packing up the loft and his life in the Big Apple."

"It is a big change he is making—that you are both making. But, I think, the right one. A fresh start can be very beneficial."

"Yes," Grania agreed. "And I don't think I ever thanked you for knowing me better than I knew myself. You made me see the mistakes I'd made."

"Attchh! I did nothing," Hans refuted modestly. "The trick is not only to know your failings, but to strive to put them right. And that is exactly what you have done, Grania."

"Well, I try, but that pride of mine will never completely disappear," she sighed.

"You are with someone who understands you, probably far better than he ever did before. Matt is a good man, Grania. You must take care of him."

"I know, and I will, Hans, I promise."

"What are you two talking about?" said Aurora, arriving back at the table. "Can we go up to the room now? I want to phone Granny and tell her all about my new house."

"Aurora tells me she's decided she wants to live in Cadogan House," said Kathleen, when Aurora had finished chewing her granny's ear off and passed the phone to Grania.

"Yes."

"You do know that's where Mary, your great-grandmother—"

"Yes, I do."

"Well now, I'm a-wondering; do you remember, during the telling of Mary's tale, that when Lawrence Lisle brought his little baby girl home with him, he asked that a suitcase be stored upstairs until the baby's mother came to collect it? You don't think . . . ?"

"Well, there's only one way to find out," said Grania. "Next time I go, I'll take a look."

A week later, when Matt had arrived in London, Grania took Aurora and Matt to Cadogan House. Aurora provided Matt with a guided tour, after which he came downstairs to the kitchen and put his arms around Grania.

"Hey, honey, it's a good thing I don't have the same problem as you." He whistled. "This house would even make my pop sit up and be impressed. It's like, amazing! And I'm gonna be living in it rent free." He smiled. "Will I be able to cope?"

"Well, it's not mine either, Matt, is it? It's Aurora's."

"I'm teasing you, baby." Matt hugged her.

"Are you sure you're OK about it, Matt?" Grania looked up at him. "Can you be comfortable here?"

"Lady"—he held his hands up—"I get to be with you and pursue the career I love. And if my wife and child can provide the creature comforts along the way, I have no problem with that."

"Good. Now, do you think you could make yourself useful, and come up to the attic with me? I've brought a torch. There's something I want to look for."

With Aurora happily ensconced in the drawing room, listening to a barely audible *Swan Lake* on the ancient gramophone, Matt and Grania climbed the stairs to the top of the house.

"There," Grania pointed to a square cutout on the ceiling, "that must be it."

Matt looked up at it. "I'll need something to stand on to reach it."

They duly dragged a wooden chair from one of the attic bedrooms. Matt stood on it precariously, reached above him and struggled with the rusty catch. He yanked and it gave way, freeing the opening in a cloud of dust and cobwebs.

"Man, I don't think this place has been visited for decades," Matt said as he poked his head into the hole. "Pass me the torch." Grania did so, and Matt shone it around the attic. "Don't think you're gonna like it up here, baby. Why don't you tell me what it is you're looking for and I'll see if I can find it?"

"From what my mam told me, you're looking for a small and very old suitcase."

"OK." Matt used the strength in his arms to haul himself up, and sat on the edge of the hole, his legs dangling beneath. There was an instant noise of pattering from above them.

"Mice, or worse, rats." Matt blanched. "Better tell the surveyor to take a look when he comes round."

"In that case, perhaps we can get someone else to clear everything out another day," Grania suggested with a shudder.

"Hey, no way! At least I'm useful for something." Matt smiled down at her. "Stay there and I'll go and have a poke around." He swung his legs over the threshold and gingerly stood up. "Think some of these boards are rotten, honey. Wow, this place is packed with old stuff."

Grania stood below, listening to Matt's feet above her.

"OK, I've found a couple of trunks . . . but they are real heavy."

"No," Grania shouted up, "it was a small suitcase."

"What's in it anyway that's so important?" he called. "Hell, the cobwebs are out of a horror movie! Even I'm getting spooked."

Grania heard thumps as Matt moved objects above her. Then finally . . .

"I think I've found something—what's left of it. I'll hand it down to you."

Matt's hands appeared through the hole, holding a small suitcase, its color indeterminate due to the layers of dust on it.

"OK, I've had enough. I'm getting out of here." Matt emerged, his hair turned gray by cobwebs. "Jesus!" he said as he levered himself down onto the chair. "I'd only do that for love."

"Thanks, darling," Grania said, turning her attention to the suitcase. As she rubbed the dust off the top of the worn leather, she could see a vague imprint of initials in the top. Matt knelt next to her.

"I think that's an *L* and a *K*," she said.

"Whose suitcase is this anyway?"

"If it's the right one, it belonged to Aurora's great-grandmother. Lawrence Lisle arrived home with a baby," explained Grania, "telling his staff that the mother would arrive to collect Anna *and* the suitcase. She never did, so Anna never knew anything of her real mother."

"Well now, those rusty locks are gonna take some opening. Let me have a try."

Eventually, they took the suitcase down to the kitchen to find a suitable implement. Grania found a knife in the drawer and Matt eventually pried open the locks.

"OK, you ready to look inside?" asked Matt.

"I think it should be Aurora who does that. This is technically hers, after all." Grania collected Aurora from the drawing room and brought her downstairs to the kitchen.

"What is that?" Aurora eyed the filthy leather suitcase with distaste.

"We think it was your great-grandmother's, who never arrived to collect it. It was left here almost a hundred years ago," explained Grania. "Would you like to open it?"

"No, you do it, there might be spiders inside." Aurora wrinkled her nose.

Grania looked equally unenthusiastic.

"OK, ladies, guess it's the man's job." Gingerly, Matt levered the top open, with a crackle of old leather, to reveal the suitcase's contents.

All three of them peered inside.

"Pooh! It smells of old," said Aurora. "There's not much in here, is there?"

"No." Grania felt disappointed. In the suitcase was a silk-covered bundle—nothing else.

Sensing his girls' reticence, Matt put his hand around the bundle and drew it out, placing it on the table. "You want me to unwrap it?"

The girls nodded.

Tentatively, Matt unwrapped the contents from the thin, faded silk surrounding them.

Aurora and Grania gazed down at what Matt had revealed.

"It's a pair of ballet shoes," whispered Aurora in awe. She picked one up to inspect it. As she did so, a moldering envelope fluttered to the floor.

Grania bent down to retrieve it. "It's a letter, and it's addressed to . . ." Grania tried to decipher the faint ink.

"Looks like *Anastasia* to me," said Matt, leaning over Grania's shoulder.

"Anna . . . my grandmother's name was Anna!" Aurora said excitedly.

"Yes, it was. Perhaps Lawrence Lisle shortened it," suggested Grania.

"That's a Russian name, isn't it?" Aurora asked.

"It is. And Mary, who looked after Anna when she was a baby, always said she suspected Anna was brought by Lawrence Lisle from Russia."

"Shall I open the letter?" said Aurora.

"Yes, but be very careful, it looks fragile," cautioned Matt.

Aurora's small fingers opened the envelope. She glanced down at the words and frowned. "I can't understand what it says."

"That's because it's written in Russian," said Matt from behind them. "I took the language for three years in high school, but that was a long time ago, so I'm rusty. But I reckon, with the help of a dictionary, I could decipher it."

"You're full of hidden talents, sweetheart." Grania turned around and placed a kiss on Matt's cheek. "Why don't we stop off at a bookshop on our way home?"

When they arrived in Kensington at Alexander's pretty town house, where they would live while Cadogan House was renovated, there was another letter, addressed to Aurora, waiting for her on the mat.

"It's from the Royal Ballet School!" Aurora picked it up and looked at Grania, hope and fear in her eyes. "Here." She handed it to her. "Can you open it for me, Mummy? I'm too nervous."

"Of course. Right." Grania tore the envelope open, unfolded its contents and began to read.

"What does it say, Mummy?" Aurora's hands were fisted with tension under her chin.

"It says . . ." Grania looked at Aurora and smiled. "It says you'd better start packing as soon as possible, because they have offered you a place at the school, starting in September."

"Oh, *Mummy*!" Aurora threw herself into Grania's arms. "I am *so* happy!"

"Well done, sweetheart," said Matt, joining in the hug.

Once all three of them had calmed down, Matt took himself off upstairs with his newly purchased dictionary to try to translate the letter.

Aurora sat at the kitchen table, still clutching the ballet shoes and talking excitedly about the future as Grania prepared supper for the three of them. "I wish Matt would hurry up, I can't wait to find out who my great-grandmother was. Especially today, when I know I'll be following in her footsteps," she added.

"Well, there's a lot you don't know about your history, Aurora. And, one day, I'll sit down and tell you. And the really weird thing is that, for almost a hundred years, it seems to have been entwined with mine. Mary, my great-grandmother, eventually adopted Anna, your grandmother."

"Gosh!" Aurora's eyes were wide. "That's a coincidence, isn't it? Because you've done the same with me, Mummy."

"Yes, I have." Grania dropped a tender kiss on top of Aurora's head.

Two hours later, Matt arrived downstairs and announced he'd managed to decipher most of the letter. He handed Aurora the typed translation.

"There you go, sweetheart. It's not perfect, but I've done my best."

"Thank you, Matt. Shall I read it out loud?" suggested Aurora.

"If you'd like to," said Grania.

"All right." Aurora cleared her throat. "Here goes."

Paris

17th September 1918

My precious Anastasia,

If you are reading this, you will know that I am no longer on the earth. My kind friend, Lawrence, has been instructed to give this to you if I do not return to retrieve it, and when you are old enough to understand. I do not know what he will have told you about your mama, but the important thing for you to know is that I love you more than any mother could. And because of that, while our beloved Russia is in turmoil, I wanted to make sure that you were safe. My baby, it would have been easy for me to accompany Lawrence to England, leave behind the danger, as so many of my fellow Russians have done. But there is a reason I must return from Paris to our home country. The man who is your father is in great danger. In fact, I do not know whether he is still alive. So, I must go to him. I know I will risk immediate arrest, and perhaps death, but I can only pray that when you, my Anastasia, are older, you too will have the pleasure and pain of knowing what true love for a man is.

Your father is from the greatest family in Russia, but our love had to be hidden. It is with shame that I tell you that he was already married.

You were the result of our precious love.

From the shoes I have enclosed with this letter, you will guess that I am a ballerina. I danced with the Mariinsky Ballet and I'm famous in our home country. And that is how I met your father. He came to watch me perform The Dying Swan *and, from then on, pursued me.*

I am in Paris now, because I understand my connection to our Imperial Family has put you and me in grave danger. So, I took a contract with Diaghilev's Ballets Russes *to give me the opportunity to leave Russia and bring you to a place of safety.*

My friend Lawrence, my kind English gentleman (I think perhaps he is a little in love with me too!) acted as my savior and said he would bring you to London and take care of you for me.

My sweetest child, it is my fervent hope that the madness in our country will end soon. And I will be free to come to you in London, then take you back to our beloved homeland and introduce you to your father. But, while all is in chaos, I know I must sacrifice my own feelings and send you away.

Godspeed, my precious little one. In a few hours' time, Lawrence Lisle will arrive to take you on your journey to safety. It is only fate that can decide whether we will meet again, so I say good-bye, my Anastasia, and may fortune favor you.

Know always that you were born out of love.

Your loving Mama,
Leonora

Silence reigned in the kitchen.

Matt cleared his throat and surreptitiously wiped a tear from his eye. "Wow," he whispered, not knowing what else to say.

Grania put her arms around Aurora as tears fell down her cheeks too.

"Isn't it . . . beautiful, Grania?" Aurora whispered.

"Yes, it is," she agreed.

"Leonora died when she went back to Russia, didn't she?"

"Yes, I think she probably did. If she was famous, we may be able to find out what happened to her. And who Anastasia's father was," pondered Grania.

"If Anastasia's father was a member of the Russian Imperial family, they were all shot very soon after Leonora wrote that letter," put in Matt.

"Leonora could have escaped, left with her baby and Lawrence and come to England," Aurora said. "But she didn't, because she loved Anastasia's daddy so much." Aurora shook her head. "She had to make a terrible choice, giving her poor baby away to a stranger."

"Yes," Grania agreed, "but then, sweetheart, I'm sure Leonora didn't believe she would die. We all make decisions as though we will live forever. She did the best thing she could at that moment, to make sure Anastasia was safe."

"I don't know whether I'd have been so brave," sighed Aurora.

"Well, that's because you haven't learned yet what us humans will sacrifice for love." Matt put an arm tightly around Grania's shoulders and planted a kiss on top of Aurora's head. "Isn't that right, Grania?"

"Yes," Grania smiled up at him, "it is."

Aurora

Doesn't that sound like the perfect ending?

The true Happily Ever After moment. The sort I love.

Grania and Matt reunited and starting on a new life together, financially secure for the rest of their lives. And me with them, pursuing my dream of becoming a great ballerina, launched from within the security of the loving family I'd always craved.

What could be more perfect?

I know! A baby for them, and a brother or sister for me?

And yes, a year later, that happened too.

Now, I'm pondering whether to end the story here, not destroy it with "After the Happily Ever . . ."

But, you see, that wouldn't finish my *story.*

And, I confess, I may have deceived you.

I'm not really "old," although my body feels as if it is.

At least a hundred years old.

But, unlike Aurora in the fairy tale, I will go to sleep for a hundred years—forever, actually—and no handsome prince will be there to wake me . . .

Not here on earth, anyway.

Dear Reader, I do not wish to depress you. Sixteen years of a life well lived is better than none at all.

But if you have felt at any point during my story that I have commented on my characters from a romantic and naive viewpoint, can you forgive me? I am sixteen years old. I am too young to have been tainted by love going wrong.

Well. I'm going to die. Before I've been tainted. And so I can still believe in the magic of love. I believe that our lives, just like fairy tales—the stories that have been written by us humans, through our own experiences of living—will always have a Hero and a Heroine, a Fairy Godmother and a Wicked Witch.

And that love and goodness and faith and hope will always win the day.

Of course, I've been thinking too that even the Wicked Witch is the "Heroine" of her own story, but that's a different point altogether.

And there is always a positive side to everything, if you look for it. My illness has allowed me to document my family history. The writing of this story has been my friend and companion through some difficult, painful moments. It has also allowed me to learn about life. A sort of crash course in the short time I've been granted here.

Grania and Matt—that is, my mother and father here—find it far harder to accept the inevitable. I am calm, because I am lucky. I know I will not be alone when I cross through my gossamer curtain; I will find two pairs of loving arms waiting for me.

Spirits . . . Ghosts . . . Angels . . . whichever you wish to call them—Reader, they do *exist. I've seen them all my life, but I've learned to say nothing.*

And for all you cynics out there, just remember, there is no proof either way.

So I choose to believe. In my opinion, it's much the best option.

As I said from the start, I didn't write this to be published. My parents have seen me scribbling, asked what I am writing about, and I have declined to answer. It is mine, you see, until the end (or the beginning), which I think is very close.

So, Dear Reader, my story is almost finished.

Do not worry about me or feel sad. I'm simply on the next stage of my journey and I'm happy to undertake it. Who knows what magic I will discover on the other side of that curtain?

Please, if you will, remember me and my family's story in a tiny corner of your mind. It is your story too, because it is about humanity.

And, above all, never lose faith in the beauty and goodness of human nature.

It's always there; just, sometimes, you have to look a little harder for it.

It is now time to say good-bye.

Epilogue

Dunworley Bay, West Cork, Ireland, January

Grania stood at the top of the cliffs, the wind howling around her ears, just as it had on the afternoon she'd first met Aurora, eight years before.

Her shoulders heaved in tearless sobs as she remembered the little girl who had appeared so suddenly behind her, like a sprite, and changed her life irrevocably. Eight years ago, she'd been mourning the loss of her unborn baby. Now, she was lost in grief for another child.

"I don't understand!" she screamed to the angry waves crashing below her. *"I don't understand."* She sank to her knees, her physical strength leaving her, and put her head in her hands.

Pictures of Aurora assailed her senses—in every image, her endless vitality. Aurora dancing, spinning, skipping along the cliff top, the beach . . . her energy, her positivity and her continuous zest for life were qualities that defined Aurora's essence. In the eight years Grania had cared for her, she could scarcely remember Aurora negative or sad. Even during the past few months, when her physical strength had been drained from her, Aurora's bright face would smile at her from her hospital bed, full of hope and laughter, even through the worst moments of her illness.

Grania took her head from her hands and remembered how brave Aurora had been in this very spot, when she'd had to tell her of her father's death. Even then, Aurora had accepted and, through her sadness, found the positives.

Somehow, Grania knew she too must find the inner strength that

Aurora had possessed to pull her through this. Aurora had never needed to search for reasons why, hadn't torn herself apart at the injustice of life's lottery. Perhaps it was because she had a certainty, an inner belief that a life ended on earth was not the end of life.

Aurora had left her a letter, but in the last terrible ten days since her death, she'd been unable to open it.

Grania stood up, moved back toward the grassy rock she'd so often used as a seat and pulled the letter out of her jacket pocket. Her fingers blue from the cold, she fumbled to open it.

Mummy,

I bet I know where you are when you read this. You'll be sitting on your favorite rock on the top of Dunworley cliffs, looking out to sea. And missing me and wondering why I've gone. Mummy, I know you will be sad. Losing anybody is always painful, but perhaps losing a child is the worst, because it isn't in the proper order of nature. But, really, it's us humans who have invented the calculation of time. I think it was the Romans who made the first modern calendar and gave us days, months and years. And honestly, Mummy, I feel as though I've been alive forever.

And perhaps I have.

I never felt I belonged completely to the earth anyway. And remember, darling Mummy, that we will all end up where I am now, and it's only the skin and bones, our physical being, that makes us visible to each other. But our spirit never dies. Who's to say, as you sit on your rock, that I am not next to you, dancing around you, loving you as I always have, just because you can't actually see me?

Mummy, you mustn't allow me leaving to make you so sad that you forget to love and care for Daddy and for Florian. Thank you for naming my little brother after the Prince in The Sleeping Beauty*—and I hope one day he will find his Princess and wake her with a kiss. Please give a big hug to Granny and Grandpa and Shane. Tell him I'll be watching to make sure he takes care of Lily. She's getting older now and needs more attention.*

Mummy, try to believe that nothing is ever ended, especially love.

You've probably spoken to Uncle Hans by now, and found out that

I have left you both Dunworley House and Cadogan House. It seems right, somehow, that you should have them. They are part of our family's joint history and I'd like to think of our line of strong women combining and continuing inside their walls. The rest of my money . . . well, Uncle Hans knows what I want to do with it and I trust him to establish my charity in his usual, careful way!

I've left you another present, by the way. It's in the special drawer that Daddy always kept locked in his study—you know the one I mean. I wrote it for us, and for both of our families, as proof of the link that has joined you and me for over a hundred years.

Mummy, I know something you don't—I would check next month if I were you, but the tiny spirit is already there, nestled deep inside you. And it will be a little girl.

Mummy, thank you for everything you've given me.

See you very soon,

Your Aurora

xxx

Grania looked up slowly, her eyes clouded with tears. And saw a small, white seagull surveying her from the edge of the cliff, its head on one side.

"Grania?"

She turned slowly in the direction of the voice. Matt was standing some distance away.

"Are you OK, sweetheart?" he asked.

Grania couldn't reply. She nodded silently.

"I was worried, the storm was blowing up and . . . can I come and hold you?"

She reached out toward her husband. He bent down and put his strong arms around her, holding her tightly. He glanced down at what she was holding. "Is that the letter she left you?"

"Yes."

"What does it say?"

"Oh, many things." Grania blew her nose on an old tissue from her pocket. "She was—*is*—extraordinary. So wise, so strong . . . how could she be those things so young?"

"Perhaps, as your mother says, she's an old soul," Matt murmured.

"Or an angel . . ." Grania leaned weakly against Matt's shoulder. "She says she's written something for me and left it in the study drawer."

"Shall we go home and find it? Your hands are blue, sweetheart."

"Yes."

Matt helped her up from the rock and put an arm around her as they turned to head up the cliff.

"Aurora said something else in the letter too."

"What was that?" Matt asked as they began walking.

"She said that I—"

A gust of wind blew suddenly, snatching the letter easily from Grania's freezing hands and carrying it toward the cliff's edge.

"Oh, baby," said Matt helplessly, knowing there was no rescuing it. "I'm sorry."

Grania turned and watched as the letter spun and danced and twirled in the wind, startling the seagull into taking flight with it, and following the letter up and out to sea.

Grania felt a sudden peace descend on her. "I understand now."

"Understand what, sweetheart?"

"She'll always be with me," she murmured.

Acknowledgments

This is the page I most look forward to writing. It means the book is finished and on its way to publication, due in many different aspects to the unstinting support, advice and encouragement of all the people below.

Johanna Castillo, Judith Curr and the fantastic team at Atria, and the foreign rights girls at Penguin UK, who have brought my stories to a global audience.

Jonathan Lloyd, my fabulous agent and friend, whose patience (and huge expense account on my behalf) has finally paid off. Susan Moss and Jacquelyn Heslop, who were the only two I trusted to read the manuscript before I sent it off, and comforted me so positively until the professional verdict came in. Helene Rampton, Tracy Blackwell, Jennifer Dufton, Rosalind Hudson, Susan Grix, Kathleen Doonan, Sam Gurney, Sophie Hicks and Amy Finnegan . . . girls, what would I do without you?

Richard Madeley and Judy Finnigan, whose "Richard and Judy Book Club" gave me a wonderful platform from which to launch future novels.

The "family," who put up with me and my mad writing habits every day without (much) complaint. My ever supportive mother, Janet; my sister, Georgia; and Olivia, whose editorial typing skills, fueled with a glass of "voddy," are still beyond impeccable. And my fantastic kids, Harry, Isabella, Leonora and Kit (deserving of a special thank-you for allowing me to steal the opening line of this book from *his* first story), whose names are written in order of age, not importance. I love you all, and each of you has provided, in your different ways, so much love, laughter and *life*. I can only say I am honored I've had the privilege of bringing each of you into the world.

And my husband, Stephen; for a change, words cannot express. I can only say thank you. For it all. This is for you.

Bibliography

The Girl on the Cliff is a work of fiction, set against a historical background. The sources I've used to research the time period and detail on my characters' lives are listed below.

Nicholson, Juliet. *The Great Silence: 1918–1920, Living in the Shadow of the Great War* (John Murray, 2009).

Nicholson, Virginia. *Singled Out* (Penguin Books, 2008).

Light, Alison. *Mrs. Woolf and the Servants* (Penguin Books, 2008).

Stevenson, David. *1914–18: The History of the First World War* (Penguin Books, 2005).

———. *The Outbreak of the First World War: 1914 in Perspective (Studies in European History)* (Palgrave Macmillan, 1997).

Eldridge, Jim. *The Trenches: A First World War Soldier, 1914–1918, My Story* (Scholastic, 2008).

Faulks, Sebastian. *Birdsong* (Vintage, 2007).

Coogan, Tim Pat. *Michael Collins* (Arrow, 1991).

Lee, Joseph J. *Ireland 1912–1985: Politics and Society* (Cambridge University Press, 1990).

Figes, Orlando. *A People's Tragedy: The Russian Revolution 1891–1924* (Pimlico, 1997).

Garafola, Lynn. *Diaghilev's Ballets Russes* (De Capo Press, 1998).

Lifar, Serge. *Serge Diaghilev* (Putnam, 1945).

Daneman, Meredith. *Margot Fonteyn* (Viking, 2002).

Valois, Ninette De. *Invitation to the Ballet* (Bodley Head, 1937).

Röhrich, Lutz. *"And They Are Still Living Happily Ever After": Anthropology, Cultural History and Interpretation of Fairy Tales*, translated by Paul Washbourne (University of Vermont, 2008).